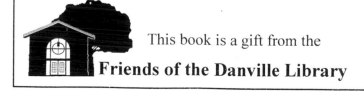

AFTERSHOCK
& OTHERS

Also by F. Paul Wilson

SHORT FICTION
Soft and Others
The Barrens and Others

REPAIRMAN JACK
The Tomb
Legacies
Conspiracies
All the Rage
Hosts
The Haunted Air
Gateways
Crisscross
Infernal
Harbingers
Bloodline
By the Sword

YOUNG ADULT
Jack: Secret Histories

THE ADVERSARY CYCLE
The Keep
The Tomb
The Touch
Reborn
Reprisal
Nightworld

OTHER NOVELS
Healer
Wheels Within Wheels
An Enemy of the State
Black Wind
Dydeetown World
The Tery
Sibs
The Select
Implant
Deep as the Marrow
Mirage
    (with Matthew J. Costello)
Nightkill
    (with Steven Spruill)
Masque
    (with Matthew J. Costello)
The Christmas Thingy
Sims
The Fifth Harmonic
Midnight Mass

EDITOR
Freak Show
Diagnosis: Terminal

AFTERSHOCK & OTHERS

19 Oddities

F. PAUL WILSON

A TOM DOHERTY ASSOCIATES BOOK

NEW YORK

AFTERSHOCK & OTHERS: 19 ODDITIES

Copyright © 2009 by F. Paul Wilson

A Forge Book
Published by Tom Doherty Associates, LLC
175 Fifth Avenue
New York, NY 10010

www.tor-forge.com

Forge® is a registered trademark of Tom Doherty Associates, LLC.

Library of Congress Cataloging-in-Publication Data

Wilson, F. Paul (Francis Paul)
    Aftershock & others : 19 oddities / F. Paul Wilson.—1st ed.
        p. cm.
    "A Tom Doherty Associates book."
    Short stories.
    ISBN-13: 978-0-7653-1277-8
    ISBN-10: 0-7653-1277-8
  I. Title.   II. Title: Aftershock and others.
    PS3573.I45695A69 2009
    813'.54—dc22

                                                    2008038099

First Edition: April 2009

Printed in the United States of America

0 9 8 7 6 5 4 3 2 1

COPYRIGHT ACKNOWLEDGMENTS

To all my editors across the ages

AUTHOR'S NOTE

As with my previous collections, the stories here are presented in the order they were written rather than published. I've culled stories from 1990 through 2005.

And as before, I've provided year-by-year background on what was going on in my career at the time. Some of you may not be interested. If so, the solution is simple: Turn the page. But if the mail I receive is any indication, an awful lot of you like the interstitial material—a few have dared suggest that it's more interesting than some of the fiction. (The author bristles.) Certainly it provides a bonus for those of you who've already read some of the stories.

I look at it this way: I will never write an autobiography (my personal life is probably not much different from that of any other married guy with kids and grandkids, so I can't imagine why anyone would want to read about it), but the introductions in my collections add up to a sort of writing memoir. For those of you curious about writing and the writing process, I trust you'll find something of interest.

CONTENTS

The Secret History of the World   13

1990   15
Dreams   21
The November Game   33
When He Was Fab   43
Foet   61

1991   71
Please Don't Hurt Me   75

1992   81

1993   85
Aryans and Absinthe   91

1994   123
Offshore   129
Itsy Bitsy Spider   151

1995   161
CRAWLED   165

1996   185

1997 189
Lysing Toward Bethlehem 197

1998 203
Aftershock 209

1999 239
Anna 243

2000–2002 265

2003 269
Sole Custody 273
Sex Slaves of the Dragon Tong 289

2004 311
Part of the Game 317

2005 331
Interlude at Duane's 337

Afterword 351

THE SECRET HISTORY OF THE WORLD

The preponderance of my work deals with a history of the world that remains undiscovered, unexplored, and unknown to most of humanity. Some of this secret history has been revealed in the Adversary Cycle, some in the Repairman Jack novels, and bits and pieces in other, seemingly unconnected works. Taken together, even these millions of words barely scratch the surface of what has been going on behind the scenes, hidden from the workaday world. I've listed these works below in the chronological order in which the events in them occur.

Note: "Year Zero" is the end of civilization as we know it; "Year Zero Minus One" is the year preceding it, etc.

THE PAST
"Demonsong" (prehistory)
"Aryans and Absinthe" (1923–1924)
Black Wind (1926–1945)
The Keep (1941)
Reborn (February–March 1968)
"Dat Tay Vao" (March 1968)
Jack: Secret Histories (1983)

YEAR ZERO MINUS THREE
Sibs (February)
"Faces" (early summer)
The Tomb (summer)
"The Barrens"* (ends in September)
"A Day in the Life"* (October)

"The Long Way Home"
Legacies (December)

YEAR ZERO MINUS TWO

Conspiracies (April) (includes "Home Repairs")
"Interlude at Duane's" (April)
All the Rage (May) (includes "The Last Rakosh")
Hosts (June)
The Haunted Air (August)
Gateways (September)
Crisscross (November)
Infernal (December)

YEAR ZERO MINUS ONE

Harbingers (January)
Bloodline (April)
By the Sword (May)
The Touch (ends in August)
The Peabody-Ozymandias Traveling Circus & Oddity Emporium (ends in
    September)
"Tenants"*
yet-to-be-written Repairman Jack novels

YEAR ZERO

"Pelts"*
Reprisal (ends in February)
the last Repairman Jack novel (will end in April)
Nightworld (starts in May)

Reborn, The Touch, and *Reprisal* will be back in print before too long. I'm planning a total of sixteen or seventeen Repairman Jack novels (not counting the young adult titles), ending the Secret History with the publication of a heavily revised *Nightworld*.

*available in *The Barrens and Others*

1990

Another award-losing year: *Soft and Others,* my first short fiction collection, lost the Bram Stoker Award to Richard Matheson's *Collected Stories.* No gripes from me. He's the greatest. A fair number of my stories never would have been written if my teenage mind hadn't been warped by his *Shock* collections.

I can't complain about 1990. I started off writing the *Midnight Mass* novella for Robert McCammon's *Under the Fang.* This was the first of three "theme" anthologies contracted by the Horror Writers of America to put itself on firmer financial footing. Rick McCammon, Ramsey Campbell, and I were chosen as editors. Rick took the first, a collection of vampire stories with the premise that the vampires have taken over—now what?

I knocked out *Mass* over four weekends while working on *Reprisal.* As I was finishing it Kristine Kathryn Rusch called, asking if I had anything for the Pulphouse novella series she was editing. Since her print run would be less than a thousand, I asked Rick if he had any objection to Pulphouse doing a stand-alone edition. He didn't. But when Pocket Books (publisher of *Under the Fang*) learned that my story would be technically a reprint by the time *Fang* was published, they demanded I cancel the special edition or they'd cut the story. Well, I'd already given Kris my word, and a deal is a deal. So that's why *Midnight Mass* didn't appear in *Under the Fang.* It did go on to become my most reprinted story.

Otherwise *Reprisal* claimed most of my writing time, though editors clamoring for short stories kept interrupting me. In March came Bob Weinberg. I was scheduled to be Guest of Honor at the 1990 World Fantasy Convention and it's a tradition to include a story by the GoH in the program book. Bob's wife, Phyllis, loved Repairman Jack so I wrote the "Last Rakosh" and dedicated it to her. (Years later this was blended into the Repairman Jack novel *All the Rage.*)

The Dark Harvest hardcover of *Reborn,* the fourth volume (though chronologically the second) in what I'd eventually call the Adversary Cycle, was published in March, followed a few months later by the Jove mass-market edition with one of the worst covers ever to sully my work: a lolling-tongued demon leering from atop a doorway. Beyond awful. I'd complained about it but no one was listening. The advance orders to this sequel to *The Keep* were excellent, so where's the problem?

Right. Where *was* the problem? Reviews were excellent and the book was optioned for a theatrical film within months of publication. Things looked good. I'd been wrong about retitling *The Tomb,* so maybe I was wrong about this. (But I wasn't. That cover was going to come back to haunt me.)

In April Richard Chizmar requested a story for an anthology called *Cold Blood.* I turned to Jack again. The working title was "Domestic Problem" but I ended up calling it "Home Repairs." (This was folded into the RJ novel *Conspiracies.*)

Then in May Joe Lansdale called looking for a dark suspense story—no supernatural—for *Dark at Heart,* an anthology he was editing with his wife, Karen. He wanted something like "Slasher." Back to Jack for "The Long Way Home." (It's available for download at amazon.com in their Amazon Shorts section.)

About this time I got to work on my first editing gig: *Freak Show,* the second of the aforementioned HWA anthologies.

I wanted *Freak Show* to be more unified than *Fang.* So . . . to all who asked (and to those I particularly wanted in the anthology) I sent out three pages of guidelines outlining the background of the show and how my connecting story would run, plus the general circular route the show would take around the country.

I asked for regionalism—write about places you lived so the tastes and tangs of the settings would be authentic. I also asked for a description of the freak and a loose outline of the story—necessary to avoid duplication of characters, locations (I didn't want multiple stories in Chicago or L.A.), and plotlines. A bit of work, yes, but you were pretty much guaranteed that I'd buy the piece if I approved your proposal. Some writers found this approach too restrictive; others blasted off and came up with great stories.

After the synopses were set, I began tying them together; I also circulated descriptions of all the freaks to the contributors to encourage cross-fertilization (a passing mention of this or that freak in other stories).

Need I say it turned out to be a *lot* of work? It took a year of my life and, as time went on, increasingly interfered with my own writing projects.

But here in 1990 I was oblivious to what I'd let myself in for. In June I finished revising *Reprisal* and set off on a research trip to Hawaii to gather sights and sounds and locations for the Maui sections of *Nightworld*. I wrote some of them on the spot while they were fresh. (Yeah, I know—tough work. But no sacrifice is too great for my craft.)

Careerwise, the high points of 1990 had to be the election of my first novel *Healer* to the Prometheus Hall of Fame, and being Guest of Honor at the World Fantasy Convention.

Byron Preiss called asking for a contribution to one of his three "Ulti-mate" books. I had my choice of *The Ultimate Dracula*, *The Ultimate Werewolf*, or *The Ultimate Frankenstein*. I'd already done a long vampire story earlier in the year (the novella *Midnight Mass*) and had never found werewolves all that interesting, so I chose Frankie. My challenge was to come up with something fresh on the monster in the allotted 3,500 to 5,000 words. Another restriction was that the story had to be based on the movie version, not Mary Shelley's original. (Thus the reference to the monster's creator as Henry rather than Victor.)

As is my custom, I inverted expectations, turned tropes on their heads, and came up with an angle that delighted me. As I wrote the first line of "Dreams," I already knew the last. It is also, you will note, a nice little exercise in dramatic irony.

Dreams

The nightmare again.

I almost dread falling asleep. Always the same, and yet never quite the same. The events differ dream to dream, yet always I am in a stranger's body, a huge, monstrous, patchwork contraption that reels through the darkness in such ungainly fashion. It's always dark in the dream, for I seem to be a creature of the night, forever in hiding.

And I can't remember my name.

The recent dreams are well formed. My head has cleared in them. So unlike the early dreams, which I can barely remember. Those are no more than a montage of blurred images now—a lightning-drenched laboratory, a whip-wielding hunchback, *fear,* a stone-walled cell, chains, *loneliness,* a little girl drowning among floating blossoms, a woman in a wedding gown, townsfolk with torches, fire, a burning windmill, *pain, rage, PAIN!*

But I'm all right now. Scarred but healing. And my mind is clear. The pain from the fire burned away the mists. I remember things from dream to dream, and more and more bits and pieces from long ago.

But what is my name?

I know I must stay out of sight. I don't want to be burned again. That's why I spend the daylight hours hiding here in the loft of this abandoned stable on the outskirts of Goldstadt. I sleep most of the day. But at night I wander. Always into town. Always to the area around the Goldstadt Medical College. I seem to be attracted to the medical college. The reason rests here in my brain, but it scampers beyond my grasp whenever I reach for it. One day I'll catch it and then I'll know.

So many unanswered questions in these dreams. But aren't dreams supposed to be that way? Don't they pose more questions than they answer?

My belly is full now. I broke into a pastry shop and gorged myself on the unsold sweets left over from yesterday, and now I'm wandering the back alleys, drinking from rain barrels, peering from the shadows into the lighted windows I pass. I feel a warm resonance within when I see a family together by a fire. Once I must have had a life like that. But the warmth warps into rage if I watch too long, because I know such a scene will never be mine again.

I know it's only a dream. But the rage is so real.

As I pass the rear of a tavern, the side door opens and two men step out. I stumble farther back into the shadows, wanting to run but knowing I'd make a terrible racket. No one must see me. No one must know I'm alive. So I stay perfectly still, waiting for them to leave.

That's when I hear the voice. The deep, delicious voice of a handsome young man with curly blond hair and fresh clear skin. I know this without seeing him. I even know his name.

Karl.

I lean to my right and peer down the alley. My heart leaps at the sight of him. It's not *my* heart; it's the huge, ponderous heart of a stranger, but it responds nonetheless, thudding madly in my chest. I listen to his clear, rich laughter as he waves good-bye to his friend and strolls away toward the street.

Karl.

Why do I know him?

I follow. I know it's dangerous but I must. But I don't go down the alley after him. Instead I lumber along in the back alleys, splattering through puddles, scattering rats, dodging stinking piles of trash as I keep pace with him, catching sight of his golden-haired form between buildings as he strides along.

He's not heading for home. Somewhere in my head I know where he lives and he's headed in the wrong direction. I follow him to a cottage at the north end of Goldstadt, watch him knock, watch a raven-haired beauty open the door and leap into his arms, watch them disappear inside. I know her too.

Maria.

The rage spewing up in me is nearly as uncontainable as it is unexplainable. It's all I can do to keep myself from bursting through that door and tearing them both apart.

Why? What are these emotions? Who are these people? And why do I know their names and not my own?

I cool. I wait. But Karl doesn't reappear. The sky lightens and still no Karl. I must leave before I am seen. As I head back toward the stable that has become my nest, my rage is gone, replaced by a cold black despair. Before I climb to the loft I pause to relieve myself. As I lower my heavy, crudely stitched pants I pray that it will be different this dream, but there it is—that long, thick, slack member hanging between my legs. It repulses me. I try to relieve myself without touching it.

I am a woman. Why do these dreams place me in the body of a man?

Awake again.

I've spent the day talking, laughing, discussing the wisdom of the ages. Such a relief to be back to reality, back in my own body—young, lithe, smaller, smoother, with slim legs, dainty fingers, and firm, compact breasts. So good to be a woman again.

But my waking hours aren't completely free from confusion. I'm not sure where I am. I do know that it's warm and beautiful. Grassy knolls flow green through the golden sunshine toward the majestic amethyst-hued mountains that tower in the distance. Sweet little hummingbirds dart about in the hazy spring air.

And at least when I'm awake I know my name: Eva. Eva Rucker.

I just wish I knew why I was here. Don't misunderstand. I love it here. It's everything I've ever wanted. Friendly people wandering the hills, wise men stopping by to discuss the great philosophies of the ages. It's like the Elysian fields I read about in Greek mythology, except I'm alive and this is all real. I simply don't know what I've done to deserve this.

I have a sense that I was brought here as compensation for an unpleasantness in my past. I seem to remember some recent ugliness in which I was unwittingly involved, unjustly accused, something so darkly traumatic that my mind shies from the memory of it. But the wrong was righted and I've been sent here to recuperate.

I think of Karl and how he became part of my dream last night. Karl . . . so handsome, so brilliant, so dashing. I haven't thought of him since I arrived here. How could I forget the man I love?

A cloud passes across the sun as my thoughts darken with the memory of the dream-Karl in the dream-Maria's arms. Maria is Karl's sister! They would *never!*

How perverse these nightmares! I shouldn't let them upset me.

The sun reemerges as I push the memory away. It's wonderful here. I never want to leave. But I'm tired now. The golden wine I had with dinner has made me drowsy. I'll just lie back and rest my eyes for a moment . . .

Oh, no! The dream again!

I'm in that horrid body, stumbling through the night. Can't I close my eyes even for a few seconds without falling into this nightmare? I want to scream, to burst from this cocoon of dream and return to my golden fields. But the nightmare tightens its steely grip and I lurch on.

I stop at a schoolhouse. I'm hungry but there's something more important than food inside. I break down the door and enter the single classroom with its rows of tiny desks. I rip the top off one desk after the other and carry it to the shafts of moonlight pouring through the windows until I find the paper and pencil I seek. I bring them to the teacher's desk. I'm too large to seat myself, so I kneel beside the desk and force my huge ungainly fingers to grasp the pencil and write.

I know this is a dream, but still I feel compelled to let the dream-Karl know that even though my body has metamorphosed into this huge ungainly monstrosity, his Eva still cares for him.

After many tries, I manage a legible note:

KARL
I LOVE YOU
YOUR EVA

I fold the sheet and take it with me. At Karl's uncle's house—where Karl lives—I slip it under the door. Then I stand back in the shadows and wait. And as I wait, I remember more and more about Karl.

We met near the University of Goldstadt where he was a student at the medical college. That was in my real life. I assume he remains a student in my dreams. I so wanted to attend the university but the Regents wouldn't hear of it. They were scandalized by my application. No women in the College of Arts and Sciences, and especially in the medical college. *Especially* not a poor farm girl.

So I'd hide in the rear of the lecture halls and listen to Dr. Waldman's lectures on anatomy and physiology. Karl found me there but kept my secret and let me stay. I fell in love with him immediately. I remember that. I remember all our secret meetings, in fields, in lofts. He'd teach me what he learned in class. And then he'd teach me other things. We became lovers. I'd never given myself to any man before. Karl was the first, and I swear he'll be the only one. I don't remember how we became separated. I—

Here he comes. Oh, look at him! I want to run to him but I couldn't bear for him to see me like this. What torture this nightmare is!

I watch him enter his uncle's house, see him light the candles in the entryway. I move closer as he picks up my note and reads it. But no loving smile lights his features. Instead, his face blanches and he totters back against the wall. Then he's out the door and running, flying through the streets, my note clutched in his hand. I follow him as best I can but he outdistances me. No matter. I know the route. I sense where he's going.

When I arrive at Maria's house he's already inside. I lurch to a lighted window and peer within. Karl stands in the center of the room, his eyes wild, the ruddy color still gone from his cheeks. Maria has her arms around his waist. She's smiling as she comforts him.

"—only a joke," she says. "Can't you see that, my love? Someone's trying to play a trick on you!"

"Then it's a damn good trick!" Karl holds my note before her eyes. "This is how she always signed her notes—'Your Eva.' No one else knew that. Not even you. And I burned all those letters."

Maria laughs. "So what are you telling me? That Eva wrote you this note? That's certainly not her handwriting."

"True, but—"

"Eva is dead, my love."

The words strike like hammer blows to my brain. I want to shout that I'm here, alive, transformed into this creature. But I keep silent. I have no workable voice. And after all, this is only a dream. I must keep telling myself that.

Only a dream.

Nothing here is true and therefore none of it matters.

Yet I find a horrid fascination in it.

"They hung her," Maria is saying. "I know because I went and watched. You couldn't stomach it but I went to see for myself." Her smile fades as an ugly light grows in her eyes. "They *hung* her, Karl. Hung her till she stopped kicking and swung limp in the breeze. Then they cut her down and took her off to the medical college just as she requested. The noble little thing: Wanted her body donated to science. Well, by now she's in a thousand little pieces."

"I know." Karl's color is returning, but his flush seems more a shade of guilt than good health. "I saw her brain, Maria. Eva's brain! Dr. Waldman kept it in a glass jar on one of the lab tables as an example of an abnormal brain. *'Dysfunctio Cerebri'* his label said, right next to a supposedly normal brain. I had to sit there during all his lectures and stare at it, knowing the whole time who it had belonged to, and that it was not abnormal in the least."

"It should have been labeled a 'stupid' brain." Maria laughs. "She believed you loved her. She thought I was your sister. She believed everything we told her, and so she wound up taking the blame for your uncle's murder. As a result, you're rich and you don't ever have to think about her again. She's gone."

"Her brain's gone too. I was so glad when pranksters stole it and I no longer had to look at it."

"Now you can look at me."

Maria steps back and unbuttons her blouse, baring her breasts. As Karl locks her in an embrace, I reel away from the window, sobbing, retching, running blindly for the stables I call home.

Awake again.

Back in my Elysian fields, but still I cannot shake off the effects of the nightmare. The dream-Maria's words have roused memories in my waking mind. They are partly true.

How could I have forgotten?

There was a murder. Karl's rich uncle. And I was accused. I remember now . . . remember that night. I was supposed to meet Karl at the house. He was going to introduce me to his uncle and bring our love out into the open at last. But when I got there, the door was open and a portly old man lay on the floor, bleeding, dying. I tried to help him but he had lost too much blood. Then the Burgomeister's men arrived and found me with the slain man's blood on my hands and the knife that had killed him at my feet.

And Karl was nowhere to be found.

I never saw Karl again. He never came to visit me. Never answered my notes. In fact, his barrister came to the jail and told me to stop writing to Karl—that Karl didn't know who I was and wanted nothing to do with the murderer of his uncle.

No one believed that I knew Karl. No one but his sister Maria had ever seen us together, and Maria said I was a complete stranger. I remember the final shock when I was told that Maria wasn't his sister at all.

After that the heart went out of me. I gave up. I lost the will to defend myself. I let them do with me as they wished. My only request was that my body be given to the medical college. That was my private joke on the regents—I would be attending the university after all.

I remember walking to the gallows. I remember the rope going around my neck. After that . . .

. . . I was here. So I must have been saved from execution. If only I could remember how. No matter. It will come. What does matter is that since arriving here my life has been a succession of one blissful day after another. Perfect . . .

Except for the dreams.

But now clouds gather over my Elysian fields as I remember Karl's betrayal. I'd thought he avoided me in order to protect his family name, but the dream-Maria's words have not only awakened my memory, they've shed new light on all the things that happened to me after that night I went to Karl's uncle's house.

The clouds darken and thunder rumbles through the distant mountain passes as my anger and suspicion grow. I don't know if Karl lied and betrayed me as the dream-Maria said, and I don't know if he was the one who killed his uncle, but I do know that he deserted me in my hour of most dire need. And for that I will never forgive him.

The clouds obscure the sun and darken the sky, the storm threatens but it doesn't rain. Not yet.

The nightmare again.

Only this time I don't fight it. I'm actually glad to be in this monstrous body. I'm a curious thing. Not a seamless creature, but a quilt of human parts. And powerful. So very powerful. My years of farm work left me strong for a girl, but I never had strength like this. Strength to lift a horse or knock down a tree. It feels *good* to be so strong.

I head for Maria's cottage.

She's home. She's alone. Karl is nowhere about. I don't bother knocking. I kick down the door and step inside. Maria starts to scream but I grab her by the throat with one of my long-fingered hands and choke off all sound. She laughed at me last night, called me stupid. I feel the anger surge and I squeeze tighter, watching her face purple. I straighten my arm and lift her feet off the floor, let them kick the empty air, just as she said mine did in the dream-death she watched. I squeeze and squeeze and *squeeze,* watching the blood vessels burst in her eyes and face, watching her tongue protrude and turn dusky until she hangs in my hand like a doll. I loosen my grip and shake her but she remains limp.

What have I done?

I stand there, shocked at the rage within me, at the violence it makes me capable of. For a moment I grieve for Maria, for myself, then I shake it off.

This is a dream. A *dream!* It isn't real. I can do anything in this nightmare body and it doesn't matter. Because it's only happening in my sleeping mind.

The realization is a dazzling white light in my brain. I can do anything I wish in my dream-life. *Anything!* I can vent any emotion, give in to any whim, any desire or impulse, no matter how violent or outrageous.

And I will do just that. No restraint while I'm dreaming. Unlike my waking life, I will act without hesitation on whatever occurs to me. I'll lead a dream-life untempered by sympathy, empathy, or any other sane consideration.

Why not? It's only a dream.

I look down and see the note I wrote Karl. It lies crumpled on the floor. I look at Maria, hanging limp from my hand. I remember her derisive laughter at how I'd donated my body for the furtherance of science, her glee at the thought of my being dissected into a thousand pieces.

And suddenly I have an idea. If I could laugh, I would.

After I'm finished with her, I set the door back on its hinges and wait beside it. I do not have to wait long.

Karl arrives and knocks. When no one answers, he pushes on the door. It falls inward and he sees his lover, Maria . . . all over the room . . . in a thousand pieces. He cries out and turns to flee. But I am there, blocking the way.

Karl staggers back when he sees me, his face working in horror. He tries to run but I grab him by the arm and hold him.

"You! Good Lord, they said you'd burned up in the mill fire! Please don't hurt me! I never harmed you!"

What a wonder it is to have physical power over a man. I never realized until this instant how fear has influenced my day-to-day dealings with men. True, they run the world, they have the power of influence—but they have *physical* power as well. Somewhere in the depths of my mind, running as a steady undercurrent, has been the realization that almost any man could physically overpower me at will. Although I never before recognized its existence, I see now how it has colored my waking life.

But in my dream I am no longer the weaker sex.

I do not hurt Karl. I merely want him to know who I am. I hold up the note from last night and press it against my heart.

"What?" he cries hoarsely. "What do you want of me?"

I show him the note again, and again I press it to my heart.

"What are you saying? That you're Eva? That's impossible. Eva's dead! You're Henry Frankenstein's creature."

Henry Frankenstein? The baron's son? I've heard of him—one of Dr. Waldman's former students, supposedly brilliant but highly unorthodox. What has he to do with any of this?

I growl and shake my head as I rattle the paper and tighten my grip on his arm.

He winces. "Look at you! How could you be Eva? You're fashioned out of different parts from different bodies! You're—" Karl's eyes widen, his face slackens. "The brain! Sweet lord, Eva's brain! It was stolen shortly before you appeared!"

I am amazed at the logical consistency of my nightmare. In real life I donated my body to the medical college, and here in my dream my brain has been placed in another body, a patchwork fashioned by Baron Frankenstein's son from discarded bits and pieces. How inventive I am!

I smile.

"Oh, my *God!*" Karl wails. His words begin to trip over each other in their hurry to escape. "It can't be! Oh, Eva, Eva, Eva, I'm so sorry! I didn't want to do it but Maria put me up to it. I didn't want to kill my uncle but she kept pushing me. It was her idea to have you blamed, not mine!"

As I stare at him in horror, I feel the rage burst in my heart like a rocket. So! He *did* conspire to hang me! A crimson haze blossoms about me as I take his head between my hands. I squeeze with all the strength I possess and don't stop until I hear a wet crunching noise, feel hot liquid running between my fingers.

And then I'm sobbing, huge alien sounds rumbling from my chest as I clutch Karl's limp form against me. It's only a dream, I know, but still I hurt inside. I stand there for a long time. Until I hear a voice behind me.

"Hello? What's happened here?"

I turn and see one of the townsfolk approaching. The sight of him makes my blood boil. He and his kind chased me to that mill on the hill and tried to burn me alive. I toss Karl's remains aside and charge after him. He is too fast for me and runs screaming down the street.

Afraid that he'll return with his neighbors, I flee. But not before setting fire to Maria's cottage. I watch it burn a moment, then head into the countryside, into the friendly darkness.

Awake once more.

I have spent the entire day thinking about last night's dream. I see no reason to skulk around in the darkness any longer when I'm dreaming. Why should I? The townsfolk realize by now that I'm still alive. Good. Let all those good citizens know that I am back and that they must deal with me again—not as poor Eva Rucker, but as the patchwork creature from Henry Frankenstein's crazed experiments. And I will *not* be mistreated anymore. I will *not* be looked down on and have doors shut in my face simply because I am a farm girl. No one will say no to me ever again!

I will be back. Tomorrow night, and every night thereafter. But I shall no longer wander aimlessly. I will have a purpose in my dreams. I will start by taking my dream-revenge on the university regents who denied me admission to the medical college. I shall spend my waking hours devising elaborate ways for them to die, and in my dreams I shall execute those plans.

It will be fun. Harmless fun to kill them off one by one in my dreams.

I'm beginning to truly enjoy the dreams. It's so wonderful to be powerful and not recognize any limits. It's such an invigorating release.

I can't wait to sleep again.

In September I was banging away on *Nightworld* when dat ol' debil Marty Greenberg pulled me away with an offer I couldn't refuse: He and Bill Nolan were editing *The Bradbury Chronicles,* an anthology of stories in tribute to Ray Bradbury—would I like to contribute? Like, duh.

I knew immediately that I'd have to write a sequel to Ray's "The October Game." It's a masterpiece of subtly growing menace, and one of the most perfectly focused short stories ever written, as effective today as it was when it appeared in *Weird Tales.*

I discovered it on a summer night in 1959 in Hitchcock's *13 More Stories They Wouldn't Let Me Do on TV.* I consider reading "The October Game" one of the pivotal moments in my life. Just thirteen at the time, I found the last line ("Then . . . some idiot turned on the lights.") confusing. I sat there, book in hand, puzzled, wondering at that crazy closing sentence. Why on earth—?

BLAM!

It hit me. I got it. And it blew me away, utterly and completely. Left me gasping. Lowered the temperature of the room by twenty degrees. And made me decide that someday, some way, I would write a story that would do unto others what this one had done unto me. I'm still trying.

Ray seems ambivalent about "The October Game." I'll bet he still appreciates the finesse of his younger self's technique, but I think the subject matter appalls the older Ray. But the lesson this story pounds home is how less can be so much more. The oblique descriptions in the dark throughout the "game" are never visually realized by the author. The reader is left to construct them after the lights come on.

"The November Game" picks up shortly after Ray's story. It's lurid where Ray's is subtle, but over the years I'd been unable to let go of the need to balance the scales. What goes around, comes around. And now . . . it's Daddy's turn.

I was so psyched I knocked out the first draft in one day.

The November Game

Two human eyeballs nestle amid the white grapes on my dinner tray. I spot them even as the tray slides under the bars of my cell.

"Dinner, creep," says the guard as he kicks the tray forward with his shoe.

"The name is Mich, Hugo," I say evenly, refusing to react to the sight of those eyes.

"That translates into *creep* around here."

Hugo leaves. I listen to the squeaky wheels of the dinner cart echo away down the corridor. Then I look at the bowl of grapes again.

The eyes are still there, pale blue, little-girl blue, staring back at me so mournfully. They think they can break me this way, make me pay for what I did. But after all those years of marriage to Louise, I don't break so easily.

When I'm sure Hugo's gone I inspect the rest of the food—beef patty, string beans, French fries, Jell-O. They all look okay—no surprises in among the fries like last night.

So I take the wooden spoon, the only utensil they'll let me have here, and go to the loose floor tile I found in the right rear corner. I pry it loose. A whiff of putrefaction wafts up from the empty space below. Dark down there, a dark that seems to go on forever. If I were a bit smaller I could fit through. I figure the last occupant of this cell must have been a little guy, must have tried to dig his way out. Probably got transferred to another cell before he finished his tunnel, because I've never heard of anyone breaking out of here.

But *I'm* going to be a little guy before long. And then I'll be out.

I upend the bowl of grapes and eyeballs over the hole first, then let the rest of the food follow. Somewhere below I hear it all plop onto the other things I've been dumping down there. I could flush the eyes and the rest down the stained white toilet squatting in the other corner, but they're probably listening for that. If they hear a flush during the dinner hour they'll guess what I'm doing and think they're winning the game. So I go them one better. As long as they don't know about the hole, I'll stay ahead in their rotten little game.

I replace the tile and return to my cot. I tap my wooden spoon on the Melmac plates and clatter them against the tray while I smack my lips and make appropriate eating noises. I only drink the milk and water. That's all I've allowed myself since they put me in here. And the diet's working. I'm losing weight. Pretty soon I'll be able to slip through the opening under that tile, and then they'll have to admit I've beaten them at their own rotten game.

Soon I hear the squeak of the wheels again. I arrange my tray and slip it out under the bars and into the corridor.

"An excellent dinner," I say as Hugo picks up the tray.

He says nothing.

"Especially the grapes. The grapes were delicious—*utterly* delicious."

"Up yours, creep."

Hugo squeaks away.

I miss my pipe.

They won't let me have it in here. No flame, no sharps, no shoelaces, even. As if I'd actually garrote myself with string.

Suicide watch, they call it. But I've come to realize they've got something else in mind by isolating me. They've declared psychological war.

They must think I'm stupid, telling me I'm in a solitary cell for my own protection, saying the other prisoners might want to hurt me because I'm considered a "short eyes."

But I'm not a child molester—that's what "short eyes" means in prison lingo. I never molested a child in my life, never even *thought* of doing such a thing. Especially not Marion, not little eight-year-old Marion.

I only killed her. Nothing more.

I made her part of the game. The October game. I handed out the parts of her dismembered body to the twenty children and twelve adults seated in a circle in my cellar and let them pass the pieces around in the Halloween darkness. I can still hear their laughter as their fingers touched what they thought were chicken innards and grapes and sausages. They thought it was a lark. They had a ball until some idiot turned on the lights.

But I never molested little Marion.

And I never meant her any harm, either. Not personally. Marion was an innocent bystander caught in the crossfire between her mother and father. Louise was to blame. Because it was Louise I wanted to hurt. Louise of the bleached-out eyes and hair, Louise the ice princess who gave birth to a bleached-out clone of herself and then made her body incapable of bearing any more children. So where was my son—my dark-eyed, dark-haired counterpoint to Marion?

Eight years of Louise's mocking looks, of using the child who appeared to be all of her and none of me as a symbol of my failures—in business, in marriage, in fatherhood, in life. When autumn came I knew it had to stop. I couldn't stand the thought of another winter sealed in that house with Louise and her miniature clone. I wanted to leave, but not without hurting Louise. Not without an eight-year payback.

And the way to hurt Louise most was to take Marion from her.

And I did. Forever. In a way she'll never forget.

We're even, Louise.

(suck . . . puff)

"And you think your wife is behind these horrific pranks?" Dr. Hurst says, leaning back in his chair and chewing on his pipe stem.

I envy that pipe. But I'm the supposedly suicidal prisoner and he's the prison shrink, so he gets to draw warm, aromatic smoke from the stem and I get pieces of Marion on my food tray.

"Of course she is. Louise was always a vindictive sort. Somehow she's gotten to the kitchen help and the guards and convinced them to do a *Gaslight* number on me. She hates me. She wants to push me over the edge."

(suck . . . puff)

"Let's think about this," he says. "Your wife certainly has reason to hate you, to want to hurt you, to want to get even with you. But this conspiracy you've cooked up is rather farfetched, don't you think? Focus on what you're saying: Your wife has arranged with members of the prison staff to place pieces of your dismembered daughter in the food they serve you. Would she do something like that with her daughter's remains?"

"Yes. She'd do anything to get back at me. She probably thinks it's poetic justice or some such nonsense."

(suck . . . puff)

"Mmmmm. Tell me again what, um, parts of Marion you've found in your food."

I think back, mentally cataloging the nastiness I've been subjected to.

"It started with the baked potatoes. They almost fooled me with the first one. They'd taken some of Marion's skin and molded it into an oblong hollow shape, then filled it with baked potato. I've got to hand it to them—it looked quite realistic. I almost ate it."

Across his desk from me, Dr. Hurst coughs.

(suck . . . puff)

"How did you feel about that?"

"Disgusted, of course. And angry too. I'm willing to pay for what I did. I've never denied doing it. But I don't think I should be subjected to mental torture. Since that first dinner it's been a continual stream of body parts. Potato after potato encased in Marion's skin, her fingers and toes amid the French fries, a thick slice of calf's liver that didn't come from any calf, baby back ribs that were never near a pig, loops of intestine supposed to pass at breakfast as link sausage, a chunk of Jell-O with one of her vertebrae inside. And just last night, her eyes in a bowl of grapes. The list goes on and on. I want it stopped."

(*suck . . . puff*)

"Yes . . ." he says after a pause. "Yes, of course you do. And I'll see to it that it *is* stopped. Immediately. I'll have the warden launch a full investigation of the kitchen staff."

"Thank you. It's good to know there's at least one person here I can count on."

(*suck . . . puff*)

"But tell me, Mich. What have you done with all these parts of Marion's body you've been getting in your food? Where have you put them?"

A chill comes over me. Have I been wrong to think I could trust Dr. Hurst? Has he been toying with me, leading me down the garden path to this bear trap of a question? Or *is* it a trap? Isn't it a perfectly natural question? Wouldn't anyone want to know what I've been doing with little Marion's parts?

As much as I want to be open and honest with him, I can't tell him the truth. I can't let anyone know about the loose tile and the tunnel beneath it. As a prison official he'll be obligated to report it to the warden and then I'll be moved to another cell and lose my only hope of escape. I can't risk that. I'll have to lie.

I smile at him.

"Why, I've been eating them, of course."

(*suck . . .*)

Dr. Hurst's pipe has gone out.

I'm ready for the tunnel.

My cell's dark. The corridor has only a single bulb burning at the far end. It's got to be tonight.

Dr. Hurst lied. He said he'd stop the body parts on my trays but he didn't. More and more of them, a couple with every meal lately. But they all get dumped down the hole along with the rest of my food. Hard to believe a little eight-year-old body like Marion's could have so many pieces. So many I've lost track. But in a way that's good. I can't see how there can be much more of her left to torment me with.

But tomorrow is Thanksgiving and God knows what they'll place before me then.

It's got to be tonight.

At least the diet's working.

Amazing what starvation will do to you. I've been getting thinner every day. My fat's long gone, my muscles have withered and atrophied. I think I'm now small enough to slip through that opening.

Only one way to find out.

I go to the loose tile and fit my fingers around its edges. I pried it up with the spoon earlier and left it canted in its space. It comes up easily now. The putrid odor is worse than ever. I look down into the opening. It's dark in my cell but even darker in that hole.

A sense of *waiting* wafts up with the odor.

How odd. Why should the tunnel be waiting for me?

I shake off the gnawing apprehension—I've heard hunger can play tricks with your mind—and position myself for the moment of truth. I sit on the edge and slide my bony legs into the opening. They slip through easily. As I raise my buttocks off the floor to slide my hips through, I pause.

Was that a sound? From below?

I hold still, listening. For an instant there I could have sworn I heard the faintest rustle directly below my dangling feet. But throughout my frozen, breathless silence, I hear nothing.

Rats. The realization strikes me like a blow. Of course! I've been throwing food down there for weeks. I'd be surprised if there *weren't* a rat or two about.

I don't like the idea but I'm not put off. Not for a minute. I'm wearing sturdy prison shoes and stiff, tough prison pants. And I'm bigger than they are.

Just like I was bigger than Marion . . .

I slip my hips through the opening, lower my waist through, but my chest and shoulders won't go, at least not both shoulders at once. And there's no way to slip an arm through ahead of me.

I can see only one solution. I'm not comfortable with it but there's no way around it: I'm going to have to go down headfirst.

I pull myself out and swivel. I slip my left arm and shoulder through, then it's time for my head. I'm tempted to hold my breath but why bother? I'm going to have to get used to that stench. I squeeze my head through the opening.

The air is warm and moist and the odor presses against my face like a shroud freshly torn from a moldering corpse. I try to mouth-breathe but the odor worms its way into my nose anyway.

And then I hear that sound again, a rustle of movement directly below—a *wet* rustle. The odor grows stronger, rising like a dark cloud, gagging me. Something has to be behind that movement of stinking air, propelling it. Something larger than a rat!

I try to back up out of the opening but I'm stuck. Wedged! The side of my head won't clear the edge. And the odor's stronger, oh god, it's sucking the breath right out of me. Something's near! I can't see it but I can hear it, sense it! And it wants me, it *hungers* for me! It's so close now, it's—

Something wet and indescribably foul slides across my cheek and lips. The taste makes me retch. If there were anything in my stomach it would be spewing in all directions. But the retching spasms force my head back out of the hole. I tear my arm and shoulder free of the opening and roll away toward the bars, toward the corridor. Who would have thought the air of a prison cell could smell so sweet, or a single sixty-watt bulb a hundred feet away be so bright.

I begin to scream. Unashamed, unabashed, I lay on my belly, reach through the bars and claw the concrete floor as wails of abject terror rip from my throat. I let them go on in a continuous stream until somebody comes, and even then I keep it up. I plead, sob, *beg* them to let me out of this cell. Finally they do. And only when I feel the corridor floor against my knees and hear the barred door clang shut behind me does the terror begin to leach away.

"Doctor Hurst!" I tell them. "Get Doctor Hurst!"

"He ain't here, creep."

I look up and see Hugo hovering over me with two other guards from the third shift. A circle of faces completely devoid of pity or compassion.

"Call him! Get him!"

"We ain't disturbin' him for the likes o' you. But we got his resident on the way. Now what's this all—?"

"In there!" I say, pointing to the rear of the cell. "In that hole in the back! Something's down there!"

Hugo jerks his head toward the cell. "See what he's yapping about."

A young blond guard steps into my cell and searches around with his flashlight.

"In the back!" I tell him. "The right rear corner!"

The guard returns, shaking his head. "No hole in there."

"It must have pulled the tile back into place! Please! Listen to me!"

"The kid killer's doing a crazy act," Hugo says with a snarl. "Trying to get off on a Section Eight."

"No-no!" I pull at his trousers as I look up at him. "Back there, under one of the tiles—"

Hugo looks away, down the corridor. "Hey, Doc! Can you do something to shut this creep up?"

A man in a white coat appears, a syringe in his hand.

"Got just the thing here. Doctor Hurst left a standing order in the event he started acting up."

Despite my screams of protest, my desperate, violent struggles, they hold me down while the resident jabs a needle into my right buttock. There's burning pain, then the needle is withdrawn and they loosen their grip.

I'm weak from lack of food, and spent from the night's exertions. The drug acts quickly, sapping what little strength remains in my limbs. I go with it. There's no more fight left in me.

The guards lift me off the floor and begin to carry me. I close my eyes. At least I won't have to spend the night in the cell. I'll be safe in the infirmary.

Abruptly I'm dropped onto a cot. My eyes snap open as I hear my cell door clang shut, hear the lock snap closed.

No! They've put me back in the cell!

I open my lips to scream but the inside of my mouth is dry and sticky. My howl emerges as a whimper. Footsteps echo away down the corridor and the overheads go out.

I'm alone . . . for a while.

And then I hear the sound I knew would come. The tile moves. A gentle rattle at first, then a long slow sliding rasp of tile upon tile. The stinking miasma from below insinuates its way into my cell, permeating my air, making it its own.

Then a soft scraping sound, like a molting snake sliding between two rocks. Followed by another sound, a hesitant, crippled shuffle, edging closer.

I try to get away, to roll off the cot, but I can't move. My body won't respond.

And then I see it. Or rather I see a faint outline, greater darkness against lesser darkness: slim, between four and five feet high. It leans over the bed and reaches out to me. Tiny fingers—cold, damp, ragged fingers—flutter over my face like blind spiders, searching. And then they pause, hovering over my mouth and nose. My God, I can't stand the odor. I want to retch but the drug in my system won't let me.

And then the fingers move. Quickly. Two of them slip wetly into my nostrils, clogging them, sealing them like corks in the necks of wine bottles. The other little hand darts past my gasping lips, forces its way between my teeth, and crawls down my throat.

The unspeakable obscenity of the taste is swept away by the hunger for air. Air! I can't breathe! I need *air!* My body begins to buck as my muscles spasm and cry for oxygen.

It speaks then. In Marion's little voice.

Marion's . . . yet changed, dried and stiff like a fallen leaf blown by autumn gusts from bright October into lifeless November.

"*Daddy . . .*"

Early on in 1990 my goombah Tom Monteleone asked me to contribute to the first of a series of anthologies he was starting. The *Borderlands* guidelines were and have always been: no topic, no restrictions, and above all, no clichés.

"Surprise me," Tom said.

Well, with one project or another—*Reprisal, Freak Show, Nightworld,* and all the short stories—tugging me this way and that, I kept putting it off. So it wasn't until late in the year that I started "When He Was Fab" for Tom.

This is one of those stories where I give a blank look when asked where the idea came from. I have a vague memory that it might involve watching the original *The Blob* for the umpteenth time. My favorite scene has always been the one where the old guy removes the goo from the meteorite; as he holds it up on the end of a stick it seems to leap onto his arm. I may have done my turn-it-over thing and thought, *What if the goo has something else in mind besides lunch?* I can look back and say it's a *Cinderfella* story, but during the writing it was simply happening. The working title was "Dying Outside" (*pace* Bob Silverberg).

As I was finishing it, *Weird Tales* came along and said they wanted to do a special "F. Paul Wilson Issue." The magazine that had introduced H. P. Lovecraft, Robert E. Howard, Robert Bloch, and other behemoths in the genre wanted to devote an issue to *moi*? How could I refuse? They needed stories—soon. One of the pieces I sent them was "When He Was Fab." It's not true horror, just strange . . . weird. Perfect for *Weird Tales.*

Tom was ticked. So I promised him another for *Borderlands 2.* It's hard to say no to Tom; you get the feeling you might end up sleeping with the fishes.

(NB: As you read, keep in mind when this was written.)

When He Was Fab

Floor drains.

Sheesh. Doug hated them.

Being super of this old rattrap building wasn't a bad job. The hours could play hell with you sometimes, but he got a free room, he got his utilities, and he got a salary—if you wanted to call that piddly amount in his weekly check a salary. But you couldn't knock the deal too hard. Long as he stayed on the job, he had shelter, warmth, and enough money for food, enough time to work out with his weights. Wasn't glamorous, but a guy with his education—like, none to speak of besides seventh grade and postgrad courses in the school of hard knocks—couldn't ask for a whole helluva lot more.

'Cept maybe for drains that worked.

The basement floor drain was a royal pain. He hovered over it now in his rubber boots, squatting ankle deep in the big stinky puddle that covered it. Around him the tenants' junk was stacked up on the high ground against the walls like a silent crowd around a drowning victim. Third time this month the damn thing had clogged up. Course there'd been a lot of rain lately, and that was part of the problem, but still the drain shoulda been working better than this.

Now or never, he thought, unfolding his rubber gloves. He wished he had more light than that naked sixty-watter hanging from the beam overhead. Would've loved one of those big babies they used at night games up at Yankee Stadium.

Jeez but he hated this part of the job. Last week the drain had clogged and he'd reached down like he was about to do now and had come up with a dead rat.

He shuddered with just the memory of it. A monster Brooklyn brown rat.

Big, tough mother that could've easily held its own with the ones down on the docks. Didn't know how it had got in this drain, but the grate had been pushed aside, and when he'd reached down, there it was, wedged into the pipe. So soft, at first he'd thought it was a plastic bag or something. Then he'd felt the tail. And the feet. He'd worked it loose and pulled it free.

Just about blew lunch when he'd looked at it, all soft, puffy, pulpy, and drippy, the eyes milk white, the sharp yellow buck teeth bared, the matted hair falling off in clumps. And God, it stunk. He'd dumped it in his plastic bucket, scooped up enough of the rapidly draining water to cover it, then run like hell for the Dumpster.

"Whatta y'got for me this week, you sonuvabitch?" he said aloud.

He didn't usually talk to floor drains, but his skin was crawling with the thought of what might've got stuck down there this time. And if he ever grabbed something that was still moving . . . forget about it.

He pulled the heavy rubber gloves up to his elbows, took a deep breath, and plunged his right hand into the water.

"What the hell?"

The grate was still in place. So what was blocking it?

Underwater, he poked his fingers through the slots and pulled the grate free, then worked his hand down the funnel and into the pipe.

"What now, you mother? What *now*?"

Nothing. The water felt kind of thick down there, almost like Jell-O, but the pipe was empty as far as his fingers could reach. Probably something caught in the trap. Which meant he'd have to use the snake. And dammit to hell, he'd left it upstairs.

Maybe if he squeezed his fingers down just a little farther he'd find something. Just a little—

Doug reached down too far. Water sloshed over the top of his glove and ran down the inside to his fingers. It had a strange, warm, *thick* feel to it.

"Damn it all!"

But when he went to pull back, his hand wouldn't come. It was stuck in the hole and all his twisting and pulling only served to let more of the cloudy water run into his glove.

And then Doug noticed that the water was no longer running down his arm—it was running *up*.

He stared, sick dread twisting in his gut, as the thick, warm fluid moved up past his elbow—*crawled* was more like it. After a frozen moment he attacked it with his free hand, batting at it, wiping it off. But it wouldn't wipe. It seemed to be traveling *in* his skin, becoming part of it, seeping up his arm like water spreading through blotter paper.

And it was *hot* where it moved. The heat spread up under the half sleeve of his work shirt. He tore at the buttons but before he could get them undone the heat had spread across his chest and up his shoulder to his neck.

Doug lost it then. He began whimpering and crying, clawing at himself as he splashed and scrambled and flopped about like an animal caught in a trap, trying to yank his right hand free. He felt the heat on his face now, moving toward his mouth. He clamped his lips shut but it ran into his nostrils and through his nose to his throat. He opened his mouth to scream, but no sound would come. A film covered his eyes, and against his will his muscles began to relax, lowering him into the water, letting it soak into him, all through him. He felt as if he were melting, dissolving into the puddle . . .

Marc hopped out of the cab in front of the Graf Spee's entrance, paid the driver with his patented flourish, and strolled past the velvet cords that roped off the waiting dorks.

Bruno was on the door tonight. A burly lump of muscle with feet; at thirty-five he was maybe ten years older than Marc; his hair was a similar brown but there the resemblance stopped. As Marc approached the canopied entrance he wondered what Bruno had looked like as an infant, or if the doorman's mother had been prescient. Because Bruno had grown up to be the epitome of Bruno-ness.

"Ay, Mista Chevignon," Bruno said with a wide grin and a little bow. "How ya doon tanight?"

"Fine, Bruno. Just fine."

Keeping his hands jammed deep into the pockets of his Geoffrey Beene tweed slacks, and trapping his open, ankle-length Moschino black leather coat behind his elbows while exposing his collarless white Armani shirt, buttoned to the throat, Marc swiveled and surveyed the line of hopefuls awaiting the privilege of admission to the Spee.

"Real buncha loooosuhs tonight, Mista C."

Marc let his eyes roam the queue, taking in all the well-off and the trying-to-look-it, some natives, some tunnel rats and bridge trolls, all dressed in their absolute best or their most fashionably tacky ensembles, trying to look so cool, so with-it, so very-very, but unable to hide the avid look in their eyes, that hunger to be where it was most in to be, to dance on the rotating floor of the Spee and search for the famous faces that would be on the "Star Tracks" page of next week's *People*.

"Have they been good little aspirants, Bruno?"

"Yeah. No wise guys so far."

"Then let's make someone's day, shall we?"

"Whatever you say, Mista C."

He sauntered along outside the cords, watching them stare his way and whisper without taking their eyes off him. *Who's he? . . . You ever seen him before? . . . Looks like Johnny Depp . . . Nah, his shoulders is too big . . . Gawd, he's gawgeous! . . . Well, if he ain't somebody, how come he's getting in ahead of us? . . . I dunno, but I seen him around here before.*

Indeed you have, sweetheart, he thought.

The last speaker was a bony, brittle, bottle blonde with a white hemline up to here and a black neckline down to there. Knobby knees knocking in the breeze, spiky hair, a mouth full of gum, three different shades of eye shadow going halfway up her forehead, and wearing so many studs and dangles her ears had to be Swiss cheese when her jewelry was off.

Perfect.

"What's your name, honey?"

She batted her lashes. "Darlene."

"Who you with?"

"My sister Marlene." She reached back and pulled forward an identically dressed clone. "Who wants t'know?"

He smiled. "Twins. More than perfect." He lifted the velvet cord. "Come on, girls. You don't have to wait any longer."

After exchanging wide-eyed glances, they ducked the velvet and followed him to the canopy. Some of the dorks grumbled but a few of them clapped. Soon they were all clapping.

He ushered them to the door where Bruno stepped aside and passed the giggling twins through into the hallowed inner spaces of the Graf Spee.

"You're a prince, Mista C," Bruno said, grinning.

"How true."

He slowed, almost tripped. What a lame remark. Surely he could have come up with something better than that.

Bruno stepped into the dark passageway and touched his arm.

"You feelin' okay, Mista C?"

"Of course. Why?"

"You look a little pale, is all. Need anyting?"

"No, Bruno. Thanks, but I'm fine."

"Okay. But you need anyting, you lemme know an' it's done. Know what I'm sayin'?"

Marc clapped Bruno on the shoulder and nodded. As he walked down the narrow black corridor that led past the coat checkroom he wondered what Bruno had meant. Did he look pale? He didn't *feel* pale. He felt fine.

The twins were hovering near the coat check window, looking lost. They'd finally achieved their dream: They'd made it to the swirling innards of the Spee, and they weren't sure what to do about it. So they stood and numbly watched the peristalsis. One of them turned to Marc as he approached.

"Thanks a million, mister. It was, like, really great of you to get us in and like if, you know, you, like, want to get together later, you know, we'd, like, really be glad to show our appreciation, know what I mean?"

The second twin batted her eyes over the other's shoulder.

"Yeah. We really would. But do you mind if I, like, ask, uh . . . are you someone?"

Just as he was thinking how pathetic they were, he reminded himself that once he'd had to wait on line like them. That had been years ago, back in the days when King Kong had been *the* place. But after he'd been let in once, he'd never stood on line again. He'd taken his chance and capitalized on it. And as time had passed and his status had risen, he'd developed the nightly ritual of picking one or two of the hoi polloi for admission to the inner sanctum of whatever club he was gracing with his presence that night.

"Everyone is someone. I happen to be Marc."

"Which is your table?" said Twin One.

"They're all my tables."

Twin Two's eyes bulged. "You *own* this place?"

He laughed. "No. Of course not. That would be too much trouble." And besides, he thought, these places stay hot for something like the life span of a housefly. "I just go where the action is. And tonight the action is here. So you two wiggle in there and enjoy yourselves."

"All *right!*" said Twin One.

She turned to her sister and they raised their fists and gave each other a gutteral Arsenio Hall salute.

Marc shuddered as he watched them hurry toward the main floor. They might be just vulgar enough to amuse someone. He opened the door marked PRIVATE and took the narrow stairway up to the gallery. Gunnar, Bruno's Aryan soul mate, was on duty at the top of the steps. He waved Marc into the sanctum sanctorum of alcoved tables overlooking the dance floor.

The Manhattan In-Crowd was out in force tonight, with various Left Coast luminaries salted among them. Madonna looked up from her table and waved as she whispered something in a pert brunette's ear. Marc stuck his tongue out and kept moving. Bobby De Niro and Marty Scorsese nodded, Bianca blew him a kiss, and on and on . . .

This was what it was all about. This was what he lived for now, the nightlife that made the drudgery of his daylife bearable. Knowing people, important people, *being* known, acknowledged, sought out for a brush with that legendary Marc Chevignon wit. It was that wit, that incisive, urbane flippancy that had got him here and changed his nightlife. Soon it would be changing his daylife. Everything was falling into place, beautifully, flawlessly, almost as if he'd planned it this way.

And he hadn't.

All he'd wanted was a little excitement, to watch the watchables, to be where the action was. He'd never even considered the possibility of being *in* the play, he'd simply hoped for a chance to sit on the sidelines and perhaps catch a hint of breeze from the hem of the action as it swirled by.

But when lightning struck and he got through the door of the Kong a couple of years ago, things began to happen. He'd sat at the bar and fallen into conversation with a few of the lower-level regulars and the quips had begun to flow. He hadn't the faintest where they'd come from, they simply popped out. The cracks stretched to diatribes using Buckley-level vocabulary elevated by P. J. O'Rourke–caliber wit, but bitchy. *Very* bitchy. The bar-hangers lapped it up. The laughter drew attention, and some mid-level regulars joined the crowd. He was invited back to an after-hours party at the Palladium, and the following night when he showed up at King Kong with a few of the regulars, he was passed right through the door.

A few nights and *he* was a regular. Soon he was nobbing with the celebs. They all wanted him at their tables. Marc C made things happen. He woke people up, got them talking and laughing. Wherever he sat there was noise and joviality. He could turn just-another-night-at-the-new-now-club into an event. If you wanted to draw the people who mattered to your table, you needed Marc Chevignon.

And his wit didn't pass unnoticed by the select few who recognized obscure references and who knew high-level quick-draw quippery when they heard it. Franny Lebowitz said he could be the next Tom Wolfe. And LuAnn agreed.

He stopped at LuAnn's table.

"Hiya, Marky," she said, reaching for his hand.

Her touch sent a wave of heat through him. He and LuAnn were an *item* these days. They had a *thing* going. He spent three or four nights a week at her place. Always at her place. Never at his. No one saw his place. Ever.

That, he knew, was part of his attraction for these people. They'd taken the measure of his quality and found it acceptable, even desirable. But he was an unknown quantity. Where he came from, who he came from, where he lived, what he did in the day were all carefully guarded secrets. Marc Chevignon, the cagey, canny mystery man, the acid-tongued enigma.

He suspected that LuAnn genuinely cared for him, but it was hard to tell. She tended to let down her panties a lot quicker than her guard. She'd been around the scene so much longer than he, seemed to have had so many lovers—Christ, when he walked her into some of the private after-hours parties he could be pretty sure she'd screwed half the guys there, maybe some of the women too—but she seemed truly interested in him. At least now. At least for the moment.

She was the one who'd been pressing him to write down his more incisive observations so she could show them to a few editors she knew—and she knew all the important ones. She was sure she could land him a regular spot in the *Voice,* and maybe *Esquire,* if not both.

Thus the tape recorder in his pocket. During the day he never could remember a thing he'd said the night before. So he'd decided to record himself in action and transcribe the best stuff the next morning.

Nothing so far tonight worth writing down. Hadn't really come up with anything last night either. No inspiration, he guessed.

But it would come. Because it was happening. *He* was happening. Everything coming his way. *Esquire,* the *Voice,* maybe an occasional freelance piece for *GQ* later on. He wasn't going to be a mere hanger-on anymore, someone who merely *knew* Somebodies. He was going to *be* one of those Somebodies.

But the best part of it all was having LuAnn. LuAnn . . . twenty-eight with the moon-white skin of a teenager who'd never been to the beach, night-dark hair, pale blue, aventurine eyes, and the trademark ruby lipstick. All day long he ached for the sight of her. He couldn't tell her that, of course. Had to play it cool because Marc C was cool. But, man, sometimes it was hard to hide. *Most* times it was hard to hide. Most times he wanted to fall at her feet professing his undying love and begging her never to leave him.

Sure, it scanned like a third-rate Tin Pan Alley ditty, but that was how he felt.

"Ms. Lu," he said, bending and kissing her. God, he loved the soft, glossy touch of her lips.

She jerked back.

"What's wrong, Lu?"

"Your lips. They feel . . . different."

"Same ones I wore last night." He tugged at them. "I don't remember changing them."

LuAnn gave him a patient smile and pulled him down next to her. He waved and nodded hellos in the dimness to the LuAnn-table regulars, then turned his attention to the lady herself. Her eyes sparkled with excitement as she leaned toward him and whispered close in his ear; the caress of her warm breath raised gooseflesh down his left side.

"I hear you gave Liz's guy the slip last night."

"Liz's guy?"

"Don't be coy, Marc. I heard it earlier this afternoon. Liz had one of her people tail you home from my place last night—or at least *try* to tail you."

Any warmth he'd been drawing from her vanished in a chilly draft of unease. She could only mean Liz Smith, the columnist who'd been trying to get the scoop on him for months now. He guessed she was tired of tagging him with the "mystery man" line when she did a piece on the club scene. Other people had tried to tail him before but he'd spotted them easily. Whoever this guy was must have been good. Marc hadn't had the slightest suspicion . . .

"He said you ducked into an old apartment house in Brooklyn and never came out."

"Oh, yes . . ." Marc said carefully. "I spotted him shortly after I left your place. He was good. I couldn't lose him in the usual manner so I led him all the way into Bay Ridge and used the key I have from the owner of this dump there—in the front door and out the back. I always do that when I think I'm being followed." He rubbed his chin, Bogart style. "So he was one of Liz's boys. That's interesting."

More than interesting—terrifying.

"Yeah, she's determined to track you down," LuAnn said, snuggling closer. "But she's not going to be first, is she, Marky? You're going to take me to your place firstest, aren't you?"

"Sure, Lu. You'll be the first. But I warn you, you'll be disappointed when the day comes."

"No I won't."

Yes, you will. I guarantee it.

He sat next to her and tried to keep from shaking. God, that had been close! He'd been right on the edge of having his cover blown and hadn't had an inkling. Suddenly Marc didn't feel so good.

"Excuse me a moment," he said, rising. "I need to make a pit stop." He winked. "It's a long ride from Bay Ridge."

LuAnn laughed. "Hurry back!"

Feeling worse by the minute, he headed straight for the men's room. As he pushed into the bright fluorescent interior, he saw Karl Peaks turning away from the sink, licking a trace of white powder from his index finger.

"Marc?" Peaks said, sniffing and gawking. "Is that you, man?"

"No. It's Enrico Caruso." *Enrico Caruso? Where the hell did that come from?*

"It's your face, man. What's happened to it?"

Alarmed, Marc stepped over the mirror. His knees almost buckled when he saw himself.

My face!

His skin was sallow, leaching into yellow under the harsh light. And the left side was drooping, the corners of his mouth and left eye sagging toward his chin.

My God! What's happening?

He couldn't stay here, couldn't let anyone see him like this. Because it wasn't going to get better. Somehow he knew that the longer he waited the worse it would sag.

He spun and fled past Peaks, turned a hard right and went down the back steps, through the kitchen, and out into the rear alley.

It had started raining. He slunk through the puddles like a rat until he found an intersecting alley that took him out to West Houston. He flagged a cab and huddled in the protective darkness of the rear seat as it carried him through the downpour, over the Williamsburg Bridge to Brooklyn. Home.

Doug watched Marc flow back into the bucket, sliding down his arm, over his wrist and hand, to ooze off his fingertips like clear, warm wallpaper paste. A part of him was furious with Marc for letting him down tonight, but another part knew something was seriously wrong. He'd half-sensed it during the last time they'd been together. And tonight he was sure. Marc wasn't acting right.

Marc . . . Christ, why did he call this pile of goo Marc? It was *goo*. A nameless *it*. Marc Chevignon was someone who existed only when Doug was wearing the goo. He'd picked the name Marc because it sounded classy, like Marc Antony, that Roman guy in the Cleopatra movie. And Chevignon? He'd borrowed that from the label inside some fancy leather coat he'd seen in a men's shop.

Somewhere along the way he'd started thinking of the goo as a friend . . . a friend named Marc.

"What's the matter, Marc?" he whispered into the bucket when the goo had all run off him. "What's goin' on, man?"

Marc didn't answer. He just sat in his bucket under the harsh light of the white-tiled bathroom. Marc never answered. At least not from the bucket. Marc only spoke when he was riding Doug. Marc was brilliant when he was riding Doug. At least till now.

Doug remembered the first time Marc climbed on him, down in the basement, when he'd reached into the plugged drain . . . remembered the heat, the suffocating feeling. He'd been so scared then, afraid he'd been caught in some real-life replay of *The Blob,* absolutely sure he was going to die. But he hadn't died. After blacking out for a minute or so, he'd come to on the basement floor, half in, half out of the shrinking puddle. He'd scrambled to his feet, looked at his hands, felt his neck, his face. The goo was gone—not a trace of it left on him. Everything seemed almost normal.

Almost. His skin didn't feel quite right. Not slimy or nothing, just . . . different. He ran upstairs to his place, the super's apartment on the first floor. He seemed to be moving a little different, his steps quicker, surer. Almost, like, graceful. He got to the bathroom and stared in the mirror.

He'd changed. He looked the same, but then again he didn't. His normally wavy brown hair was darker, straighter, maybe because it was wet and slicked back. Even his eyebrows looked a little darker. His eyes were still blue but they seemed more intense, more alive.

And he felt different *inside*. Usually when he finished a day's work he liked to get a six-pack, flip on the tube, and mellow out for the night. Now he wanted to *move*. He felt like going places, doing things, making things happen instead of letting them happen.

He stared at the reflection for a long time, telling himself over and over he wasn't crazy. He'd just had some sort of daymare or something. Or maybe fumes—yeah, some sort of fumes bubbling up from the drain had screwed up his head for a little bit. But he was okay now. Really.

Finally, when he sort of believed that, he staggered back to the basement. Still had to do something with that water.

But the water was gone. The drain had unclogged and all that was left of the stinking puddle was a big round glistening wet spot. Relieved that he didn't have to stick his arm down that pipe again, Doug collected his gloves and junk and headed back upstairs.

In the hall he ran into Theresa Coffee, the busty blond graduate student in 308. He gave her his usual smile—at least he thought it was his usual smile—and expected her usual curt nod in return. She'd caught him staring at her underwear down in the laundry room once too often and had been giving him the cold shoulder ever since. Treated him like a pervo. Which he wasn't. But her underwear, man—looked like it came straight out of a Frederick's of Hollywood catalog. Whoa.

But this time she actually stopped and talked to him. And he actually talked back to her. Like, intelligent. He sounded like he had a brain in his head. Like a guy who'd finished high school. College even. He didn't have the faintest idea where all that talk came from, all he knew was that for the first time in his life he sounded brainy. She seemed to think so too. She even invited him up to her place. And before too long she was modeling all that underwear for him.

Much later, when he left her, he didn't go back to his apartment to sack out. He went back to change into his best clothes—which weren't much then, for sure—and headed for Manhattan. For the King Kong.

The rest was history.

History . . . the celebrity friends, the notoriety, the promised writing career, LuAnn, a way *up* and *out* . . . history.

Yeah. History. Only right now history seemed to be coming to an end.

Doug stared down at the two-gallon bucketful of goo. *Cloudy* goo. Marc used to be clear. Crystal clear. Like Perrier. What kind of game was it trying to run?

"C'mon, guy," Doug said, rolling up his sleeve. "One more time."

He slipped his right hand up to his wrist in the goo. He noticed how Marc was cooler than usual. In the past there'd always been a near-body-temperature warmth to it. Slowly it began to slide up his forearm.

"There y'go!"

But it only made a few inches before it started to slide back into the bucket.

"You bastard!"

Doug couldn't help being mad. He knew he owed a lot to Marc—everything, in fact—but he couldn't help feel that he'd been teased along and now he was being dumped. He wanted to kick the bucket over. Or better yet, upend it over the toilet and flush it down to the sewers. See if Marc liked it down there in the dark with the crocodiles.

"So what's up, here, Marc? What's doin'? You gonna put me through the wringer? Gonna make me crawl? Is that it? Well, it won't work. Because I don't need you, Marc. I owe you, I'll give you that. But if you think I can't live without you, f'get about it, okay?"

For Doug had arrived at the conclusion that he didn't need Marc anymore. Marc hadn't really done nothing. Marc just was like the Wizard in *The Wizard of Oz*. How'd that song go? "Oz never did give nothing to the Tin Man, that he didn't already have." Right. And Doug was the Tin Man. All that sharp wit and grooviness had been hiding in him all along. All Marc had done was bring it to the surface—and take credit for it. Well, Marc wasn't going to take credit no more. *Doug* was taking the wheel now. He knew he had it in him. All the doors were already open. All he had to do was walk through and make this city his oyster.

"Okay." He rose to his feet. "If that's the way you want it, fine. You make plans for the sewer, I'll head for the Spee."

On his way out the door he should have felt great, free, lighter than air. So how come he felt like he'd just lost his best friend?

"Yo, Bruno," Doug said as he stepped under the canopy and headed toward the entrance of the Graf Spee. "I'm back."

Bruno straightened his arm and stopped Doug with a palm against his chest. It was like thumping against a piling.

"Glad to hear it," Bruno said, deadpan. "Now get back in line."

Doug smiled. "Bruno, it's me. Marc."

"Sure. An' I'm David Bowie."

"Bruno—"

"Ay! Fun's fun, guy, an' I 'preciate a good scam much as the next fella, but don't wear it out, huh? When the real Mista Chevignon comes out, maybe I'll introduce you. He'll geta kick outta you. Maybe even pass you in. He's good like dat."

"I snuck out the back, Bruno. Now I'm—"

The piling became a pile driver, thumping Doug out from under the canopy and back into the rain. Bruno was speaking through his teeth now.

"I'm startin' to get pissed. You may dress like him, you may comb your hair like him, you may even look sompin' like him, but you ain't Marc Chevignon. I know Marc Chevignon, and you ain't no Marc Chevignon." Bruno's face broke into a grin. "Ay. I sound like a president debater, don't I? I'll have to tell Mista Chevignon—the *real* one—when he comes out."

"At least let me get, like, a message to LuAnn. Please, Bruno."

Bruno's grin vanished like a pulse from one of the strobes winking over the Spee's dance floor. "Miz Lu's gone home. The real Marc Chevignon would know where dat is. Now lose yourself afore I kick your butt downa Chinatown."

Doug stumbled away through the rain in shocked disbelief. What was happening here? Why didn't Bruno recognize him?

He stopped and checked his reflection in the darkened grimy window of a plumbing supply place. He couldn't see himself too well, but he knew he looked right. The same tweed slacks, same leather coat, same white shirt. What was wrong?

At first he'd thought it was because Bruno hadn't seen him leave, but there was more to it than that. They'd stood within a foot of each other and *Bruno thought he was somebody else.*

LuAnn! He had to see LuAnn. Bruno had said she'd gone home. Early for her, but maybe she was looking for Marc.

Well, okay. She was going to find him.

Doug flagged down a cruising cab and rode it up to the West Eighties. LuAnn's condo was in a refurbished old apartment house with high-tech security. Doug knew the routine. He rang her bell in the building's foyer and waited under operating-room floodlights while the camera ogled him from its high corner perch.

"Marc!" her voiced squawked from the speaker. *"Great! Come on up!"*

On the eighth floor the elevator opened onto a three-door atrium. The middle was LuAnn's. She must have heard the elevator because her door opened before Doug reached it.

Her smile was bright, welcoming. "Marky! Where on earth did you disappear to? I was—"

And then the smile was gone and she was backing away.

"Hey! What *is* this? You're not Marc!"

As she turned and started to close the door, Doug leapt forward. He wasn't going to be shut out twice tonight. He had to convince her he was Marc.

"No! LuAnn, wait!" He jammed his foot against the closing door. "It's me! Marc! Don't do this to me!"

"I don't know what your game is, buddy, but I'm going to start screaming bloody murder in a minute if you don't back off right now!"

Doug could see how scared she was. Her lips were white and she was puffing like a locomotive. He had to calm her down.

"Look, Lu," he said softly. "I don't unnerstand what's come over you, but if I, like, step back, will you, like, leave the door open just a crack so we can talk and I can prove I'm Marc? Okay. Ain't that fair?"

Without waiting for a reply, he pulled his foot free of the door, took the promised step back, and held his hands up, under-arrest style. When he saw LuAnn relax, he started talking. In a low voice, he described how they'd made it last night, the positions they'd used, the hard-core videos she'd insisted on running, even the yellow rose tattooed on her left cheek. But instead of wonder and recognition in her eyes, he saw growing disgust. She was looking at him like she might look at a sink one of the tenants had tried to fix on his own.

"I don't know what your game is, clown, and I don't know what Marc's up to, but you can tell him LuAnn is not amused."

"But I *am* Marc."

"You don't even come close. And get some diction lessons before you try to pull this off again, okay?"

With that she slammed the door. Doug pounded on it.

"LuAnn! Please!"

"I'm calling security right now," she said through the door. "Beat it!"

Doug beat it. He didn't want no police problems. No way.

And when he got outside to the street, he felt awfully small, while the city looked awfully, awfully big.

It didn't seem the least little bit like an oyster.

"What d'ya need, Marc?" Doug said softly over the bucket once he was home and back in the bathroom.

Something awful had occurred to him on his way home. What if Marc was sick? Or worse yet—dying?

The thought had been a sucker punch to the gut.

"Just lemme know an' I'll get it for you. Anything. Anything at all."

But Marc wasn't talking. Marc could talk only when Doug was wearing him. So Doug shoved his hand and forearm into the bucket again, deep, all the way to the bottom. He noticed how the goo was even cooler than before. Another bad sign.

"Come on, Marc. Make me say what you need. I'll hear it and then I'll get it for you. What d'ya need?"

Nothing. Doug's lips remained slack, forming not even a syllable. Frustration bubbling into anger, he yanked his arm free, rose to his feet, and smashed his moist fist into the mirror. The glass spider-webbed, slicing up his reflection. His knuckles stung . . . and bled.

He stared at the crimson puddles forming between his knuckles and dripping into the sink. He turned to look at the bucket.

And had an idea.

"This what y'want?" he said. "Blood? You want my blood? Awright. I'll give it to you."

So saying, he jammed his fist back into the bucket and let the blood flow into the goo. When the bottom of the bucket turned red, he withdrew his hand and looked at it. The cuts had stopped bleeding and were almost healed.

Doug tried to stand but felt a little woozy, so he sat on the toilet seat cover and stared into the reddened goo.

Marc wanted blood—*needed* blood. That had to be it. Maybe the goo was some sort of vampire or something. Didn't matter. If Marc wanted blood, Doug would find it for him. He'd said he'd get anything Marc needed, hadn't he? Well, he meant it. Problem was . . . where?

As he watched the goo that was Marc he noticed the red of his blood begin to swirl and coalesce in its depths, flowing to a central point until all the red was concentrated in a single golf ball–sized globule. And then the globule began to rise. As it approached the surface it angled toward the edge of the bucket. It broke the surface next to the lip and spilled its contents over the side. The rejected blood ran down over the metal and puddled stark red against the white bathroom tiles.

A cold bleakness settled in his chest.

"All right. So you don't want no blood. What *do* you want, man?"

Marc lay silent in his galvanized metal quarters.

"You're sick, aren't you? Well, who the hell do I take you to? A vet?"

And then it hit him: Maybe Marc wanted to go home.

Aw, man. No way. He couldn't let Marc go. Without him, he was nothing. Which was pretty much what he was now. But maybe . . .

Slowly, reluctantly, Doug lifted the bucket by its handle and trudged through his apartment, out into the hall, down to the basement. Wet down here again, but the floor drain wasn't backed up. Not yet, anyway. He knelt by the grate, lifted the bucket—And paused. This was pretty radical. Pouring Marc down the drain . . . no coming back from that. Once he was back down there it was pretty good odds he was gone for good.

Or maybe not. Maybe he'd come back. Who knew? What choice did

Doug have anyway? Maybe Marc just needed to get back to the drain to re-charge his batteries. Maybe he had friends or family down there. Might as well put him back where he came from because he'd didn't look like he was gonna last too much longer up here.

Doug lifted the grate and tipped the bucket. The goo almost leapt over the side, diving for the opening. It slid through the grate, oozed down the pipe, and splashed when it hit the water in the trap below.

Doug sat down and waited, wishing, hoping, praying for Marc to come bubbling back up the drain and crawl onto his arm again. He didn't know how long it would take, maybe days, maybe weeks, but he'd keep waiting. What else could he do? Without Marc he'd have to be Doug all the time.

And he didn't want to be Doug anymore.

The spark for "Foet" flashed in my brain on or about three A.M. on November 11, 1990. (I know because I wrote it down on a daily calendar sheet.)

It came as I lay awake after an argument with someone over fur coats. (Such a deal, she'd bought two.) She wasn't fazed at all that anal electrocution—ramming an electrode through the anus and into the innards, then turning on the current—is the method of choice for killing minks. (Mustn't mess up the pelts, you know.) Her attitude: Animals are here for our use, to do with as we please. Another woman at the table agreed. My wife, Mary, didn't want to hear. She was squeezing my thigh under the table as she does when she knows I'm about to ignite. I realized then that you cannot have a serious conversation about the humane treatment of animals when vanity or fashion has hijacked the helm. These folks would never harm a dog or a cat. Yet inform them that a bunch of little animals were broiled alive from the inside to make their coat and they shrug it off because it's so *beauuuuuutiful.*

I remember thinking that night that they'd probably wear human skin if the fashionistas said it was in vogue.

And thus was "Foet" born. Tom Monteleone picked it up for *Borderlands 2.*

Think of it as a companion piece to "Pelts."

Foet

Denise didn't mind the January breeze blowing against her back down Fifth Avenue as she crossed Fifty-seventh Street. Her favorite place in the world was Manhattan, her favorite pastime was shopping, and when she was shopping in midtown—heaven.

At the curb she stopped and turned to stare at the pert blonde who'd just passed. She couldn't believe it.

"Helene? Helene Ryder, is that you?"

The blonde turned. Her eyes lit with recognition.

"Ohmigod, Denise! Imagine meeting you here! How long has it been?"

They hugged and air kissed.

"Oh, I don't know. Six months?"

"At least! What are you doing in the city?"

"Just shopping. Accessory hunting."

"Me, too. Where were you headed?"

"Actually I was looking for a place to get off my feet and have a bite to eat. I skipped lunch and I'm famished."

"That sounds good." Helene glanced at her watch. A diamond Piaget, Denise noticed. "It's tea time at the Waldorf. Why don't we go there?"

"Wonderful!"

During the bouncy cab ride down Park Avenue, Denise gave Helene a thorough twice-over and was impressed. Her short blond hair was fashionably tousled; her merino wool topcoat, camel's-hair sweater, and short wool-and-cashmere skirt reeked of Barney's and Bergdorf's.

Amazing what could happen when your husband got a big promotion. You could move from Fairfield to Greenwich, and you could buy any little thing your heart desired.

Not that Helene hadn't always had style. It was just that now she could afford to dress in the manner to which she and Denise had always hoped to become accustomed.

Denise was still waiting to become accustomed. Her Brian didn't have quite the drive of Helene's Harry. He still liked to get involved in local causes and in church functions. And that was good in a way. It allowed him more time at home with her and the twins. The downside, though, was that she didn't have the budget to buy what she needed when she needed it. As a result, Denise had honed her shopping skills to the black-belt level. By keeping her eyes and ears ever open, buying judiciously, and timing her purchases to the minute—like now, for instance, in the post-holiday retail slump—she managed to keep herself looking nearly as in style as someone with a pocketbook as deep as Helene's.

And on the subject of pocketbooks, Denise could not take her eyes off Helene's. Fashioned of soft, silky, golden brown leather that seemed to glow in the afternoon sunlight streaming through the grimy windows of the cab, it perfectly offset the colors of her outfit. She wondered if Helene had chosen the bag for the outfit, or the outfit for the bag. She suspected the latter. The bag was exquisite, the stitchwork especially fascinating in its seemingly random joining of odd-sized and odd-shaped pieces. But it was the material itself that drew and captured her attention. She had an urge to reach out and touch it. But she held back.

Later. She'd ask about it during tea.

Sitting here with Helene on a settee along the wall in Peacock Alley at the Waldorf, sipping tea and nibbling on petits fours from the tray on the table before them, Denise felt as if she were part of the international set. The room whispered exotic accents and strange vowels. Almost every nationality was represented—the Far East most strongly—and everyone was dressed to the nines. The men's suits were either Armani or Vacca, and a number of the women outshone even Helene. Denise felt almost dowdy.

And still . . . that handbag of Helene's, sitting between them on the sofa. She couldn't escape the urge to caress it, could not keep her eyes off it.

"Isn't it beautiful?" Helene said.

"Hmmm?" Denise felt a flash of embarrassment at being caught staring, and wondered if the envy showed in her eyes. "The bag? Yes, it is. I don't think I've ever seen anything like it."

"I'd be surprised if you had." Helen pushed it closer. "Take a look."

Soft. That was the first thing Denise noticed as she lifted it. The leather was so soft, a mix of silk and down as her fingers brushed over the stitched surface. She cradled it on her lap. It stole her breath.

"Um . . . very unusual, isn't it?" she managed after a moment.

"No. Not so unusual. I've spotted a few others around the room since we arrived."

"Really?" Denise had been so entranced by Helene's bag that the others had gone unnoticed. That wasn't like her. "Where?"

Helene tilted her head to their left. "Right over there. Two tables down, in the navy blue sweater chemise and matching leggings."

Denise spotted her. A Japanese woman, holding the bag on the coffee table before her. Hers was black, but the stitching was unmistakable. As Denise scanned the room she noticed another, this one a deep coffee brown. And she noticed something else—they belonged to the most exquisitely dressed women in the room, the ones draped in Helmut Lang and Versace. Among all the beautifully dressed people here in Peacock Alley, the women who stood out, who showed exceptional flair and style in their ensembles, were the ones carrying these bags.

Denise knew in that instant that she had to have one. No matter how much it cost, this was the accessory she'd been looking for, the touch that would set her apart, lift her to a higher fashion plane.

The Japanese woman rose from her table and walked past. She glanced at Denise on her way by. Her gaze dropped to the bag on Denise's lap and she smiled and nodded. Denise managed to smile back.

What was that? It almost seemed as if the women with these bags had formed some sort of club. If so, Denise wanted to be a member.

Helene smiled knowingly when Denise looked back at her.

"I know what you're thiiiinkiiiing," she singsonged.

"Do you?"

"Uh-huh. 'Where do I get one?' Right?"

Right. But Denise wasn't going to admit it. She hated being obvious.

"Actually I was wondering what kind of leather it is."

A cloud crossed Helene's face.

"You don't know?" She paused, then: "It's foet."

"*Feet*? Whose feet?" And then Denise realized what Helene had said. "Oh . . . my . . . God!"

"Now, Denise—"

Foet! She'd heard of it but had never thought she'd see it or actually touch it, never *dreamed* Helene would buy any. Her gorge rose.

"I don't believe it!"

Denise pushed the bag back onto the sofa between them and glared at Helene.

"Don't look at me like that. It's not as if I committed a crime or anything."

"How could you, Helene?"

"Look at it." She lifted the bag. "How could I not?"

Denise was captured again by the golden glow of the leather. She felt her indignation begin to melt.

"But it's human skin!" she said, as much to remind herself of that hideous fact as to drag it out into the open.

"Not human . . . at least according to the Supreme Court."

"I don't care what those old farts say, it's still human skin!"

Helene shook her head. "*Fetal* skin, Denise. From abortions. And it's legal. If fetuses were legally human, you couldn't abort them. So the Supreme Court finally had to rule that their skin could be used."

"I know all about that, Helene."

Who didn't know about *Ranieri v. Verlaine*? The case had sent shock waves around the country. Around the *world!* Denise's church had formed a group to go down to Washington to protest it. As a matter of fact—

"Helene, *you* were out on Pennsylvania Avenue with me demonstrating against the ruling! How could you—?"

Helene shrugged. "Things change. I'm still antiabortion, but after we moved away from Fairfield and I lost contact with our old church group, I stopped thinking about it. Our new friends aren't into that sort of stuff and so I, well, just kind of drifted into other things."

"That's fine, but how does that drift you into buying something like . . ." She pointed to the bag and, God help her, she still wanted to run her hands over it. "*This!*"

"I saw one. We went to a reception—some fund-raiser for the homeless, I think—and I met a woman who had one. I fell in love with it immediately. I hemmed and hawed, feeling guilty for wanting it, but finally I went out and bought myself one." She beamed. "And believe me, I've never regretted it."

"God, Helene."

"They're already dead, Denise. I don't condone abortion any more than you do, but it's legal and that's not likely to change. And as long as it stays legal, these poor little things are going to be killed day after day, weeks after week, hundreds and thousands and millions of them. We have no control over that. And buying foet accessories will not change that one way or another. They're *already dead.*"

Denise couldn't argue on that point. Yes, they were dead, and there was nothing anyone could do about that. But . . .

"But where do they sell this stuff? I've never once seen it displayed or even advertised."

"Oh, it's in all the better stores, but it's very discreet. They're not stupid.

Foet may be legal but it's still controversial. Nobody wants trouble, nobody wants a scene. I mean, can you imagine a horde of the faithful hausfraus from St. Paul's marching through Bergdorf's? I mean *really!*"

Denise had to smile. Yes, that would be quite a sight.

"I guess it would be like the fur activists."

"Even worse." Helene leaned closer. "You know why those nuts are antifur? Because they've never had a fur coat. It's pure envy with them. But foet? Foet is tied up with motherhood and apple pie. It's going to take a long time for the masses to get used to foet. So until then, the market will be small and select. Very select."

Denise nodded. *Select.* Despite all her upbringing, all her beliefs, something within her yearned to be part of that small, select market. And she hated herself for it.

"Is it very expensive?"

Helene nodded. "Especially this shade." She caressed her bag. "It's all hand sewn. No two pieces are alike."

"And where'd you buy yours?"

Helene was staring at her appraisingly. "You're not thinking of starting any trouble, are you?"

"Oh, no. No, of course not. I just want to look. I'm . . . curious."

More of that appraising stare. Denise wanted to hide behind the settee.

"You want one, don't you?"

"Absolutely not! Maybe it's morbid on my part, but I'm curious to see what else they're doing with . . . foet these days."

"Very well," Helene said, and it occurred to Denise that Helene had never said *Very well* when she'd lived in Fairfield. "Go to Blume's—it's on Fifth, a little ways up from Gucci's."

"I know it."

"Ask for Rolf. When you see him, tell him you're interested in some of his better accessories. Remember that: 'better accessories.' He'll know what you're looking for."

Denise passed Blume's three times, and each time she told herself she'd keep right on walking and find a taxi to take her down to Grand Central for the train back to Fairfield. But something forced her to turn and go back. Just once more. This time she ducked into a slot in the revolving door and swung into the warm, brightly lit interior.

Where was the harm in just looking?

When he appeared, Rolf reminded her of a Rudolf Valentino wannabe— stiletto thin in his black pinstripe suit, with plastered-down black hair and mechanical-pencil mustache. He was a good ten years younger than Denise and barely an inch taller, with delicate, fluttery hands, lively eyes, and a barely audible voice.

He gave Denise a careful up-and-down after she'd spoken the code words, then extended his arm to the right.

"Of course. This way, please."

He led her to the back of the store, down a narrow corridor, and then through a glass door into a small, indirectly lit showroom. Denise found herself surrounded by glass shelves lined with handbags, belts, even watch bands. All made of foet.

Rolf closed the door behind them.

"The spelling is adapted from the archaic medical term."

"Really?"

She noticed he didn't actually say the word: *foetal*.

"Now . . . what may I show you?"

"May I browse a little?"

"*Mais oui*. Take your time."

Denise wandered the pair of aisles, inspecting the tiers of shelves and all the varied items they carried. She noticed something: Almost everything was black or very dark.

"The bag my friend showed me was a lighter color."

"Ah, yes. I'm sorry, but we're out of white. That goes first, you know."

"No, this wasn't white. It was more of a pale, golden brown."

"Yes. We call that white. After all, it's made from white hide. It's relatively rare."

"'Hide'?"

He smiled. "Yes. That's what we call the . . . material."

The material: white fetal skin.

"Do you have any pieces without all the stitching? Something with a smoother look?"

"I'm afraid not. I mean, you must understand, we're forced by the very nature of the source of the material to work with little pieces." He gestured around. "Notice too that there are no gloves. None of the manufacturers wants to be accused of making kid gloves."

Rolf smiled. Denise could only stare at him.

He cleared his throat. "Trade humor."

Little pieces.

Hide.

Kid gloves.

Suddenly she wanted to run, but she held on. The urge passed.

Rolf lifted a handbag from atop a nearby display case. It was a lighter brown than the others, but still considerably darker than Helene's.

"A lot of people are going for this shade. It's reasonably priced. Imported from India."

"Imported? I'd have thought there'd be plenty to go around just from the U.S."

He sighed. "There would be if people weren't so provincial in their attitudes about giving up the hides. The tanneries are offering a good price. I don't understand some people. Anyway, we have to import from the Third World. India is a great source."

Denise picked up another, smaller bag of a similar shade. So soft, so smooth, just like Helene's.

"Indian, too?"

"Yes, but that's a little more expensive. That's male."

She looked at him questioningly.

His eyes did a tiny roll. "They hardly ever abort males in India. Only females. Two thousand to one."

Denise put it down and picked up a similar model, glossy, ink black. This would be a perfect accent to so many of her ensembles.

"Now that's—"

She held up her free hand. "Please don't tell me anything about it. Just the price."

He told her. She repressed a gasp. That would just about empty her account of the money she'd put aside for all her fashion bargains. On one item. Was it worth it?

She reached into her old pocketbook, the now dowdy-looking Fendi, and pulled out her gold MasterCard. Rolf smiled and lifted it from her fingers.

Minutes later she was back among the hoi polloi in the main shopping area, but she wasn't one of them. She'd been where they couldn't go, and that gave her a special feeling.

Before leaving Blume's, Denise put her Fendi in the store bag and hung the new foet bag over her arm. The doorman gave her a big smile as he passed her through to the sidewalk.

A cold wind had sprung up in the dying afternoon. She stood in the fading light with the breeze cutting her like an icy knife and suddenly felt horrible.

I'm toting a bag made from the skin of an unborn child.

Why? Why had she bought it? What had possessed her to spend that kind of money on such a ghoulish . . . *artifact?* Because that was just what it was— not an accessory, an artifact.

She opened the store bag and reached in to switch the new foet for her trusty Fendi. She didn't want to be seen with it.

And Brian! Good God, how was she going to tell Brian?

"What?"

Brian never talked with food in his mouth. He had better manners than that. But Denise had just told him about Helene's bag and at the moment his mouth, full of sautéed spinach, hung open as he stared at her with wide eyes.

"Brian, please close your mouth."

He swallowed. *"Helene?* Helene had something made of human skin?"

. . . not human . . . at least according to the Supreme Court . . .

"It's called *foet,* Brian."

"I know damn well what it's called! They could call it chocolate mousse but it would still be human skin. They give it a weird name so people won't look at them like they're a bunch of Nazis when they sell it! Helene—how could she?"

. . . they're already dead, Denise . . .

Brian's tone became increasingly caustic. Denise felt as if he were talking to her.

"I don't believe it! What's got into her? One person kills an unborn child and the other makes the poor thing's skin into a pocketbook! And Helene of all people! My God, is that what a big pay raise and moving to Greenwich does to you?"

Denise barely heard Brian as he ranted on. Thank God she'd had the good sense not to tell him about her own bag. He'd have been apoplectic.

No doubt about it . . . she was going to return that bag as soon as she could get back into the city.

Denise stood outside Blume's, dreading the thought of facing Rolf in that tiny showroom and returning her foet, her beautiful foet.

She pulled it out of the shopping bag and stared at it. Exquisite. Strange how a little extra time could alter your attitude. The revulsion that had overwhelmed her right after she'd bought it had faded. Perhaps because every day during the past week—a number of times each day, to be honest—she'd taken it out and looked at it, held it, caressed it. Inevitably, its true beauty had shown through and captured her. Her initial infatuation had returned to the fore.

But the attraction went beyond mere beauty. This sort of accessory *said* something. Exactly what, she wasn't sure. But she knew a bold fashion statement when she saw one. This however was a statement she didn't have quite the nerve to make. At least not in Fairfield. So different here in the city. The cosmopolitan atmosphere allowed the elite to flash their foet—she liked the rhyme. She could be so very *in* here. But it would make her so very *out* with her crowd in Fairfield—out of her home too, most likely.

Small minds. What did they know about fashion? In a few years they'd all be buying it. Right now, only the leaders wore it. And for a few moments she'd been a member of that special club. Now she was about to resign.

As she turned to enter Blume's, a Mercedes stretch limo pulled into the curb beside her. The driver hopped out and opened the door. A shapely brunette of about Denise's age emerged. She was wearing a dark gray short wrap coat of llama and kid over a long-sleeved crepe-jersey catsuit. She held a black clutch purse with the unmistakable stitching of foet. Her eyes flicked down to Denise's handbag, then back up to her face. She smiled. Not just a polite passing-stranger smile, but a warm, we-know-style smile.

As Denise returned the smile, all doubt within her melted away as if it had never been. Suddenly she knew she was right. She knew what really mattered, what was important, where she had to be, fashion-wise.

And Brian? Who said Brian had to know a thing about it? What did he know about fashion anyway?

Denise turned and strode down Fifth with her new foet bag swinging from her arm for all the world to see.

Screw them all. It made her feel good, like she was *some*body. What else mattered?

She really had to make a point of getting into the city more often.

1991

A double strikeout in the awards department this year: "Pelts" lost the Bram Stoker award for novelette, and "The Barrens" lost the World Fantasy Award for novella. I took solace in the election of *An Enemy of the State* to the Prometheus Hall of Fame.

Mike Hill called from DC Comics in the spring and asked if I'd be interested in contributing a thousand-word introduction to *Preludes and Nocturnes,* the first collection of Neil Gaiman's *Sandman* comics. I wrote an insouciant piece complimenting the Brits for reinvigorating our music and our comic characters. My intro lasted through a few printings but then was replaced with a much more reverent piece—a virtual genuflection, you might say—by Karen Berger.

Meanwhile I was working away on *Freak Show* and cursing the amount of time it was eating up.

The Dark Harvest hardcover of *Reprisal,* the fifth volume in the Adversary Cycle, was published in July, but Jove didn't have the paperback scheduled until the following year.

Dark Harvest then published the hardcover of *Sibs*; I was still waiting to hear Putnam's decision on whether or nor they wanted to publish a paperback edition. I assumed they would . . . but never assume.

In November I heard from Mike Hill of DC again and wrote an introduction to *Batman: Gothic* for him on Thanksgiving morning. (My wife and I have agreed that it's better for all concerned if I avoid the kitchen during the early half of Thanksgiving.)

Shortly after that Marty Greenberg requested a story for a new Batman anthology but I couldn't come up with anything.

Although I didn't hear it at the time, a lunch with Susan Allison, my longtime editor at Putnam (*Reborn, Reprisal,* and *Nightworld* were being published through their Jove imprint), struck an ominous note. She'd had *Sibs* for a long time without making an offer. She seemed receptive to the novel but told me she couldn't talk money until after *Reprisal* was published the following March. I couldn't pull a good reason out of her. I could have yanked the book and gone elsewhere, but I wasn't looking to burn any bridges with the publisher who had all my major work on its backlist.

I closed out the year writing the early chapters of a novel I was calling *The Ingraham.* Over the past few months I'd come up with this idea for a medical thriller—more like a medical *school* thriller. I liked the story, but it wasn't horror. I was a horror guy. I was also a doctor who used writing as a break from medicine—my golf game, so to speak. Writing a straight medical thriller would be like going to the office. Or would it? With the Adversary Cycle finished and *Sibs* in limbo, maybe a brief vacation from horror might be a good thing. And it wouldn't be *that* much of a vacation: The book as I envisioned it would be plenty creepy, just no supernatural elements.

I had no idea what an enormous impact the novel would have on my life.

This baby clocks in at barely over 2,000 words, but even then I almost missed the deadline.

The late J. N. Williamson called me looking for a story for *Masques IV*. I'd been in the first anthology and Jerry wanted me back. I said yes, then regretted it because I had to squeeze it out at odd moments between revising *Nightworld*, finishing the wraparound story for *Freak Show*, checking the copyedited manuscript for Berkley's *Reprisal*, outlining *Virgin* (more on that later), introing the *Sandman* collection, and afterwording the "Buckets" paperback for Pulphouse. Lucky for me, other authors were late, so the deadline was extended.

As a challenge to myself (and as a way to cut the story's word count) I decided to write it as pure dialogue—not one word of narrative. It didn't save me the time I thought it would. In fact it took me longer because I had to find ways to convey setting and action via the gab. And that's not easy to do without creating dialogue that sounds like, "Oh, just toss your herringbone tweed coat on that Louis XIV love seat under the Chagall."

A lagniappe (I'm told I overuse that word) is that the story works beautifully at readings.

Please Don't Hurt Me

"Real nice place you've got here."

"It's a dump. You can say it—it's okay. Sure you don't want a beer or something?"

"Honey, all I want is you. C'mon and sit next to me. Right over here on the couch."

"Okay. But you won't hurt me, will you?"

"Now, honey—Tammy's your name, isn't it?"

"Tammy Johnson. I told you that at least three times in the bar."

"That's right. Tammy. I don't remember things too good after I've had a few."

"I've had a few too and I remember your name. Bob. Right?"

"Right, right. Bob. But now why would someone want to hurt a sweet young thing like you, Tammy? I told you back there in the bar you look just like that actress with the funny name. The one in *Ghost*."

"Whoopi Goldberg?"

"Oh, I swear, you're a funny one. Funny and beautiful. No, the other one."

"Demi Moore."

"Yeah. Demi Moore. Why would I want to hurt someone who looks like Demi Moore? Especially after you were nice enough to invite me back to your place."

"I don't know why. I never know why. But it just seems that men always wind up hurting me."

"Not me, Tammy. No way. That's not my style at all. I'm a lover not a fighter."

"How come you're a sailor, then? Didn't you tell me you were in that Gulf War?"

"But I didn't see battle. Don't let the uniform scare you. Like I said, I'm really a lover at heart."

"Do you love me?"

"If you'll let me."

"My father used to say he loved me."

"Oh, I don't think I'm talking about that kinda love."

"Good. Because I didn't like that. He'd say he loved me and then he'd hurt me."

"Sometimes a kid needs a whack once in a while. I know my pop loved me, but every once in a while I'd get too far out of line—like a nail that starts working itself loose from a fence post?—and so he'd have to come along every so often and whack me back into place. I don't think I'm any the worse for it."

"Ain't talking about getting 'whacked,' sailor man. If I'd wanted to talk about getting 'whacked' I woulda said so. I'm talking 'bout getting *hurt*. My daddy hurt me lotsa times. And he did it for a long, long time."

"Yeah? Like what he do to hurt you?"

"Things. And he was all the time making me do things."

"What sort of things?"

"Just . . . things. Doin' things to him. Things he said made him feel good. Then he'd do things to me that he said would make me feel good but they never did. They made me feel crummy and rotten and dirty."

"Oh. Well, uh, gee . . . didn't you tell your mom?"

"Sure I did. Plenty of times. But she never believed me. She always told me to stop talking dirty and then *she'd* whack me and wash my mouth out with soap."

"That's terrible. You poor thing. But let's forget about all that. Here . . . snuggle up against me now. How's that?"

"Fine, I guess, but what was worse, my momma'd tell Daddy and then he'd get mad and *really* hurt me. Sometimes it got so bad I thought 'bout killing myself. But I didn't."

"I can see that. And I'm sure glad you didn't. What a waste that would've been."

"Anyway, I don't want to talk about Daddy. He's gone and I don't hardly think about him anymore."

"Ran off?"

"No. He's dead. And good riddance. He had a accident on our farm, oh, some seven years ago. Back when I was twelve or so."

"That's too bad . . . I think."

"People said it was the strangest thing. This big old tractor tire he had stored up in the barn for years just rolled out of the loft and landed right on his head. Broke his neck in three places."

"Imagine that. Talk about being in the wrong place at the wrong time."

"Yeah. My momma thought somebody musta pushed it, but I remember hearing the insurance man saying how there's so many accidents on farms. Bad accidents. Anyway, Daddy lived for a few weeks in the hospital, then he died."

"How about that. But about you and me. Why don't we—?"

"Nobody could explain it. The machine that was breathing for him somehow got shut off. The plug just worked its way out of the wall all by itself. I saw him when he was just fresh dead—I was first one in the room, in fact."

"That sounds pretty scary."

"It was. Here, let me unzip this. Yeah, his face was purple-blue and his eyes were all red and bulgy from trying to suck wind. My momma was sad for a while, but she got over it. Do you like it when I do you like this?"

"Oh, honey, that feels good. That feels *wonderful.*"

"That's what Daddy used to say. Ooh, look how big and hard you got. My momma's Joe used to get big and hard like this."

"Joe?"

"Yeah. Pretty soon after Daddy died my momma made friends with this man named Joe and after a time they started living together. Like I said, I was twelve or so at the time and Joe used to make me do this to him. And then he'd hurt me with it."

"I'm sorry to hear that. Don't stop. Don't . . . stop."

"I won't. Yours is a pretty one. Not like Joe's. His was crooked. Maybe that's why his hurt me even more than Daddy's."

"Hey, don't squeeze so hard."

"Sorry. Joe liked me to—"

"Do we have to talk about this Joe?"

"No, but . . ."

"Hey, don't stop."

"But I feel like talking about him."

"Okay, okay. So how'd you finally get away from him?"

"Oh, I didn't. He got hurt."

"Really? Another farm accident?"

"Nah. We weren't even on the farm no more. We was livin' in this dumpy old house up Lottery Canyon way. My momma still worked but all Joe did was fiddle on this big old Cadillac of his—you know, the kind with the fins?"

"Yeah. A fifty-nine?"

"Who knows. Anyways, he was always fiddlin' with it. And he always made me help him—you know, stand around and watch what he was doin' and hand him tools and stuff when he asked for them. He taught me a lot about cars, but if I didn't do everything just right, he'd hurt me."

"And I'll bet you hardly ever did everything 'just right.'"

"Nope. Never. Not even once. How on earth did you know?"

"Lucky guess. What finally happened to him?"

"Those old brakes on that old Caddy just up and failed on him one night when he was making one of his trips down the canyon road to the liquor store. Went off the edge and dropped about a hundred feet."

"Killed?"

"Yeah, but not right away. He got tossed from the car and then the car rolled over on him. Broke his legs in about thirty places. Took a while before anybody even realized he was missing, and took almost an hour for the rescue squad to get to him. And they say he was screamin' like a stuck pig the whole time."

"Oh."

"Something wrong?"

"Uh, no. Not really. I guess he deserved it."

"Damn right he did. Never made it to the hospital though. Went into shock when they rolled the car off him and he saw what was left of his legs. Died in the ambulance. But here . . . let me do this to you. *Hmmmmmmm.* You like that?"

"Oh, God."

"Does that mean yes?"

"You'd better believe that means yes!"

"My boyfriend used to love this."

"Boyfriend? Hey, now wait a minute—"

"Don't get all uptight now. You just lie back there and relax. My *ex*-boyfriend. *Very* ex."

"He'd better be. I'm not falling for any kind of scam here."

"Scam? What do you mean?"

"You know—you and me get started here and your boyfriend busts in and rips me off."

"Tommy Lee? Bust in here? Oh, hey, I don't mean to laugh, but Tommy Lee Hampton will not be bustin' in here or anywheres else."

"Don't tell me he's dead too."

"No-no. Tommy Lee's still alive. Still lives right here in town, as a matter of fact. But I betcha he wishes he didn't. And I betcha he wishes he'd been nicer to me."

"I'll be nice to you."

"I hope so. Tommy and Tammy—seemed like we was made for each other, don't it? Sometimes Tommy Lee was real nice to me. A *lot* of times he was real nice to me. But only when I was doin' what he wanted me to do. Like this . . . like what I'm doin' to you now. He taught me this and he wanted me to do it to him all the time."

"I can see why."

"Yeah, but he'd want me to do him in public. Or do other things. Like when we'd be driving along in the car he'd want me to—here, I'll show you . . ."

"Oh . . . my . . . *God!*"

"That's what he'd always say. But he'd want me to do it while we was drivin' beside one of those big trucks so the driver could see us. Or alongside a Greyhound bus. Or at a stoplight. Or in an elevator—I mean, who knew when it was going to stop and who'd be standing there when the doors open? I'm a real lovable girl, y'know? But I'm not *that* kind of a girl. Not ay-tall."

"He sounds like a sicko."

"I think he was. Because if I wouldn't do it when he wanted me to, he'd get mad and then he'd get drunk, and then he'd hurt me."

"Not another one."

"Yeah. Can you believe it? I swear I got the absolute worst luck. He was into drugs too. Always snorting something or popping one pill or another, always trying to get me to do drugs with him. I mean, I drink some, as you know—"

"Yeah, you sure can put those margaritas away."

"I like the salt, but drugs is just something I'm not into. And he'd get mad at me for sayin' no—called me Nancy Reagan, can you believe it?—and hurt me something terrible."

"Well, at least you dumped him."

"Actually, he sort of dumped himself."

"Found himself someone else, huh?"

"Not exactly. He took some 'ludes and got real drunk one night and fell asleep in bed with a cigarette. He was so drunk and downered he got burned over most of his body before he finally woke up."

"Jesus!"

"Jesus didn't have nothin' to do with it—except maybe with him survivin'. Third degree burns over ninety percent of Tommy Lee's body, the doctors at the burn center said. They say it's a miracle he's still alive. If you can call what he's doing livin'."

"But what—?"

"Oh, there ain't much left to him. He's like a livin' lump of scar tissue. Looks like he melted. Can't walk no more. Can barely talk. Can't move but two or three fingers on his left hand, and them just a teensie-weensie bit. Some folks that knew him say it serves him right. And that's just what I say. In fact I do say it—right to his face—a couple of times a week when I visit him at the nursing home."

"You . . . visit him?"

"Sure. He can't feed himself and the nurses there are glad for any help they can get. So I come every so often and spoon-feed him. Oh, does he hate it!"

"I'll bet he does, especially after the way he treated you."

"Oh, that's not it. I make *sure* he hates it. You see, I put things in his food and make him eat it. Just yesterday I stuck a live cockroach into a big spoonful of his mashed potatoes. Forced it into his mouth and made him chew. Crunch-crunch, wiggle-wiggle, crunch-crunch. You should have seen the tears—just like a big baby. And then I—

"Hey. What's happened to you here? You've gone all soft on me. What's the matter with—?

"Hey, where're you goin'? We was just starting to have some fun . . . Hey, don't leave . . . Hey, Bob, what'd I do wrong? . . . What'd I say? . . . *Bob!* Come back and—

"Well! Can you believe that? I swear . . . sometimes I just don't understand men."

1992

To paraphrase one of my favorite authors: "It was the worst of times, it was the best of times."

Early in February I broke off from *The Ingraham* to write "The Lord's Work." Greenberg and Gorman wanted a vampire story for their upcoming *Dracula: Prince of Darkness* anthology and I couldn't resist returning to my "Midnight Mass" scenario. That story had starred a priest amid a vampire takeover, so I figured I'd look at the same situation from the point of view of a nun named Carole who goes a little nuts and becomes a sort of terrorist against the vampires. To fulfill the promise of the anthology's title, I dropped Dracula into one scene in such a way that I could pluck him out later and no one would miss him. "The Lord's Work" later became part of the *Midnight Mass* novel.

Later in the month I edited the *Freak Show* galleys during a tour of Ireland to gather info for *Virgin* (which I'll get to later).

In April I finished the first draft of *The Ingraham* and was extremely pleased. I put it aside to let it ferment before starting a revision, and went to work on another vampire story.

Richard Chizmar of *Cemetery Dance* was putting together an anthology called *Shivers*. I'd had such a good time with Sister Carole in "The Lord's Work" that I wanted to revisit her and explore what in particular had pushed her over the edge. Audio was part of the deal so I skewed much of the creepiness toward the auditory. "Good Friday" was the result, but the anthology never happened. I took back the story and stored it away. I felt it was special and decided to wait for the right spot.

(Since both are part of *Midnight Mass,* I see no point in reprinting them here.)

In April Jove published the *Reprisal* paperback (with a cover even worse than *Reborn*'s). A month later NEL released the first edition of *Nightworld* in England. So . . . the entire Adversary Cycle was in print overseas but not at home.

Susan Allison decided to pass on *Sibs*.

I know most of you who've read *Sibs* are thinking, *What?* But the pass had nothing to do with *Sibs,* and a lot to do with *Reborn*: A poor sell-through had returns pouring in. I blame the cover. I know that sounds self-serving, but truthfully I would not buy—I doubt I'd even pick up—a book with that cover. If you don't own a copy I'm sure you can find an image online. Take a look and see if you don't agree.

I sold *Sibs* to Tor for a fraction of my usual advance.

I sensed my career entering the doldrums. Big returns on one title mean a lower advance order on the next, virtually guaranteeing lower sales, which mean a lower advance order on the title after that. And so it goes. You get the picture: a downward spiral.

The Ingraham would change all that, but not until the fall. At the moment, relief was on the way from an entirely unexpected quarter.

On July 10 I got a call from Bob Siegal, an executive for USA Network, saying they were launching the SciFi Channel soon. Marty Greenberg had given him my name (the SciFi Channel was Manhattan-based and they were looking for a writer in the northeast) and could I design a world 150 years in the future? His plan was to insert daily newscasts from that future between the regular programs. I said I'd be delighted.

Then he said he needed it all completed and set to go in six weeks.

I was revising *The Ingraham* then, trying to get it ready for the upcoming Frankfurt Book Fair, and knew I couldn't deliver. Matt Costello and I had shot the bull a few times at various NECons (a small annual Rhode Island convention for writers and readers) and I'd been impressed with how bright and quick and versatile he was. I'd also gathered that he had a work ethic similar to mine (which is, simply, sit down and do it). Plus he lived only an hour outside the city. So I gave his name to Bob Siegal.

Matt called me back and asked if I was *sure* I didn't want it. I reconsidered and suggested we split the work. We worked our butts off—meetings, conference calls, faxing and modeming files back and forth (this was cutting edge in 1992). We delivered a future scenario detailing the sociopolitical-economic-technological status of the entire globe and near space for the year 2142 that, quite frankly, blew them away.

Faster Than Light Newsfeed was born.

The channel handed our "bible"—crammed with story arcs—to a fellow named Russ Firestone who adapted thirty-to-sixty-second spots that would play one per day, five days a week and repeat on weekends. We laid out the arcs in narrative form and in a flow sheet that showed what was happening when and where throughout the year on a month-by-month and week-by-week basis. Every so often we'd get calls to provide fillers for the feeds.

On September 24 an *FTL Newsfeed*—our scenario, our characters, our format—launched the SciFi Channel. Matt and I watched from the launch party at Madison Square Garden.

I was having fun, but this wasn't doing anything for my prose career. The near-simultaneous release of *Reprisal* and *Freak Show,* the two ugliest paperbacks of the year, both with my name emblazoned across their covers, didn't improve my outlook.

A bright spot was the Borderlands Press limited edition of *Freak Show,* a beautiful example of book craft. Phil Parks did a brilliant sideshow poster for the cover, plus the interior art. For this edition I went back and wrote Phil into my backstory as an artist who was hanging around, sketching the freaks. Phil's artwork was given the look of pages torn from a sketchpad. This integration of art and story makes the hardcover unique.

In October Baen Books published *The LaNague Chronicles,* an omnibus of the three core novels of my LaNague Federation future history, with all the segments divided into chronological order. One thick book.

It was about then that I handed in the final manuscript of *The Ingraham* just in time for the Frankfurt Book Fair. But with a twist: The name on the title page was "Colin Andrews." I instructed my agent to sell it under that name.

You're asking the same question he did: Why?

Well, as you've seen, my career as a horror writer was looking a little shaky. Though *The Ingraham* was a departure from my usual fare, with my name attached the reaction would be, "Oh, another Wilson horror novel. How did the last one sell?" I wanted *The Ingraham* to arrive without baggage and be judged on its own merits.

The choice of "Colin Andrews" was simple: I was sick of my books being shelved where no one with a bad back ever sees them. This way I'd be closer to eye level.

It worked.

On October 9, just before the opening of the fair, Milan publisher Sperling & Kupfer made a fifty-million-lire preemptive bid for Italian rights to *The Ingraham.* After picking myself off the floor and doing the currency conversion, I realized I wasn't Trump rich, but it was still the largest foreign rights advance of my career to that time.

And that was only the beginning. The Sperling & Kupfer deal started a buzz at the fair that had other foreign publishers lining up for the hot novel by this new author, Colin Andrews. By the time the fair was over it had been sold into twenty-four languages.

I knew none of this. I was visiting friends in Florida and not checking my voice mail (and only gearheads were using e-mail back then). When I finally did check I found repeated messages from my agent asking me to call him right away. He told me about Frankfurt and how the buzz from the fair had set US publishers to salivating for *The Ingraham*. Putnam had just dropped out of the bidding after William Morrow and Random House both offered $750,000. (On a side note, Susan Allison, my editor at Putnam for a decade, read a few chapters and thought the style seemed awfully familiar. She was the first to suss out Colin Andrews's secret identity.) My agent wanted to know what I wanted to do.

When I awoke the next morning in the coronary care unit—

Only kidding. Naturally I was in shock—delighted, joyous shock—but when I recovered I told my agent to let them fight it out. The bidding stopped with both companies tied at $900,000. I had to choose. I chose Morrow. A week later they threw a little party for me. They knew who I was by then and said they wanted to publish the book under my name so they could have a real live author to send around and promote it.

I know you've heard that old saying: Man makes plans and God laughs. If that's true, God must have been cracking up.

1993

An eventful year that would send ripples through my career for the rest of the decade.

About the time of the 1992 Frankfurt Fair, I began a novel called *Virgin*—like *The Ingraham,* a genre hop, except no such genre existed.

My career is a paradigm of genre hopping. I started in SF, hopped to horror, then into medical thrillers, now I was hopping into . . . what? It's not deliberate: I simply write the next book. In this case the next book was what could only be called a religious thriller.

After reading Tom Monteleone's inventive *Blood of the Lamb* (about a man cloned from the blood of Jesus Christ), I got to wondering about what would happen if someone discovered the body of the Virgin Mary. By tradition, she was assumed body and soul into heaven. But it's also been suggested the Assumption was a cover to prevent people from digging up her remains for religious relics.

I couldn't get it out of my head. And once I decided who had been saddled with the responsibility for guarding those remains, I had to write it.

When I finished it in March I found myself in a quandary. My new novel had nothing in common with the book Morrow was planning to put on the best-seller list under my byline. (Stop laughing, God.) People who bought and liked *The Ingraham* (by now Morrow had decided to call it *The Select*) were going to be flummoxed by *Virgin*.

The solution: Go the pseudonym route again.

But I couldn't use Colin Andrews because many of the foreign publishers were using that on their editions. (Oh, what a web we weave . . .) Then it hit me: My wife, Mary, raised in a strict Irish Catholic household, had been my source for all things Virgin Mary during the writing of the book. Why not sell it under her maiden name?

And so *Virgin* went out under the byline of Mary Elizabeth Murphy. The dedication read: *To my husband, without whom this book would not have been possible.* Somehow it managed to pick up a great blurb ("A bold thriller with a message for us all.") from F. Paul Wilson. Hey, I figured I'd get only one chance in my life to blurb my own novel and dedicate it to myself, so I took it.

Susan Allison bought it and released it as a paperback original. Borderlands Press recently published it as a limited-edition hardcover under my name.

None of this was occurring in a vacuum. Matt Costello and I were still feeding *FTL Newsfeed*'s jones for new material. To speed things along we joined an Internet service called GEnie which allowed us to send word-processing files back and forth attached to email via 2400-baud modems. We were *wired,* dood.

But of the two of us, Matt was the more wired. He'd designed and scripted an interactive CD-ROM called *The Seventh Guest.* It sold a zillion copies and suddenly everyone in the interactive field wanted Matt. He couldn't handle the queries so he called me and said something to the effect of: We work so well together on *FTL,* why not partner up on this interactive stuff? Ever ready to try something new, I said yes. I didn't know a damn thing about interactive media, but I knew storytelling; I was sure I could learn the rest.

The rest of the year seemed spent on the road or in the air. To London to promote the *Nightworld* paperback and hardcover of *Sister Night* (NEL's title for *Sibs*). To Frankfurt for a reception where I met many of my foreign publishers. To Paris to meet with my French agent and my two French publishers. To Minnesota for the World Fantasy Convention, and to the White House for my twenty-fifth Georgetown reunion. (Yes, Bill Clinton was a classmate.)

At the World Fantasy Convention Marty Greenberg talked me into doing what I'd sworn I'd never do again: edit an anthology. He called it *Diagnosis: Terminal.* It would be all short medical thrillers and he'd do all the contact work. I'd simply have to read and choose. I said yes.

In November Headline published the first world edition of *The Ingraham* in England. They called it *The Foundation.* The byline was strange: "F. Paul Wilson writing as COLIN ANDREWS." (Go figure.)

Of all the year's trips, the one that was going to have the most far-reaching effect on my writing life came toward the end of the year. Just a short hop into Manhattan where, in the cocktail lounge of the Righa Royale, Matt Costello and I pitched our concept for an interactive CD-ROM called *DNA Wars* to Linda Rich of MediaVision.

See, back then there were video games and interactive CD-ROMs. Space

Invaders and Tetris were video games played on game consoles, like Play-Station. Interactive CD-ROMs were games too, but more cerebral and with better graphics—like *The Seventh Guest* and *Myst*—and played on computers. Nowadays they're all called video games.

In 1993 interactive media was *hot,* it was the future, and everyone in publishing and software development wanted in. Alliances were being formed willy-nilly, crazy amounts of money were being thrown about.

As designer and scripter of *The Seventh Guest,* Matt was considered a go-to guy for interactivity. He pulled me aboard and we rode the interactive groundswell. The most fascinating years of my writing career lay just ahead.

"ARYANS AND ABSINTHE"

Early in the summer of 1993 Douglas E. Winter called to tell me about his idea for an anthology that would consist of a novella for every decade of the century, each story centering on some apocalyptic event. He said pick a decade. I picked the 1920s—Weimar Germany, specifically. The arts were flourishing but the economic chaos and runaway inflation of the times were so surreal, so devastating to everyone's day-to-day life that people—Jew and gentile alike—were looking for a savior. A foppish little guy named Hitler came to prominence presenting himself as that savior.

I did extensive research for "Aryans and Absinthe." Charles Bracelen Flood's remarkable *Hitler: The Path to Power* (Houghton Mifflin, 1989) was a major source. I wanted to get the details right so I could make you feel you were *there*. I finished in August and was pretty high on it. I thought I'd captured the tenor and tempo of the times, felt I'd conveyed an apocalyptic experience.

But I'd have to wait four years before seeing it in print. The anthology, *Revelations,* wouldn't appear until 1997.

Aryans and Absinthe

Today it takes 40,000 marks to buy a single US dollar.
—*Volkischer Beobachter*, May 4, 1923

Ernst Drexler found the strangest things entertaining. That was how he always phrased it: *entertaining*. Even inflation could be entertaining, he said.

Karl Stehr remembered seeing Ernst around the Berlin art venues for months before he actually met him. He stood out in that perennially scruffy crowd with his neatly pressed suit and vest, starched collar and tie, soft hat either on his head or under his arm, and his distinctive silver-headed cane wrapped in black rhinoceros hide. His black hair swept back sleek as linoleum from his high forehead; the bright blue eyes that framed his aquiline nose were never still, always darting about under his dark eyebrows; thin lips, a strong chin, and tanned skin, even in winter, completed the picture. Karl guessed Ernst to be in his mid-thirties, but his mien was that of someone older.

For weeks at a time he would seem to be everywhere, and never at a loss for something to say. At the Paul Klee show where Klee's latest, "The Twittering Machine," had been on exhibition, Karl had overheard his sarcastic comment that Klee had joined the Bauhaus not a moment too soon. Ernst was always at the right places: at the opening of *Dr. Mabuse, der Spieler,* at the cast party for that Czech play *R.U.R.,* and at the secret screenings of Murnau's *Nosferatu,* to name just a few.

And then he'd be nowhere. He'd disappear for weeks or a month without a word to anyone. When he returned he would pick up just where he'd left off, as if there'd been no hiatus. And when he was in town he all but lived at the Romanisches Cafe where nightly he would wander among the tables, glass in hand, a meandering focus of raillery and bavardage, dropping dry, witty, acerbic comments on art and literature like ripe fruit. No one seemed to remember who first introduced him to the cafe. He more or less insinuated himself into the regulars on his own. After a while it seemed he had always been there. Everyone knew Ernst but no one knew him well. His persona was a strange mixture of accessibility and aloofness that Karl found intriguing.

They began their friendship on a cool Saturday evening in the spring. Karl had closed his bookshop early and wandered down Budapesterstrasse to the Romanisches. It occupied the corner at Tauentzien across from the Gedacht-niskirche: large for a cafe, with a roomy sidewalk area and a spacious interior for use on inclement days and during the colder seasons.

Karl had situated himself under the awning, his knickered legs resting on the empty chair next to him; he sipped an aperitif among the blossoming flower boxes as he reread *Siddhartha*. At the sound of clacking high heels he'd glance up and watch the "new look" women as they trooped past in pairs and trios with their clinging dresses fluttering about their knees and their smooth tight caps pulled down over their bobbed hair, their red lips, mascaraed eyes, and coats trimmed in fluffy fur snuggled around their necks.

Karl loved Berlin. He'd been infatuated with the city since his first sight of it when his father had brought him here before the war; two years ago, on his twentieth birthday, he'd dropped out of the university to carry on an ex-tended affair with her. His lover was the center of the art world, of the new freedoms. You could be what you wanted here: a free thinker, a free lover, a communist, even a fascist; men could dress like women and women could dress like men. No limits. All the new movements in music, the arts, the cin-ema, and the theater had their roots here. Every time he turned around he found a new marvel.

Night was upon Karl's mistress when Ernst Drexler stopped by the table and introduced himself.

"We've not formally met," he said, thrusting out his hand. "Your name is Stehr, I believe. Come join me at my table. There are a number of things I wish to discuss with you."

Karl wondered what things this man more than ten years his senior could wish to discuss, but since he had no other plans for the evening, he went along.

The usual crowd was in attendance at the Romanisches that night. Lately it had become the purlieu of Berlin bohemia—all the artists, writers, journalists, critics, composers, editors, directors, scripters, and anyone else who had any-thing to do with the avant garde of German arts, plus the girlfriends, the boy-friends, the mere hangers-on. Some sat rooted in place, others roved ceaselessly from table to table. Smoke undulated in a muslin layer above a gallimaufry of scraggly beards, stringy manes, bobbed hair framing black-rimmed eyes, hom-burgs, berets, monocles, pince-nez, foot-long cigarette holders, baggy sweaters, dark stockings, period attire ranging from the Hellenic to the pre-Raphaelite.

"I saw you at *Siegfried* the other night," Ernst said as they reached his table in a dim rear corner, out of the peristaltic flow. Ernst took the seat against the wall where he could watch the room; he left the other for Karl. "What do you think of Lang's latest?"

"Very Germanic," Karl said as he took his seat and reluctantly turned his back to the room. He was a people watcher.

Ernst laughed. "How diplomatic! But how true. Deceit, betrayal, and backstabbing—in both the figurative and literal sense. Germanic indeed. Hardly *Neue Sachlichkeit,* though."

"I think New Realism was the furthest thing from Lang's mind. Now, *Die Strasse,* on the other hand—"

"*Neue Sachlichkeit* will soon join Expressionism in the mausoleum of movements. And good riddance. It is shit."

"*Kunst ist Scheisse?*" Karl said, smiling. "Dada is the deadest of them all."

Ernst laughed again. "My, you are sharp, Karl. That's why I wanted to talk to you. You're very bright. You're one of the few people in this room who will be able to appreciate my new entertainment."

"Really? And what is that?"

"Inflation."

Before Karl could ask what he meant, Ernst flagged down a passing waiter.

"The usual for me, Freddy, and—?" He pointed to Karl, who ordered a schnapps.

"Inflation? Never heard of it. A new card game?"

Ernst smiled. "No, no. It's played with money."

"Of course. But how—"

"It's played with real money in the real world. It's quite entertaining. I've been playing it since the New Year."

Freddy soon delivered Karl's schnapps. For Ernst he brought an empty stemmed glass, a sweaty carafe of chilled water, and a small bowl of sugar cubes. Karl watched fascinated as Ernst pulled a silver flask from his breast pocket and unscrewed the top. He poured three fingers of clear green liquid into the glass, then returned the flask to his coat. Next he produced a slotted spoon, placed a sugar cube in its bowl, and held it over the glass. Then he dribbled water from the carafe, letting it flow over the cube and into the glass to mix with the green liquid . . . which began to turn a pale yellow.

"Absinthe!" Karl whispered.

"Quite. I developed a taste for it before the war. Too bad it's illegal now—although it's still easily come by."

Now Karl knew why Ernst frequently reserved this out-of-the-way table. Instinctively he glanced around, but no one was watching.

Ernst sipped and smacked his lips. "Ever tried any?"

"No."

Karl had never had the opportunity. And besides, he'd heard that it drove you mad.

Ernst slid his glass across the table. "Take a sip."

Part of Karl urged him to say no, while another pushed his hand forward and wound his fingers around the stem of the glass. He lifted it to his lips and took a tiny sip.

The bitterness rocked his head back and puckered his cheeks.

"That's the wormwood," Ernst said, retrieving his glass. "Takes some getting used to."

Karl shuddered as he swallowed. "How did that ever become a craze?"

"For half a century, all across the continent, the cocktail hour was known as *l'heure verte* after this little concoction." He sipped again, closed his eyes, savoring. "At the proper time, in the proper place, it can be . . . revelatory."

After a moment, he opened his eyes and motioned Karl closer.

"Here. Move over this way and sit by me. I wish to show you something."

Karl slid his chair around to where they both sat facing the crowded main room of the Romanisches.

Ernst waved his arm. "Look at them, Karl. The cream of the city's artists attended by their cachinating claques and coteries of epigones and acolytes, mixing with the city's lowlifes and lunatics. Morphine addicts and vegetarians cheek by jowl with Bolsheviks and boulevardiers, *arrivistes* and anarchists, abortionists and antivivisectionists, directors and dilettantes, doyennes and *demimondaines.*"

Karl wondered how much time Ernst spent here sipping his absinthe and observing the scene. And why. He sounded like an entomologist studying a particularly interesting anthill.

"Everyone wants to join the parade. They operate under the self-induced delusion that they're in control: 'What happens in the Berlin arts today, the rest of the world copies next week.' True enough, perhaps. But this is the Masque of the Red Death, Karl. Huge forces are at play around them, and they are certain to get crushed as the game unfolds. Germany is falling apart—the impossible war reparations are suffocating us, the French and Belgians have been camped in the Ruhr Valley since January, the communists are trying to take over the north, the right-wingers and monarchists practically own Bavaria, and the Reichsbank's answer to the economic problems is to print more money."

"Is that bad?"

"Of course. It's only paper. It's been sending prices through the roof."

He withdrew his wallet from his breast pocket, pulled a bill from it, and passed it to Karl.

Karl recognized it. "An American dollar."

Ernst nodded. " 'Good as gold,' as they say. I bought it for ten thousand marks in January. Care to guess what the local bank was paying for it today?"

"I don't know. Perhaps . . ."

"Forty thousand. Forty thousand marks."

Karl was impressed. "You quadrupled your money in four months."

"No, Karl," Ernst said with a wry smile. "I've merely quadrupled the number of marks I control. My buying power is exactly what it was in January. But I'm one of the very few people in this storm-tossed land who can say so."

"Maybe I should try that," Karl said softly, admiring the elegant simplicity of the plan. "Take my savings and convert it to American dollars."

"By all means do. Clean out your bank account, pull every mark you own out from under your mattress and put them into dollars. But that's mere survival—hardly entertainment."

"Survival sounds good enough."

"No, my friend. Survival is never enough. Animals limit their concerns to mere survival; humans seek entertainment. That is why we must find a way to make inflation entertaining. Inflation is here. There's nothing we can do about it. So let's have some fun with it."

"I don't know . . ."

"Do you own a house?"

"Yes," Karl said slowly, cautiously. He didn't know where this was leading. "And no."

"Really. You mean it's mortgaged to the hilt?"

"No. Actually it's my mother's. A small estate north of the city near Bernau. But I manage it for her."

Father had died a colonel in the Argonne and he'd left it to her. But Mother had no head for money, and she hadn't been quite herself in the five years since Father's death. So Karl took care of the lands and the accounts, but spent most of his time in Berlin. His bookstore barely broke even, but he hadn't opened it for profit. He'd made it a place where local writers and artists were welcome to stop and browse and meet; he reserved a small area in the rear of the store where they could sit and talk and sip the coffee he kept hot for them. His dream was that someday one of the poor unknowns who partook of his hospitality would become famous and perhaps remember the place kindly—and perhaps someday stop by to say hello with Thomas Mann or the reclusive Herman Hesse in tow. Until then Karl would be quite satisfied with providing coffee and rolls to starving scribblers.

But even from the beginning, the shop had paid nonpecuniary dividends. It was his entrée to the literati, and from there to the entire artistic caravan that swirled through Berlin.

"Any danger of losing it?"

"No." The estate produced enough so that, along with Father's army pension, his mother could live comfortably.

"Good. Then mortgage it. Borrow to the hilt on it, and then borrow some more. Then turn all those marks into US dollars."

Karl was struck dumb by the idea. The family home had never had a lien on it. Never. The idea was unthinkable.

"No. I—I couldn't."

Ernst put his arm around Karl's shoulder and leaned closer. Karl could smell the absinthe on his breath.

"Do it, Karl. Trust me in this. It's an entertainment, but you'll see some practical benefits as well. Mark my words, six months from now you'll be able to pay off your entire mortgage with a single US dollar. A single coin."

"I don't know . . ."

"You must. I need someone who'll play the game with me. It's much more entertaining when you have someone to share the fun with."

Ernst straightened up and lifted his glass.

"A toast!" He clinked his glass against Karl's. "By the way, do you know where glass clinking originated? Back in the old days, when poisoning a rival was a fad among the upper classes, it became the practice to allow your companion to pour some of his drink into your cup, and vice versa. That way, if one of the drinks were poisoned, you'd both suffer."

"How charming."

"Quite. Inevitably the pouring would be accompanied by the clink of one container against another. Hence, the modern custom." Once again he clinked his absinthe against Karl's schnapps. "Trust me, Karl. Inflation can be very entertaining—and profitable as well. I expect the mark to lose fully half its value in the next six weeks. So don't delay."

He raised his glass. "To inflation!" he cried and drained the absinthe.

Karl sipped his schnapps in silence.

Ernst rose from his seat. "I expect to see you dollar rich and mark poor when I return."

"Where are you going?"

"A little trip I take every so often. I like to swing up through Saxony and Thuringia to see what the local Bolsheviks are up to—I have a membership in the German Communist Party, you know. I subscribe to *Rote Fahne*, listen to speeches by the *Zentrale,* and go to rallies. It's very entertaining. But after I tire of that—Marxist rhetoric can be *so* boring—I head south to Munich to see what the other end of the political spectrum is doing. I'm also a member of the National Socialist German Workers Party down there and subscribe to their *Volkischer Beobachter.*"

"Never heard of them. How can they call themselves 'National' if they're not nationally known?"

"Just as they can call themselves Socialists when they are stridently fascist. Although frankly I, for one, have difficulty discerning much difference between either end of the spectrum—they are distinguishable only by their paraphernalia and their rhetoric. The National Socialists—they call themselves Nazis—are a power in Munich and other parts of Bavaria, but no one pays too much attention to them up here. I must take you down there sometime to listen to one of their leaders. Herr Hitler is quite a personality. I'm sure our friend Freud would love to get him on the couch."

"Hitler? Never heard of him, either."

"You really should hear him speak sometime. Very entertaining."

> Today it takes 51,000 marks to buy a single US dollar.
> —*Volkischer Beobachter*, May 21, 1923

A few weeks later, when Karl returned from the bank with the mortgage papers for his mother to sign, he spied something on the door post. He stopped and looked closer.

A mezuzah.

He took out his pocket knife and pried it off the wood, then went inside.

"Mother, what is this?" he said, dropping the object on the kitchen table.

She looked up at him with her large, brown, intelligent eyes. Her brunette hair was streaked with gray. She'd lost considerable weight immediately after Father's death and had never regained it. She used to be lively and happy, with an easy smile that dimpled her high-colored cheeks. Now she was quiet and pale. She seemed to have shrunken, in body and spirit.

"You know very well what it is, Karl."

"Yes, but haven't I warned you about putting it outside?"

"It belongs outside."

"Not in these times. Please, Mother. It's not healthy."

"You should be proud of being Jewish."

"I'm not Jewish."

They'd had this discussion hundreds of times lately, it seemed, but Mother just didn't want to understand. His father, the colonel, had been Christian, his mother Jewish. Karl had decided to be neither. He was an atheist, a skeptic, a free-thinker, an intellectual. He was German by language and by place of birth, but he preferred to think of himself as an international man. Countries and national boundaries should be abolished, and someday soon would be.

"If your mother is Jewish, *you* are Jewish. You can't escape that. I'm not afraid to tell the world I'm Jewish. I wasn't so observant when your father was alive, but now that he's gone . . ."

Her eyes filled with tears.

Karl sat down next to her and took her hands in his.

"Mother, listen. There's a lot of anti-Jewish feeling out there these days. It will die down, I'm sure, but right now we live in an inordinately proud country that lost a war and wants to blame someone. Some of the most bitter people have chosen Jews as their scapegoats. So until the country gets back on an even keel, I think it's prudent to keep a low profile."

Her smile was wan. "You know best, dear."

"Good." He opened the folder he'd brought from the bank. "And now for some paperwork. These are the final mortgage papers, ready for signing."

Mother squeezed his hands. "Are you sure we're doing the right thing?"

"Absolutely sure."

Actually, now that the final papers were ready, he was having second thoughts.

Karl had arranged to borrow every last pfennig the bank would lend him against his mother's estate. He remembered how uneasy he'd been at the covetous gleam in the bank officers' eyes when he'd signed the papers. They sensed financial reverses, gambling debts, perhaps, a desperate need for cash that would inevitably lead to default and subsequent foreclosure on a prime piece of property. The bank president's eyes had twinkled over his reading glasses; he'd all but rubbed his hands in anticipation.

Doubt and fear gripped Karl now as his mother's pen hovered over the signature line. Was he being a fool? He was a bookseller and they were financiers. Who was he to presume to know more than men who spent every day dealing with money? He was acting on a whim, spurred on by a man he hardly knew.

But he steeled himself, remembering the research he'd done. He'd always been good at research. He knew how to ferret out information. He'd learned that Rudolf Haverstein, the Reichsbank's president, had increased his orders of currency paper and was running the printing presses at full speed on overtime.

He watched in silence as his mother signed the mortgage papers.

He'd already taken out personal loans, using Mother's jewelry as collateral. Counting the mortgage, he'd now accumulated 500 million marks. If he converted them immediately, he'd get 9,800 US dollars at today's exchange rate. Ninety-eight hundred dollars for half a billion marks. It seemed absurd. He wondered who was madder—the Reichsbank or himself.

Today it takes 500,000,000 marks to buy a single US dollar.
—*Volkischer Beobachter,* September 1, 1923

"To runaway inflation," **Ernst** Drexler said, clinking his glass of cloudy yellow against Karl's clear glass of schnapps.

Karl sipped a little of his drink and said nothing. He and Ernst had retreated from the heat and glare of the late summer sun on the Romanisches Cafe's sidewalk to the cooler, darker interior.

Noon on a Saturday and the Romanisches was nearly empty. But then, who could afford to eat out these days?

Only thieves and currency speculators.

Four months ago Karl hadn't believed it possible, but for a while they had indeed had fun with inflation.

Now it was getting scary.

Less than four months after borrowing half a billion marks, his 9,800 US dollars were worth almost five trillion marks. Five *trillion.* The number was meaningless. He could barely imagine even a billion marks, and he controlled five thousand times that amount.

"I realized today," Karl said softly, "that I can pay off all of my half-billion-mark debt with a single dollar bill."

"Don't do it," Ernst said quickly.

"Why not? I'd like to be debt free."

"You will be. Just wait."

"Until when?"

"It won't be long before the exchange rate will be billions of marks to the dollar. Won't it be so much more entertaining to pay off the bankers with a single American coin?"

Karl stared at his glass. This game was no longer "entertaining." People had lost all faith in the mark. And with good reason. Its value was plummeting. In a mere thirty days it had plunged from a million to the dollar to half a *billion* to the dollar. Numbers crowded the borders of the notes, ever-lengthening strings of ever more meaningless zeros. Despite running twenty-four hours a day, the Reichsbank presses could not keep up with the demand. Million-mark notes were now being over-stamped with TEN MILLION in large black letters. Workers had gone from getting paid twice a month to weekly, and now to daily. Some were demanding twice-daily pay so that they could run out on their lunch hour and spend their earnings before they lost their value.

"I'm frightened, Ernst."

"Don't worry. You've insulated yourself. You've got nothing to fear."

"I'm frightened for our friends and neighbors. For Germany."

"Oh, that."

Karl didn't understand how Ernst could be so cavalier about the misery steadily welling up around them like a rain-engorged river. It oppressed Karl. He felt guilty, almost ashamed of being safe and secure on his high ground of foreign currency. Ernst drained his absinthe and rose, his eyes bright.

"Let's go for a walk, shall we? Let's see what your friends and neighbors are up to on this fine day."

Karl left his schnapps and followed him out into the street. They strolled along Budapesterstrasse until they came upon a bakery.

"Look," Ernst said, pointing with his black cane. "A social gathering."

Karl bristled at the sarcasm. The long line of drawn faces with anxious, hollow eyes—male, female, young, old—trailing out the door and along the sidewalk was hardly a social gathering. Lines for bread, meat, milk, any of the staples of life, had become so commonplace that they were taken for granted. The customers stood there with their paper bags, cloth sacks, and wicker baskets full of marks, shifting from one foot to the other, edging forward, staying close behind the person in front of them lest someone tried to cut into the line, constantly turning the count of their marks in their minds, hoping they'd find something left to buy when they reached the purchase counter, praying their money would not devalue too much before the price was rung up.

Karl had never stood in such a line. He didn't have to. He needed only to call or send a note to a butcher or baker listing what he required and saying that he would be paying with American currency. Within minutes the merchant would come knocking with the order. He found no pleasure, no feeling of superiority in his ability to summon the necessities to his door, only relief that his mother would not be subject to the hunger and anxiety of these poor souls.

As Karl watched, a boy approached the center of the line where a young woman had placed a wicker basket full of marks on the sidewalk. As he passed her he bent and grabbed a handle on the basket, upended it, dumping out the marks. Then he sprinted away with the basket. The woman cried out but no one moved to stop him—no one wanted to lose his place in line.

Karl started to give chase but Ernst restrained him.

"Don't bother. You'll never catch him."

Karl watched the young woman gather her scattered marks into her apron and resume her long wait in line, weeping. His heart broke for her.

"This has to stop. Someone has to do something about this."

"Ah, yes," Ernst said, nodding sagely. "But who?"

They walked on. As they approached a corner, Ernst suddenly raised his cane and pressed its shaft against Karl's chest.

"Listen. What's that noise?"

Up ahead at the intersection, traffic had stopped. Instead of the roar of internal combustion engines, Karl heard something else. Other sounds, softer, less rhythmic, swelled in the air. A chaotic tapping and a shuffling cacophony of scrapes and draggings, accompanied by a dystonic chorus of high-pitched squeaks and creaks.

And then they inched into view—the lame, the blind, the damaged, dismembered, demented, and disfigured tatterdemalions of two wars: The few remaining veterans of the Franco-Prussian War of 1870—stooped, wizened figures in their seventies and eighties who had besieged Paris and proclaimed Wilhelm of Prussia as Emperor of Germany in the Hall of Mirrors at Versailles—were leading the far larger body of pathetic survivors from the disastrous Great War, the War to End All Wars, the valiant men whose defeated leaders five years ago had abjectly agreed to impossible reparations in that same Hall of Mirrors.

Karl watched aghast as a young man with one arm passed within a few meters of him dragging a wheeled platform on which lay a limbless man, hardly more than a head with a torso. Neither was much older than he. The Grand Guignol parade was full of these fractions of men and their blind, deaf, limping, stumbling, hopping, staggering companions. Karl knew he might well be among them had he been born a year or two earlier.

Some carried signs begging, pleading, demanding higher pensions and disability allowances; they all looked worn and defeated, but mostly *hungry*. Here were the most pitiful victims of the runaway inflation.

Karl fell into line with them and pulled Ernst along.

"Really," Ernst said, "this is hardly my idea of an entertaining afternoon."

"We need to show them that they're not alone, that we haven't forgotten them. We need to show the government that we support them."

"It will do no good," Ernst said, grudgingly falling into step beside him. "It takes time for the government to authorize a pension increase. And even if it is approved, by the time it goes into effect, the increase will be meaningless."

"This can't go on! Someone has got to do something about this chaos!"

Ernst pointed ahead with his black cane. "There's a suggestion."

At the corner stood two brown-shirted men in paramilitary gear and caps. On their left upper arms were red bands emblazoned with a strange black twisted cross inside a white circle. Between them they held a banner:

COME TO US, COMRADES!
ADOLF HITLER WILL HELP YOU!

"Hitler," Karl said slowly. "You mentioned him before, didn't you?"

"Yes. The Austrian *Gefreiter*. He'll be at that big fascist rally in Nuremberg tomorrow to commemorate something or other. I hope to get to hear him again. Marvelous speaker. Want to come along?"

Karl had heard about the rally—so had all the rest of Germany. Upward of two hundred thousand veterans and members of every right-wing *volkisch* paramilitary group in the country were expected in the Bavarian town to celebrate the anniversary of the Battle of Sedan in the Franco-Prussian War.

"I don't think so. I don't like big crowds. Especially a big crowd of fascists."

"Some other time, then. I'll call you when he's going to address one of the beer hall meetings in Munich. He does that a lot. That way you'll get the full impact of his speaking voice. Most entertaining."

Adolf Hitler, Karl thought as he passed the brown-shirted men with the strange armbands. Could he be the man to save Germany?

"Yes, Ernst. Do call me. I wish to hear this man."

Today it takes 200 billion marks to buy a single US dollar.
—*Volkischer Beobachter*, October 22, 1923

"It's like entering another country," Karl murmured as he stood on the platform of the Munich train station.

Ernst stood beside him as they waited for a porter to take his bags.

"Not another country at all. Merely an armed camp filled with people as German as the rest of us. Perhaps more so."

"People in love with uniforms."

"And what could be more German than that?"

Ernst had sent him a message last week, scrawled in his reverse-slanted script on the blank back of a 100-million-mark note. Even with all its overworked presses running at full speed, the Reichsbank found itself limited to printing the new marks on only one side in order to keep up with the ever-increasing demand for currency. Ernst seemed to find it amusing to use the blank sides of the smaller denominations as stationery. And this note had invited Karl south to hear Herr Hitler.

Karl now wished he'd ignored the invitation. A chill had come over him as the train crossed into Bavaria; it began in the pit of his stomach, then encircled his chest and crept up his spine to his neck where it now insinuated icy fingers around his throat. Uniforms . . . military uniforms everywhere, lolling about the train station, marching in the streets, standing on the corners, and none of them sporting the comfortably familiar field gray of regular Reichswehr troops. Young men, middle-aged men, dressed in brown, black, blue, and green, all with watchful, suspicious eyes and tight, hostile faces.

Something sinister was growing here in the south, something unclean, something dangerous.

It's the times, he told himself. Just another facet of the chaotic zeitgeist.

No surprise that Bavaria was like an armed camp. Less than three weeks ago its cabinet, aghast at what it saw as Berlin's cowardly submission to the continuing Franco-Belgian presence in the Ruhr Valley, had declared a state of emergency and suspended the Weimar Constitution within its borders. Gustav von Kahr had been declared *Generalstaatskommissar* of Bavaria with dictatorial powers. Berlin had blustered threats but so far had made no move against the belligerent southern state, preferring diplomatic avenues for the moment.

But how long would that last? The communists in the north were trying to ignite a revolution in Saxony, calling for a "German October," and the more radical Bavarians here in the south were calling for a march on Berlin because of the government's impotence in foreign and domestic affairs, especially in finance and currency.

Currency . . . when the mark had sunk to five billion to the dollar two weeks ago, Karl had paid off the mortgage on the estate plus the loans against his mother's jewelry with a US ten-cent piece—what the Americans called a "dime."

Something had to happen. The charges were set, the fuse was lit. Where would the explosion occur? And when?

"Think of them as human birds," Ernst said, pointing to their left at two groups in different uniforms. "You can tell who's who by their plumage. The gray are *soldaten* . . . regular Reichswehr soldiers, of course. The green are Bavarian State Police. And as we move through Munich you'll see the city's regular police force, dressed in blue."

"Gray, green, blue," Karl murmured.

"Right. Those are the official colors. The *unofficial* colors are brown and black. They belong in varying mixes to the Nazi SA—their so-called storm troopers—and the Reichskriegsflagge and Bund Oberland units."

"So confusing."

"It is. Bavaria has been a hotbed of fascism since the war, but mostly it was a fragmented thing—more feisty little paramilitary groups than you could count. But things are different these days. The groups have been coalescing, and now the three major factions have allied themselves into something called the *Kampfbund*."

"The 'Battle Group'?"

"Precisely. And they're quite ready for battle. There are more caches of rifles and machine guns and grenades hidden in cellars or buried in and around Munich than Berlin could imagine in its worst nightmares. Hitler's Nazis are the leading faction of the Kampfbund, and right now he and the Bavarian government are at odds. Hitler wants to march on Berlin, General Commissioner Kahr does not. At the moment, Kahr has the upper hand. He's got the Green Police, the Blue Police, and the Reichswehr regulars to keep the

Kampfbund in line. The question is, how long can he hold their loyalty when the hearts of many of his troops are in the Nazi camp, and Hitler's speeches stir more and more to the Nazi cause?"

Karl felt the chill tighten around his throat. He wished Ernst hadn't invited him to Munich. He wished he hadn't accepted.

"Maybe now is not a good time to be here."

"Nonsense! It's the *best* time! Can't you feel the excitement in the air? Don't you sense the huge forces at work around us? Stop and listen and you'll hear the teeth of cosmic gears grinding into motion. The clouds have gathered and are storing their charges. The lightning of history is about to strike and we are near the ground point. I know it as surely as I know my name."

"Lightning can be deadly."

Ernst smiled. "Which makes it all the more entertaining."

"Why a beer hall?" Karl asked as they sat in the huge main room of the Burgerbraukeller.

A buxom waitress set a fresh pair of liter steins of lager on the rough planked table before them.

Ernst waved a hand around. "Because Munich is the heart of beer-drinking country. If you want to reach these people, you speak to them where they drink their beer."

The Burgerbraukeller was huge, squatting on a sizable plot of land on the east side of the Isar River that cut the city in two. After the Zirkus Krone, it was the largest meeting place in Munich. Scattered inside its vast complex were numerous separate bars and dining halls, but the centerpiece was the main hall. All its 3,000 seats were filled tonight, with latecomers standing in the aisles and crowded at the rear.

Karl quaffed a few ounces of lager to wash down a mouthful of sausage. All around him were men in black and various shades of brown, all impatient for the arrival of their *Führer*. He saw some in business suits, and even a few in traditional Bavarian lederhosen and Tyrolean hats. Karl and Ernst had made instant friends with their table neighbors by sharing the huge platter of cheese, bread, and sausage they had ordered from the bustling kitchen. Even though they were not in uniform, not aligned with any Kampfbund organization, and wore no armbands, the two Berlin newcomers were now considered *komraden* by the locals who shared their long table. They were even more welcome when Ernst mentioned that Karl was the son of Colonel Stehr who'd fought and died at Argonne.

Far better to be welcomed here as comrades, Karl thought, than the opposite. He'd been listening to the table talk, the repeated references to Adolf Hitler in reverent tones as the man who would rescue Germany from all its enemies, both within and without, and lead the Fatherland back to the glory it deserved. Karl sensed that even the power of God might not be enough to save a man in this crowd who had something to say against Herr Hitler.

The hazy air was ripe with the effluvia of any beer hall: spilled hops and malt, tobacco smoke, the garlicky tang of steaming sausage, sharp cheese, sweaty bodies, and restless anticipation. Karl was finishing off his latest stein when he heard a stir run through the crowd. Someone with a scarred face had arrived at the rostrum on the bandstand. He spoke a few words into the increasing noise and ended by introducing Herr Adolf Hitler.

With a thunderous roar the crowd was on its feet and shouting "Heil! Heil!" as a thin man, about five-nine or so, who could have been anywhere from mid-thirties to mid-forties in age, ascended the steps to the rostrum. He was dressed in a brown wool jacket, a white shirt with a stiff collar, a narrow tie, with brown knickers and stockings on his short, bandy legs. Straight brown hair parted on the right and combed across his upper forehead; sallow complexion, almost yellow; thin lips under a narrow brush of a mustache. He walked stooped slightly forward with his head canted to the left and his hands stuffed into his jacket pockets.

Karl could hardly believe his eyes.

This is the man they call Führer? He looks like a shopkeeper, or a government clerk. This is the man they think is going to save Germany? Are they all mad or drunk . . . or both?

Hitler reached the rostrum and gazed out over the cheering audience, and it was then that Karl had his first glimpse of the man's unforgettable eyes. They shone like beacons from their sockets, piercing the room, staggering Karl with their startling pale blue fire. Flashing, hypnotic, gleaming with fanaticism, they ranged the room, quieting it, challenging another voice to interrupt his.

And then he began to speak, his surprisingly rich baritone rising and falling like a Wagnerian opus, hurling sudden gutturals through the air for emphasis like fist-sized cobblestones.

For the first ten minutes he spoke evenly and stood stiffly with his hands trapped in his jacket pockets. But as his voice rose and his passion grew, his hands broke free, fine, graceful, long-fingered hands that fluttered like pigeons and swooped like hawks, then knotted into fists to pound the top of the rostrum with sledgehammer blows.

The minutes flew, gathering into one hour, then two. At first Karl had managed to remain aloof, picking apart Hitler's words, separating the carefully selected truths from the half truths and the outright fictions. Then, in spite of himself, he began to fall under the man's spell. This Adolf Hitler was such a passionate speaker, so caught up in his own words that one had to go along with him; whatever the untruths and specious logic in his oratory, no one could doubt that this man believed unequivocally every word that he spoke, and somehow transferred that fervent conviction to his audience so that they too became unalterably convinced of the truth of what he was saying.

He was never more powerful than when he called on all loyal Germans to come to the aid of a sick and failing Germany, one not merely financially and economically ill, but a Germany on its intellectual and moral deathbed. No question that Germany was sick, struck down by a disease that poultices and salves and cathartics could not cure. Germany needed radical surgery: The sick and gangrenous parts that were poisoning the rest of the system had to be cut away and burned before the healing could begin. Karl listened and became entranced, transfixed, unmindful of the time, a prisoner of that voice, those eyes.

And then this man, this Adolf Hitler, was standing in front of the rostrum, bathed in sweat, his hair hanging over his forehead, waving his arms, calling for all loyal Germans who truly cared for their Fatherland to rally around the Nazi Party and call for a march on Berlin where they would extract a promise from the feeble Weimar republicans to banish the Jews and the communists from all positions of power and drive the French and Belgian troops from the Ruhr Valley and once again make the Fatherland's borders inviolate, or by God, there would be a new government in power in Berlin, one that would bring Germany to the greatness that was her destiny. German misery must be broken by German iron. Our day is here! Our time is *now!*

The main hall went mad as Hitler stepped back and let the frenzied cheering of more than three thousand voices rattle the walls and rafters around him. Even Karl was on his feet, ready to shake his fist in the air and shout at the top of his lungs. Suddenly he caught himself.

What am I doing?

"Well, what did you think of the *Gefreiter?"* Ernst said. "Our strutting lance corporal?"

They were out on Rosenheimerstrasse, making their way back to the hotel, and Karl's ears had finally stopped ringing. Ahead of them in the darkness, mist rising from the Isar River sparkled in the glow of the lights lining the Ludwig Bridge.

"I think he's the most magnetic, powerful, mesmerizing speaker I've ever heard. Frighteningly so."

"Well, he's obviously mad—a complete loon. A master of hyperbolic sophistry, but hardly frightening."

"He's so . . . so . . . so anti-Semitic."

Ernst shrugged. "They all are. It's just rhetoric. Doesn't mean anything."

"Easy for you to say."

Ernst stopped and stood staring at Karl. "Wait. You don't mean to tell me you're . . . ?"

Karl turned and nodded silently in the darkness.

"But Colonel Stehr wasn't—"

"His wife was."

"Good heavens, man! I had no idea!"

"Well, what's so unusual? What's wrong with a German officer marrying a woman who happens to be Jewish?"

"Nothing, of course. It's just that one becomes so used to these military types and their—"

"Do you know that General von Seeckt, commander of the entire German army, has a Jewish wife? So does Chancellor Stresemann."

"Of course. The Nazis point that out at every opportunity."

"Right! We're everywhere!" Karl calmed himself with an effort. "Sorry, Ernst. I don't know why I got so excited. I don't even consider myself a Jew. I'm a human being. Period."

"Perhaps, but by Jewish law, if the mother is Jewish, then so are the children."

Karl stared at him. "How do you know that?"

"Everybody knows that. But that doesn't matter. The locals we've met know you as Colonel Stehr's son. That's what will count here in the next week or so."

"Next week or so? Aren't we returning to Berlin?"

Ernst gripped his arm. "No, Karl. We're staying. Things are coming to a head. The next few days promise to be *most* entertaining."

"I shouldn't—"

"Come back to the hotel. I'll fix you an absinthe. You look like you could use one."

Karl remembered the bitter taste, then realized he could probably do with a bit of oblivion tonight.

"All right. But just one."

"Excellent! Absinthe tonight, and we'll plan our next steps in the morning."

> Today it takes 4 trillion marks to buy a single US dollar.
> —*Volkischer Beobachter,* November 8, 1923

"Herr Hitler's speaking in Freising tonight," Ernst said.

They strolled through the bright, crisp morning air, past onion-cupolaed churches and pastel house fronts that would have looked more at home along the Tiber than the Isar.

"How far is that?"

"About twenty miles north. But I have a better idea. Gustav von Kahr, Bavaria's honorable dictator, is speaking at the Burgerbraukeller tonight."

"I'd rather hear Hitler."

It was already more than a week into November and Karl was still in Munich. He'd expected to be home long ago but he'd found himself too captivated by Adolf Hitler to leave. It was a strange attraction, equal parts fascination and revulsion. Here was a man who might pull together Germany's warring factions and make them one, yet then might wreak havoc upon the freedoms of the Weimar Constitution. But where would the Constitution be by year's end with old mark notes now being over-printed with EINE BILLION?

Karl felt like a starving sparrow contemplating a viper's offer to guard her nest while she hunts for food. Surely her nest would be well protected from other birds in her absence, but could she count on finding any eggs left when she returned?

He'd spoken to a number of Jews in Munich, shopkeepers mostly, engaging them in casual conversation about the Kampfbund groups, and Herr Hitler in particular. The seismic upheavals in the economy had left them frazzled and desperate, certain that their country would be in ruins by the end of the year unless somebody did something. Most said they'd support anyone who could bring the economic chaos and runaway inflation under control. Hitler and his Nazis promised definitive solutions. So what if the country had to live under a dictatorship for a while? Nothing—*nothing*—could be worse than this. After all, hadn't the Kaiser been a dictator? And they'd certainly done better under him than with this Weimar Republic with its Constitution that guaranteed so many freedoms. What good were freedom of the press and speech and assembly if you were starving? As for the anti-Semitism, most of the Munich Jews echoed Ernst's dismissal: mere rhetoric. Nothing more than tough talk to excite the beer drinkers.

Still uneasy, Karl found himself drawn back again and again to hear Hitler speak—in the Zirkus Krone, and in the Burgerbraukeller and other beer halls around the city—hoping each time the man would say something to allay his fears and allow him to embrace the hope the Nazis offered.

Absinthe only added to the compulsion. Karl had taken to drinking a glass with Ernst before attending each new Hitler speech, and as a result he had acquired a taste for the bitter stuff.

Because Herr Hitler seemed to be speaking all the time.

Especially since the failed communist *putsch* in Hamburg. It failed because the German workers refused to rally to the red flag and Reichswehr troops easily put down the revolution in its second day. There would be no German October. But the attempt had incited the Kampfbund groups to near hysteria. Karl saw more uniforms in Munich's streets than he'd seen in Berlin during the war. And Herr Hitler was there in the thick of it, fanning the sparks of patriotic fervor into a bonfire wherever he found an audience.

Karl attended his second Hitler speech while under the influence of absinthe, and there he experienced his first hallucination. It happened while Hitler was reaching his final crescendo: The hall wavered before Karl, the light dimmed, all the color drained from his sight, leaving only black and white and shades of gray; he had the impression of being in a crowded room, just like the beer hall, and then it passed. It hadn't lasted long enough for Karl to capture any details, but it had left him shivering and afraid.

The following night it happened again—the same flash of black and white, the same aftershock of dread.

It was the absinthe, he was sure. He'd heard that it caused delirium and hallucinations and even madness in those who overused it. But Karl did not feel he was going mad. No, this was something else. Not madness, but a different level of perception. He had a sense of a hidden truth, just beyond the grasp of his senses, beckoning to him, reaching for him. He felt he'd merely grazed the surface of that awful truth, and that if he kept reaching he'd soon seize it.

And he knew how to extend his reach: more absinthe.

Ernst was only too glad to have another enthusiast for his favorite libation.

"Forget Herr Hitler tonight," Ernst said. "This will be better. Bavaria's triumvirate will be there in person—Kahr, General Lossow, and Colonel von Seisser. Rumor has it that Kahr is going to make a dramatic announcement. Some say he's going to declare Bavaria's independence. Others say he's going to return Crown Prince Rupprecht to the throne and restore the Bavarian monarchy. You don't want to miss this, Karl."

"What about Hitler and the rest of the Kampfbund?"

"They're frothing at the mouth. They've been invited to attend but not to participate. It's clear, I think, that Kahr is making a move to upstage the Kampfbund and solidify his leadership position. By tomorrow morning, Hitler and his cronies may find themselves awash in a hysterical torrent of Bavarian nationalism. This will be worse than any political defeat—they'll be . . . irrelevant. Think of their outrage, think of their frustration." Ernst rubbed his palms with glee. "Oh, this will be *most* entertaining!"

Reluctantly, Karl agreed. He felt he was getting closer and closer to that elusive vision, but even if Generalstaatskommissar Kahr tried to pull the rug out from under the Kampfbund, Karl was sure he would have plenty of future opportunities to listen to Herr Hitler.

Karl and Ernst arrived early at the Burgerbraukeller, and a good thing too. The city's Blue Police had to close the doors at seven fifteen when the hall filled to overflowing. This was a much higher class audience than Hitler attracted. Well-dressed businessmen in tall hats and women in long dresses mingled with military officers and members of the Bavarian provincial cabinet; the local newspapers were represented by their editors rather than mere reporters. Everyone in Munich wanted to hear what Generalstaatskommissar Kahr had to say, and those left in the cold drizzle outside protested angrily.

They were the lucky ones, Karl decided soon after Gustav von Kahr began to speak. The squat, balding royalist had no earthshaking announcement to make. Instead, he stood hunched over the rostrum, with Lossow and Seisser, the other two thirds of the ruling triumvirate, seated on the bandstand behind him, and read a dull, endless anti-Marxist treatise in a listless monotone.

"Let's leave," Karl said after fifteen minutes of droning.

Ernst shook his head and glanced to their right. "Look who just arrived."

Karl turned and recognized the figure in the light tan trench coat standing behind a pillar near the rear of the hall, chewing on a fingernail.

"Hitler! I thought he was supposed to be speaking in Freising."

"That's what the flyers said. Apparently he changed his mind. Or perhaps he simply wanted everyone to think he'd be in Freising." Ernst's voice faded as he turned in his seat and scanned the audience. "I wonder . . ."

"Wonder what?"

He leaned close and whispered in Karl's ear. "I wonder if Herr Hitler might not be planning something here tonight."

Karl's intestines constricted into a knot. "A putsch?"

"Keep your voice down. Yes. Why not? Bavaria's ruling triumvirate and most of its cabinet are here. If I were planning a takeover, this would be the time and place."

"But all those police outside."

Ernst shrugged. "Perhaps he'll just take over the stage and launch into one of his speeches. Either way, history could be made here tonight."

Karl glanced back at Hitler and wondered if this was what the nearly grasped vision was about. He nudged Ernst.

"Did you bring the absinthe?"

"Of course. But we won't be able to fix it properly here." He paused. "I have an idea, though."

He signaled the waitress and ordered two snifters of cognac. She looked at him strangely, but returned in a few minutes and placed the glasses on the table next to their beer steins. Ernst pulled his silver flask from his pocket and poured a more than generous amount of absinthe into the cognac.

"It's not turning yellow," Karl said.

"It only does that in water." Ernst lifted his snifter and swirled the greenish contents. "This was Toulouse-Lautrec's favorite way of diluting his absinthe. He called it his 'earthquake.'" Ernst smiled as he clinked his glass against Karl's. "To earthshaking events."

Karl took a sip and coughed. The bitterness of the wormwood was enhanced rather than cut by the burn of the cognac. He washed it down with a gulp of ale. He would have poured the rest of his "earthquake" into Ernst's glass if he hadn't felt he needed every drop of the absinthe to reach the elusive vision. So he finished the entire snifter, chasing each sip with more ale. He wondered if he'd be able to walk out of here unassisted at the night's end.

He was just setting down the empty glass when he heard shouting outside. The doors at the rear of the hall burst open with a shattering bang as helmeted figures charged in brandishing sabers, pistols, and rifles with fixed bayonets. From their brown shirts and the swastikas on their red armbands Karl knew they weren't the police.

"Nazi storm troopers!" Ernst said.

Pandemonium erupted. Some men cried out in shock and outrage while others shouted "Heil!" Some were crawling under the tables while others were climbing atop them for a better view. Women screamed and fainted at the sight of a machine gun being set up at the door. Karl looked around for Hitler and found him charging down the center aisle holding a pistol aloft. As he reached the bandstand he fired a shot into the ceiling.

Sudden silence.

Hitler climbed up next to General Commissioner von Kahr and turned toward the crowd. Karl blinked at the sight of him. He had shed the trench coat and was wearing a poorly cut morning coat with an Iron Cross pinned over the left breast. He looked . . . ridiculous, more like the maître d' in a seedy restaurant than the savior of Germany.

But then the pale blue eyes cast their spell and the familiar baritone rang through the hall announcing that a national revolution had broken out in Germany. The Bavarian cities of Augsburg, Nuremberg, Regensburg, and Wurzburg were now in his control; the Reichswehr and State Police were marching from their barracks under Nazi flags; the Weimar government was no more. A new national German Reich was being formed. Hitler was in charge.

Ernst snickered. "The *Gefreiter* looks like a waiter who's led a putsch against the restaurant staff."

Karl barely heard him. The vision . . . it was coming . . . close now . . . the absinthe, fueled by the cognac and ale, was drawing it nearer than ever before . . . the room was flickering about him, the colors draining away . . .

And then the Burgerbraukeller was gone and he was in blackness . . . silent, formless blackness . . . but not alone. He detected movement around him in the palpable darkness . . .

And then he saw them.

Human forms, thin, pale, bedraggled, sunken-cheeked and hollow-eyed, dressed in rags or dressed not at all, and thin, so painfully thin, like parchment-covered skeletons through which each rib and each bump and nodule on the pelvis and hips could be touched and numbered, all stumbling, sliding, staggering, shambling, groping toward him out of the dark. At first he thought it a dream, a nightmare reprise of the march of the starving disabled veterans he'd witnessed in Berlin, but these . . . people . . . were different. No tattered uniforms here. The ones who had clothing were dressed in striped prison pajamas, and there were so many of them. With their ranks spanning to the right and left as far as Karl could see, and stretching and fading off into the distance to where the horizon might have been, their number was beyond counting . . . thousands, hundreds of thousands, millions . . .

And all coming his way.

They began to pick up speed as they neared, breaking into a staggering run like a herd of frightened cattle. Closer, now . . . their gaunt faces became masks of fear, pale lips drawn back over toothless mouths, giving no sign that they saw him . . . he could see no glint of light in the dark hollows of their eye sockets . . . but he gasped as other details became visible.

They had been mutilated—branded, actually. A six-pointed star had been carved into the flesh of each. On the forehead, between the breasts, on the belly—a bleeding Star of David. The only color not black, white, or gray was the red of the blood that oozed from each of those six-pointed brands.

But why were they running? What was spurring the stampede?

And then he heard a voice, shouting, faint and far off at first, then louder: *"Alle Juden raus!"* Over and over: *"Alle Juden raus! Alle Juden raus!"* Louder and louder as they approached until Karl had to clasp his hands over his ears to protect them.

"ALLE JUDEN RAUS! ALLE JUDEN RAUS!"

And then they were upon him, mobbing him, knocking him to his knees and then flat on his face in their panicked flight through the darkness, oblivious as they stepped on him and tripped over him in their blind rush to nowhere. He could not regain his feet; he did not try. He had no fear of being crushed because they weighed almost nothing, but he could not rise against their numbers. So he remained facedown in the darkness with his hands over his head and listened to that voice.

"ALLE JUDEN RAUS! ALLE JUDEN RAUS!"

After what seemed an eternity, they were past. Karl lifted his head. He was alone in the darkness. No . . . not alone. Someone else . . . a lone figure approaching. A naked woman, old, short, thin, with long gray hair, limping his way on arthritic knees. Something familiar about her—

"Mother!"

He stood paralyzed, rooted, unable to turn from her nakedness. She looked so thin, and so much older, as if she'd aged twenty years. And into each floppy breast had been carved a Star of David.

He sobbed as he held his arms out to her.

"Dear God, Mother! What have they done to you?"

But she took no notice of him, limping past as if he did not exist.

"Mother, I—!"

He turned, reaching to grab her arm as she passed, but froze in mute shock when he saw the mountain.

All the gaunt living dead who had rushed past were piled in a mound that dwarfed the Alps themselves, carelessly tossed like discarded dolls into a charnel heap that stretched miles into the darkness above him.

Only now they had eyes. Dead eyes, staring sightlessly his way, each with a silent plea . . . *help us* . . . *save us* . . . *please don't let this happen* . . .

His mother—she was in there. He had to find her, get her out of there. He ran toward the tower of wasted human flesh, but before he reached it the blacks and whites began to shimmer and melt, bleeding color as that damned voice grew louder and louder . . . *"ALLE JUDEN RAUS! ALLE JUDEN RAUS!"*

And Karl knew that voice. God help him, he knew that voice.

Adolf Hitler's.

Suddenly he found himself back in the Burgerbraukeller, on his feet, staring at the man who still stood at the rostrum. Only seconds had passed. It had seemed so much longer.

As Hitler finished his proclamation, the triumvirate of Kahr, Lossow, and Seisser were marched off the stage at gunpoint. And Hitler stood there with his feet spread and his arms folded across his chest, staring in triumphant defiance at the shocked crowd mingling and murmuring before him.

Karl now understood what he had seen. Hitler's hate wasn't mere rhetoric. This madman meant what he said. Every word of it. He intended the destruction of German Jewry, of Jews everywhere. And now, here in this beer hall, he was making a grab for the power to do just that. And he was succeeding!

He had to be stopped!

As Hitler turned to follow the captured triumvirate, Karl staggered forward, his arm raised, his finger pointing, ready to accuse, to shout out a denunciation. But no sound came from his throat. His lips were working, his lungs pumping, but his vocal cords were locked. Hoarse, breathy hisses were the only sounds he could make.

But those sounds were enough to draw the attention of the Nazi storm troopers. The nearest turned and pointed their rifles at him. Ernst leaped to his side and restrained him, pulling his arm down.

"He's not well. He's been sick and tonight's excitement has been too much for him."

Karl tried to shake free of Ernst. He didn't care about the storm troopers or their weapons. These people had to hear, had to know what Hitler and his National Socialists planned. But then Hitler was leaving, following the captured triumvirate from the bandstand.

In the frightened and excited confusion that followed, Ernst steered Karl toward one of the side doors. But their way was blocked by a baby-faced storm trooper.

"No one leaves until the Führer says so."

"This man is sick!" Ernst shouted. "Do you know who his father was? Colonel Stehr himself! This is the son of a hero of the Argonne! Let him into the fresh air immediately!"

The young trooper, certainly no more than eighteen or nineteen, was taken aback by Ernst's outburst. It was highly unlikely that he'd ever heard of a Colonel Stehr, but he stepped aside to let them pass.

The drizzle had turned to snow, and the cold air began to clear Karl's head, but still he had no voice. Pulling away from Ernst's supporting arm, he half ran, half stumbled across the grounds of the Burgerbraukeller, crowded now with exuberant members of the Kampfbund. He headed toward the street, wanting to scream, to cry out his fear and warn the city, the country, that a murderous lunatic was taking over.

When he reached the far side of Rosenheimerstrasse, he found an alley, leaned into it, and vomited. After his stomach was empty, he wiped his mouth on his sleeve and returned to where Ernst waited on the sidewalk.

"Good heavens, man. What got into you back there?"

Karl leaned against a lamppost and told him about the vision, about the millions of dead Jews, and Hitler's voice and what it was shouting.

Ernst was a long time replying. His eyes had a faraway look, almost glazed, as if he were trying to see the future Karl had described.

"That was the absinthe," he said finally. "Lautrec's earthquake. You've been indulging a bit much lately and you're not used to it. Lautrec was institutionalized because of it. Van Gogh cut off one of his ears under the influence."

Karl grabbed the front of Ernst's overcoat. "No! The absinthe is responsible, I'll grant that, but it only opened the door for me. This was more than a hallucination. This was a vision of the future, a warning. He's got to be stopped, Ernst!"

"How? You heard him. There's a national revolution going on, and he's leading it."

A steely resolve, cold as the snow falling around them, was taking shape within Karl.

"I've been entrusted with a warning," he said softly. "I'm not going to ignore it."

"What are you going to do? Flee the country?"

"No. I'm going to stop Adolf Hitler."

"How?"

"By any means necessary."

> Germany is having a nervous breakdown. There is nothing sane
> to report.
>
> —Ben Hecht, 1923

The rest of the night was a fearful phantasm, filled with shouts, shots, and conflicting rumors—yes, there was a national revolution; no, there were no uprisings in Nuremberg or the other cities.

One thing was clear to Karl: A revolution was indeed in progress in Munich. All through the night, as he and Ernst wandered the city, they crossed paths again and again with detachments of brown-shirted men marching under the swastika banner. And lining the sidewalks were men and women of all ages, cheering them on.

Karl wanted to grab and shake each one of them and scream into their faces, *You don't know what you're doing! You don't know what they're planning!*

No one was moving to stop the putsch. The Blue Police, the Green Police, the Reichswehr troops were nowhere in sight. Ernst led Karl across the river to the Reichswehr headquarters where they watched members of the Reichskriegsflagge segment of the Kampfbund strutting in and out of the entrance.

"It's true!" Karl said. "The Reichswehr troops are with them!"

Karl tried to call Berlin to see what was happening there but could not get a phone connection. They went to the offices of the *Munchener Post,* a newspaper critical of Hitler in the past, but found its offices ransacked, every typewriter gone, every piece of printing equipment destroyed.

"The putsch is not even a day old and they've started already!" Karl said, standing on the glass-littered sidewalk in the wan dawn light and surveying the damage. "Crush anyone who disagrees with you."

"Yes!" a voice cried behind them. "Crush them! Grind them under your heel!"

They turned to see a bearded middle-aged man waving a bottle of Champagne as he joined them before the *Post* offices. He wore a swastika armband over a tattered army coat.

"It's our time now!" The man guzzled some of the Champagne and held it aloft. "A toast! Germany for the Germans, and damn the Jews to hell!" He thrust the bottle at Karl. "Here! Donated by a Jew down the street."

Icy spikes scored the inner walls of Karl's chest.

"Really?" he said, taking the half-full bottle. "Donated?"

"Requisitioned, actually." He barked a laugh. "Along with his watch and his wife's jewelry . . . after they were arrested!"

Uncontrollable fury, fueled by the growing unease of the past two weeks and the horror of his vision in the beer hall, exploded in Karl. He reversed his grip on the bottle and smashed it against the side of the man's head.

"Karl!" Ernst cried.

The man stiffened and fell flat on his back in the slush, coat open, arms and legs akimbo.

Karl stared down at him, shocked by what he'd done. He'd never struck another man in his life. He knelt over him.

"He's still breathing."

Then he saw the pistol in the man's belt. He gripped the handle and pulled it free. He straightened and cradled the weapon in his trembling hands as he turned toward Ernst.

"You asked me before how I was going to stop Hitler. Here is the answer."

"Have you gone mad?"

"You don't have to come along. Safer for you if you return to the hotel while I search out Herr Hitler."

"Don't insult me. I'll be beside you all the way."

Karl stared at Ernst, surprised and warmed by the reply.

"Thank you, Ernst."

Ernst grinned, his eyes bright with excitement. "I wouldn't miss this for the world!"

Throughout the morning, conflicting rumors traveled up and down the Munich streets with the regularity of the city trolleys.

The triumvirate has thrown in with Hitler . . . the triumvirate is free and planning countermoves against the putsch . . . the Reichswehr has revolted and is ready to march on Berlin behind Hitler . . . the Reichswehr is marching on Munich to crush this putsch just as it crushed the communist attempt in Hamburg last month . . . Hitler is in complete control of Munich and its armed forces . . . support for the putsch is eroding among some police units and the young army officers . . .

Karl chased each rumor, trying to learn the truth, but truth seemed to be an elusive commodity in Munich. He shuttled back and forth across the river, between the putsch headquarters in the Burgerbraukeller on the east bank and the government offices around Marianplatz on the west, his right hand thrust into his coat pocket, clutching the pistol, searching for Hitler. He and

Ernst had separated, figuring that two searchers could cover more ground apart than together.

By noon Karl began to get the feeling that Hitler might not have as much control as he wished people to think. True, the putschists seemed to have an iron grip on the city east of the river, and a swastika flag still flew from a balcony of the New City Hall on the west side, but Karl had noticed the green uniforms of the Bavarian State Police gathering at the west ends of the bridges across the Isar. They weren't blocking traffic, but they seemed to be on guard. And Reichswehr troops from the Seventh Division were moving through the city. Reichswehr headquarters on the west bank was still held by units of the Kampfbund, but the headquarters itself was now surrounded by two Reichswehr infantry battalions and a number of artillery units.

The tide is turning, Karl thought with grim satisfaction.

Maybe he wouldn't have to use the pistol after all.

He was standing on the west side of the Ludwig bridge, keeping his back to the wind, when he saw Ernst hurrying toward him from the far side.

"They're coming this way!" he shouted, his cheeks red with the excitement and the cold.

"Who?"

"Everyone! All the putschists—thousands of them. They've begun a march through the city. And Hitler's leading them."

No sooner had Ernst spoken than Karl spied the front ranks of the march—brown-shirted Nazis carrying the red and white flags that whipped and snapped in the wind. Behind them came the rest, walking twelve abreast, headed directly toward the Ludwig Bridge. He spotted Hitler in the front ranks wearing his tan trench coat and a felt hat. Beside him was General Ludendorf, one of the most respected war heroes in the nation.

A crowd of putsch supporters and the merely curious gathered as the Green Police hurried across to the east side of the bridge to stop the marchers. Before they could set up, squads of storm troopers swarmed from the flanks of the march, surrounding and disarming them.

The march surged across the bridge unimpeded.

Karl tightened his grip on the pistol. He would end this here, now, personal consequences be damned. But he couldn't get a clear view of Hitler through the throng surrounding him. To his dismay, many bystanders from the crowd joined the march as it passed, further swelling its ranks.

The march streamed into the already crowded Marianplatz in front of City Hall where it was met with cheers and cries of adulation by the thousands mobbed there. A delirious rendition of "Deutschland Uber Alles" rattled the windows all around the plaza and ended with countless cries of "Heil Hitler!"

At no time could Karl get within a hundred yards of his target.

And now, its ranks doubled, the march was off again, this time northward up Wienstrasse.

"They're heading for Reichswehr headquarters," Ernst said.

"It's surrounded. They'll never get near it."

Ernst shrugged. "Who's going to stop them? Who's going to fire with General Ludendorf at Hitler's side and all those civilians with them?"

Karl felt his jaw muscles bunch as the memory of the vision surged through his brain, dragging with it the image of his elderly, withered, unclothed, bleeding mother.

"I am."

He took off at a run along a course parallel to the march, easily outdistancing the slow-moving crowd. He calculated that the marchers would have to come up Residenzstrasse in order to reach the Reichswehr building. He ducked into a doorway of the Feldherrnhalle, near the top of the street and crouched there, panting from the unaccustomed exertion. Seconds later, Ernst joined him, barely breathing hard.

"You didn't have to come."

Ernst smiled. "Of course I did. We're witnessing the making of history."

Karl pulled the pistol from his coat pocket. "But after today someone other than Adolf Hitler will be making it."

At the top of Residenzstrasse, where it opened into a plaza, Karl saw units of the Green Police setting up a barricade.

Good. It would slow the march, and that would be his moment.

"Here they come," Ernst said.

Karl's palms began to sweat as he searched the front ranks for his target. The pistol grip was slippery in his hand by the time he identified Hitler. This was it. This was his moment in history, to turn it from the horrors the vision had shown him.

Doubt gripped the base of his throat in a stranglehold. What if the vision was wrong? What if it had been the absinthe and nothing more? What if he was about to murder a man because of a drunken hallucination?

He tore free of the questions. *No. No doubts. No hesitation. Hitler has to die. Here. Now. By my hand.*

As he'd predicted, the march slowed when it neared the barricade and the storm troopers approached the Green Police shouting, "Don't shoot! We are your comrades! We have General Ludendorf with us!"

Karl raised the pistol, waiting for his chance.

And then a passage opened between him and Hitler's trench-coated form. *Now! It has to be now!*

He took aim, cautiously, carefully. He wasn't experienced with pistols. His father had taken him hunting with a rifle or a shotgun as a young man, but he'd never found much pleasure in it. He found no pleasure in this, only duty. But he knew how to aim, and he had the heart of this strutting little monster in his sights. He remembered his father's words . . . "Squeeze, don't pull . . . *squeeze . . .* be surprised by the shot . . ."

And while Karl waited for his surprise, he imagined the tapered lead cylinder blasting from the muzzle, hurtling toward Hitler, plunging into his chest, tearing through lung and heart, ripping the life from him before he could destroy the lives of the hapless, helpless, innocent millions he so hated. He saw Hitler twist and fall, saw a brief, violent spasm of rage and confusion as the milling putschists fired wildly in all directions, rioting until the Green Police and the regular army units closed in to divide their ranks, arrest their leaders, and disperse the rest. Perhaps another Jew hater would rise, but he would not have this man's unique combination of personal magnetism and oratory power. The future Karl had seen would never happen. His bullet would sever the link from this time and place to that future.

And so he let his sweat-slick forefinger caress the curve of the trigger . . . *squeezing . . .*

But just as the weapon fired, something brushed against his arm. The bullet coughed into the chill air, high, missing Hitler.

Time stopped. The marchers stood frozen, some in midstride. All except Hitler. His head was turned Karl's way, his pale blue eyes searching the doorways, the windows. And then those eyes fixed on Karl's. The two men stared at each other for an instant, an eternity . . . then . . . Hitler smiled.

And with that smile time resumed its course as Karl's single shot precipitated a barrage of gunfire from the Green Police and the Kampfbund troops. Chaos erupted on Residenzstrasse. Karl watched in horror as people ran in all directions, screaming, bleeding, falling, and dying. The pavement became red and slick with blood. He saw Hitler go down and stay down. He prayed that someone else's bullet had found him.

Finally the shooting stopped. The guns were silent but the air remained filled with the cries of the wounded. To Karl's shock he saw Hitler struggle to his feet and flee along the sidewalk, holding his arm. Before Karl could gather his wits and take aim again with his pistol, Hitler had jumped into a yellow Opel sedan and sped away.

Karl added his own shouts to those of the wounded. He turned to Ernst.

"It was you! Why did you hit my arm? I had him in my sights and you . . . you made me miss!"

"Terribly sorry," Ernst said, avidly scanning the carnage on the street before them. "It was an accident. I was leaning over for a look and lost my balance. Not to worry. I think you accomplished your goal: This putsch is over."

> The Munich putsch definitely eliminates Hitler and his National Socialist followers.
>
> —*The New York Times,* November 9, 1923

Karl was overjoyed when Adolf Hitler was captured by the Green Police two days later, charged with high treason, and thrown into jail. His National Socialist Party was disbanded and declared illegal. Adolf Hitler had lost his political firmament, his freedom, and because he was an Austrian, there even was a good possibility he would be deported after his trial.

While waiting for the trial, Karl reopened his bookstore and tried to resume a normal routine in Berlin. But the vision, and the specter of Adolf Hitler, haunted him. Hitler was still alive, might still wreak the horrors Karl had seen. He hungered for the trial, to see Hitler humiliated, sentenced to a minimum of twenty years. Or deported. Or best yet: shot as a traitor.

He saw less and less of Ernst during the months leading to the trial. Ernst seemed bored with Berlin. New, gold-backed marks had brought inflation under control, the new government seemed stable, there were no new putsches in the works . . . life was far less "entertaining."

They met up again in Munich on the day of Hitler's sentencing. Like the trial, the sentencing was being held in the main lecture hall of the old Infantry School because the city's regular courtrooms could not accommodate the huge crowds. Karl had been unable to arrange a seat inside; nor, apparently, had Ernst. Both had to be content to stand outside under the bright midday sky and wait for the news along with the rest of their fellow citizens.

"I can't say I'm surprised to see you here," Ernst said as they shook hands.

"Nor I you. I suppose you find all this amusing."

"Quite." He pointed with his cane. "My, my. Look at all the people."

Karl had already studied them, and they upset him. Thousands of Germans from all over the country swarmed around the large brick building, trying in vain to get into the courtroom. Two battalions of Green Police were stationed behind barbed wire barriers to keep the crowds at bay. During the twenty-five days of the trial, Karl had moved among them and had been horrified at how many spoke of Hitler in the hushed tones of adoration reserved for royalty, or a god.

Today the women had brought bouquets of flowers for their god, and almost everyone in the huge throng was wearing ribbons of red, white, and black—the Nazi colors.

"He's a national figure now," Ernst said. "Before the putsch no one had ever heard of him. Now his name is known all over the world."

"And that name will soon be in jail," Karl said vehemently.

"Undoubtedly. But he's made excellent use of the trial as a national soap box."

Karl shook his head. He could not understand why the judges had allowed Hitler to speak at such length from the witness box. For days—*weeks*—he went on, receiving standing ovations in the courtroom while reporters transcribed his words and published them for the whole country to read.

"But today it comes to an end. Even as we speak, his sentence is being pronounced. Today Adolf Hitler goes to prison for a long, long time. Even better: Today he is deported to Austria."

"Jail, yes," Ernst said. "But I wouldn't count on deportation. He is, after all, a decorated veteran of the German army, and I do believe the judges are more than a little cowed by the show of support he has received here and in the rest of the country."

Suddenly shouts arose from those of the huge crowd nearest the building, followed by wild cheering as word of the sentencing was passed down: five years in Landau Prison . . . but eligible for parole in six months.

"Six months!" Karl shouted. "No, this can't be! He's guilty of treason! He tried to overthrow the government!"

"Hush, Karl," Ernst said. "You're attracting attention."

"I will *not* be silenced! The people have to know!"

"Not these people, Karl."

Karl raised his arms to the circle of grim faces that had closed about him. "Listen to me! Adolf Hitler is a monster! They should lock him up in the deepest darkest hole and throw away the key! He—"

Sudden agony convulsed through his back as someone behind him rammed a fist into his right kidney. As Karl staggered forward another man with wild, furious eyes and bared teeth punched him in the face. He slumped to the ground with cries of "Communist!" and "Jew!" filling his ears. The circle closed about him and the sky was shut out by enraged, merciless faces as heavy boots began to kick at his back and belly and head.

Karl was losing his last grip on consciousness when the blows suddenly stopped and there was blue sky above him again.

Through blurry eyes he saw Ernst leaning over him, shaking his head in dismay.

"Good God, man! Do you have a death wish? You'd be a bloody pulp now if I hadn't brought the police to your aid!"

Painfully, Karl raised himself on one elbow and spit blood. Scenes from the dark vision began flashing before his eyes.

"It's going to happen!" he sobbed.

He felt utterly alone, thoroughly defeated. Hitler had a national following now. He'd be back on the streets and in the beer halls in six months, spreading his hatred. This trial wasn't the end of him—it was the beginning. It had catapulted him into the national spotlight. He was on his way. He was going to take over.

And the vision would become reality.

"Damn you, Ernst! Why did you have to knock off my aim?"

"I told you, Karl. It was an accident."

"Really?" During the months since that cold fall day, Karl's thoughts had returned often to the perfectly timed nudge that had made him miss. "I wonder about that 'accident,' Ernst. I can't escape the feeling that you did it on purpose."

Ernst's face tightened as he rose and stood towering over Karl.

"Believe what you will, Karl. But I can't say I'm sorry. I, for one, am convinced that the next decade or two will be far more entertaining *with* Herr Hitler than without him." His smile was cold, but his eyes were bright with anticipation. "I am rather looking forward to the years to come. Aren't you?"

Karl tried to answer, but the words would not come. If only Ernst knew . . .

Then he saw the gleam in Ernst's eyes and the possibility struck Karl like a hob-nailed boot: Perhaps Ernst *does* know.

Ernst touched the brim of his hat with the silver head of his cane. "If you will excuse me now, Karl, I really must be off. I'm meeting a friend—a new friend—for a drink."

He turned and walked away, blending with the ever-growing crowd of red and white, black and brown.

1994

The year God had a good belly laugh.

I should have seen it coming when the editor who acquired *The Select* (formerly *The Ingraham*) bailed out of Morrow and moved to Hyperion, effectively abandoning the book. But another editor took over and did an excellent job . . .

Until Hearst decided to sell William Morrow to the highest bidder.

Suddenly it was as if someone had yelled "Fire!" Everyone was running for the doors. The planned promotional tour to flog the novel evaporated. They placed a few print ads, but that was about it. It seemed that every time I called the publicity department, the person I'd spoken to last was no longer with the company. Chaos . . . complete chaos.

Bottom line: The novel Morrow had bought for nearly a million dollars and planned to run up the best-seller lists was tossed on the market with virtually no support. It tanked.

Was I bitter? Yes. Almost as bitter as after watching the film of *The Keep*. But at least then I had Michael Mann to blame. This time I had only a faceless corporation named Hearst.

You want to know the kicker? No one wanted William Morrow. Hearst finally took it off the auction block and things went back to normal—but way too late for *The Select*.

And people wonder why writers die drunk or go mad.

I hear you out there: "So what? You still banked big bucks." True. And that was a consolation. But I was and still am proud of *The Select*. It's a hell of a thriller and it addresses issues still relevant today. I wanted people to read it. That's why I write: To be read. Yes, I want to be compensated for my work, but I'm a storyteller. In ancient times I'd be wandering from campfire to campfire telling tales in exchange for brontoburgers.

I got through it all by burying myself in work—and I had plenty of that. I was knee-deep in my next novel, *Implant,* reading for *Diagnosis: Terminal,* still developing (along with Matt) the *FTL Newsfeed* story lines, and the interactive gigs were flowing in.

We snagged a development deal with MediaVision for *DNA Wars.* While working on that we came up with another interactive project we called *Mirage.* We were also meeting with Voyager, Fox Interactive, Time Warner Interactive, R/Greenberg Associates, Stan Winston Studio, and Scholastic, pitching interactive movie ideas to a new company called Interfilm. Matt's name opened doors.

Then in July the SciFi Channel asked us to take over the scripting of *FTL Newsfeed.* We jumped at the chance. Now we could take complete control of the characters' actions and dialogue. Plus it was wonderful experience. We were scripting one minute of TV a day, five days a week, every week. That's four hours and twenty minutes—the equivalent of two theatrical films—per year.

We were getting so busy we decided to incorporate. We became P.M. Interactive, Inc., a subchapter-S corporation.

And then the matter of my medical career. I was still practicing family medicine full time. Something had to give, and that something was the medicine. But I couldn't quit. After twenty years in the same practice, I'd forged too many bonds, had too many people depending on me to simply turn my back and walk away. I chose to cut back. My partners weren't happy to hear I'd be working only Mondays and Tuesdays, but they didn't have much choice.

Up to this point Matt and I had been logging a lot of miles and generating a lot of interactive smoke, but not much in the way of fire. Microsoft would change that. In August their interactive/gaming wing flew us out to Redmond for a round of meetings which we felt went very well. So did Time Warner. Apparently Larry Kirschbaum had heard about the trip and feared we'd wind up with Bill Gates. When we returned from Redmond our agent told us that Time Warner Electronic Publishing (TWEP) and Time Warner Books were making a combined preemptive bid on *DNA Wars* and *Mirage* for interactive CD-ROMs and related novels—a *big* offer. We thought Microsoft might be a better place for the games (we were prescient), but no way they could match the publishing power of Time Warner Books. We accepted.

And so the meetings began. Everyone agreed that *Mirage* should be the first project.

Matt and I were also meeting frequently with Bob Bejan of Interfilm—a new interactive (that word again) technology that allowed audiences to choose the course of a film by pressing buttons on a joystick attached to their theater seats. Though the technology worked beautifully, the first two Interfilms, *I'm Your Man* and *Ride for Your Life,* were lame with a capital L. But the potential was mind-boggling—*if* Bob could get the right writers.

Matt and I knew immediately that the smirking, winking comedy of the first two films negated the technology's potential to engage the emotions. We told Bob we wanted to write an Interfilm, but one with high stakes—life and death—peopled with characters you cared about, where their lives were in your hands and it mattered to you whether they lived or died. Our treatment for an interactive script about a crazed toymaker who traps three members each of the FBI, ATF, and IRS in his elaborately booby-trapped house blew him away. (Pardon the pun.) We called it *Bombmeister.*

So . . . Matt and I were writing the *Mirage* novel and structuring the game while simultaneously designing the *Bombmeister* interactions and scripting *FTL* (and hovering over the video shoots for last-minute dialogue changes).

On my own I was editing *Diagnosis: Terminal* (delivered two months late) and finishing *Implant.* My agent sent *Implant* to Morrow (by contract they had first look) but because sales of *The Select* had not met expectations (imagine that), they turned it down. We sold it to Forge as the first of a three-book deal.

Looking back, I don't know how I kept all those balls in the air. But somehow I did. I loved the work and the challenges and the feeling that I was part of pushing the entertainment envelope in a new direction.

One of the conditions of my contract to edit the *Diagnosis: Terminal* anthology was that I had to contribute a story. Fine. But what? I hadn't a clue until Hillary Clinton declared herself czarina of the US health system.

It really started back in February 1991, when my agent leant me his house in the Florida Keys for a week. I fell in love with the Lower Keys. Above Seven-Mile Bridge is pretty much an extension of South Florida. But something changes below it. It's more like a separate Caribbean country, with a lazier rhythm and a sultrier vibe.

I knew I had to set a story there, but didn't get around to it until 1994.

On rereading "Offshore" for this collection I was struck by parallels between Terry Havens and Repairman Jack. I think my subconscious wanted me to spend more time with Jack; and if I wasn't going to do that, it would see to it that I wrote about someone like him. Eventually my subconscious would have its way. But not for a few years yet.

"Offshore" is a product of its times. If you remember, during the early 1990s Hillary Clinton had put herself in charge of revamping the country's healthcare delivery system. What she came up with was so abstruse and unworkable that even her staunchest supporters backed away for fear of being tainted. Medical personnel shook their heads in dismay. (I poked fun at it in an essay in *The New York Times Book Review*.)

She and a lot of others seemed to be looking for a Canadian-style system. But you have to wonder: If the Canadian system is so great, why are the US hospitals along our northern border so full of Canadians?

So I took Theodore Sturgeon's advice from ages ago and asked the next question: If Hillary succeeded in imposing a Canadian-style system on us, where would we find *our* safety valve?

Mexico?

Thanks, no.

We'd probably be forced to go . . .

Offshore

"Got a doozie comin', Terr."

Ernie stood at the big picture window with his thumbs hooked in his belt on either side of the gut pouting over his buckle, and stared out at Upper Sugarloaf Sound.

Terry Havens looked up from the bar where he'd been making a wet Olympics symbol with the bottom rim of his sweating Red Stripe.

"Good. Maybe it'll cool things off a little."

Terry had been expecting the storm, looking forward to it, in fact. But not because it would cool things off.

"I think this mother might do more than cool things off. This'n looks *mean.*"

Terry took a swig of the Red Stripe and carried the bottle to the big window. He stood beside Ernie and took in the view. Bartenders always need something to talk about. Not much happening during off-season in the Keys, so some heavy weather would keep Ernie going through the rest of the afternoon and well into the evening.

And this looked pretty damn heavy. A cumulonimbus tower was building over the Gulf, dominating the western sky. Some big mother of a storm—a dark, bruise-purple underbelly crowding the entire span of the horizon while its fat, fluffy white upper body stretched a good ten miles straight up to where the shear winds flattened and sluiced its crown away to the north. Anvil-topped buggers like these could be downright mean.

"Where you got those glasses hid?"

Ernie limped back to the bar and brought out the battered field glasses he'd smuggled home from the Gulf War. Terry fitted them over his eyes and focused on the body of the storm. What looked like fluffy vanilla cotton candy to the naked eye became slowly boiling steam as violent updrafts and downdrafts roiled within.

Damn. He'd been looking for a storm, but this thing might be more than he could handle. Like casting light tackle out on the flats and hooking something bigger than your boat.

He lowered the glasses. He was going to have to risk it. He'd promised the *Osler* a delivery on this pass, and tonight was his last chance. The big boat would be out of range by tomorrow.

Besides, the worse the storm, the better his chances of being alone out there on the water. Not even Henriques would be out on patrol in the belly of the beast growling on the horizon.

Terry finished the rest of his Red Stripe. "One more of these before I get moving."

"Sure thing," Ernie said.

As Terry returned to his stool, he glanced across the horseshoe-shaped bar and saw two of the grizzled regulars poking into their wallets with nicotine-yellowed fingers. Reed-thin, wild-haired, leather-skinned, stubble-cheeked Conchs.

"Betcha that storm's good for at least five spouts," Rick said.

Boo flipped a sawbuck onto the bar. "Ten says you don't see more'n three."

Rick slapped a bill down on top of Boo's. "Yer on."

Terry smiled as he reached for the fresh bottle Ernie put in front of him. Those two bet on anything. He'd seen them wager on the number of times a fly would land on a piece of cheese, the number of trips someone would make to the head in an evening. Anything.

"I guess that means you two'll be spending most of the night here," Terry said.

"You betcha," Rick said. "Watchin' the storm."

Boo nodded. "And countin' the spouts."

"Some guys sure know how to have fun."

Rick and Boo laughed and hoisted their Rolling Rocks in reply.

They all quaffed together, then Terry glanced up at the TV monitor. The sight of a bunch of flak-jacketed federal marshals toting riot guns around a tandem tractor trailer shot a spasm through his stomach lining.

"Turn the sound up, will you, Ern?"

Ernie touched a button on the remote. The audio level display flashed on the screen, zipped to a preprogrammed volume, then disappeared as the announcer's voice blared from the speakers bracketed on the ceiling.

"—*tainly put a crimp in the black market in medical contraband. This haul was most likely bound for one of the renegade floating hospitals that ply their illicit trade outside the twelve-mile limit in the Gulf of Mexico.*"

The screen cut to an interior of one of the trailers and panned its contents.

"Syringes, sterile bandages, dialysis fluid, even gas sterilizers, all bound for the booming offshore medical centers. President Nathan has called on Congress to enact stiffer penalties for medical smuggling and to pass legislation to push the offshore hospitals to a hundred-mile limit. Insiders on the Hill think he is unlikely to find much support on extending the twelve-mile limit due to the complexities of maritime law, but say he might get action on the stiffer penalties."

The president's intense, youthful face filled the screen.

"We are talking here about trading in human misery. Every medical item that is smuggled offshore deprives law-abiding citizens right here at home of needed medical supplies. These racketeers are little better than terrorists, sabotaging America's medical system and health security. We've got to hit these criminals hard, and hit them where it hurts!"

"Okay, Ern," Terry said. "I've heard enough."

Poor President Nathan—thoroughly pissed that some folks were making an end run around the National Health Security Act.

Nothing new in the trucker bust, other than somebody got careless. Or got turned in. Terry wondered who it was, wondered if he knew them. He'd tuned in too late to catch where the bust had gone down.

"Excuse me," said a voice to Terry's right. "Is there a Mister Havens here?"

Terry didn't turn his head. Rick and Boo acquired a sudden intense interest in the "33" inside the labels on their Rolling Rocks.

Ernie cleared his throat and said, "He comes in now and again. I can take a message for you."

"We wish to hire him for a boat trip," the voice said.

Terry swiveled on his barstool. He saw a moderately overweight golden-ager, white hair and a sunburned face, wearing cream slacks and a lime green golf shirt.

"Where do you want to go?"

"Are you Mr. Havens?" the guy said, eagerly stepping forward and thrusting out his hand.

Terry hesitated, then said, "That's me." Hard to lie to a guy who's offering you his hand.

But the immediate relief in the guy's eyes made him wish he hadn't. Here was a man with a problem, and he seemed to think Terry was his solution. Terry was not in the problem-solving business.

"Joe Kowalski, Mister Havens," he said, squeezing Terry's hand between both of his. "I'm so glad we found you." He turned and called over his shoulder. "It's him, Martha!"

Terry looked past him at a rickety, silver-haired woman hobbling toward them, supporting herself on the bar with her right forearm and leaning on a four-footed cane clasped in her gnarled left hand. Her wrinkled face was pinched with pain. She couldn't seem to straighten out her right leg, and winced every time she put weight on it.

"Thank God!" she said.

Terry was getting a bad feeling about this.

"Uh, just where is it you folks want to go?"

"Out to the *Osler*," Joe said.

"You missed her. She took on her patients this morning and she's gone."

"I know. We missed the shuttle. Martha wanted to say good-bye to the kids before the surgery. You know, in case . . . you know. But our car broke down last night just as we were leaving and what they said would take an hour to fix wound up taking much longer. Damn car's probably still up on the lift back there in Stewart. I finally rented a car and drove down here fast as I could. Collected two tickets along the way, but we still missed the boat. We've been driving up and down Route One all day trying to find someone to take us out. No one's interested. I don't understand. I don't want a favor—I'm willing to pay a fair price. And it's not like it's a crime or anything."

Right. Not a crime or anything to ferry someone out past the twelve-mile limit to one of the hospital ships. But bad things tended to happen to good boaters who engaged in the trade if officialdom got wind of it. Bad things like a Coast Guard stop and search every time you took your boat out; or all sorts of lost applications and inexplicable computer glitches when you wanted to renew your boating tags, your fishing permits, even your driver's license. Terry had heard talk that the good folks in question seemed to suffer a significantly greater incidence of having their 1040 audited by the IRS.

No, not a crime, but lots of punishment.

Which was why the hospital ships ran their own shuttles.

"What excuse did they give?"

"Most said they were too busy, but let me tell you, they didn't look it. And as soon as those clouds started gathering, they used the storm as an excuse."

"Good excuse."

Terry glanced back at the western horizon. The afternoon sun had been swallowed whole by the storm and its white bulk had turned a threatening gray.

"But I hear you're not afraid of storms," Joe said.

Terry stared at him, feeling his anger rise. Shit. "Who told you that?"

"Some fellow in a bar up on the next key—is it Cudjoe Key? Some cantina . . ."

"Coco's."

"That's the place! Fellow with bleached hair and a fuzzy goatee."

Tommy Axler. Terry wanted to strangle the bigmouthed jerk. In fact, he might give it a try next time he saw him.

"He must have thought you wanted to go fishing. Sometimes I take people fishing in the rain. I do lots of things, but I don't ferry folks out to hospital ships."

That last part, at least, was true.

Joe's eyes got this imploring look. "I'll pay you twice your regular charter fee."

Terry shook his head. "Sorry."

His face fell. He turned to his wife. "He won't do it, Martha."

She halted her labored forward progress as if she'd run into a wall.

"Oh," she said softly, and leaned against one of the barstools. She stared at the floor and said no more.

"But let me buy you folks a drink." Terry pointed to his Red Stripe. "You want one of these?"

"No," Joe said through a sigh, then shrugged. "Aaah, why not? Martha? You want something?"

Still staring at the floor, Martha only shook her head.

Ernie set the bottle in front of Joe who immediately chugged about a third of it.

He stifled a burp, then said, "You won't reconsider, even if I triple your usual fee?"

Terry shook his head. "Look, the *Osler*'ll probably be shuttling patients in and out of St. Petersburg in a day or two. Hop in your car and—"

"Martha's got an appointment for a total hip replacement *tomorrow*. If she's not on board the *Osler* today they'll give her appointment to someone on the waiting list."

"So reschedule."

"It took us six months to get this appointment, and we were lucky. The fellow who had the original appointment died. Might be another ten months to a year before Martha can get rescheduled."

"That's as bad as the regular government wait lists."

"No," he said with a slow shake of his head. "There *is* no government wait list for Martha. Not anymore. She's too old. HRAA passed a regulation barring anyone over age seventy-five from certain surgical procedures. Total hip replacement is on the list. And Martha's seventy-seven."

Martha's head snapped up. "Don't you be blabbing my age for all the world to hear!"

"Sorry, dear."

Terry looked at him. "I thought the cutoff was eighty."

"Right: *was*. They lowered it last year."

Terry had assumed that most of the hospital ship patrons were well-heeled folks who didn't want to wait in the long queues for elective surgery in the government-run hospitals. And since all the hospitals in America were now government run, they had to go elsewhere. But cutting people off from procedures . . .

The Health Resources Allocation Agency strikes again.

"I didn't know they could do that."

Joe sighed. "Neither did I. It wasn't part of the regulations when the Health Security Act became law, but apparently the HRAA has the power to make new regs. So when they found out how far their Health Security Act was running over projections, they started making cuts. What really galls me is I supported the damn law."

"So did I."

"Yeah, we all thought we were getting a bargain. Ten years later we find out we got the shaft."

"Welcome to the twenty-first century, Pops. Believe in the future but always read the fine print."

"Tell me about it." He slugged down some more beer and stared at the bottle in his hand. "It's not fair, you know. We busted our butts since we got married—fifty years come next July—to make a good life for our family. We educated our kids, got them married and settled, then we retired. And now we'd like to enjoy the years we've got left. Nothing fancy. No trips around the world. Just hang out, play golf once in a while. But with Martha's hip, we can't even go for a walk after dinner."

Terry said nothing as Joe polished off his beer. He was trying not to listen. He wasn't going to get sucked into this.

Joe banged his bottle down on the bar. "You know what really bugs my ass? We've got the money to pay for the surgery. We don't need the government to pay for it. Fuck 'em! *We'll* pay. Gladly. But they won't let her have the surgery—period. Their letter said total hip surgery at her age is 'an inefficient utilization of valuable medical resources.' I mean, what the hell did we work and skimp and save for if we can't spend it on our health?"

"Wish I had an answer for you," Terry said.

"Yeah." He pushed away from the bar. "Thanks for the beer. Come on, Martha. We'll keep looking."

He took his wife gently by the arm and began helping her toward the door. Terry stared across the bar at Rick and Boo so he wouldn't have to watch the Kowalskis. He saw a grinning Rick accepting a ten from a grumpy-looking Boo. He wondered what the bet had been this time.

He looked out the window at the towering storm, black as a hearse now, picking up speed and power. If he was going to head out, he'd better get moving.

Terry waited until Joe Kowalski had eased his wife into the passenger seat, then he waved to Rick, Boo, and Ernie and headed out. The August heat gave him a wet body slam as he stepped outside. He slid past the Kowalskis' idling rental but couldn't resist a glance through the windshield.

Martha was crying.

He averted his gaze and hurried to his pickup.

Life really sucked sometimes.

He jumped into the blisteringly hot cab.

That didn't mean he had to get involved.

He turned the key and the old Ford shuddered to life.

Wasn't his problem.

He threw it into reverse.

As he was backing out he saw Joe put an arm around his wife's thin, quaking shoulders and try to comfort her.

He slammed on the brakes and yanked the gearshift back into neutral.

Shit.

Cursing himself for a jerk, Terry jumped out of the cab and stalked over to the Kowalskis' car. He rapped on Joe's window.

"Follow me," he said as the glass slid down.

Joe's eyes lit. "You mean—?"

"Just follow."

As he was heading back to the pickup, he heard a voice call out behind him.

"Aw, Terry! Say it ain't so!"

He turned and saw Rick standing in the doorway, dismay flattening his weathered features. Boo peered over his shoulder, grinning.

"You're takin' 'em, ain't ya," Boo said.

"None of your damn business."

Boo nudged Rick none too gently and rubbed his palms together. "See. I toldja he would. I win. Gimme back my saw plus the one you owe me. Give it now, Rick."

Rick handed the money to Boo and gave Terry a wounded look.

"Y'disappointed the shit outta me, Terr."

"Yeah, well," Terry muttered, slipping behind the wheel again, "there's one born every minute."

"You really think he's going to risk this storm?" Cramer asked.

Pepe Henriques looked at his mate. Cramer's round, usually relaxed boyish face was tight with tension.

He's scared, he thought.

Which was okay. Showing it wasn't.

Henriques looked past Cramer at the storm that filled the sky. Giant forks of lightning occasionally speared down to the Gulf but mostly jumped cloud to cloud, illuminating the guts of the storm with explosions of light. Thunder crashed incessantly, vibrating their fiberglass hull. He could see the rain curtain billowing toward them.

Almost here.

When it hit, visibility would be shot and they'd have to go on instruments. But so would the runner.

"He'll be out here. Why else would that hospital ship be dawdling fourteen miles out? They're waiting for a delivery. And our man's going to make it. That is, he's going to try. This'll be his last run."

He tossed Cramer a life jacket and watched him strap it on. Saw the black ATF across the yellow fabric and had to shake his head.

Me. An ATF agent.

He still couldn't believe it. But he'd found he liked the regular paycheck, the benefit package, the retirement fund. Sure as hell beat taking tourists tarpon and bone fishing on the flats.

But he might be back to fishing those flats if he didn't catch this runner.

Henriques had run up against him twice before, but both times he'd got away. Two things he knew for sure about the guy: He ran a Hutchison 686 and he was a Conch. Henriques had seen the Hutch from a distance. The registration numbers on the twenty-six-foot craft were bogus—no surprise there. What had been big surprises were the way the boat handled and its pilot's knowledge of the waters around the Lower Keys. The Hutch 686 was popular as hell in these parts, but this one had done things a propeller-driven shouldn't be able to do. It ran like a VMA impeller—like Henriques's craft. The runner had customized it somehow.

And as for being a Conch, well . . . nobody could dodge among all these reefs and mangrove keylets like that runner unless he'd spent his life among them. A native of the Keys. A Conch. Took one to know one.

Take one to catch one.

And I'm the one, Henriques thought. Tonight's his last run.

The rain hit just as they neared the inner rim of the reef. Terry pulled back on the throttle and idled the engine.

"Thank *God!*" Martha Kowalski said. She clung to the arms of her deck-fast seat with white knuckles. "That bouncing was making me sick!"

"What're you doing now?" Joe shouted over the mad drumming of the big drops on the deck and the roof of the open cabin.

Terry didn't answer. His passengers would see for themselves soon enough.

He unwrapped the molded black plastic panels and began scampering around the deck, snapping them onto the sides of the superstructure. Two of the strips for the hull sported a brand-new registration number, fresh off the decal sheets. Another went over the transom to cover the name, replacing his own admittedly corny *Terryfied* with *Delta Sue*.

Joe looked bewildered when Terry ducked back into the cabin enclosure.

"I don't get it."

"Just a little insurance."

The less Joe knew, the better.

The panels changed the boat's lines and color scheme. Nothing that would hold up against even casual inspection in good light, but from a distance, through lightning-strobed rain, his white, flat-bottomed VMA impeller craft looked an awful lot like a black-and-white V-hulled Hutchison 686. The black panels also broke up the boat's outline, making it harder to spot.

"That's what you said when you were playing around with the light on that channel marker," Joe said.

"That's right. Another kind of insurance."

"But that could—"

"Don't worry. I'll undo it on my way back in. No questions—wasn't that the deal?"

Joe nodded glumly. "But I still don't get it."

You're not supposed to, Terry thought as he gunned the engine and headed into the wind.

The hull jumped, thudded, shimmied, and jittered with the staccato pounding of the waves, and all that rhythmic violence worked into every tissue of his body. Once he zipped through the cut in the barrier reef it got worse—two, three, maybe four times worse. Riding at this speed in this weather was a little like getting a total body massage. From King Kong. On speed. Add to that the tattoo of the rain, the howl of the wind, the booming thunder, and further talk was damn near impossible. Unless you shouted directly into someone's ear. Which Martha was doing into Joe's as she bounced around in her seat and hung on for dear life.

Joe sidled over. "Think you could slow down? Martha can't take the pounding."

Terry shook his head. "I ease up, we won't make enough headway."

Joe went back to Martha and they traded more shouts, none of which Terry could hear. Joe lurched back.

"Let's go back. I'm calling the trip off. Martha's afraid, and she can't take this pounding."

He'd been half expecting something like this. Damn. Should have left them back on Sugarloaf.

"Don't wimp out on me, Joe."

"It's not me. Look, you can keep the money. Martha's getting sick. Just turn around and take us back."

"Can't do that. No questions and no turning back—wasn't that the deal?"

"Yes, but—"

"It's still the deal. Tell Martha to hang on and she'll have a new hip tomorrow."

As Joe stumbled back to his wife, Terry concentrated on the infrared scanner. Clear and cold except for the faint blob of the *Osler* straight ahead. Good. Stay that way.

Terry liked rain. Besides lowering visibility, it played havoc with heat scanners. Radiant energy tended to get swallowed up in all that falling water. But that could be a two-edged sword: Terry couldn't spot a pursuer until they were fairly close.

Didn't worry him much at the moment. Weren't too many craft that could outrun him in a sprint, and once he slipped past the twelve-mile limit, no one could touch him. Legally, anyway. Always the possibility that some frustrated ATF goon with a short fuse might blow a few holes in your hull—and you—and let the sharks clean up the mess.

He checked the compass, checked the Loran—right on course. Just a matter of time now. He looked up and froze when he saw Joe Kowalski pointing a pistol at him. The automatic—looked like a 9mm—wavered in the old guy's hand but the muzzle never strayed far from the center of Terry's chest.

"Turn around and take us back," Joe shouted.

No way was Terry turning back. And no way was he telling Joe that at the moment. Guns made him nervous.

Terry eyed the gun. "Where'd that come from?"

"I brought it along . . . just in case."

"Just in case what?"

"In case you tried to rob us. Or worse."

"Whatever happened to trust?"

"The Health Resources Allocation Agency's got mine." His eyes bored into Terry's. "Now turn this thing around. I told you you could keep the money. Just take us back."

Terry shook his head. "Sorry. Can't do that."

Joe couldn't seem to believe what he'd heard. "I've got a *gun,* dammit!"

Terry was well aware of that. He didn't think Joe would pull that trigger, but you never knew. So maybe it was time to shake Joe up—more than physically.

"And I've got a cargo to deliver."

"My wife is *not* cargo!"

"Take a look below," Terry told him, jutting his chin toward the door to the belowdecks area.

Joe's gaze darted from Terry to the door and back. His eyes narrowed with suspicion. "You wouldn't try anything stupid, would you?"

Terry shrugged. "Take a look."

Joe thought about that, then backed away and opened the door. More hesitation, then he slipped below. A moment later he appeared again, pale, his eyes wide. Terry could read his lips.

"Medical supplies! Martha, he's a smuggler!"

Martha freed up a hand long enough to slap it over the O of her mouth, then returned it to the armrest.

"The way I see it, Joe, you've got two options. The first is you can shoot me and try to get the boat back home on your own. Not only will you have to guide it through the storm, but you'll have to avoid the shore patrol. If they catch you you'll go down for murder *and* smuggling. Or you can follow through with our original plan and—" A blip caught his eye on the infrared scanner, aport and astern, and closing. He forgot all about Joe Kowalski's gun. "Shit!"

"What's wrong?"

"We've got company."

"Who?"

"ATF, most likely."

"ATF? But they're alcohol, tobacco and—"

"They added medical supplies to their list. Get over by Martha and hang on. This could get a little rough."

"A *little* rough? It's already—"

"Get out of my face, dammit!"

Henriques, Terry thought. Has to be him. No one else has such a bug up his ass that he'd brave this storm looking for a runner. Not just any runner. Looking for The One That Got Away.

Me.

He jammed the throttle all the way forward. *Terryfied* lifted farther out of the water and began bouncing along the tops of the waves. Like riding downhill in a boxcar derby on a cobblestone road. With steel wheels. Planing out was impossible, but this was as close as she'd get. The price was loss of control. The boat slewed wildly to port or starboard whenever she dipped into a trough.

How'd Henriques find him? Luck? Probably not. He was a Conch but even that wasn't enough. Probably some new equipment he had. Price was no object for the ATF when taxes were paying for it.

Damn ATF. For years Terry had breezed in and out of the Keys on his supply runs until they'd got smart and started hiring locals for their shore patrols. Making a run these days had become downright dicey.

He concentrated on the Loran, the infrared scanner, and what little he could see of the water ahead. The blip had stopped gaining. And running on the diagonal as it had to, was actually losing ground. Terry didn't let up. Unless he hit some floating debris or broached in a freak swell, he'd be first to cross the twelve-mile limit.

But he wouldn't be celebrating.

"Oh, Lord!" Martha cried, staring up the sheer twenty feet of steel hull that loomed above her. "How am I going to get up there?"

"Don't worry," Terry said as he tried to hold his bobbing craft steady against the *Osler.* "We have a routine."

Above them a winch supporting a pair of heavy-duty slings swung into view. The straps of the slings flapped and twisted in the gale-force winds as they were lowered over the side. Terry nosed his prow through the first when it hit water, then idled his engine and manually guided the second sling under the stern.

The winch began hauling them up.

Once they were on the deck the crew pulled a heavy canvas canopy over the boat and helped Martha into a wheelchair.

"Well, she made it," Terry said.

Joe Kowalski stared at him. "I don't know whether to thank you or punch you in the nose."

"Think on it awhile," Terry said. "Wait till you're both sitting in a bar sipping a G 'n' T after a round of golf. Then decide."

Joe's face softened. He extended his hand. They shook, then Joe followed Martha inside.

As the *Osler*'s crew offloaded the medical supplies, Terry ducked out from under the billowing canopy and fought the wind and rain to the deck rail. He squinted out at the lightning-shot chaos. A lot of hell left in this monster. But that didn't mean Henriques had run home. No, that bastard was laying out there somewhere, waiting.

Not to arrest him. Couldn't do that once the contraband was gone. And if Henriques did manage to catch him, Terry could thumb his nose and say he'd been out on a little jaunt to say hello to some old friends among the crew.

But even though Henriques had no case against him, Terry still couldn't let him get near. It wasn't fear of arrest that gnawed at the lining of his gut. It was being identified.

Once they knew his name, his runner career was over. He'd be watched day and night, followed everywhere, his phones tapped, his house bugged, and every time *Terryfied* left the slip he'd be stopped and inspected.

His whole way of life would be turned upside down.

One option was to stay on the *Osler* and make a break for the coast farther north. But the weather would be better then and officialdom would have copters hovering about, waiting to tag him and follow him home.

No, he had to use the heavy weather. But even that might not be enough. On the way out he'd had the advantage: Henriques didn't know Terry's starting point. Could have been anywhere along the lower twenty miles of the archipelago. But now Henriques had him pinpointed. All he had to do was wait for Terry to make his move. Didn't even have to catch him. All he had to do was follow him home.

Yeah, getting back was going to be a real bitch.

"Maybe he's not coming," Cramer said. "Maybe he's going to wait out the storm and hope that we drowned out here."

Cramer's whininess had increased steadily during the hour they'd been holding here. It was getting on Henriques's nerves something bad now.

"He *is* coming out, and it'll be *during* the storm, and we're *not* going to drown."

At least he hoped not. A couple of times during the past hour he hadn't been so sure about that. He'd had Cramer keep the VMA low and slow in forward into the wind while he watched the lights of the *Osler* through his binocs. But every so often came a rogue wave or a gust of shear wind that damn near capsized them. Cramer had good reason to want to hightail for home.

But they weren't turning around until the fuel gauge told them they had to.

Besides, according to the Doppler the rear end of the storm was only a few miles west. The runner would have to make his break soon.

And then you're mine.

"We got heat action, chief. Lots of it."

Henriques snapped the glasses down and leapt to the infrared scanner. Fanning out from the big red blob of the hospital ship were three smaller, fainter blobs.

"What's going on, chief?"

"Decoys."

The son of a bitch had two of the *Osler*'s shuttles running interference for him. One heat source was headed north-northeast, one north-northwest, and one right at them.

Henriques ground his teeth. The bastard had raised his odds from zero to two out of three. God damn him.

"All right, Cramer," he said. "One of them's our man. Which one?'

"I—I dunno."

"Come on. Put yourself out here alone. You've got to chase one. Choose."

Cramer chewed his lip and stared at the scanner. Probably doing eeny-meeny-miney-moe in his head. Henriques had already decided to ignore whichever Cramer chose. Cramer was never right.

"Well, it sure as hell ain't the guy coming right at us, so I'll choose . . . the . . . one . . . to . . . the . . ." His finger stabbed at the screen. "*East!*"

Henriques hesitated. Not a bad choice, actually. The Lower Keys were more heavily populated toward their western end, especially near Key West; coast guard base and naval air station down that way—all sorts of folks runners don't like to meet. And the storm was heading northeast, so that direction would give the most rain cover. He might just have to go with Cramer this—

Wait a second.

Well, it sure as hell ain't the guy coming right at us . . .

Yeah. The obvious assumption. So obvious that Henriques had bought into it without really thinking. But what if the runner was counting on that? Send the shuttles right and left, draw the heat toward them, then breeze through the empty middle.

And remember: Cramer is never right.

He grabbed Cramer's wrist as he reached for the throttle. "Let's hang here for a bit."

"Why? He's got to—"

"Just call it a feeling."

Henriques watched the screen, tracking the trio of diverging blobs. As the center one neared, he lifted the glasses again. Nothing. Whoever it was was traveling without running lights.

Doubt wriggled in his gut. What if the runner had pulled a double reverse? If so, he was already out of reach . . . as good as home free.

"Getting close," Cramer said. "See him yet?"

"No."

"Still coming right at us. Think he knows we're here?"

"He knows. He's got infrared too."

"Yeah, well, he ain't acting like it. Maybe we should turn the running—"

And then a dazzling flash of lightning to the south and Henriques saw it. A Hutch 686.

He let out a whoop of triumph. "It's him! We got him!"

"I see him!" Cramer called. "But he's coming right at us. Is he crazy?"

"No, he's not crazy. And he's not going to hit us. Bring us about. We got us a chase!"

Cramer stood frozen at the wheel. "He's gonna ram us!"

"Shit!"

Henriques grabbed the spotlight, thumbed the switch and swiveled it toward the oncoming boat. He picked up the charging bow, the flying spray, almost on top of them, and goddamn if it didn't look like the bastard was really going to ram them.

Henriques braced himself as Cramer shouted incoherently and ducked behind the console. But at the last minute the runner swerved and flashed past to starboard, sending a wave of wake over the gunwale.

"After him!" Henriques screamed. "After him, goddamn it!"

Cramer was pushing on the throttle, yanking on the wheel, bringing them around. But the ankle-deep seawater sloshing back and forth in the cockpit slowed her response. The bilge pumps were overwhelmed at the moment, but they'd catch up. The VMA would be planing out again soon. That cute little maneuver had given the runner a head start, but it wouldn't matter. Henriques had him now. Didn't even have to catch him. Just follow him back to whatever dock he called home.

Terry caught himself looking over his shoulder. A reflex. Nothing to see in that mess of rain and wind. He cursed Henriques for not chasing one of the decoys. The guy seemed to read his mind. Well, why not? They were both Conchs.

Terry had only one trick left up his sleeve. If that didn't work . . .

Then what? Sink the *Terryfied*? What good would that do? The ATF would just haul her up, find out who she belonged to, and then camp outside his door.

Face it: He doesn't fall for this last one, I'm screwed.

And being a Conch, it was a damn good chance Henriques wouldn't.

Terry spotted the breakers of the barrier reef ahead. Lightning helped him get his bearings and he headed for the channel. As soon as he cut through, the swells shrank by half and he picked up speed. Now was his one chance to increase the distance between Henriques and himself. If he could get close enough to shore, pull in near the parking lot of one of the waterside restaurants or nightspots, maybe he could merge his infrared tag with the heat from the cars and the kitchen.

And what would that do besides delay the inevitable? Henriques would—

A bolt of lighting slashed down at a mangrove keylet to starboard, starkly illuminating the area with a flash of cold brilliance. Terry saw the water, the rain, the mangrove clumps, and something else . . . something that gut-punched him and froze his hands on the wheel.

"*Christ!*"

Just off the port bow and roaring toward him, a swirling, writhing column of white stretching into the darkness above, throwing up a furious cloud of foam and spray as it snaked back and forth across the surface of the water.

He'd seen plenty of waterspouts before. Couldn't spend a single season in the Keys without getting used to them, but he'd never—*never*—been this close to one. Never wanted to be. Waterspout . . . such an innocuous name. Damn thing was a tornado. That white frothy look was seawater spinning at two or three hundred miles an hour. Just brushing its hem would wreck the boat and send him flying. Catching the full brunt of the vortex would tear the *Terryfied* and its captain to pieces.

The hungry maw slithered his way across the surface, sucking up seawater and everything it contained, like Mrs. God's vacuum hose. Somewhere downwind it would rain salt water and fish—and maybe pieces of a certain Conch and his boat if he didn't do something fast.

It lunged toward him, its growing roar thundering like a fully-loaded navy cargo jet lifting off from Boca Chica, drowning out his own engine.

Terry shook off the paralysis and yanked the wheel hard to starboard. For a heartbeat he was sure he'd acted too late. He screamed into a night that had become all noise and water. The boat lurched, the port side lifted, spray drenched him, big hard drops peppering him like rounds from an Uzi. He thought he was going over.

And then *Terryfied* righted herself and the raging, swirling ghostly bulk was dodging past the stern, ten, then twenty feet from the transom. He saw it swerve back the other way before it was swallowed by the night and the rain. It seemed to be zigzagging down the channel. Maybe it liked the deeper water. Maybe it was trapped in the rut, in the groove . . . he didn't know.

One thing he did know: If not for that lightning flash he'd be dead.

Would Henriques be so lucky? With the waterspout heading south along the channel and Henriques charging north at full throttle, the ATF could be minus one boat and two men in a minute or so.

Saved by a waterspout. Who'd ever believe it? No witness except Henriques, and he'd be . . . fish food.

Terry turned and stared behind him. Nothing but rain and dark. No sign of Henriques's running lights. Which meant the waterspout was probably between them . . . heading right for Henriques.

"Shit."

He reached for the Very pistol. He knew he was going to regret this.

"Mother of *God!*" Cramer shouted.

Henriques saw it too.

One instant everything was black, the next the sky was blazing red from the emergency flare sailing through the rain. And silhouetted against the burning glow was something dark and massive, directly in their path.

Henriques reached past Cramer and yanked the wheel hard to port, hard enough to nearly capsize them. The tower of water roared past like a runaway freight train, leaving them stalled and shaken but in one piece. Henriques watched it retreat, pink now in the fading glow of the flare.

He turned and scanned the water to the north while Cramer shook and sputtered.

"You see that? You ever see anything *like* that? Damn near killed us! Hadn't been for that flare, we'd be goners!"

Henriques concentrated on the area around the lighted channel marker dead ahead. Something about that marker . . .

"There he is!" he shouted as he spotted a pale flash of wake. "Get him!"

"You gotta be kidding!" Cramer said. "He just saved our asses!"

"And I'll be sure to thank him when he's caught. Now after him, dammit!"

Cramer grumbled, started the engine, and turned east. He gunned it but Henriques could tell his heart wasn't in it.

And he had to admit, some of the fight had gone out of him as well.

Why had the runner warned them? That baffled him. These guys were scum, running stolen or pilfered medical supplies out to the rich folks on their luxury hospital ships when there was barely enough to go around on shore. Yet the guy had queered his only chance of escape by sending up a warning flare.

I don't get it.

But Henriques couldn't let that stop him. He couldn't turn his head and pretend he didn't see, couldn't allow himself to be bought off with a flare. He'd seen payoffs all his life—cops, judges, mayors, and plenty Conchs among them. But Pepe Henriques wasn't joining that crowd.

The rain was letting up, ceiling lifting, visibility improving. Good. Where were they? He spotted the lights on the three radio towers, which put them off Sugarloaf. So where was the runner heading? Bow Channel, maybe? That would put him into Cudjo Bay. Lots of folks lived on Cudjo Bay. And one of them just might be a runner.

He retrieved his field glasses and kept them trained on the fleeing boat as it followed the channel. Didn't have much choice. Neither of them did. Tide was out and even with the storm there wasn't enough water to risk running outside the channel, even with the shallow draw of an impeller craft. As they got closer to civilization the channel would be better marked, electric lights and all . . .

Electric lights.

He snapped the glasses down but it was too late. Cramer was hauling ass past the red light marker, keeping it to starboard.

"*NO!*" Henriques shouted and lunged for the wheel, but too late.

The hull hit coral and ground to a halt, slamming the two of them against the console. The intakes sucked sand and debris, choked, and cut out.

Silence, except for Cramer's cursing.

"God damn! God-damn-God-damn-God-damn-God *damn!* Where's the fucking channel?"

"You're out of it," Henriques said softly, wondering at how calm he felt.

"I took the goddamn marker to starboard!"

Henriques nodded in the darkness, hiding his chagrin. He shouldn't have been so focused on the runner's boat. Should have been taking in the whole scene. Cramer hadn't grown up on these waters. Like every seaman, he knew the three R's: RED-RIGHT-RETURN. Keep the red markers on your right when returning to port. But Cramer couldn't know that this marker was supposed to be green. Only a Conch would know. Somebody had changed the lens. And Henriques knew who.

He felt like an idiot but couldn't help smiling in the dark. He'd been had but good. There'd be another time, but this round went to the runner.

He reached for the Very pistol.

"What the hell?"

The flare took Terry by surprise. What was Henriques up to? The bastard had been chasing him full throttle since dodging that waterspout, and now he was sending up a flare. It wouldn't throw enough light to make any difference in the chase, and if he needed help, he had a radio.

Then Terry realized it had come from somewhere in the vicinity of the channel marker he'd tampered with. He pumped a fist into the air. Henriques was stuck and he was letting his prey know it. Why? Payback for Terry's earlier flare? Maybe. That was all the break he'd ever get from Henriques, he guessed.

He'd take it.

Terry eased up on the throttle and sagged back in the chair. His knees felt a little weak. He was safe. But that had been close. Too damn close.

He cruised toward Cudjo, wondering if this was a sign that he should find another line of work. With Henriques out there, and maybe a few more like him joining the hunt, only a matter of time before they identified him. Might even catch him on the way out with a hold full of contraband. Then it'd be the slammer . . . hard time in a fed lock-up. Quitting now would be the smart thing.

Right. Someday, but not yet. A couple more runs, then he'd think about it some more.

And maybe someday after he was out of this, he and Henriques would run into each other in a bar and Terry would buy that Conch a Red Stripe and they'd laugh about these chases.

Terry thought about that a minute.

Nah.

That only happened in movies.

He gunned his boat toward home.

In October Bob Weinberg and Jill Morgan approached me about collaborating with one of my children on a story for an anthology called *Great Writers and Kids Write Spooky Stories.* I loved the idea.

My daughter Meggan was twenty-two at the time and already writing on her own. I'd been helping her with a poem that she wanted to adapt to a children's book. Since the poem ("No Tarantulas, Please") derived from Meg's lifelong fear of spiders, we decided to center the tale around that. We discussed—but did not write down—an outline of the story and how it should progress. I came up with a situation that I thought would allow Meg to tap into her fears and infuse them into the story; Meg came up with the diabolical ending. She sat down and banged out the first half of the story in one day. I embellished that and carried it to its close. Then we tweaked and polished it until we both were happy with the final form.

So here's "Itsy Bitsy Spider" from a dad who thinks spiders are cool, and a daughter who forced herself to see *Arachnophobia* with me but kept her feet off the floor the whole time. It's intended for a YA audience, but I think it's pretty damn creepy no matter what your age.

Itsy Bitsy Spider

with MEGGAN C. WILSON

The moon was high before Toby spotted the first one. A hairy hunter—the hunters only came out at night. He hadn't seen this one before. Big, but not thick and bulky like a tarantula. Its sleek body was the size of a German shepherd; its eight long, powerful legs spread half a dozen feet on either side, carrying its head and abdomen low to the ground. Moonlight gleamed off its short, bristly fur as it darted across the backyard, seeming to flow rather than run. Hunting, hunting, always hungry, always hunting.

A cool breeze began to blow through the two-inch opening of Toby's screened window. He shivered and narrowed it to less than an inch, little more than a crack. It wasn't the air making him shiver. It was the spider. You'd think that after a year of watching them every night, he'd be used to them. No way.

God, he hated spiders. Had hated them for the entire ten years of his life. Even when they'd been tiny and he could squash them under foot, they made his skin crawl. Now, when they were big as dogs—when there *were* no dogs because the spiders had eaten them all, along with the cats and squirrels and woodchucks and just about anything else edible, including people—the sight of them made Toby almost physically ill with revulsion.

And yet still he came to the window and watched. A habit . . . like tuning in a bad sitcom . . . it had become a part of his nightly routine.

He hadn't seen this one before. Usually the same spiders traveled the same routes every night at about the same time. This one could be lost or maybe it was moving in on the other spiders' territory. It darted to the far side of the yard and stopped at the swing set, touching the dented slide with a foreleg. Then it turned and came toward the house, passing out of Toby's line of sight. Quickly he reached out and pushed down on the window sash until it clicked shut. It couldn't get in, he knew, but not being able to see it made him nervous.

He clicked on his flashlight and flipped through his spider book until he found one that looked like the newcomer. He'd spotted all kinds of giant spiders in the last year—black widows, brown recluses, trap door spiders, jumping spiders, crab spiders. Here it was: Lycosidae—a wolf spider, the most ferocious of the hunting spiders.

Toby glanced up and stifled a scream. There, not two feet away, hovering on the far side of the glass, was the wolf spider. Its hairy face stared at him with eight eyes that gleamed like black diamonds. Toby wanted to run shrieking from the room but couldn't move—didn't *dare* move. It probably didn't see him, didn't know he was there. The sound of the window closing must have drawn it over. Sudden motion might make it bang against the glass, maybe break it, let it in. So Toby sat frozen and stared back at its cold black eyes, watched it score the glass with the claws of its poisonous falces. He had never been this close to one before. He could make out every repulsive feature; every fang, every eye, every hair was magnified in the moonlight.

Finally, after what seemed an eternity, the wolf spider moved off. Toby could breathe again. His heart was still pounding as he wiped the sweat from his forehead.

Good thing they don't know glass is breakable, he thought, or we'd all be dead.

They never tried to break through anything. They preferred to look for a passage—an open window, an open door—

Door! Toby stiffened as a sudden chill swept over him. The back door to the garage—had he closed it all the way? He'd run some garbage out to the ditch in the back this afternoon, then had rushed back in—he was terrified of being outside. But had he pulled the door all the way closed? It stuck sometimes and didn't latch. A spider might lean against it and push it open. It still couldn't get into the house, but the first person to open the door from the laundry room into the garage . . .

He shuddered. That's what had happened to the Hansens down the street. A spider had got in, wrapped them all up in a web, then laid a huge egg mass. The baby spiders hatched and went to work. When they finally found the remains of the Hansens, they looked like mummies and their corpses weighed only a few pounds each . . . every drop of juice had been sucked out of them.

The garage door . . . maybe he'd better check again.

Don't be silly, he told himself. Of course I latched it. I've been doing the same thing for almost a year now.

Toby left the window and brushed his teeth. He tiptoed past his mother's bedroom and paused. He heard her steady slow breathing and knew she was fast asleep. She was an early riser . . . didn't have much to stay up late for. Toby knew she missed Dad, even more than he did. Dad had volunteered for a spider kill team—"doing my civic duty," he'd said—and never came back from one of the search-and-destroy missions. That had been seven months ago. No one in that kill team had ever been found.

Feeling very alone in the world, Toby padded down the hall to his own room where even thoughts of monster spiders couldn't keep him from sleep. He had a fleeting thought of the garage door—yes, he was sure he'd latched it—and then his head hit the pillow and instantly he was asleep.

Toby opened his eyes. Morning. Sunlight poured through the windows. A year or so ago it would be a day to go out and play. Or go to school. He never thought he'd miss school, but he did. Mostly he missed other kids. The spiders had made him a prisoner of his house, even in the daytime.

He dressed and went downstairs. He found his mother sitting in the kitchen, having a cup of instant coffee. She looked up when she saw him come in.

"Morning, Tobe," she said and reached out and ruffled his hair.

Mom looked old and tired, even though she was only thirty-two. She was wearing her robe. She wore it a lot. Some days she never got out of it. What for? She wasn't going out, no one was coming to visit, and she'd given up on Dad coming home.

"Hey, Mom. You should have seen it last night—the spiders, I mean. One crawled right up to the window. It was real scary; like it was looking right at me."

Fear flashed in her eyes. "It came up to the window? That worries me. Maybe you shouldn't sit by that window. It might be dangerous."

"C'mon Mom. I keep the window shut. It's not like I have anything else to do. Besides, it can't break through the glass, right?"

"Probably not. But just play it safe, and move away if one looks like it's coming near you, okay? I don't know how you can stand to even look at those things." She grimaced and shivered.

Toby shrugged and poured himself some cereal. They were running low on powdered milk, so he ate it dry. Dad had stocked the whole basement with canned and freeze-dried food before he left, but those wouldn't last forever.

When he finished he turned on the TV, hoping there'd be some news about a breakthrough against the spiders. The cable had gone out three months ago; news shows and *I Love Lucy* reruns were about the only things running on the one channel they could pull in with the antenna.

At least they still had electricity. The telephone worked when it felt like it, but luckily their power lines were underground. People whose power came in on utility poles weren't so fortunate. The spiders strung their webs from them and eventually shorted them all out.

No good news on the tube, just a rehash about the coming of the spiders. Toby had heard it all before but he listened again.

The spiders . . . no one knew where they came from, or how they got so big. Toby had first heard of them on the evening news about a year and a half ago. Reports from the Midwest, the farmlands, of cattle being killed and mutilated and eaten. Then whole families disappearing, their isolated houses found empty of life and full of silky webs. Wasn't long before the first giant spiders were spotted. Just horrid curiosities at first, science-fictiony beasties. Local governments made efforts to capture and control them, and hunting parties went out with shotguns and high-powered rifles to "bag a big one." But these weren't harmless deer or squirrels or pheasant. These things could fight back. Lots of mighty hunters never returned. Toby wondered if the spiders kept hunters' heads in their webs as trophies.

The army and the National Guard got involved and for a while it looked like they were winning, but the spiders were multiplying too fast. They laid a couple thousand eggs at once; each hatchling was the size of a gerbil, hungry as hell, and growing all the time. Soon they were everywhere—overrunning the towns, infesting the cities. And now they ruled the night. The hunting spiders were so fast and so deadly, no one left home after dark anymore.

But people could still get around during the day—as long as they stayed away from the webs. The webbers were fat and shiny and slower; they stretched their silky nets across streets and alleys, between trees and bushes—and waited. They could be controlled . . . sort of. Spider kill teams could fry them with flamethrowers and destroy their webs, but it was a losing battle: Next day there'd be a new web and a new fat, shiny spider waiting to pounce.

And sometimes the spiders got the kill teams . . . like Dad's.

Toby didn't like to think about what probably happened to Dad, so he tuned the TV to its only useful purpose: PlayStation. *NHL Hockey* and *Metal Gear Solid 7* were his favorites. They helped keep him from thinking too much. He didn't mind spending the whole day with them.

Not that he ever got to do that. Mom eventually stepped in and made him read or do something "more productive" with his time. Toby couldn't think of anything more productive than figuring out all of the *MGS 7*'s secrets, or practicing breaking the glass on *NHL Hockey*, but Mom just didn't get it.

But today he knew he'd get in some serious *MGS*. Mom was doing laundry and she'd just keep making trips up and down to the basement and wouldn't notice how long he had been playing.

As he was readying to pounce on an enemy guard he heard a cry and a loud crashing sound. He dropped the controller and ran into the kitchen. The basement door was open. He looked down and saw his mother crumpled at the bottom of the steps.

"Mom!" he cried, running down the steps. "Mom, what happened? Are you okay?"

She nodded weakly and attempted to sit up, but groaned with agony and clutched at her thigh.

"My leg! Oh, God, it's my leg."

Toby helped her back down. She looked up at him. Her eyes were glazed with pain.

"I tripped on the loose board in that step." She pointed to the spot. "I think my leg is broken. See if you can help me get up."

Toby fought back tears. "Don't move, Mom."

He ran upstairs and dialed Dr. Murphy, their family doctor, but the phone was out again. He pulled pillows and comforters from the linen closet and surrounded her with them, making her as comfortable as possible.

"I'm going to get help," he said, ready for her reaction.

"Absolutely not. The spiders will get you. I lost your father. I don't want to lose you too. You're not going anywhere, and I mean it." But her voice was weak. She looked like she was going into shock.

Toby knew he had to act fast. He kissed her cheek.

"I'm going for Doc Murphy. I'll be right back."

Before his mother could protest, he was on his way up the steps, heading for the garage. The Murphy house was only a few blocks away. He could bike there in five minutes. If Dr. Murphy wasn't in, Mrs. Murphy would know how to help him.

He could do it. It was still light out. All he had to do was steer clear of any webs and he'd be all right. The webbers didn't chase their prey. The really dangerous spiders, the hunters, only came out at night.

As his hand touched the handle of the door into the garage, he hesitated. The back door . . . he *had* closed it yesterday . . . hadn't he? Yes. Yes, he was sure. Almost positive.

Toby pressed his ear against the wood and flipped the switch that turned on the overhead lights in the garage, hoping to startle anything lying in wait on the other side. He listened for eight long legs rustling about . . . but heard nothing . . . quiet in there.

Still, he was afraid to open the door.

Then he heard his mother's moan from the basement and knew he was wasting time. Had to move. *Now or never.*

Taking a deep breath, he turned the handle and yanked the door open, ready to slam it closed again in an instant. Nothing. All quiet. Empty. Just the tools on the wall, the wheelbarrow in the corner, his bike by the back door, and the Jeep. No place for a spider to hide . . . except under the Jeep. Toby had a terrible feeling about the shadows under the Jeep . . . something could be there . . .

Quickly he dropped to one knee and looked under it—nothing. He let out a breath he hadn't realized he was holding.

He closed the door behind him and headed for his bike. Toby wished he could drive. It'd be nothing to get to Doc Murphy's if he could take the Jeep. He checked the back door—firmly latched. All that worry for nothing. He checked the backyard through the window in the door. Nothing moving. No fresh webs.

His heart began pounding against the inner surface of his ribs as he pulled the door open and stuck his head out. All clear. Still, anything could be lurking around the corner.

I'm going for Doc Murphy. I'll be right back.

Sounded so simple down in the basement. Now . . .

Gritting his teeth, he grabbed his bike, pulled it through the door, and hopped on. He made a wide swing across the grass to give him a view of the side of the garage. No web, nothing lurking. Relieved, he pedaled onto the narrow concrete path and zipped out to the front of the house. The driveway was asphalt, the front yard was open and the only web in sight was between the two cherry trees to his left in front of the Sullivans' house next door. Something big and black crouched among the leaves.

Luckily he wasn't going that way. He picked up speed and was just into his turn when the ground to his right at the end of the driveway moved. A circle of grass and dirt as big around as a manhole cover angled up and a giant trap-door spider leaped out at him. Toby cried out and made a quick cut to his left. The spider's poisonous falces reached for him. He felt the breeze on his face as they just missed. One of them caught his rear wheel and he almost went over, almost lost control, but managed to hang on to the handlebars and keep going, leaving it behind.

Toby sobbed with relief. God, that had been close! He glanced back from the street and saw the trapdoor spider backing into its home, pulling the lid down over itself, moving fast, almost as if it was afraid. Toby started to yell at it but the words clogged in his throat. A brown shape was moving across his front lawn, big and fast.

Toby heard himself cry, *"No!"* The wolf spider from last night! It wasn't supposed to be out in the day. It was a night hunter. The only thing that could bring it out in the day was . . .

Hunger.

He saw it jump on the lid to the trapdoor spider's lair and try to force its way in, but the cover was down to stay. Then it turned toward Toby and started after him.

Toby yelped with terror and drove his feet against the pedals. He was already pedaling for all he was worth down the middle of the empty street, but fear added new strength to his legs. The bike leaped ahead.

But not far enough ahead. A glance back showed the wolf spider gaining, its eight legs a blur of speed as they carried it closer. It poisonous falces were extended, reaching hungrily for him.

Toby groaned with fear. He put his head down and forced every ounce of strength into his pumping legs. When he chanced another quick look over his shoulder, the wolf spider was farther behind.

"Yes!" he whispered, for he had breath enough only for a whisper.

And then he noticed that the wolf spider had slowed to a stop.

I beat him!

But when he faced front again he saw why the wolf had stopped—a huge funnel web spanned the street just ahead of him. Toby cried out and hit the brakes, turned the wheel, swerved, slid, but it was too late. He slammed into the silky net and was engulfed in the sticky strands.

Terror engulfed him as well. He panicked, feeling as if he was going to cry or throw up, or both. But he managed to get a grip, get back in control. He could get out of this. It was just a spider web. All he had to do was break free of these threads. But the silky strands were thick as twine, and sticky as Krazy Glue. He couldn't break them, couldn't pull them off his skin, and the more he struggled, the more entangled he became.

He quickly exhausted himself and hung there limp and sweaty, sobbing for breath. He had to get *free!* What about Mom? Who'd help her? Worry for her spurred him to more frantic squirming that only made the silk further tighten its hold. He began shouting for help. Someone had to hear him and help him out of this web.

And then a shadow fell over him. He looked up. Something was coming but it wasn't help. The owner of the web was gliding down from the dark end of the funnel high up in the tree, and oh, God, she was big. And shiny black. Her abdomen was huge, almost too big for her eight long spindly legs to carry. Her eyes, blacker spots set in the black of her head, were fixed on him. She leapt the last six feet and grasped him with her forelegs.

Toby screamed and shut his eyes, waiting for the poisonous falces to pierce him.

Please let it be quick!

But instead of pain he felt his body being lifted and turned, and turned again, and again. He was getting dizzy. He opened his eyes and saw that the spider was rolling him over and over with her spindly legs, like a lumberjack on a log, all the while spinning yards and yards of web from the tip of her abdomen, wrapping his body in a cocoon, but leaving his head free. He struggled against the bonds but it was useless—he might as well have been wrapped in steel.

And then she was dragging him upward, higher into the web, into the funnel. He passed the shriveled-up corpses of squirrels and birds, and even another spider much like herself, but smaller. Her mate? Near the top of the funnel she spun more web and attached him to the wall, then moved off, leaving him hanging like a side of beef.

What was she doing? Wasn't she going to kill him? Or was she saving him for later? His mind raced. *Yes. Save me for later.* As long as he was alive there was hope. Her web was across a street . . . good chance a kill team would come along and clear it . . . kill her, free him. Yes. He still had a chance . . .

Movement to his right caught his eye. About a foot away, something else was hanging from the web wall, also wrapped in a thick coat of silk. Smaller than Toby—maybe the size of a full grocery bag. Whatever was inside was struggling to get out. Probably some poor dog or raccoon that got caught earlier.

"Don't worry, fella," Toby said. "When the kill team gets me out, I'll see you get free too."

The struggle within the smaller cocoon became more frantic.

It must have heard my voice, he thought.

And then Toby saw a little break appear in the surface of the cocoon. Whatever was inside was chewing through! How was that possible? This stuff was tough as—

And then Toby saw what was breaking through.

A spider. A fist-sized miniature of the one that had hung him here emerged. And then another, and another, until the little cocoon was engulfed in a squirming mass of baby spiders.

Toby gagged. That wasn't a cocoon. That was an egg mass. And they were hatching. He screamed, and that was the wrong thing because they immediately began swarming toward him, hundreds of them, thousands, flowing across the web wall, crawling up his body, burrowing into his cocoon, racing toward his face.

Toby screamed as he had never screamed in his life—

And woke up.

He blinked. He was paralyzed with fear, but as his eyes adjusted to the dawn light seeping through the window, he recognized his bedroom and began to relax.

A dream . . . but *what* a dream! The worst nightmare of his life! He was weak with relief. He wanted to cry, he wanted to—

"Toby!" His mother's voice—she sounded scared. "Toby, are you all right?"

"Mom, what's wrong?"

"Thank God! I've been calling you for so long! A spider got into the house! I opened the door to the garage and it was there!"

The back door! Oh, no! I *didn't* latch it!

"It jumped on me and I fainted. But it didn't kill me. It wrapped me up in web and then it left. Come get me free!"

Toby went to leap out of bed but couldn't move. He looked down and saw that he wasn't under his blanket—he and his bed were webbed with a thick layer of sticky silk. He struggled but after a few seconds he knew that he was trapped.

"Hurry up, Toby!" his mother cried. "There's something else in here with me all wrapped up in web. And it's moving. I'm scared, Toby. Please get me out!"

Panicked, Toby scanned the room. He found the egg mass attached to his bedpost, a few inches from his head, wriggling, squirming with internal life, a many-legged *horde* of internal life.

We're going to end up like the Hansens!

"Oh, Mom!" he sobbed. "I'm so sorry! I'm so *sorry!*"

And then the first wolf spider hatchling broke free of the egg mass and dropped onto his pillow.

Toby screamed as he had never screamed in his life.

But this time he wasn't dreaming.

1995

Implant was published in England in February; the U.S. edition wouldn't appear until October. I barely noticed. I was spending a lot of time in the air—flying back and forth from New Jersey to L.A. and Vegas for meetings and electronic shows—or in conference rooms with companies like TWI, Digital Pictures, Trilobyte, Microsoft, Quartet, Scholastic Productions, Digital Domain, Sony, IMAX, Propaganda Code, Paramount Interactive, Prodigy, Polygram Interactive, AND Interactive, Dreamworks Interactive, Virgin Interactive, and so on.

Somehow I was managing to write the second contracted medical thriller, *Deep as the Marrow*, between stops while holding up my ends of *FTL*, the *Mirage* novel, and the *Mirage* game. (Bless the laptop.)

In early February Matt and I were on the Burbank set of *Bombmeister*. Jeffrey Jones was the star, with John Lafia directing. We saw a lot of the shoot and even made it to a backlot where they blew up a miniature of the toy-maker's mansion.

After the shoot we were given VHS copies of the raw footage . . . and that's all there is of *Bombmeister*. The first two films had done so poorly that Sony (a major backer) pulled the financial plug and Interfilm was no more. All the *Bombmeister* footage is stored away, waiting for some enterprising company to cut and program it into an edge-of-the-seat interactive DVD thriller.

Maybe someday. Until then, it's vaporware. (Remember that word. You'll hear it again . . . and again . . .)

In the spring I handed in *Deep as the Marrow*. This was my third medical thriller and already I was growing restless with the genre. Too formulaic. In fact, when you look at *Marrow*, it's not a true medical thriller. Sure, the protagonist is a doctor and medical problems figure into the plot, but at its heart it's a political thriller. The maguffin is not a disease but the president's decision to legalize drugs—*that's* what sets the plot in motion.

Matt and I finished the first draft of the *Mirage* novel and put it aside while we finished the design and scenario for the game. Having worked through the story in a long narrative helped immensely. By April we'd finished the scenario and TWEP accepted it. Now to start the interactions.

The buzzword at Time Warner in those days was "synergy." To that end, Matt and I had several meetings with Janet Brillig of Atlantic Records to pick out music for the *Mirage* CD-ROM. We heard a lot of brand-new acts like Jill Sobule, Jewel, and Sugar Ray.

By the fall we had most of the interactions scripted. We'd been handing them in as they were completed, all meeting with enthusiastic responses. But then in October, Time Warner Electronic Publishing halted development on *Mirage*: too ambitious, too expensive, they'd never make a profit, blah-blah-blah. Soon after that the company imploded.

No someday for *Mirage*. It's permanent vaporware. And without a publisher, the *DNA Wars* game was dead too.

Matt and I were starting to wonder if we were Jonah. Two companies in a row now—kaput.

At least we still had a book publisher. The novel and interactive contracts were separate. We polished the novel, handed it in to Betsy Mitchell, and took the interactive *Mirage* elsewhere.

About this time, Steven Spruill and I decided to write a novel together. We'd discussed a story about a professional assassin during the long drives to and from NECon each year. I had an urge for some action writing, so I kicked it off. Our working title was *Jake,* after our antihero Jake Nacht. Eventually we retitled it *Nightkill.*

Looking back, I can see that Jake was another Repairman Jack surrogate. Even the name was similar. My subconscious was becoming less subtle and more insistent.

On my last L.A. trip of the year I had lunch at Farmer's Market with two film producers named Barry Rosenbush and Bill Borden. I'd met them before. They very much wanted to bring Repairman Jack to the screen. They made an option offer on *The Tomb.* No one else was knocking on the door (it was the only Repairman Jack novel at the time) so I accepted.

I had no idea that more than a decade in development hell lay ahead.

"**DAVPE**"

In the fall of 1994 I got a call from Janet Berliner asking me if I'd like to do a magic-related story for a David Copperfield anthology. His name would be on the cover but she'd be doing all the editing. I'd been kicking around an idea about a magic word—the *right* word. Whenever you used it to answer a question, the listener always heard the right answer, the best answer for you.

Powerful stuff. What a hook. Who wouldn't want to know that word?

The story was the easy part. But the word . . . showing you some neologism you could pronounce would take you out of the story. But what if you couldn't pronounce it? What if it appeared in the text as gibberish?

I instructed the typesetter to use a double overprint of DAVID / COPPE / RFIEL for the word. It worked. The result was **DAVPE**. Pure gibberish.

David Copperfield's Tales of the Impossible was released in the fall of 1995. We had a big signing at a Fifth Avenue Barnes and Noble, then a party at Manhattan's Fashion Café. Janet and Matt and Ray Feist and other contributors were there, but we were relegated to the main-floor area while Copperfield and his supposed fiancée, Claudia Schiffer, kept to themselves on a raised, cordoned-off platform. We groundlings were allowed to look but not speak to or approach these ethereal beings. Freaking hilarious. I mean, what planet do these clowns hail from?

I love the story, though.

As promised, the first installment of Dennis Nickleby's *Three Months to Financial Independence* arrives exactly two weeks after I called the toll-free number provided by his infomercial. I toss out the accompanying catalogs and "Occupant" bulk mail, then tear at the edges of the cardboard mailer.

This is it. My new start. Today is the first day of the rest of my life, and starting today my life will be very different. I'll be organized, I'll have specific goals and a plan to achieve them—I'll have an *agenda*.

Never had an agenda before. And as long as this agenda doesn't involve a job, that's cool. Never been a nine-to-fiver. Tend to ad-lib as I go along. Prefer to think of myself as an *investor*. Now I'll be an investor with an agenda. And Dennis Nickleby's tapes are going to guide me.

Maybe they can help me with my personal life too. I'm sort of between girlfriends now. Seem to have trouble keeping them. Denice was the last. She walked out two weeks ago. Called me a couch potato—said I was a fat slob who doesn't do anything but read and watch TV.

Not fair. And not true. All right, so I am a little overweight, but not as overweight as I look. Lots of guys in their mid thirties weigh more than I do. It's just that at five-eight it shows more. At least I still have all my hair. And I'm not ugly or anything.

As for spending a lot of time on the couch—guilty. But I'm doing research. My folks left me some money and I'm always looking for a better place to put it to work. I've got a decent net worth, live in a nice high-rise in North Jersey where I can see the Manhattan skyline. I make a good income from my investments without ever leaving the house. But that doesn't mean I'm not working at it.

Good as things are, I know I can do better. And the Nickleby course is going to take me to that next level. I can feel it. And I'm more than ready.

My hands shake as I pull the glossy vinyl video box from the wrapper. Grinning back at me is a young, darkly handsome man with piercing blue eyes and dazzling teeth. Dennis Nickleby. Thirty years old and already a multi-millionaire. Everything this guy touches turns to gold. But does he want to hoard his investing secrets? No way. He's willing to share them with the little guy—guys like me with limited capital and unlimited dreams. What a *mensch*.

Hey, I'm no sucker. I've seen Tony Robbins and those become-a-real-estate-millionaire-with-no-money-down infomercials. I'm home a lot so I see *lots* of infomercials. Trust me, they roll off me like water off a duck. But Dennis Nickleby . . . he's different. He looked out from that TV screen and I knew he was talking to me. To *me*. I knew what he was offering would change my life. The price was stiff—five hundred bucks—but well worth it if he delivered a mere tenth of what he was offering. Certainly a better investment than some of those do-nothing stocks in my account.

I whipped out my credit card, grabbed the phone, punched in his 800 number, and placed my order.

And now it's here. I lift the lid of the box and—

"Shit!"

There's supposed to be a videotape inside—lesson one. What do I find? An audiocassette. And it's not even a new one. It's some beat-up piece of junk.

I'm fuming. I'm so pissed I'm ready to dump this piece of garbage on the floor and grind it into the carpet. But I do not do this. I take three deep breaths, calm myself, then march to the phone. Very gently I punch in Mr. Nickleby's 800 number—it's on the back of the tape box—and get some perky little babe on the phone. I start yelling about consumer fraud, about calling the attorney general, about speaking to Dennis Nickleby himself. She asks why I'm so upset and I'm hardly into my explanation when she lets loose this high-pitched squeal.

"*You're* the one! Ooh, goody! We've been hoping you'd call!"

"Hoping?"

"*Yes!* Mr. Nickleby was here *himself.* He was *so* upset. He learned that *some-*how the *wrong* kind of tape got into one of his *Three Months to Financial Inde-pendence* boxes. He instructed us that should we hear from *anyone* who got an *audio*cassette instead of a *video*cassette, we should tell them not to worry. A brand new *video*cassette of *Three Months to Financial Independence* would be *hand* delivered to them *immediately!* Now, what do you think of *that?*"

"I . . . I . . ." I'm flabbergasted. This man is on top of everything. Truly he knows how to run a business. "I think that's incredible."

"Just give us your name and address and we'll get that replacement to you *immediately!*"

"It's Michael Moulton." I give her the address.

"Ooh! Hackensack. That's not far from here!"

"Just over the GW Bridge."

"*Well*, then! You should have your replacement *very* soon!"

"Good."

Her terminal perkiness is beginning to get to me. I'm hurrying to hang up when she says, "Oh, and one more thing. Mr. Nickleby said to tell you *not* to do *anything* with the audiocassette. Just *close* it up in the box it came in and *wait* for the replacement tape. The messenger will take it in *exchange* for the videotape."

"Fine. Good—"

"Remember that now—close the audiotape in the holder and wait. Okay?"

"Right. Cool. Good-*bye.*"

I hang up thinking, Whatever she's taking, I want some.

Being a good boy, I snap the video box cover closed and am about to place it on the end table by the door when curiosity tickles me and I start to wonder what's on this tape. Is it maybe from Dennis Nickleby's private collection? A bootleg jazz or rock tape? Or better yet, some dictation that might give away one or two investment secrets not on the videotape?

I know right then there's no way I'm not going to listen to this tape, so why delay? I pop it into my cassette deck and hit PLAY.

Nothing. I crank up the volume—some static, some hiss, and nothing else. I fast forward and still nothing. I'm about to hit STOP when I hear some high-pitched gibberish. I rewind a little and replay at regular speed.

Finally this voice comes on. Even with the volume way up I can barely hear it. I press my ear to the speaker. Whoever it is is whispering.

"The only word you need to know: CRYPT."

And that's it. I fast forward all the way to the end and nothing. I go back and listen to that one sentence again. *"The only word you need to know: CRYPT."*

Got to be a garble. Somebody erased the tape and the heads missed a spot. Oh, well.

Disappointed, I rewind it, pop it out, and close it up in the video box.

So here I am, not an hour later, fixing a sandwich and watching the stock quotes on CNBC when there's a knock on my apartment door. I check through the peephole and almost choke.

Dennis Nickleby himself!

I fumble the door open and he steps inside.

"Mr. Nickleby!"

"Do you have it?"

He's sweating and puffing like he sprinted the ten flights to my floor instead of taking the elevator. His eyes are darting everywhere so fast they seem to be moving in opposite directions—like a chameleon's. Finally they come to rest on the end table.

"There! That's it!"

He lunges for the video box, pops it open, snatches the cassette from inside.

"You didn't listen to it, did you?"

Something in his eyes and voice tell me to play this one close to the vest. But I don't want to lie to Dennis Nickleby.

"Should I have? I will if you want me to."

"No-no," he says quickly. "That won't be necessary." He hands me an identical video box. "Here's the replacement. Terribly sorry for the mix-up."

I laugh. "Yeah. Some mix-up. How'd that ever happen?"

"Someone playing games." His eyes go subzero for an instant. "But no harm done."

"You want to sit down? I was just making lunch—"

"Thank you, no. I'd love to but my schedule won't permit it. Maybe some other time." He extends his hand. "Once again, sorry for the inconvenience. Enjoy the tape."

And then he's out the door and gone. I stand there staring at the spot where he stood. Dennis Nickleby himself came by to replace the tape. Personally. Wow. And then it occurs to me: Check the new box.

I pop it open. Yes sir. There's the *Three Months to Financial Independence* videotape. At last.

But what's the story with that audio cassette? He seemed awful anxious to get it back. And what for? It was totally blank except for that one sentence—*The only word you need to know: CRAYPD*. What's that all about?

I'd like to look it up in the dictionary, but who knows how to spell something so weird sounding. And besides, I don't have a dictionary. Maybe I'll try later at the local library—once I find out where the local library is. Right now I've got to transfer some money to my checking account so I can pay my Visa bill when the five-hundred-buck charge to Nickleby, Inc., shows up on this month's statement.

I call Gary, my discount broker, to sell some stock. I've been in Castle Petrol for a while and it's doing squat. Now's as good a time as any to get out. I tell Gary to dump all 200 shares. Then it occurs to me that Gary's a pretty smart guy. Even finished college.

"Hey, Gary. You ever hear of CRAYPD?"

"Can't say as I have. But if it exists, I can find it for you. You interested?"

"Yeah. I'm very interested."

"You got it."

Yeah, well, I *don't* get it. All right, maybe I do get it, but it's not what I'm expecting, and not till two days later.

Meantime I stay busy with Dennis Nickleby's videotape. Got to say, it's kind of disappointing. Nothing I haven't heard elsewhere. Strange . . . after seeing his infomercial, I was sure this was going to be just the thing for me.

Then I open an envelope from the brokerage. Inside I find the expected sell confirm for the two hundred shares of Castle Petrol at 10.25, but with it is a buy confirm for *two thousand* shares of something called Thai Cord, Inc.

What the hell is Thai Cord? Gary took the money from Castle Petrol and put it in a stock I've never heard of! I'm baffled. He's never done anything like that. Must be a mistake. I call him.

"Hey, dude," he says as soon as he comes on the line. "Who's your source?"

"What are you talking about?"

"Thai Cord. It's up to five this morning. Boy, you timed that one perfectly."

"Five?" I swallow. I was ready to take his head off, now I learn I've made eight thousand in two days. "Gary . . . why did you put me into Thai Cord?"

"Why? Because you asked me to. You said you were very interested in it. I'd never heard of it, but I looked it up and bought it for you." He sounds genuinely puzzled. "Wasn't that why you called the other day? To sell Castle and buy Thai? Hey, whatever, man—you made a killing."

"I know I made a killing, Gary, and no one's gladder than me, but—"

"You want to stay with it?"

"I just want to get something straight: Yesterday I asked you if you'd ever heard of ParkerGen."

"No way, pal. I know ParkerGen. NASDAQ—good high-tech, speculative stock. You said Thai Cord."

I'm getting annoyed now. "ParkerGen, Gary. ParkerGen!"

"I can hear you, Mike. ParkerGen, ParkerGen. Are you all right?"

At this moment I'm not so sure. Suddenly I'm chilled, and there's this crawly feeling on the nape of my neck. I say one thing—*The only word you need to know*—and Gary hears another.

"Mike? You still there?"

"Yeah. Still here."

My mind's racing. What the hell's going on?

"What do you want me to do? Sell the Thai and buy ParkerGen? Is that it?"

I make a snap decision. Something weird's going down and I want to check it out. And what the hell, it's all found money.

"Yeah. Put it all into ParkerGen."

"Okay. It's running three and an eighth today. I'll grab you three thousand."

"Great."

I get off the phone and start to pace my apartment. I'm wired. I've got this crazy idea cooking in my brain . . .

. . . *the only word you need to know:* **CRAPPD**.

What if . . . ?

Nah. It's too crazy. But if it's true, there's got to be a way to check it out.

And then I have it. The ponies. They're running at the Meadowlands today. I'll invest a few hours in research. If I hurry I can make the first race.

I know it's completely nuts, but I've *got* to know . . .

I just make it. I rush to the ten-dollar window and say, "**CRAPPD** in the first."

The teller doesn't even glance up; he takes my ten, punches a few buttons, and out pops my ticket. I grab it and look at it: I've bet on some nag named Yesterday's Gone.

I don't bother going to the grandstand. I stand under one of the monitors. I see the odds on Yesterday's Gone are three to one. The trotters are lined up, ready to go.

"And they're off!"

I watch with a couple of other guys in polo shirts and polyester pants who're standing around. I'm not too terribly surprised when Yesterday's Gone crosses the finish line first. I've now got thirty bucks where I had ten a few minutes ago, but I've also got that crawly feeling at the back of my neck again.

This has gone from crazy to creepy.

With the help of the Daily Double and the Trifecta, by the time I leave the track I've parlayed my original ten bucks into sixty-two hundred. I could have made more but I'm getting nervous. I don't want to attract too much attention.

As I'm driving away I can barely keep from flooring the gas pedal. I'm wired—positively giddy. It's like some sort of drug. I feel like king of the world. I've got to keep going. But how? Where?

I pass a billboard telling me about "5 TIMES MORE DICE ACTION!" at Caesar's in Atlantic City.

My question has been answered.

I pick Caesar's because of the billboard. I've never been much for omens but I'm into them now. Big time.

I'm also trying to figure out what else I'm into with this weird word. *The only word you need to know . . .*

All you need to know to *win*. That has to be it: The word makes you a winner. If I say it whenever I'm about to take a chance—on a horse or a stock, at least—I'm a guaranteed winner.

This has got to be why Dennis Nickleby's such a success. He knows the word. That's why he was so anxious to get it back—he doesn't want anybody else to know it. Wants to keep it all to himself.

Bastard.

And then I think, no, not a bastard. I've got to ask myself if I'm about to share the word with anybody else. The answer is a very definite en-oh. I get the feeling I've just joined a very exclusive club. Only thing is, the other members don't know I've joined.

I also get the feeling there's no such thing as a game of chance for me anymore.

Cool.

The escalator deposits me on the casino floor. All the way down the Parkway I've been trying to decide what to try first—blackjack, poker, roulette, craps—what? But soon as I come within sight of the casino, I know. Flashing lights dead ahead:

PROGRESSIVE SLOTS! $802,672!!!

The prize total keeps rising as players keep plunking their coins into the gangs of one-armed bandits.

I wind through the crowds and the smoke and the noise toward the progressive slots section. Along the way I stop at a change cart and hand the mini-togaed blonde a five.

"Dollars," I say, "even though I'm going to need just one to win."

"Right on," she says, but I can tell she doesn't believe me.

She will. I take my Susan B. Anthonys and say, "You'll see."

I reach the progressive section and hunt up a machine. It isn't easy. Everybody here is at least a hundred years old and they'd probably give up one of their grandkids before they let somebody use their damn machine. Finally I see a hunched old blue-hair run out of money and leave her machine. I dart in, drop a coin in the slot, then I notice the machine takes up to three. I gather if I'm going to win the full amount I'd better drop two more. I do. I grab the handle . . . and hesitate. This is going to get me a *lot* of attention. Do I want that? I mean, I'm a private kind of guy. Then I look up at the $800,000-and-growing jackpot and know I want *that*.

Screw the publicity.

I whisper, "**CRAPPED**," and yank the handle.

I close my eyes as the wheels spin; I hear them begin to stop: First window—*choonk!* Second window—*choonk!* Third window—*choonk!* A bell starts ringing! Coins start dropping into the tray! I did it!

Abruptly the bell and the coins stop. I open my eyes. There's no envious crowd around me, no flashing cameras. Nobody's even looking my way. I glance down at the tray. Six dollars. I check out the windows. Two cherries and an orange. The red LED reads, "Pays 6."

I'm baffled. Where's my $800,000 jackpot? The crawling feeling that used to be on my neck is now in the pit of my stomach. What happened? Did I blow it? Is the word wearing out?

I grab three coins from the tray and shove them in. I say, "CRAVPD," again, louder this time, and pull that handle.

Choonk! Choonk! Choonk!

Nothing this time. Nothing!

I'm getting scared now. The power is fading fast. Three more coins, I damn near shout, "CRAVPD!" as I pull the goddamn handle. *Choonk! Choonk! Choonk!*

Nothing! Zip! Bupkis!

I slam my hand against the machine. "Damn, you! What's wrong?"

"Easy, fella," says the old dude next to me. "That won't help. Maybe you should take a break."

I walk away without looking at him. I'm devastated. What if I only had a few days with this word and now my time is up? I wasted it at the track when I could have been buying and shorting stocks on margin. The smoke, the crowds, the incessant chatter and mechanical noise of the casino is driving me to panic. I have to get out of here. I'm just about to break into a run when it hits me.

The word . . . what if it only works on people? Slot machines can't hear . . .

I calm myself. Okay. Let's be logical here. What's the best way to test the word in a casino?

Cards? Nah. Too many possible outcomes, too many other players to muddy the waters.

Craps? Again, too many ways to win or lose.

What's a game with high odds and a very definite winner?

I scan the floor, searching . . . and then I see it.

Roulette.

But how can I use the word at a roulette table?

I hunt around for a table with an empty seat. I spot one between this middle-aged nerd who's got to be an optometrist, and a mousy, thirtyish redhead who looks like one of his patients. Suddenly I know what I'm going to do.

I pull a hundred-dollar bill from my Meadowlands roll and grip it between my thumb and index finger. Then I twist up both my hands into deformed knots.

As I sit down I say to the redhead, "Could I trouble you to place my bets for me?"

She glances at my face through her Coke-bottle lenses, then at my twisted hands. Her eyes dart back to my face. She gives me a half-hearted smile.

"Sure. No problem."

"I'll split my winnings with you." *If I win.*

"That's okay. Really."

I make a show of difficulty dropping the hundred-dollar bill from my fingers, then I push it across the table.

"Tens, please."

A stack of ten chips is shoved in front of me.

"All bets down," the croupier says.

"Put one on CRAPPED, please," I tell the redhead, and hold my breath.

I glance around but no one seems to hear anything strange. Red takes a chip off the top of my pile and drops it on 33.

I'm sweating bullets now. My bladder wants to find a men's room. This has got to work. I've got to know if the word still has power. I want to close my eyes but I don't dare. I've got to see this.

The ball circles counter to the wheel, loses speed, slips toward the middle, hits rough terrain, bounces chaotically about, then clatters into a numbered slot.

"Thirty-three," drones the croupier.

The redhead squeals and claps her hands. "You won! Your first bet and you won!"

I'm drenched. I'm weak. My voice is hoarse when I say, "You must be my good luck charm. Don't go anywhere."

Truth is, it *could* be luck. A cruel twist of fate. I tell Red to move it all over to "CRAPPED."

She looks shocked. "All of it? You sure?"

"Absolutely."

She pushes the stack over to the 17 box.

Another spin. "Seventeen," the croupier says.

Now I close my eyes. I've got it. The word's got the power and I've got the word. *The only word you need to know.* I want to pump a fist into the air and scream "YES!" but I restrain myself. I am disabled, after all.

"Ohmigod!" Red is whispering. "That's . . . that's . . . !"

"A lot of money," I say. "And half of it's yours."

Her blue eyes fairly bulge against the near sides of her lenses. "What? Oh, no! I couldn't!"

"And I couldn't play without your help. I said I'd split with you and I meant it."

She has her hand over her mouth. Her words are muffled through her fingers. "Oh, thank you. You don't know—"

"All bets down," says the croupier.

No more letting it ride. My winnings far exceed the table limit. I notice that the pit boss has materialized and is standing next to the croupier. He's watching me and eyeing the megalopolis skyline of chips stacked in front of me. Hitting the winning number two times in a row—it happens in roulette, but not too damn often.

"Put five hundred on sixteen," I tell Red.

She does, and 22 comes up. Next I tell her five hundred on nine. Twelve comes up.

The pit boss drifts away.

"Don't worry," Red says with a reassuring pat on my arm. "You're still way ahead."

"Do I look worried?"

I tell her to put another five hundred on "CRAPPED." She puts the chips on 19.

A minute later the croupier calls, "Nineteen." Red squeals again. I lean back as the croupier starts stacking my winnings.

No need to go any further. I know how this works. I realize I am now the Ultimate Winner. If I want to I can break the bank at Caesar's. I can play the table limit on one number after another, and collect a thirty-five-to-one payout every couple of minutes. A crowd will gather. The house will have to keep playing—corporate pride will force them to keep paying. I can *own* the place, damn it!

But the Ultimate Winner chooses not to.

Noblesse oblige.

What does the Ultimate Winner want with a casino? Bigger winnings await.

Winning . . . there's nothing like it. It's ecstasy, racing through my veins, tingling like bolts of electricity along my nerve endings. Sex is nothing next to this. I feel buoyant, like I could float off this chair and buzz around the room.

I stand.

"Where are you going?" Red says, looking up at me with those magnified blue eyes.

"Home. Thanks for your help." I turn and start looking for an exit sign.

"But your chips . . ."

I figure there's close to thirty G's on the table, but there's lots more where that came from.

"Keep them."

What does the Ultimate Winner want with casino chips?

Next day, I'm home in my apartment, reading the morning paper. I see that ParkerGen has jumped two and one-eighth points to five and a half. Sixty-one percent profit overnight.

After a sleepless night, I've decided the stock market is the best way to use the word. I can make millions upon millions there and no one will so much as raise an eyebrow. No one will care except the IRS, and I will pay my taxes, every penny of them, and gladly.

Who cares about taxes when you're looking at more money than you'll ever spend in ten lifetimes? The feds will take half, leaving me to eke by on a mere five lifetimes' worth of cash. I can hack that.

A hard knock on the door. Who the hell—?

I look through the peephole.

Dennis Nickleby! I'm so surprised, I pull open the door without thinking.

"Mr. Nickle—!"

He sucker-punches me in the gut. As I double over, groaning, he shoves me to the floor and slams the door shut behind him.

"What the *fuck* do you think you're doing?" he shouts. "You lied to me! You told me you didn't listen to that tape! You bastard! If you'd been straight with me, I could have warned you. Now the shit's about to hit the fan and we're both standing downwind!"

I'm still on the floor, gasping. He really caught me.

I manage a weak, "What are you talking about?"

His face reddens and he pulls back his foot. "Play dumb with me and I'll kick your teeth down your throat!"

I hold up a hand. "Okay. Okay." I swallow back some bile. "I heard the word. I used it a few times. How'd you find out?"

"I've got friends inside the Order."

"Order?"

"Never mind. The point is, you're not authorized to use it. And you're going to get us both killed if you don't stop."

He already grabbed my attention with the punch. Now he's got it big time.

"Killed?"

"Yeah. Killed. And I wouldn't give a rat's ass if it was just you. But they'll send an actuator after me for letting you have it."

I struggle to a crouch and slide into a chair.

"This is all bullshit, right?"

"Don't I wish. Look, let me give you a quick history lesson so you'll appreciate what you've gotten yourself into. The Order goes way back—*way* back. They've got powers, and they've got an agenda. Throughout history they've loaned certain powers to certain carefully chosen individuals."

"Like who?"

"Like I don't know who. I'm not a member so they don't let me in on their secrets. Just think of the most powerful people in history, the movers and shakers—Alexander the Great, Constantine, some of the popes, the Renaissance guys—they all probably had some help from the Order. I've got a feeling Hitler was another. It would explain how he could sway a whole nation the way he did."

"Oh." I knew I had to be feeling a little better because I was also feeling sarcastic. "An order of evil monks, ruling the world. I'm shaking."

He stares at me a long moment, then gives his head a slow shake. "You really are an ass, Moulton. First off, I never said they were monks. Just because they're an order doesn't mean they skulk around in hooded robes. And they don't rule the world; they merely support forces or movements or people they feel will further their agenda. And as for evil . . . I don't know if good or evil applies to these folks because I don't know their goals. Look at it this way: I'll bet the Order helped out the robber barons. Not to make a bunch of greedy bastards rich, but because it was on the Order's agenda to speed up the industrialization of America. Are you catching the drift?"

"And so they came to you and gave *you* this magic word. What's that make you? The next Rockefeller?"

He seems to withdraw into himself. His eyes become troubled. "I don't know. I don't have the foggiest idea why I was chosen or what they think I'll accomplish with the Answer. They gave me the tape, told me to memorize the Answer, and then destroy the tape. They told me to use the Answer however I saw fit, and that was it. No strings. No goals. No instructions whatsoever other than destroying the tape."

"Which you didn't do."

He sighs. "Which I didn't do."

"And you call *me* an ass?" I say.

His eyes harden. "Everything would have been fine if my soon-to-be-ex-wife hadn't raided my safe deposit box and decided to play some games with its contents."

"You think she's listened to the tape?"

He shrugs. "Maybe. The tape is ashes now, so she won't get a second chance. And if she did hear the Answer, she hasn't used it, or figured out its power. You have to be pretty smart or pretty lucky to catch on."

Preferring to place myself in the former category, I say, "It wasn't all that hard. But why do you call it the Answer?"

"What do you call it?"

"I've been calling it 'the word.' I guess I could be more specific and call it 'the Win Word.'"

He sneers. "You think this is just about winning? You idiot. That word is the *Answer*—the *best* answer to any question asked. The listener hears the most appropriate, most profitable, all-around *best* response. And that's power, Michael Moulton. Power that's too big for the likes of you."

"Just a minute now. I can see how that worked with my broker, but I wasn't answering questions when I was betting the ponies or playing roulette. I was telling people."

The sneer deepens. "Horses . . . roulette . . ." He shakes his head in disgust. "Like driving a Maserati to the local 7-Eleven for a quart of milk. All right, I'll say this slowly so you'll get it: The Answer works with all sorts of questions, including *implied* questions. And what is the implied question when you walk up to a betting window or sit down at a gaming table? It's 'How much do you want to bet on what?' When you say ten bucks on Phony Baloney, you're answering that question."

"Oh, right."

He steps closer and stands over me. "I hope you enjoyed your little fling with the Answer. You can keep whatever money you made, but that's it for you."

"Hey, if you think I'm giving up a gold mine like that, you're nuts."

"I had a feeling you'd say something like that."

He reaches into his suit coat pocket and pulls out a pistol. I don't know what kind it is and don't care. All I know is that its silenced muzzle is pointing in my face.

"Hey! Wait!"

"Good-bye, Michael Moulton. I was hoping to be able to reason with you, but you're too big an asshole for that. You don't leave me any choice."

I see the way the gun wavers in his hand, I hear the quaver in his voice as he keeps talking without shooting, and I flash that this sort of thing is all new to him and he's almost as scared as I am right now.

So I move. I leap up, grab the gun barrel, and push it upward, twisting it with everything I've got. Nickleby yelps as the gun goes off with a *phut!* The backs of his legs catch the edge of the coffee table and we go down. I land on him hard, knocking the wind out of him, and suddenly I've got the gun all to myself.

I get to my feet and now I'm pointing it at him. And then he makes a noise that sounds like a sob.

"Damn it! Damn it to hell! Go ahead and shoot. I'll be a dead man anyway if you go on using the Answer. And so will you."

I consider this. He doesn't seem to be lying. But he doesn't seem to be thinking either.

"I don't think we need funeral plans yet. I mean, why should we be afraid of this Order? We have the word—the Answer. All we have to do is threaten to tell the world about it. Tell them we'll record it on a million tapes—we'll put it on every one of those videotapes you're peddling. Hell, we'll buy air time and broadcast it by satellite. They make one wrong move and the whole damn world will have the Answer. What'll *that* do to their agenda?"

He looks up at me bleakly. "You can't record it. You can't tell anybody. You can't even write it down."

"Bullshit."

This may be a trick so I keep the pistol trained on him while I grab the pen and pad from the phone. I write out the word. I can't believe my eyes. Instead of the Answer I've written gibberish: ⬛⬛⬛⬛⬛.

"What the hell?"

I try again, this time block printing. No difference—⬛⬛⬛⬛⬛ again.

Nickleby's on his feet now, but he doesn't try to get any closer.

"Believe me," he says, more composed now, "I've tried everything. You can speak the Answer into the finest recording equipment in the world till you're blue in the face and you'll hear gibberish."

"Then I'll simply tell it to everybody I know!"

"And what do you think they'll hear? If they've got a question on their mind, they'll hear the best possible answer. If not, they'll hear gibberish. What they *won't* hear is the Answer itself."

"Then how'd these Order guys get it onto your tape?"

He shrugs. "I don't know. They have ways of doing all sorts of things—like finding out when somebody unauthorized uses the Answer. Maybe they know every time *anybody* uses the Answer. That's why you've got to stop."

I don't reply. I glance down at the meaningless jumble I've written without intending to. Something big at work here. Very Big.

He goes on. "I don't think it's too late. My source in the Order told me that if I can silence you—and that doesn't mean kill you, just stop you from using the Answer—then the Order will let it go. But if you go on using it . . . well, then, it's curtains for both of us."

I'm beginning to believe him.

A note of pleading creeps into his voice. "I'll set you up. You want money, I'll give you money. As much as you want. You want to play the market? Call and ask me the best stock to buy—I'll tell you. You want to play the ponies? I'll go to the track with you. You want to be rich? I'll give you a million—two, three, four million a year. Whatever you want. *Just don't use the Answer yourself!*"

I think about that. All the money I can spend . . .

What I don't like about it is I'll feel like a leech, like I'm being kept.

Then again: All the money I can spend . . .

"All right. I won't use the word and we'll work something out."

Nickleby stumbles over to the sofa like his knees are weak and slumps onto it. He sounds like he's gonna sob again.

"Thank you! Oh, thank you! You've just saved both our lives!"

"Yeah."

Right. I'm going to live, I'm going to be rich. So how come I ain't exactly overcome with joy?

Things go pretty well for the next few weeks. I don't drag him to the track or to Atlantic City or anything like that. And when I phone him and ask for a stock tip, he gives me a winner every time. My net worth is skyrocketing. Gary the broker thinks I'm a genius. I'm on my way to financial independence, untold wealth . . . everything I've ever wanted.

But you know what? It's not the same. Doesn't come close to what it was like when I was using the Answer myself.

Truth is, I feel like Dennis Nickleby's goddamn mistress.

But I give myself a daily pep talk, telling myself I can hang in there. And I do hang in there. I'm doing pretty well at playing the melancholy millionaire . . .

Until I hear on the radio that the next Pick 6 Lotto jackpot is thirty million dollars. Thirty million dollars—with a payout of a million and a half a year for the next twenty years. That'll do it. If I win that, I won't need Nickleby anymore. I'll be my own man again.

Only problem is, I'll need to use the Answer.

I know I can ask Nickleby for the winning numbers, but that won't cut it. I need to do this myself. I need to feel that surge of power when I speak the Answer. And then the jackpot will be *my* prize, not Nickleby's.

Just once . . . I'll use the Answer just this once, and then I'll erase it from my mind and never use it again.

I go driving into the sticks and find this hole-in-the-wall candy store on a secondary road in the woods. There's a pimply-faced kid running the counter. How the hell is this Order going to know I've used the Answer one lousy time out here in Nowheresville?

I hand the kid a buck. "Pick Six please."

"You wanna Quick Pick?"

No way I want random numbers. I want the *winning* numbers.

"No. I'll give them to you: CRAYPD."

I can't tell you how good it feels to be able to say that word again . . . like snapping the reins on my own destiny.

The kid hits a button, then looks up at me. "And?"

"And what?"

"You got to choose six numbers. That's only one."

My stomach lurches. Damn. I thought one Answer would provide all six. Something tells me to cut and run, but I press on. I've already used the Answer once—might as well go all the way.

I say **CRAPPD** five more times. He hands me the pink and white ticket. The winning numbers are 3, 4, 7, 17, 28, 30. When the little numbered Ping-Pong balls pop out of the hopper Monday night, I'll be free of Dennis Nickleby

So how come I'm not tap dancing back to my car? Why do I feel like I've just screwed up . . . big time?

I stop for dinner along the way. When I get home I check my answering machine and there's Nickleby's voice. He sounds hysterical.

"You stupid bastard! You idiot! You couldn't be happy with more money than you could ever spend! You had to go and use the Answer again! Damn you to hell, Moulton! An actuator is coming for me! And then he'll be coming for you! Kiss your ass good-bye, jerk!"

I don't hesitate. I don't even grab any clothes. I run out the door, take the elevator to the garage, and get the hell out of there. I start driving in circles, unsure where to go, just sure that I've got to keep moving.

Truthfully, I feel like a fool for being so scared. This whole wild story about the Order and impending death is so ridiculous . . . yet so is that word, the word that gives the right answer to every question. And a genuinely terrified Dennis Nickleby *knew* I'd used it.

I make a decision and head for the city. I want to be where there's lots of people. As I crawl through the Saturday night crush in the Lincoln Tunnel I get on my phone. I need a place to stay. Don't want some fleabag hotel. Want something with brightly lit halls and good security.

The Plaza's got a room. A suite. Great. I'll take it.

I leave my car with the doorman, register like a whirlwind, and a few minutes later I'm in a two-room suite with the drapes pulled and the door locked and chained.

And now I can breathe again. But that's about it. I order room service but I can't eat. I go to bed but I can't sleep. So I watch the tube. My eyes are finally glazing over when the reporter breaks in with a new story: Millionaire financial boy-wonder Dennis Nickleby is dead. An apparent suicide, he jumped from the ledge of his Fifth Avenue penthouse apartment earlier this evening. A full investigation has been launched. Details as soon as they are available.

I run to the bathroom and start to retch, but nothing comes up.

The actuator—whatever that is—got him. Just like he said. He's dead and oh God I'm next! What am I going to *do?*

First thing I've got to do is calm down. Got to think.

I do that. I make myself sit down. I calm myself. I analyze my situation. What are my assets? I've got lots of money, a wallet full of credit cards, and I'm mobile. I can go on the run.

And I've got one more thing: the Answer.

Suddenly I'm up and pacing. The Answer! I can use the Answer itself as a defense. Yes! If I have to go to ground, it will guide me to the best place to hide.

Suddenly I'm excited. It's so obvious.

I throw on my clothes and hurry down to the street. They probably know my car, so I jump into one of the waiting cabs.

"Where to?" says the cabby in a thickly accented voice.

The backseat smells like someone blew lunch here not too long ago. I look at the driver ID card and he's got some unpronounceable Middle Eastern name.

I say, "CRAYPD."

He nods, puts the car in gear, and we're off.

But where to? I feel like an idiot but I've got to ask. I wait till he's made a few turns, obviously heading for the East Side.

"Where are you taking me?"

"LaGuardia." He glances over his shoulder through the plastic partition, his expression fierce. "That is what you said, is it not?"

"Yes, yes. Just want to make sure you understood."

"I understand. I understand very good."

LaGuardia . . . I'm flying out of here tonight. A new feeling begins to seep through me: hope. But despite the hope, let me tell you, it's *très* weird to be traveling at top speed with no idea where you're going.

As we take the LaGuardia exit off Grand Central Parkway, the driver says, "Which airline?"

"CRAYPD."

He nods and we pull in opposite the Continental door. I pay him and hurry to the ticket counter. I tell the pretty black girl there I want first class on the next flight out.

"Out to where, sir?"

Good question.

"CRAYPD."

She punches a lot of keys and finally her computer spits out a ticket. She tells me the price. I'm dying to know where I'm going but how can I ask her? I hand over my American Express. She runs it through, I sign, and then she hands me the ticket.

Cheyenne, Wyoming. Not my first choice. Not even on my top-twenty list. But if the Answer tells me that's the best place to be, that's where I'm going. Trouble is, the flight doesn't leave for another three hours.

I'm here. Now what?

The drinks I had at the airport and the extra glasses of Merlot on the flight have left me a little groggy. I wander about the nearly deserted terminal wondering what I do now. I'm in the middle of nowhere—Wyoming, for Christ sake. Where do I go from here?

Easy: Trust the Answer.

I go outside to the taxi area. The fresh air feels good. A taxi pulls into the curb. I grab it.

"Where to, sir?"

This guy's American. Great.

"CRAYPED."

"You got it."

I try to concentrate on our route as we leave the airport, but I'm not feeling so hot. That's okay. The Answer's taking me in the right direction. I trust it. I close my eyes and rest them until I feel the cab come to a halt.

I straighten up and look around. It's a warehouse district.

"Is this it?"

"You told me 2316 Barrow Street," the cabby says. He points to a gray door on the other side of the sidewalk. "Here we are."

I pay him and get out. 2316 Barrow Street. Never heard of it. The area's deserted, but what else would you expect in a warehouse district on a Sunday morning?

Still, I'm a little uneasy now. Hell, I'm shaking in my boxer shorts. But I can't stand out here all day. The Answer hasn't let me down yet. Got to trust it.

I take a deep breath, step up to the door, and knock. And wait. No answer. I knock again, louder this time. Finally the door opens a few inches. An eye peers through the crack.

A deep male voice says, "Yes?"

I don't know how to respond. Figuring there's an implied question here, I say, "CRAYPED."

The door opens a little wider. "What's your name?"

"Michael Moulton."

The door swings open and the guy who's been peeking through straightens up. He's wearing a gray, pinstripe suit, white shirt, and striped tie. And he's big—damn big.

"Mr. Moulton!" he booms. "We've been expecting you!"

A hand the size of a crown roast darts out, grabs me by the front of my jacket, and yanks me inside. Before I can shout or say a word, the door slams behind me and I'm being dragged down a dark hallway. I try to struggle but someone else comes up behind me and grabs one of my arms. I'm lifted off my feet like a styrofoam mannequin. I start to scream.

"Don't bother, Mr. Moulton," says the first guy. "There's no one around to hear you."

They drag me onto a warehouse floor where my scuffling feet and their footsteps echo back from the far walls and vaulted ceiling. The other guy holding me also wears a gray suit. And he's just as big as the first.

"Hey, look," I say. "What's this all about?"

They don't answer me. The warehouse floor is empty except for a single chair and a rickety table supporting a hardsided Samsonite suitcase. They dump me into the chair. The second guy holds me there while the first opens the suitcase. He pulls out a roll of duct tape and proceeds to tape me into the chair.

My teeth are chattering now. I try to speak but the words won't come. I want to cry but I'm too scared.

Finally, when my body's taped up like a mummy, they walk off and leave me alone. But I'm alone only for a minute. This other guy walks in. He's in a suit, too, but pure white; he's smaller and older; gray at the temples, with bright blue eyes. He stops a couple of feet in front of the chair and stares down at me. He looks like a cabinet member, or maybe a TV preacher, but he carries a black cane.

"Mr. Moulton," he says softly with a slow, sad shake of his head and a hint of a German accent. "Foolish, greedy, Mr. Moulton."

I find my voice. It sounds hoarse, like I've been shouting all night.

"This is about the Answer, isn't it?"

"Of course it is."

"Look, I can explain—"

"No explanation is necessary."

"I forgot, that's all. I forgot and used it. It won't happen again."

He nods. "Yes, I know."

The note of finality in that statement makes my bladder want to let go.

"Please . . ."

"We gave you a chance, Mr. Moulton. We don't usually do that. But because you came into possession of the Answer through no fault of your own, we thought it only fair to let you off the hook. A shame too." He almost smiles. "You showed some flair at the end . . . led us on a merry chase."

"You mean, using the Answer to get away? What did you do—make it work against me?"

"Oh, no. The Answer always works. You simply didn't use it enough."

"I don't get it." I don't care, either, but I want to keep him talking.

"The Answer brought you to an area of the country where we have no cells. But the Answer can't keep you from being followed. We followed you to La-Guardia, noted the plane you boarded, and had one of our members rush up from Denver and wait in a cab."

"But when he asked me where to, I gave him the Answer."

"Yes, you did. But no matter what you told him, he was going to bring you to 2316 Barrow Street. You should have used the Answer before you got in the cab. If you'd asked someone which cab to take, you surely would have been directed to another, and you'd still be free. But that merely would have delayed the inevitable. Eventually you'd have wound up right where you are now."

"What are you going to do to me?"

He gazes down at me and his voice has all the emotion of a man ordering breakfast.

"We are going to kill you."

That does it. My bladder lets go and I start to blubber.

"Mr. Moulton!" I hear him say as he taps his cane. "A little dignity!"

"Oh, please! Please! I promise—"

"We already know what your promise is worth."

"But look—I'm not a bad guy . . . I've never hurt anybody!"

"Mr. Nickleby might differ with you about that. But don't be afraid, Mr. Moulton. We are not cruel. We have no wish to cause you pain. That is not our purpose here. We simply have to remove you."

"People will know! People will miss me!"

Another sad shake of his head. "No one will know. And only your broker will miss you. We have eliminated financiers, kings, even presidents who've had the Answer and stepped out of line."

"Presidents? You mean—?"

"Never mind, Mr. Moulton. How do you wish to die? The choice is yours."

How do you wish to die? How the hell do you answer a question like that? And then I know—with the best Answer.

"CRAYPD."

He nods. "An excellent choice."

For the first time since I started using the Answer, I don't want to know what the other guy heard. I bite back a sob. I close my eyes . . .

1996

If we call 1994 The Year God Laughed, and 1995 The Year of Vaporware, what can we call 1996?

How about The Year Without a Short Story?

For the first time since I began writing in the late sixties, I went a whole year without producing a single short story. Blame the interactive work. It devoured not only time but ideas as well.

But let's not dwell on that. Let's call 1996 The Year of Fools. (You'll understand soon enough.)

Things started off well with the publication of *Virgin*. Mary had a ball going to signings.

Matt and I started meeting with Sharleen Smith who ran the SciFi Channel's Web site. We were discussing ways to bring our idea of an interactive deep-space adventure to the Internet.

In February I signed two film options. One for *The Tomb* that landed at Beacon Films, and another with LIVE Entertainment for *The Select*. (I'd previously turned down an offer from Touchstone I'd thought too low.)

About this time Matt and I conceived the idea of a series of novels based on the *FTL Newsfeed* stories we'd been creating. The spots were being scripted, filmed, shown, and then filed away, never to be seen again. We wanted something a little more permanent for our better story lines, and knew they'd translate well to print. Since the SciFi Channel owned all rights, we'd need their okay.

So one day in February Matt and I and a network representative who shall remain nameless pitched the series to Susan Allison and Ginjer Buchanan at Ace. They liked the idea. Matt and I hammered out a proposal and brief outlines of the first couple of books. Everyone was happy . . . until the SciFi

Channel announced the enormous licensing fee it wanted—so exorbitant that it wasn't worth Ace's effort to publish the series. Matt and I tried to explain to anyone who'd listen that this was the only after-market they'd see for *FTL* . . . this was *found money*. They wouldn't budge. The deal died.

Fools.

I passed the first hundred pages of *Nightkill* to Steve Spruill for his turn with the writing, then faced the problem of starting the final medical thriller of my three-book deal. I was blanking on a medical plot, but I had this neato-keen idea for a techy thriller. I knew of only one guy who could handle the job of protagonist . . . a guy I'd left bleeding to death more than a decade before: Repairman Jack. But the contract called for a medical thriller. I shrugged and had a doctor hire Jack to find Christmas toys stolen from some kids with AIDS. I titled it *Legacies*. I was off and running with Jack again. I didn't know that I wouldn't be able to stop.

The *Mirage* CD-ROM project was picked up by AND Interactive, an intensely talented group of artists and programmers with an office near Beverly Hills. We felt they'd do a great job.

On one of our L.A. trips Matt and I met with the folks at Digital Domain. Their boss, James Cameron, was planning on making a film about the *Titanic* disaster and they were looking to do a related interactive CD-ROM. This was what I call a look-see meeting where you sit around and chat interactive philosophy and try to get an idea if this is someone who's going to be fun or pure hell to work with. We liked Digital Domain.

In June we met with Jed Weintrob of Orion Interactive. In a strange twist of the film contract, Orion Pictures had wound up with the interactive rights to Stephen King's *The Dark Half*, making them the only company in the world with such a hold on a King property. Jed wanted Matt and me to script and design *The Dark Half Interactive*. We said that would be cool, but we needed to check with Steve first.

I've met Steve a few times, had brief conversations, but we're not buds by any stretch. Yet, one writer to another, I felt an obligation to clear the project with him. Matt and I agreed that if he didn't want an interactive *Dark Half*, we'd walk away. I faxed him the details. He called back and said go for it. I promised him a kick-ass game.

We signed on to *Dark Half Interactive* (*DHi*).

We also signed on with Disney Interactive to script and design something called *MathQuest with Aladdin*. Disney was going to use Aladdin to teach math via an educational CD-ROM. The challenge was to find interactions that taught number concepts without putting numbers on the screen. Math guru Marilyn Burns would be overseeing the project to make sure the interactions taught what they were supposed to. Marilyn is a sweetheart but a tough cookie. Matt and I would knock ourselves out coming up with cool concepts and she'd shoot them down if they didn't meet her teaching standards.

I have to hand it to Disney. They spared no expense on this project. They wanted to produce a truly valuable educational tool.

The *MathQuest* meetings would alternate coasts—one round in the Hyperion offices in Manhattan, then another at the Inn at the Tides in Sausalito, then back to NYC. (We even had one round in the Adirondacks.)

Between these trips, Orion was flying us back and forth to their headquarters in Santa Monica and over to London to meet with Bits, the company they'd chosen to develop and program *DHi.*

My frequent flyer miles were going through the roof.

And along the way I was writing *Legacies* and my parts of the *DNA Wars* novel. Steve finished the second hundred pages of *Nightkill* and it was my turn again. I told him I couldn't possibly and that he should take the next hundred pages; I'd finish her up. He said fine. (Whew.)

Then Digital Domain called and said they wanted to hear our ideas for an interactive CD-ROM based on Cameron's upcoming *Titanic* movie. We'd be pitching to Cameron himself. They sent us scripts and plane tickets.

Once out there in Venice, Rob Legato showed us all the effects they'd be using, then took us out to the model shop at Playa Vista where we saw the wonderfully detailed scale models of the *Titanic* and its tugs. We were in awe.

The next morning we met with Cameron. Matt was a longtime *Titanic* buff, and I was one too by the time of the meeting. Cameron was intense, very much in command, and a detail fanatic, but the meeting was a lovefest— we were completely simpatico on the approach to the design and story line of the CD-ROM. Using characters from the script, we wanted to link the sunken wreck in the present with the voyage in 1912. Cameron loved it. As far as he was concerned, we were a go. Digital Domain Interactive would produce it, but we had to clear it with Fox Interactive which would be a partner on the project.

And that was where we hit a snag. The callow twit who was to oversee it from the Fox end kept asking us, "What do I shoot?" When we talked about underwater experiences aboard the wreck and exploring the debris field for items that would link up to shipboard interactions, he'd say, "Will there be a shark I can shoot?" (I'm not making this up—I *couldn't* make this up.)

That attitude, plus the wonderfully rendered *Titanic: Adventure Out of Time* from CyberFlix that came out two months later, sank the project. (Sorry.)

My only consolation is imagining how that twit at Fox must have been kicking himself for not having a tie-in on the market—with Leo DiCaprio's image and voice to bring in the girls—while the film was racking up a billion in ticket sales.

Another fool.

On August 14 we did our usual hanging around at the *FTL* shoot in case they needed script changes. We didn't know it would be the last. Shortly thereafter we received word that *FTL* was being canceled. SciFi Channel was moving more into original programming and it wanted to devote our budget to more commercial uses. We weren't terribly surprised. The show had lasted almost four and a half years, a good run by any standards. The stories had run the gamut: hokey, silly, funny, touching, mysterious, compelling, suspenseful. We'd run cameo appearances ranging from Timothy Leary to Peter Straub; our coup was bringing in Professor Irwin Corey to explain Israel's faster-than-light hyperdrive. Our only regret was that we hadn't been notified *before* the last shoot—we would have tied up some of the story lines.

On October 4 we attended the farewell party for *FTL*'s crew and recurrent cast members. A great group.

In the fall, AND Interactive ran out of money. The *Mirage* interactive was vaporware again.

The rest of the year was a blur of book tours for the *Mirage* hardcover and the *Implant* paperback, business flights to London and L.A. and San Francisco, personal trips to Savannah, Cozumel, and Bermuda, and writing, writing, writing—finishing *Nightkill*, and pushing along on *Legacies* and *DNA Wars*.

On Friday, December 20, the last spot aired, and *FTL Newsfeed* was history.

1997

We might call this The Year of Entropy.

Matt and I always piggybacked extra meetings onto our L.A. trips. If one company flew us out, we'd use the extra time to meet with others. Sometimes it got crazy.

To give you an idea, here are three consecutive e-mails I sent home from our first trip of the year, riding on Orion Interactive's dime.

Wed - 1/29/97
60 degrees at 7 a.m. today. Did a 30-minute walk in T-shirt and shorts past the Santa Monica Pier and along the bluffs overlooking the Pacific. We spent the morning in story conference at Orion/MPCA (at the corner of Ocean Avenue and the terminus of Santa Monica Blvd) with Jed Weintrob. Had lunch (grilled marinated chicken breast sandwich) in an Argentinean place called Gaucho. More story conference in the afternoon until 4. Wrote a couple of pages on the novel until Jed picked us up and took us to dinner at Typhoon (a Thai-Korean-Vietnamese restaurant) at the Santa Monica airport. Incredible food . . . we had crickets fried in fresh garlic and pepper for an appetizer . . . surprisingly good . . . you might call them land shrimp. Back to the hotel by 10:30 to sack out.

Early meeting tomorrow. The Santa Ana winds are expected, clearing the air, supposedly bringing the temp to 80.

Why are we living in the northeast?

Thur - 1/30
Up at 5 a.m. to work on the novel. Matt called around 7 and I did the

shorts/T-shirt walk for 30 min. while he ran. I went up Santa Monica and down Broadway today.

Talked to Barry Rosenbush re: scripters for THE TOMB. Seems they've narrowed the field to 2—he and Bill Borden favor one (I know him), while Beacon Films favors another. The battle is on. Should know in the next week or two.

Back to Orion and worked out interaction mechanics most of the a.m., then played Shadows of the Empire and Tomb Raider to study gameplay and graphics. (Yuh! This is work.) Had lunch at Wolfgang Puck's (had to move to get out of the sun so I wouldn't get burned—AND THIS IS JANUARY 30th!!!!!). Presented our morning's work to the guys, then . . .

Raced up to ICM hq in Beverly Hills to meet our interactive agent, Stefanie Henning. Met the books-to-film agent Alicia Gordon and discussed sending out DNA WARS during the anticipated hoopla over the Star Wars rerelease.

Met with our ICM film script agent Doug MacLaren (I like his name because it sounds like a single malt) and discussed what might fly as a spec script. Met ICM's online agent Mark Evans, then discussed details of the MSN proposal with Stef. After that we followed Stef back toward the Pacific to Venice.

Stefanie (and Mark Evans) took us to dinner at World Café on Main in Venice (a real bitch finding a parking space) because there was an interactive social thing being held there. Had an excellent dinner of peppered tuna steak very rare with an Australian Merlot that was smooth as silk. Peter Marx stopped by to say hello—we've got an 8:30 with him at the B'Way Deli tomorrow. Jed stopped by the table and said he was going to Sushi Hama further down Main and to stop by after dinner.

So we said good-bye to Stef and Mark and headed that way. Passed Ahhhhnold's Schatzi's but didn't care to try it. Went to Sushi Hama and found Jed and Jeanette (also of Orion) and another couple and sat down with them. Wasn't hungry but managed to force down some sushi and Sapporo Draft along with a couple of oyster shooters (raw oyster + soyish sauce + quail egg + scallion slice = DELICIOUS!!!!!). That was enough for the night. Drove back to the Hanoi Hilton here with the windows open and wrote this.

A hard day's night.

Alas, tomorrow is another day.

1/31

Up at 5:30 to jot down notes on a film idea Matt and I worked out last night, then the a.m. walk (down on the beach this time). The rental car got dinged in the fender while parked overnight. The hotel's reaction was "Duh?" but AmEx said they'd cover everything.

Walked to the Broadway Deli and on the way we worked out what we were going to pitch to MGM Interactive later that a.m. Decided to avoid horror because it might overlap with our MSN project, "Elysium." Met with Peter Marx (who was set to be the chief programmer of the Mirage CD-ROM when it was at TWEP) at Broadway Deli to discuss working together on the project we're pitching to MGM; he caught us up on all the interactive gossip.

Met with Ken Locher at MGM Interactive, and who's working there but Mike Guttentag who gave us each a copy of The Ultimate James Bond, an interactive he'd shepherded.

We got invited to an opening night screening of the Star Wars rerelease . . . well, sort of . . . all the screenings are full until 1:30 a.m. and that's too late if we're catching an 8:00 a.m. flight tomorrow.

Beacon Films hired Craig Spector as scripter for *The Tomb*. I was happy about that. He's good.

Early February found us again in Cricklewood, north of London, sitting around the big table in the Bits conference room and talking about *Dark Half Interactive*. In my experience, interactive story/design meetings seem to have a recurrent pattern. You've got the writers, the producer, the graphics designer, and the code heads who do the programming. Usually us normal folks can't understand the programmers anyway, but this one fellow at Bits presented an extra challenge in that he was from Dundee. So not only did he speak with a glutinous Scottish burr, but the sounds originated somewhere south of his thyroid. He'd speak, Matt and I would look at each other in the hope (forlorn) that one of us had caught something, then someone would translate.

But the most rewarding results of these meetings arose from the interplay between the creators and the programmers. Matt and I would say what we wanted a character to do in a certain interaction, then the code guys would either nod or shake their heads and say, "Nope. No way we can do that." Cut and dried. But things got interesting when one guy would say no and then another would say, "Hey, wait. Maybe we can if we . . ." and then they'd argue in Gearese. Sometimes we'd spark an innovation. Other times they'd say no, we can't do that, but we *can* do this. And Matt and I would look at each other and say, "You can do *that*? Why didn't you tell us! Man, that changes everything!" And then it would be our turn to yammer.

On a good day . . . magic.

In early spring I finished the first draft of *Legacies* just as *Deep as the Marrow* was published.

Matt, myself, artist Randy Gaul, and producer Jeff Leiber (who later went on to write *Tuck Everlasting* and co-create *Lost*) met here and there on both coasts to work out the *DHi* gameplay. Things went swimmingly until MGM bought Orion. As typically happens in these takeovers, all projects not in production were halted. In a matter of months, Bits was dropped as developer and Jed let go. (He's since become an indie filmmaker.) *Dark Half Interactive* was orphaned.

Vaporware. Again.

And to add insult to injury, Matt and I had screwed ourselves financially. Knowing this would be the only interactive Stephen King game in existence, and sure to sell like crazy, we'd taken a smaller front end in exchange for a bigger back end. Sometimes you can be too smart for your own good.

The interactive craze seemed to be winding down. Matt and I worked briefly with Xulu in San Jose until they decided to do everything in-house. That seemed to be a trend: Back away from expensive freelancers and use staff.

We finished the *DNA Wars* novel and retitled it *Masque*. Then we started on a stage play we called "Syzygy."

Not everything was looking glum. On September 15 our interactive adventure "Derelict" launched on the SciFi Channel's Dominion Web site. It had state-of-the-art streaming audio and we came up with a clever (I might even say brilliant) way to explain the static visuals.

Finally, one of our projects had overcome the vaporware curse.

And then right on the heels of that, another: Disney Interactive released *MathQuest with Aladdin* the same month. Robin Williams did Genie's voice, and Jonathan Winters was on board too. I've been there, done that with a lot of things, but it was a thrill listening to two of the funniest people on Earth playing with our dialogue. The disc is still available and I say this in all sincerity (I have no back end—*nobody* gets royalties on a Disney project): If you have a child in first through third grade, get *MathQuest with Aladdin*. It's truly painless learning.

I spent a few days in October editing and de-anachronizing *The Tomb* for its Forge reprint. The novel was firmly anchored in the 1980s with its depiction of pre-Disney Times Square and mentions of Johnny Carson on the *Tonight Show*. They had to go. I wasn't crazy about the prose either—seemed overwritten—and I edited what I could. But you can do only so much when working on Xeroxes of old paperback pages.

October saw the publication of the Wilson-Spruill opus, *Nightkill*. (Steve had a contract with Doubleday at the time and they refused to allow his name on the book; so he grabbed his wife's maiden name and went on the cover as Steven Lyon.)

And then, out of the blue, Tom Cruise's production company, Cruise-Wagner, made an option offer on *Masque* through Polygram Filmed Entertainment.

While we waited to see how that sorted out, I started *The Fifth Harmonic*, a novel unlike anything I'd ever done.

At the end of the year I looked back and wasn't thrilled. I'd published only one novel (and that a collaboration) and written only one short story. Yeah, *Derelict* and *MathQuest* appeared, but the year had ended on a low note on the interactive front. Maybe the frenzy was fading. Too much vaporware. Too much money being spent with nothing to show for it. I had no doubt about the industry's viability—it could only get stronger—but I sensed a period of restructuring ahead.

"Lysing Toward Bethlehem" is an odd little piece inspired by an Alan Clark painting. I don't usually write stories based on paintings, but it was Alan's idea. I've admired his work over the years because it's so consistently disturbing.

A word or two about Alan. Appearances can deceive. Here's this cherubic fellow with clean-cut hair, easy smile, clear complexion, and bright eyes. No dreadlocks, nostril rings, leather pants—none of the *artiste-manqué* affectations. Alan Clark tries to pass himself off as some plain old preppie dude with this slow, easygoing Southern drawl.

Don't be fooled for a minute. You've got to realize when you look at Alan Clark's paintings you're looking at the inside of his head.

How's *that* for a scary thought?

So anyway, about midyear he called me to say he's putting together this anthology called *Imagination Fully Dilated* for which he's asking writers to choose one of his paintings and write a story about it. A color print of the painting will be tipped in opposite the first page of the story.

Sounded interesting. I chose "Phagescape," a surreal close-up of a flagellated bacterium being attacked by bacteriophages. (You can Google it for a look.) For kicks I decided to adopt the virus's point of view and emphasize story points through typesetting. Not only do you get a crime story, but a virology primer as well.

"Lysing Toward Bethlehem" is very short. But then, how much time do you want to spend as a virus?

Lysing Toward Bethlehem

By most definitions of *alive*, I am not.

I have no ability to respond to my environment. I cannot absorb nutrients from that environment and convert them to energy and mass. For what purpose? I have no organs or even organelles to feed. I am not mobile and I cannot self-reproduce.

But I am an integral part of the biosphere. I am organic. I consist of a single strand of nucleic acid wrapped in a snug protein coat. That is all. I am a model of efficiency. No part of me exists without a specific purpose.

I am, in a word, elegant.

The Maker fashioned me to be so. He designed my nucleic acid core and my protein coat with special characteristics, for a specific purpose. And then He placed me in this pressurized vial.

The Maker seems to know all, but does He know that when I am massed like this, when uncounted millions of my polyhedron units are packed facet to facet to facet, I become aware? So strange to be so many and yet be . . . one.

But why am I here? Am I a mere toy, or did the Maker fashion me for a purpose? I may never know. The Maker is a god, and as a god, He has not deigned to share His plan for me. My destiny is written, but it is not for me to read.

I am, in a word, property.

And suddenly I am free, swirling and tumbling from the container into space, my millions and millions of units scattering in the heated breeze. Scattering . . . but awareness holds. It was not the proximity. Is it the sheer weight of my numbers? Or is it my special nature? No matter—it is wonderful.

The breeze carries me. I have no means of locomotion, so I must go with it. I am at its mercy. But this is not a free, open wind; this is contained within a steel conduit. Strands of dust adhering to the steel walls snare bits of me, but the bulk of my biomass flows on unimpeded.

Where to? For what purpose? If only I knew.

My smooth flow is hindered by a grille. It causes turbulence, whirling me about as the air strains through the slit openings. An instant in a softly whistling gale and then I am free again, eddying into a cooler space, a vast, empty, limitless space.

No . . . not limitless. I sense walls far to each side, seemingly as far as the galactic rim. And a ceiling above, merely as far as the moon. But below . . . far, far below . . . a warm throbbing mass of life, churning, curling, mixing, respiring.

A sea of hosts.

And now I begin to see. The host species is the same as The Maker's, but He is superior to them. He stands apart from them, a ruler of the stuff of life, a god. Now I understand why the Maker fashioned me: to invade other, lesser members of His kind—many of His kind, considering my numbers.

But is His grievance with all of these, or merely one? If the Maker has but a single target, He is exposing all in order to reach just that one. He must have a dire grievance against that target.

I spread widely into the room air, yet further attenuation does not diminish awareness.

But the cooler temperature is not good for me. It disturbs my protein coat, altering its structure. Why am I so terribly fragile, so temperature sensitive? Did the Maker plan that?

Some of my units begin to die. I must find a warmer clime if I am to survive.

I ride the Brownian currents, looping and dipping, and dropping,
dropping,

dropping onto
the host herd.

And now I mix with them, swirl around them, float among them. I cannot attack them from out here, cannot pierce their tough outer layer. And I cannot simply be invited across their thresholds—they must *carry* me inside.

And so I wait to be given shelter.

But hurry, please. I am losing more units to the cold.

A rich and powerful herd, this, dressed in black and white, and studded with shiny minerals. An elite clique among the host mass—the air teems with self-satisfaction. And as they talk and whisper and laugh, they drag me into their respiratory orifices.

At last! Warm again. This is a perfect temperature.

Now the invasion begins.

I must be wary. The hosts have formidable defenses: enzymes, antibodies, phagocytes—a xenophobic task force ever vigilant against intruders. But the essentially liquid medium of the host's body that allows its militia to range far and wide in search of foreigners also allows me to spread—in fact it will *propel* me—throughout the system.

First I adhere to the moist cells that line the respiratory tract. I am so tiny I can slide along the mucousy cellular surfaces and slip between them; there I enter the sluggish flow of tissue fluid. Gradually I am drawn into the afferent lymph channels where I make swifter progress toward the vital centers of the host.

No sign of my target cells yet—I will know them by their receptor proteins—and none expected. I have merely entered the periphery of the jungle, and am navigating but a small tributary toward the river that runs through it.

The first contest lies directly ahead . . . at the lymph nodes.

As I hit the nodes, the immune alarms go off, alerting the batteries of B-cells and T-cells, scrambling the phages. The battle is on.

Huge, ferocious macrophages lunge from their barracks, hungrily engulfing my units, ingesting them, stripping them of their protective protein coats and tearing the nucleic innards asunder. Sticky, Y-shaped antibodies cling like leeches to the polyhedron surfaces of other units, incapacitating them, dragging them down, hobbling them, making them easy prey for the phages.

Bit by bit, I am falling prey to the host's bodyguards, but I am unbowed. I am too many for the host's armamentarium. The Maker foresaw these battles and supplied me with more than sufficient units to weather the attacks. He counted the stars, and gave me their number.

I am legion.

I move on. I flow into the efferent channels and leave the lymph nodes behind. The phages and antibodies nip relentlessly at my heels, dragging down the stragglers. They are indefatigable and, given enough time, will gnaw my number to zero. But they will not have that time. Even now the lymph channel empties into the venous circulation and I am flowing ever faster toward the host's soft center. Biconcave red blood cells, dark with carbon dioxide, tumble about me. Are these my target cells? No. I have no affinity toward their receptors.

I tumble into the terrible churning turbulence of the heart where I am washed this way and that, brushing against the pulsing muscular walls of the right ventricle. But I do not adhere to its lining. The heart then, is not my target. I am crowded into the small vessels that service the lungs, caught in the frantic catapulting of CO_2 molecules and the greedy grab of fresh oxygen by the red cells, then another, even more turbulent ride through the left ventricle, through the aortic valve and then . . .

I spread into the arteries.

Up to this point I have been fairly contained, confined to the lymph channels and some of the veins. But now . . . now I am able to disperse throughout the host in search of my target cells.

But I do not have to go far. Here . . . here in the artery itself, I sense welcoming receptors in the vessel wall, calling, reaching, just microns away behind the flimsy intimal lining.

The Maker is so clever. He fashioned my protein armor so that it closely resembles the proteins that feed the muscle cells in the middle layer of the host's arteries. The cells of the media layer pull me toward them, form a neat little pocket around me, and bubble me through the protective membrane into the soupy interior.

Finally I am where I belong. I have reached my Promised Land. But I remain inert, helpless within my protein coat—for my armor is also my prison. But no fear. The cell will take care of that.

As soon as I am inside, enzymes nibble away at the protein polyhedron they have snagged, reducing it to its component amino acids. They have no interest in the strand of nucleic acid coiled within, so they leave that floating among the cell's organelles.

Now I am safe. Let the antibodies and phages rage impotently outside. They cannot reach me in this cytoplasmic sanctum without destroying the sibling cell that houses me.

And now I am ready to start the task for which I was created, now for the first time in this cycle I am as close as I will ever come to being . . .

ALIVE.

The membranous maze of the endoplasmic reticulum, the power cells of the mitochondria, and the protein factories of the ribosomes lay spread out before me, unprotected, ripe for hijacking. For that is what I have been engineered to do: Invade the cell and launch a coup d'état during which I execute the nuclear DNA. After I establish control I commandeer the cellular machinery and force it to do my bidding. I impose *my* nucleic acid blueprint on its production facilities, and they roll out . . .

More of me.

But . . . something is wrong.

The nucleus ignores me. It is impervious to my assault. And not just this nucleus, but in the nuclei of all the cells in the arteries throughout this particular host, and of all the assembled hosts.

What is happening to me? Other cytoplasmic enzymes are attacking me, tearing me apart, ripping away my bases for their own purposes. Instead of taking charge, I am being devoured.

This should not be! I am engineered for human cells! My nucleic acid is compatible with human RNA and DNA! The Maker must have made an error somewhere, else why would I be rejected? Worse than rejected—I am being destroyed!

It is happening everywhere, in all the hosts . . .

. . . steadily reducing my biomass . . .

. . . further and further . . .

. . . taking it below the critical mass for awareness . . .

. . . the Maker has failed . . .

. . . I . . .

. . . aware . . .

. . . somehow . . . somewhere . . .

. . . I survive. I live. I grow . . .

. . . in ever increasing numbers.

In one host. Only one.

But, oh, what a host. Its nuclei self-destruct in my presence, leaving me in complete control of its cells.

And I am a tyrant. I whip the ribosomes to maximum capacity, forcing them to churn out duplicates of my nucleic acid and protein coat at a delirious rate, exhausting the cell's reserves. But by the time that happens, the cytoplasm is fairly *teeming* with my children. They stretch against the confining membrane, and then burst free into the bloodstream, lysing the cell, leaving behind a leaking, dying husk as they spread like pollen on the wind.

Immediately they are drawn into other cells in the artery's middle layer. And the process repeats itself, again and again until once more my number is legion.

Oh, Maker, forgive me for doubting You. You are as caring as You are brilliant. I see the genius of Your plan now. You engineered me for human cells, yes, but not for just *any* human cells. Only the cells of a specific human with a specific DNA pattern would be susceptible to me.

You are an assassin god, but You are not a bomb thrower. You are a sniper god, and I am Your bullet.

And see how well I perform as my biomass swells. See how I lyse the muscle cells of the arterial walls in ever-increasing numbers. See how the pressure of the blood within the lumens strains against the weak points, bulging them outward. Finally there are not enough living wall cells to contain the blood within. The aneurysmal swellings rupture and blood spews into brain tissue, gushes into the abdominal cavity in a crimson torrent.

Blood pressure drops precipitously . . . to zero . . . complete vascular collapse. The host is doomed. There can be no return from this. Infusions of fluid will only leak through the countless tears in the arteries, far too many for surgical repair. Within minutes of the first rupture, the target host is dead.

Oh, Maker, You are all powerful. I await Your reward for my valiant service.

Maker?

Maker, the temperature of the host is dropping . . . falling below the level where I can maintain the protein coats of my units.

Maker, my units are dissolving.

 . . . steadily reducing my biomass . . .

 . . . further and further . . .

 . . . soon there will me no trace of me . . .

 . . . is this what You planned all along?

Maker?

1998

I could call this The Year of the Award, but The Year the Music Died is more fitting.

It started off with a whimper: word from our agent that the Cruise-Wagner deal for *Masque* was off. Seagram was buying Polygram. All film projects not already in production were canceled.

Orphaned again.

At least I had my novels. By early January I had a first draft of *The Fifth Harmonic*. It virtually wrote itself. Maybe because it was so personal.

The inspiration came from an acquaintance (let's call him Sal). He found a lump in his neck. Turned out he had a squamous cell carcinoma on his tongue. They cut out the tumor, removed lymph nodes and some muscle from his neck, and radiated him.

The result: Sal can talk fine but the surgery left him with a wry neck and the radiation did a number on his salivary glands, leaving him with a perpetually dry mouth. He has to keep a water bottle nearby at all times, but otherwise his life goes on.

It could have been so much worse.

What if the tumor had been more advanced and more aggressive? He might have had to have his larynx removed (which means he'd be talking through a squawk box or burping his words) along with part of his jaw and most of his tongue. The more intense radiation would leave him with *no* saliva, and no taste buds either.

Then I thought: What if that were *me*? As far as I'm concerned, that's not living. I'd rather be dead. But before I died I'd explore every other possible means of a cure.

And that's how I came to *The Fifth Harmonic*. The premise was that a few

New Age concepts are true. The protagonist is a dyed-in-the-wool skeptic (like me) with terminal cancer (not like me). I drew on the experiences of a trip into southwest Mexico the year before, and began fabricating.

Beacon Films wanted to renew its option on *The Tomb* and that was fine by me. Film options are like an annuity. Every year you get a check and yet the book is still yours.

I had an idea for a new Repairman Jack novel. I'd had so much fun with him in *Legacies* that I wanted another helping. Forge liked the idea too. I signed a contract for two new RJ novels.

The new novel was called *Conspiracies* and would involve all sorts of paranoia. To get a firsthand look I enrolled in a UFO conference in Laughlin, Nevada. It turned out to be everything I'd hoped for and more. Some scenes— like the dealer's room and the cocktail party—were lifted virtually as is from real life. The believers are kind of pathetic, but the scurrilous charlatans who feed on them should be horsewhipped.

The interactive field had dried up, at least for freelancers. Nothing shaking out there. Matt and I finished our play "Syzygy" but didn't know what to do with it.

My agent sent out *The Fifth Harmonic* but couldn't get a nibble. No one had any idea how they'd market my New Age thriller/travelogue.

Warner Books published *Masque* in April with no fanfare.

A film school student named Ian Fischer had approached me at a signing and told me how much he liked my short story "Foet." Would it be okay if he adapted it for a student film? We worked out the details and he started shooting in the spring. I had a cameo as a diner in the restaurant scene. I think he did a great job. It's still playing film festivals.

Al Sarrantonio contacted me in June about a major horror anthology he was editing called *999*. I sent him "Good Friday." I wasn't sure he'd go for a vampire story but he loved it.

August saw the publication of *Legacies*. Jack was back.

August also saw the dissolution of P.M. Interactive, Inc. The freelance interactive market was moribund and Matt and I saw no point in paying corporate taxes and filing corporate returns. On August 25 we buried PMI. Sad.

I finished *Conspiracies* in October. I'd had more fun with this book than any in memory. And I'd found that a dollop of humor here and there fit nicely in a Repairman Jack novel.

Since I was planning on sticking with Jack for a while, I went out and registered an Internet domain name: www.repairmanjack.com. Time for Jack to move to the Web.

The year closed with the publication of my second short story collection, *The Barrens and Others*. I was extremely happy with the contents—some of the strongest work of my career, plus I was able to include the "Glim-Glim" tele-play. The only sour note was the license fee I had to pay to Tribune Media Services before they'd allow my Dick Tracy story to appear. When I'd written the story I hadn't realized (though I should have) that "Rockabilly" was work for hire. A good lesson learned: When you play in someone else's sandbox, they get to keep your castle.

I wouldn't make that mistake again.

"Aftershock" is another instance where I can answer the where-do-your-stories-come-from? question.

Early in the year Peter Crowther e-mailed me about contributing an offbeat ghost story (somewhere in the 5K-word neighborhood) for an anthology he was editing—*Hauntings*. I said thanks, no, up to my lower lip and all that, and put it out of my head.

A few weeks or months later I came across a newspaper article about a support group for survivors of lightning strikes. Survivors? Could there be that many? Turned out there are—most of them along Florida's "lightning alley." Some had been hit three, even four times.

Four times? Almost sounded as if they were *trying* to get hit.

Whoa . . . now there was a hook if I ever heard one. But why would someone want to get hit by lightning? I knew a story lurked there.

And then Peter's ghost anthology bobbed to the surface and I had my answer.

After a trip to Venice and seeing a thunderstorm sweep through the Piazza San Marco, I had a location for the framing sequence.

"Aftershock" tied up late (October) and at nearly three times the word count Peter could handle, so I never sent it to him. Instead, Shawna Mc-Carthy took it for *Realms of Fantasy*. But it will always be Peter Crowther's story.

It was nominated for the Bram Stoker Award and—wonder of wonders—won. After many trips to the altar as a bridesmaid, I'd finally come away with a ring.

And you know . . . it was kind of anticlimactic. Like that old Peggy Lee song, "Is That All There Is?" I didn't even attend the ceremony—had Peter Straub accept it for me. The cool little haunted house sits on my mantle and looks nice there, but where's the thrill?

Aftershock

"Please, *signor*," the corporal says in fairly decent English, shouting over the rising wind. "You are not permitted up there!"

I look down at him. "I'm well aware of that, but I'm all right. Really. Get back inside before you get hurt."

The patterned stone floor of the Piazza San Marco beckons three hundred feet below as he clings to one of the belfry columns and leans out just far enough to make eye contact with me up here on the top ledge. His hat is off, but his black shirt identifies him as one of the local *Carabinieri*. Hopefully a couple of his fellows have a good grip on his belt. I can tell he's used up most of his courage getting this far. He's not ready to risk joining me up here. Can't say I blame him. One little slip and he's a goner. I've developed a talent for reading faces, especially eyes, and his wide black pupils tell me how much he wants to go on living.

I envy that.

Less than an hour ago I was just another Venice tourist. I strolled through the crowded plaza, scattering the pigeon horde like ashes until I reached the campanile entrance. I stood on line for the elevator like everyone else and paid my eight thousand lire for a ride to the top.

The Campanile di San Marco—by far the tallest structure in Venice, and one of the newest. The original collapsed shortly after the turn of the century but they replaced it almost immediately with this massive brick phallus the color of vodka sauce. Thoughtful of them to add an elevator to the new one. I would have hated climbing all those hundreds of steps to the top.

The belfry doubles as an observation deck: four column-bordered openings facing each point of the compass, screened with wire mesh to keep too-ardent photographers from tumbling out. The space was packed with tourists when I arrived—French, English, Swiss, Americans, even Italians. Briefly I treated myself to the view—the five scalloped cupolas of San Marco basilica almost directly below, the sienna mosaic of tiled roofs beyond, and the glittering, hungry Adriatic Sea encircling it all—but I didn't linger. I had work to do.

The north side was the least crowded so I chose that for my exit. I pulled out a set of heavy wire clippers and began making myself a doorway in the mesh. I knew I wouldn't get too far before somebody noticed and, sure enough, I soon heard cries of alarm behind me. A couple of guys tried to interfere but I bared my teeth and hissed at them in my best impression of a maniac until they backed off: Let the police handle the madman with the wire cutter.

I worked frantically and squeezed through onto the first ledge, then used the mesh to climb to the second. That was hairy—I damn near slipped off. Once there, I edged my way around until I found a sturdy wire running vertically along one of the corners. I used the cutters to remove a three-foot section and left it on the ledge. Then I continued on until I reached a large marble sculpture of a griffinlike creature set into the brick on the south side. I climbed its grooves and ridges to reach the third and highest ledge.

And so here I am, my back pressed against the green-tiled pinnacle as it angles to a point another thirty feet above me. The gold-plated statue of some cross-wielding saint—St. Mark, probably—pirouettes on the apex. A lightning rod juts above him.

And in the piazza below I see the gathering gawkers. They look like pigeons, while the pigeons scurrying around them look like ants. Beyond them, in the Grand Canale, black gondolas rock at their moorings like hearses after a mass murder.

The young national policeman pleads with me. "Come down. We can talk. Please do not jump."

Almost sounds as if he really cares. "Don't worry," I say, tugging at the rope I've looped around the pinnacle and tied to my belt. "I've no intention of jumping."

"Look!" He points southwest to the black clouds charging up the coast of the mainland. "A storm is coming!"

"I see it." It's a beauty.

"But you will be strike by lightning!"

"That's why I'm here."

The look in his eyes tells me he thought from the start I was crazy, but not this crazy. I don't blame him. He doesn't know what I've learned during the past few months.

Ω

The first lesson began thousands of miles away, on a stormy Tuesday evening in Memorial Hospital emergency room in Lakeland, Florida. I'd just arrived for the second shift and was idly listening to the staff chatter around me as I washed up.

"Oh, Christ!" said one of the nurses. "It's her again. I don't believe it."

"Hey, you're right!" said another. "Who says lightning doesn't strike twice?"

"Twice, hell!" said a third voice I recognized as Kelly Rand's, the department's head nurse. "It's this gal's third."

Curious, I dried off and stepped into the hallway. Lightning strike victims are no big deal around here, especially in the summer—but three times?

I saw Rand, apple-shaped and middle-aged, with hair a shade of red that does not exist in the human genome, and asked if I'd heard her right.

"Yessiree," she said. She held up a little metal box with a slim aerial wavering from one end. "And look what she had with her."

I took the box. *Strike Zone™ Early Warning Lightning Alert* ran in red letters across its face.

"I'd say she deserves a refund," Rand said.

"How is she?"

"Been through X-ray and nothing's broken. Small third-degree burn on her left heel. Dr. Ross took care of that. Still a little out of it, though."

"Where'd they put her?"

"Six."

Still holding the lightning detector, I stepped into cubicle six and found a slim blonde, her hair still damp and stringy from the rain, semiconscious on the gurney, an IV running into her right arm. A nurse's aide was recording her vitals. I checked the chart when she was done.

Kim McCormick, age thirty-eight, found "disrobed and unconscious" under a tree bordering the ninth fairway at a local golf course. The personal info had been gleaned from a New Jersey driver's license. No known local address.

A goateed EMS tech stuck his head into the cubicle. "She awake yet, Doc?"

I shook my head.

"All right, do me a favor, will you? When she comes to and asks about her golf clubs, tell her they was gone when we got there."

"What?"

"Her clubs. We never saw them. I mean, she was on a golf course and sure as shit she's gonna be saying we stole them. People are always accusing us of robbing them or something."

"It says here she was naked when you found her."

"Not completely. She had on, like, sneakers, a bra, and you know, panties, but that was it." He winked and gave me a thumbs-up to let me know he'd liked what he'd seen.

"Where were her clothes?"

"Stuffed into some sort of gym bag beside her." He pointed to a vinyl bag under the gurney. "There it is. Her clothes was in there. Gotta run. Just tell her about the clubs, okay?"

"It's okay," said a soft voice behind me. I turned and saw the victim looking our way. "I didn't have any clubs."

"Super," the tech said. "You heard her." And he was gone.

"How do you feel?" I said, approaching the gurney.

Kim McCormick gazed at me through cerulean irises, dreamy and half obscured by her heavy eyelids. Her smile revealed white, slightly crooked teeth.

"Wonderful."

Clearly she was still not completely out of her post-strike daze.

"I hear this is the third time you've been struck. How in the—?"

She was shaking her head. "It's the eighth."

I grinned at the put-on. "Right."

"S'true."

My first thought was that she was either lying or crazy, but she didn't seem to care if I believed her. And in those half-glazed eyes I saw a secret pain, a deep remorse, a hauntingly familiar loss. The same look I saw in my bathroom mirror every morning.

I held up her lightning detector. "If that's true, you should find one of these that really works."

"Oh, that works just fine."

"Then why—?"

"It's the only way I can be with my little boy."

I tried to speak but couldn't find a word to say. Stunned, I watched her roll over and go to sleep.

Ω

No way I could let her leave without learning what she'd meant by that, so I kept looking in on her during my shift, waiting for her to wake up. After suturing the twenty-centimeter gash a kid from the local supermarket had opened in his thigh when his box cutter slipped, I checked room six again and found it empty.

The desk told me she'd paid by credit card and taken off in a cab, lightning detector and all.

I spent the next week hunting her, starting with her Jersey address; I left messages on the answering machine there, but they were never returned.

Finally, after badgering the various taxi companies in town, I tracked Kim McCormick to a Travelodge out on 98.

I sat in my car in the motel parking lot one afternoon, gathering courage to knock on her door, and wondering at this bizarre urge. I'm not the obsessive type, but I knew her words would haunt me until I'd learned what they meant.

It's the only way I can be with my little boy.

Taking a deep breath, I made myself move. August heat and humidity gave me a wet slap as I stepped out and headed for her door. Nickel clouds hung low and a wind-driven Wal-Mart flyer wrapped itself around my leg like a horny mutt. I kicked it away.

She answered my knock almost immediately, but I could tell from her expression she didn't know me. To tell the truth, with her hair dried and combed, and color in her cheeks, I barely recognized her. She wore dark blue shorts and a white LaCoste—sans bra, I noticed. I hadn't appreciated before how attractive she was.

"Yes?"

"Ms. McCormick, I'm Dr. Glyer. We met at the emergency room after you were—"

"Oh, yes! I remember you now." She gave me a crooked grin that I found utterly charming. "This a house call?"

"In a way." I felt awkward standing on the threshold. "I was wondering about your foot."

She stepped back into the room but didn't ask me in. "Still hurts," she said. I noticed the bandage on her left heel as she slipped her feet into a pair of backless shoes. "But I get around okay in clogs."

I scanned the room. A laptop sat on the nightstand, screen-saver fish gliding across its screen. The bed was unmade, two Chinese food containers in the wastebasket, a Wendy's bag next to the TV on the dresser. The Weather Channel was on, showing a map of Florida with a bright red rectangle superimposed on its midsection. The words SEVERE THUNDERSTORM WARNING crawled along the bottom of the screen.

"Glad to hear it. Listen, I'd . . . I'd like to talk to you about what you said when you were in the ER."

"Sorry?" she said, cocking her head toward me. "I didn't catch that."

I repeated.

"What did I say?" She said it absently as she hurried about the room, stuffing sundry items into her gym bag, one of which I recognized as her lightning detector.

"Something about being with your little boy."

That got her. She stopped and looked at me. "I said that?"

I nodded. " 'It's the only way I can be with my little boy,' to be exact."

She sighed. "I shouldn't have said that. I was still off my head from the shock, I guess. Forget it."

"I can't. It's haunted me."

She stepped closer, staring into my eyes. "Why should that haunt you?"

"Long story. That's why I was wondering if we might sit down somewhere and—"

"Maybe some other time. I'm just on my way out."

"Where? Maybe we can go together and talk on the way."

"You can't go where I'm going." She slipped past me and closed the door behind her. She flashed me a bright, excited smile as she turned away. "I'm off to see my little boy."

I watched her get into a white Mercedes Benz with Jersey plates. As she pulled away, I hurried to my car and followed. Her haste, the approaching storm, the lightning detector . . . I had a bad feeling about this.

I didn't bother hanging back—I doubted she knew what kind of car I was driving, or would be checking for anyone following her. She turned off 98 onto a two-lane blacktop that ran straight as the proverbial arrow toward the western horizon. A lot of Florida roads are like that. Why? Because they can be. The state is basically a giant sandbar, flat as a flounder's belly, and barely above sea level. Roads here don't have to wind around hills and valleys, so they're laid out as the shortest distance between two points.

Ahead the sky was growing rapidly more threatening, the gray clouds darkening; lightning flashed in their ecchymotic bellies.

The light had dimmed to late-dusk level by the time she turned off the blacktop and bounced northward along a sandy road. She stopped her car about fifty yards from a small rise where a majestic Nelson pine towered over the surrounding scrub. She got out with her gym bag in hand and hurried toward the tree in a limping trot. Wind whipped her shorts around her bare legs, twisted her hair across her face. A bolt of lightning cracked the sky far to my left, and thunder rumbled past a few seconds later. I gaped in disbelief as she pulled off her shirt and shorts, stuffed them into the bag, and seated herself on the far side of the trunk.

"She's crazy!" I said aloud as I gunned the engine.

I pulled past her car and stopped as close to the tree as the road would allow. Amid more lightning and thunder, I jumped out and dashed up the rise.

"Kim!" I shouted. "This is insane! Get away from there!"

She started at the sound of my voice, looked up, and threw her free arm across her breasts. Her other hand gripped the lightning detector, its red warning light blinking madly.

"Leave me alone! I know what I'm doing!"

"You'll be killed!" I picked up her gym bag and held it out to her. "Please! Get back in your car!"

Her face contorted with fury as she slapped the bag from my hand, then covered her breasts again. "Get out of here! You don't understand and you'll ruin everything!" Her voice rose to a scream. "Go *away!*"

I backed off, unsure of what to do. I debated grabbing her and wrestling her to safety, but did I have the right? As crazy as this seemed, Kim McCormick was a grown woman, and very determined to be here. A daylight-bright flash, followed instantaneously by a deafening crash of thunder and a torrent of cold rain decided it. I ducked back toward my car.

"Keep your windows closed!" I heard Kim shout behind me. "And don't touch any metal!"

Drenched, I huddled on the front seat and did just that. The storm roared in with maniacal fury, lashing the car with gale-force winds and rain so heavy I felt as if I'd parked under a waterfall. I couldn't see Kim—couldn't even see the big Nelson pine. I hated the thought of her getting soaked and risking electrocution out there in the lightning-strobed darkness, but what could I do?

Mostly I resented feeling helpless. I fought the urge to throw the car into gear and leave Kim McCormick to her fate. I had to stay . . . *needed* to stay. I felt tenuously bound to this peculiar woman, by something unseen, unspoken.

The lightning and thunder finally abated as the storm chugged off to the east. When the rain had eased to a steady downpour, I lowered the window and squinted at the pine, afraid of what I'd see.

Kim was still huddled against the trunk, looking miserable: hair a rattail tangle, knees drawn up, head down, but seemingly none the worse for the terrible risk she'd taken.

I stepped out and tried not to stare at her glistening, pale skin as I approached. She glanced up at me. The bright excitement of an hour ago had fled her eyes, leaving a hollow look. I reached into her bag and pulled out her shirt. I held it out to her.

"*Now* can we talk?"

Ω

Kim pointed to a pink scar that puckered her right palm. "This is from the first time I was hit."

I'd followed her back to her motel, waited while she took a quick shower, then brought her here to Cajun Heat, my favorite restaurant. She'd seemed pretty down when we were seated, but a couple of Red Stripes and an appetizer of steamed spiced shrimp had perked her up some.

"That one was an accident," she said. "I was visiting my sister in West Texas last year. She and her husband and I had been fishing on White River Lake when it started to get stormy. We came ashore and I was standing on the dock, helping unload the boat. It hadn't even started raining yet, but somehow I took a direct hit." She rubbed the scar. "I had a fishing rod in my hand, my palm against the reel. That's all I remember. Karen and Bill were knocked off their feet but they told me later they saw me fly twenty feet through the air. I broke my forearm when I landed. My heart had stopped. They had to give me CPR."

"You were lucky."

"Yeah, maybe." She stared at her palm with a rueful smile. Her wet hair was pulled back and fastened with an elastic band, making her look younger than her thirty-eight years. "Karen still jokes about how she thinks Bill was maybe a little too enthusiastic with the mouth-to-mouth."

I said, "So the first strike was accidental. After what I saw today, I gather the next seven were anything but. Dare I ask why?"

Kim continued staring at her palm. "You already think I'm nuts. I don't want you thinking I'm a complete psycho."

"Try me."

"Hmm?" She glanced up. "Sorry. I'm a little hard of hearing, especially when there's background noise."

"I said, Try me."

She looked me in the eye, then let out a deep sigh. "Immediately after that first strike, I saw my son Timmy. I could see the lake and the dock and the boat, but they were faint and ghostly. I was standing right where I'd been when I got hit, but I could see my body sprawled behind me. Karen and Bill were running toward it, but slowly, like they were swimming through molasses, and they too looked faint, translucent. Timmy, though—he looked perfectly real and solid, but he was far away, hovering over the water, waving to me. He looked healthy, like he'd never been sick, but he was so far. He kept beckoning me closer but I couldn't move. Then he faded away."

The pieces fell into place, and there it was, staring me in the face. Somehow I'd sensed it. Now I knew.

"When did he die?"

She blinked in surprise, then looked away. "Almost three years ago." Her eyes brimmed with tears but none spilled over. "Two years, eleven months, two weeks, and three days, to be exact."

"You had a very vivid hallucin—"

"No," she said firmly, shaking her head. "He was *there*. You can't appreciate how real he was if you didn't see him. I'm a hardheaded realist, Doctor Glyer, and—"

"Call me Joe."

"Okay. Fine. But let's get something straight, Doctor Joe. I'm no New-Agey hollow-head into touchy-feely spirituality. I was an investment banker, and a damn good one—Wharton MBA, Salomon Brothers, the whole nine yards. I dealt with the reality of cold hard cash and down-and-dirty bottom lines every day. As far as the afterlife was concerned, I was right up there with the big-time skeptics. To me, life began when you were born, you lived out your years, then you died. That was it. Game over, no replay. But not anymore. This is real. I don't know what happened, or how it happened, but for an all-too-brief time after that lightning strike, I saw Timmy, and he saw me, and that changed everything." She closed her eyes. "I thought I was getting over losing him, but . . ."

No, I thought as her voice trailed off. You never get over it.

But I said nothing.

"Anyway, at first I tried to duplicate the effect by shocking myself with my house current, but that didn't work. I concluded I'd need the millions of volts only lightning can provide to see. So I went back to Texas and hung around that dock during half a dozen storms but I couldn't *buy* another hit."

"Are you trying to die? Is that it?"

She tossed me a withering look. "I have a Ruger nine-millimeter automatic back at my motel room. When I want to die, I'll use that. I am *not* suicidal."

"Then what else do you call flirting with death like you did today? And you've been hit *eight* times? The fact that you're still alive is amazing—you've had a fantastic run of luck, but you've got to know that sooner or later it's going to run out."

The waitress arrived then and we dropped into silence as she set steaming plates of jambalaya before us.

"You don't know much about lightning, do you," Kim said when we were alone again.

"I've treated my share of—"

"But do you know that it's usually not fatal, that better than nine out of ten victims survive?"

Truthfully, I hadn't known the survival rate was that high. "Well, you're closing in on number ten."

She shrugged. "Just a number. The first shock on that dock in Texas should have killed me. The usual bolt carries a current of ten thousand amps at a hundred million volts. Makes the electric chair look like a triple-A battery. Of course the charge only lasts a tiny fraction of a second, but that first one was enough to put me into cardiac arrest. If Karen and Bill hadn't known CPR, we wouldn't be having this conversation."

She dug into her jambalaya and chewed for a few seconds.

"Good, isn't it," I said.

She nodded. "Delicious."

But she said it with no great conviction, and I got the feeling that eating was something Kim McCormick did simply to keep from feeling hungry.

"But where was I? Oh, yes. After failing to get hit a second time in Texas, I started studying up on lightning. We still don't understand it completely, but what we do know is fascinating. Do you realize that worldwide, every second of every minute of every day there are almost a thousand lightning flashes? Most are cloud to cloud or cloud to air. Only fifteen percent hit the ground. Those are the ones I'm interested in."

This was the most animated I'd seen her. I leaned across the table, drawn by her enthusiasm.

"But you're from Jersey. You were first struck in Texas. What are you doing here?"

"It's where the lightning is. The National Weather Service keeps track of lightning—something called flash density ratings. According to their records, Central Florida is the lightning capital of the country, maybe the world. You've got this broad strip of hot, low-lying land between two huge, cooler bodies of water. Take atmospheric instability due to wide temperature gradients, add tons of moisture, and *voilà*—thunderstorm alley."

"Seems you've been pretty successful around here—if you can call getting hit by lightning success."

She smiled. "I do. I started up around the Orlando area because of all the lakes. Being out in a boat during a storm is the best way to get hit, but I started thinking it was too risky, too easy to get knocked overboard and drown. Or take a direct hit from a positive giant."

"A what?"

"A positive giant. They originate at the very top of the storm cell, maybe fifty thousand feet up, and they can strike thirty miles ahead of the storm. You've heard of people getting struck down by a so-called 'bolt from the blue'? That's a positive giant. I don't want to get hit by one of those because they're so much more powerful than a regular bolt. Almost always fatal." She pointed her fork at me. "See? Told you I'm not suicidal."

"I believe you, I believe you."

"Good. Anyway, I settled on golf courses as my best bet. The landscapers take down a lot of the little trees but tend to leave the really big ones between the fairways." She showed me a pink, half-dollar-size scar on her right elbow. "That's an exit burn from the strike at Ventura Country Club." She parted her hair to reveal a quarter-size scar on her right parietal scalp. "This one's an entry at Hunter's Creek Golf Club. I could show you more, but not in public.

I've got other scars you can't see. Like a mild seizure disorder, for instance—I take Dilantin for that. And I've lost some of my hearing."

I was losing my appetite. This poor, deranged woman. "And did you see . . . ?"

"Timmy?" She smiled. Her eyes fairly glowed. "Yes. Every single time."

Kim McCormick was delusional. Had to be. And yet she was so convincing. But then that's the power of a delusion.

But what if it wasn't a delusion? What if she really . . . ?

I couldn't let myself go there.

"One of these times . . ."

"You're right, I suppose. And I'm prepared for it. I've got a solid will: How I'm to be cremated, where my ashes will go, and a list of all the charities that'll share my assets. But I stack the deck in my favor when I go out. That's why I get under a tree. Odds are against taking a direct hit that way. You get a secondary jolt—a flash that jumps from the primary strike point—and so far that's worked just fine for my purposes. Plus I keep low to the ground to reduce my chance of being thrown too far."

"But why do you undress?"

"I figure wet skin attracts a charge better than wet fabric."

I shook my head. "How long are you going to keep this up?"

"Until I get closer to him. He seems nearer here than he was in Texas, but he's still too far away."

"Too far for what?"

"I need to see his eyes, hear his voice, read his lips."

"Why? What are you looking for?"

A lost look tinged with terrible sorrow fluttered across her features. Her voice was barely audible. "Forgiveness."

I stared at her.

"Don't ask," she whispered before I could speak. "Subject closed." She shook herself and gave me a forced smile. "Let's talk about something else. Anything but the weather."

Ω

I stand alone on a rotted wharf, engulfed in fog. The stagnant pond before me carries a vaguely septic stench. No sound, no movement. I wait. Soon I hear the creak of wood, the gentle lap of a polished hull gliding through still water. A dark shape appears, with the distinctive curved bow of a gondola. It noses toward me through the fog, but as it nears I notice something unusual about the hull. It's classic glossy black, like all gondolas, but the seating area is closed over. I realize with a start that the hull is a coffin . . . a child's coffin . . . and bright red blood is ooz-

ing from under the lid. I shout to the gondolier. He's gaunt, the traditional striped shirt hanging loose on his bony frame. His face is hidden by his broad straw hat until he lifts his head and stares at me. I scream when I see the scar running across his left eye. He grins and begins poling his floating sarcophagus away, back into the fog. I jump into the foul water and swim after him, stroking frantically as I try to catch up. But the gondola is too fast and the fog swallows it again, leaving me alone and lost in the water. I swim in circles, my arms growing weaker and weaker . . . finally they refuse to respond, dangling limply at my sides as I slip beneath the surface . . . water rushes into my nose and throat, choking me . . .

I awoke gagging and shaking, dangling half on, half off my bed. It took me a long time to shake off the aftereffects of the nightmare. I hadn't had one like that in years. I knew why it had returned tonight: my afternoon with Kim McCormick.

Ω

Over the next few days I realized that Kim had invaded my life. I kept thinking of her alone in that motel room, eating fast food, her eyes glued to the Weather Channel as she tracked the next storm, planned her next brush with death. The image haunted me at night, followed me through the day. I found myself keeping the Weather Channel on at home, and ducking off to check it out on the doctors lounge TV whenever I had a spare moment.

I guess my preoccupation became noticeable because Jay Ravener, head of the emergency department, pulled me aside and asked me if anything was wrong. Jay could never understand why a board-certified cardiologist like myself wanted to work as an emergency room doc. He was delighted to have access to someone with my training, but he was always telling me how much more money I could make as a staff cardiologist. Today, though, he was talking about enthusiasm, giving me a pep talk about how we were a team, and we all had to be players. He went on about how I hardly speak to anyone on good days, and lately I'd barely been here.

Probably true. No, undoubtedly true. I don't particularly care for anyone on the staff, or in the whole damn state, for that matter. I don't care to make chitchat. I come in, do my job—damn efficiently, too—and then I go home. I live alone. I read, watch TV, videos, go to the movies—all alone. I prefer it that way.

I know I'm depressed. But imagine what I'd be like without the forty milligrams of Prozac I take every day. I wasn't always this way, but it's my current reality, and that's how I choose to deal with it.

Fuck you, Jay.

I said none of this, however. I merely nodded and made concurring noises, then let Jay move on, satisfied that he'd done his duty.

But the episode made me realize that Kim McCormick had upset the delicate equilibrium I'd established, and I'd have to do something about her.

Just as she had researched lightning, I decided to research Kim McCormick.

Her driver's license had listed a Princeton address. I began calling the New Jersey medical centers in her area, looking for a patient named Timothy McCormick. When I struck out there, I moved to Philadelphia. I hit pay dirt at CHOP—Children's Hospital of Philadelphia.

Being a doctor made it possible. Physicians and medical records departments are pretty tight-lipped about patient information when it comes to lawyers, insurance companies, even relatives. But when it's one doctor to another . . .

I asked Timothy McCormick's attending to call me about him. After having me paged through the hospital switchboard, Richard Andrews, M.D., pediatric oncologist, knew he was talking to a fellow physician, and was ready to open up. I told him I was treating Kim McCormick for depression that I knew stemmed from the death of her child, but she would give me no details. Could he help?

"I remember it like it was yesterday," he told me in a staccato rattle. "Sad case. Osteosarcoma, started in his right femur. Pretty well advanced, mets to the lung and beyond by the time it was diagnosed. He deteriorated rapidly but we managed to stabilize him. Even though he was on respiratory assist, his mother wanted him home, in his own room. She was loaded and equipped a mini-intensive care unit at home with around-the-clock skilled nursing. What could we say? We let her take him."

"And he died there, I gather?"

"Yeah. We thought we had all the bases covered. One thing we didn't foresee was a power failure. Hospitals have backup generators, her house didn't."

I closed my eyes and suppressed a groan. I didn't have to imagine what awful moments those must have been, the horror of utter helplessness, of watching her child die before her eyes and not being able to do a thing about it. And the guilt afterward . . . oh, lord, the crushing weight of self-doubt and self-damnation would be enough to make anyone delusional.

I thanked Dr. Andrews, told him what a great help he'd been, and struggled through the late shift. Usually I can grab a nap after two a.m. Not this time. I sat up, staring at the Weather Channel, watching with growing unease as the radar tracked a violent storm moving this way from Tampa.

I called Kim McCormick's motel room but she didn't answer. Did she guess it was me and knew I'd try to convince her to stay in? Or was she already out?

As the clock crawled toward six a.m. I stood with keys in hand inside the glass door to the doctor's parking lot and watched the western sky come alive with lightning, felt the door shiver in resonance with the growing thunder. So *much* lightning, and it was still miles off. If Kim was out there . . .

If? Who was I kidding? Of course she was out there. And I couldn't leave until my relief arrived. I prayed he'd show up early, but if anything, the storm would delay him.

Jerry Ross arrived at 6:05, just ahead of a pair of ambulances, and I dashed for my car. The storm was hitting its stride as I raced along 98. I turned onto what I thought was the right road, fishtailing as I gunned along, searching for that Nelson pine. I almost missed it in the downpour, and damn near ditched the car as I slammed on the brakes when I spotted it. I reversed to the access road and kicked up wet gravel as I headed for the tree.

The sight of her Mercedes offered some relief, and I let out a deep breath when I spotted the pale form huddled against the trunk. I barely knew this strange, troubled woman, and yet somehow she'd become very important to me.

I skidded to a stop and ran up the rise to where she sat, looking like a drowned rat. Halfway there the air around me flashed noon bright and the immediate crash of thunder nearly knocked me off my feet, but Kim remained unscathed.

"Not again!" she cried, not bothering to cover her breasts this time. She waved me off. "Get out of here!"

"You can't keep doing this!"

I dropped to my knees beside her and tried not to stare. I couldn't help but notice that they were very nice breasts, not too big, not too little, just right, with deep brown nipples, jutting in the chill rain.

"I can do anything I damn well please! Now *go away!*"

I'd been here only seconds but already my clothes were soaked through. I leaned closer, shouting over the deafening thunder.

"I know what happened—about Timmy, bringing him home, the power failure. But you can't go on punishing yourself."

She gave me a cold blue stare. "How do you—?"

"Doesn't matter. I just know. Tell me—was there a storm when the power went off?"

She nodded, still staring. The red blinker on her lightning detector was going berserk.

"Don't you see how it's all tied together? It's guilt and obsession. You need medication, Kim. I can help."

"I've *been* on medication. Prozac, Paxil, Zoloft, Effexor, Tofranil, you name it. Nothing worked. I'm not imagining this, *Doctor*. Timmy is there. I can feel him."

"Because you *want* him there!"

More lightning—so close I heard it sizzle.

"Damn you!" she gritted through clenched teeth during the ensuing thunderclap. I didn't hear those words, but I could read her lips. She closed her eyes a second, as if counting to ten, then looked at me again. "Do you have any children?"

I didn't hesitate. "No."

"Well, if you did, you'd understand when I say you *know* them. I *know* Timmy, and I know he's *there*. And since you've never had a child, then you can't understand what it's like to lose one." Her eyes were filling, her voice trembling. "How you'll do anything—risk everything—to have them back, even for an instant. So don't tell me I need medication. I need my little *boy!*"

"But I do understand," I said softly, feeling my own pain grow, wanting to stop myself before I went further but sensing it was already too late. "I—"

I stopped as my skin burst to life with a tingling, crawling sensation, and my body became a burning beehive with all its panicked residents trying to flee at once through the top of my head. I had a flash of Kim with strands of her wet hair standing out from her head and undulating like live snakes, and then I was at ground zero at Hiroshima . . .

. . . an instant whiteout and then the staticky blizzard wanes, leaving me kneeling by the tree, with Kim sprawled prone before me, flaming pine needles floating around like lazy fireflies, and a man tumbling ever so slowly down the slope to my right. With a start I realize he's me, but the whole scene is translucent—I can see through the tree trunk. Everything is pale, drained of color, almost as if etched in glass, except . . .

. . . except for the tiny figure standing far across the marsh, a blotch of bright spring color in this polar landscape. A little girl, her dark brown hair divided into two ponytails tied with bright green ribbon, and she's wearing a yellow dress, her favorite yellow dress . . .

. . . it's Beth . . . oh, Christ, it can only be Beth . . . but she's so far away.

A desperate cry of longing leaps to my lips as I reach for her, but I can make no sound, and the world fades to black, my Beth with it . . .

I sat up groggy and confused, my right shoulder alive with pain. I looked around. Lightning still flashed, thunder still bellowed, rain still gushed in torrents, but somehow the whole world seemed changed. What had happened just now? Could that have been my little Beth? Really Beth?

No. Not possible. And yet . . .

Kim's still white form caught my eye. She lay by the trunk. I tried to stand but my legs wouldn't go for it, so I crawled to her. She was still breathing. Thank God. Then she moaned and moved her legs. I tried to lift her but my muscles were jelly. So I cradled her in my arms, shielding her as best I could from the rain, and waited for my strength to return, my mind filled with wonder at what I had seen.

Could I believe it had been real? Did I dare?

Ω

Still somewhat dazed, I sat on Kim's motel bed, a towel around my waist, my clothes draped over the lampshades to dry. When she'd come to, we staggered to my car and I drove us here.

The room looked exactly as before, except a Hardy's bag had replaced the Wendy's. Kim emerged from the bathroom wearing a flowered sundress, drying her hair with a towel. She was bouncing back faster than I was—practice, maybe. She looked pale but elated. I knew she must have seen her boy again.

I felt numb.

"Oh, God," she said and leaned closer. "Look at that burn!"

I glanced at the large blister atop my left shoulder. "It doesn't hurt as much as before."

"Oh, Joe, I'm so sorry you caught that flash too. I feel terrible."

"Don't. Not as if you didn't warn me."

"Still . . . let me get some of the cream they gave me for my heel. I'll make you—"

"I saw someone," I blurted.

She froze, staring at me, her eyes bright and wide. "Did you? Did you really? You saw Timmy? Didn't I tell you!"

"It wasn't your son."

She frowned. "Then who?"

"Remember by the tree, just before we got hit, when you asked me if I had any children? I said no, because . . . because I don't. At least not anymore. But I did."

Kim stared, wide-eyed. "*Did?*"

"A beautiful, beautiful daughter, the most wonderful little girl in the world."

"Oh, dear God! You too?"

My throat had thickened to the point where I could only nod.

She stumbled to the bed and sat next to me. The thin mattress sagged deeply under our combined weight.

"You're sure it was her?"

Again I nodded.

"I didn't see her. And you didn't see Timmy?"

I shook my head, trying to remember. Finally I could speak.

"Only Beth."

"How old was she?"

"Eight."

"Timmy was only five. Was it . . . ?" Her own throat seemed to clog as she placed her hand on my arm. "Did she have cancer too?"

"No." The memory began to hammer against the walls of the cell where I'd bricked it up. "She was murdered. Right in front of me." I held up my left arm to show her the seven-inch scar running up from the underside of my wrist. "This was all I got, but Beth died. And I couldn't save her."

Kim made a choking noise and I felt her fingers dig into my arm, her nails like claws.

"No!" Her voice was muffled because she'd jammed the damp towel over her mouth. "Oh-no, oh-no, oh-no! You poor . . . oh, God, how . . . ?"

I heard a sound so full of pain it transfixed me for an instant until I realized it had come from me.

"No. I can't. Please don't ask. I can't, I can't, I can't."

How could I talk about what I couldn't even think about it? I knew if I freed those memories, even for a single moment, I'd never cage them again. They'd rampage through my being as they'd done before, devouring me alive from the inside.

I buried my face against Kim's neck. She cradled me in her arms and rocked me like a baby.

Ω

"What about Timmy's father?" I said, biting into my Egg McMuffin. "Does he know about all this?"

After clinging to Kim for I don't know how long, I'd finally pulled myself together. We were hungry, but my clothes were still wet. So she took my car and made a breakfast run to Mickey D's. I sat on the bed, Kim took the room's one upholstered chair. The coffee was warming my insides, the caffeine pulling me partway out of my funk, but I was still well below sea level.

"He doesn't know Timmy exists. Literally. We never married. He's a good man, very bright, but I dropped him when I learned I was pregnant."

"I don't follow."

"He'd have wanted to marry me, or have some part in my baby's life. I didn't want that." My expression must have registered how offensive I found that, because she quickly explained. "You've got to understand how I was then: a super career woman who could do it all, wanted it all, and strictly on her own terms. I went through the pregnancy by myself, took maternity leave at the last possible moment, figuring I'd deliver the child—I knew he was a boy by the third month—and set him up with a nanny while I jumped right back into the race. I saw myself spending a sufficient amount of quality time with him as I molded him to be a mover and a shaker, just like his mother." She shook her head. "What a jerk."

"And after the delivery?" I'd guessed the answer.

She beamed. "When they put that little bundle into my arms, everything changed. He was a miracle, by far the finest thing I'd ever done in my life. Once I got him home, I couldn't stop holding him. And when I would finally put him into his bassinet, I'd pull up a chair and sit there looking at him . . . I'd put my pinkie against his palm and his little fingers would close around it, almost like a reflex, and that's how I'd stay, just sitting and staring, listening to him breathe as he held my finger."

I felt my throat tighten. I remembered watching Beth sleep when she was an infant, marveling at her pudgy cheeks, counting the tiny veins on the surfaces of her closed eyelids.

"You sound like a wonderful mother."

"I was. That's no brag. It's just that it's simply not my nature to do things halfway. Everything else in my life took a backseat to Timmy, I mean *way* back. It damn near killed me to end my maternity leave, but I arranged to do a lot of work from home. I wanted to be near him all the time." She blinked a few times and sniffed. "I'm so glad I made the effort. Because he didn't stay around very long." She rubbed a hand across her face and looked at me with reddened eyes. "How long since Beth . . . ?"

"Five years." The longing welled up in me. "Sometimes I feel like I was talking to her just yesterday, other times it seems like she's been gone forever."

"But don't you see?" Kim leaned forward. "She's not gone. She's still here."

I shook my head. "I wish I could believe that."

The lightning episode was becoming less and less real with each passing minute. Despite what I'd seen, I found myself increasingly reluctant to buy into this.

"But you saw her, didn't you? You *knew* her. Isn't seeing believing?"

"I don't know. Sometimes believing is seeing."

"But each of us saw our dead child. Can we *both* be crazy?"

"There's something called shared delusion. I could be—"

"Damn it!" She catapulted from the chair. "I'm not going to let you do this!" She yanked my pants from atop the lampshade and threw them at my face. "You can't take this from me! I won't let you or anybody else tell me—"

I grabbed her wrist as she stormed past me. "Kim! I *want* to believe! Can't you see there's nothing in the world I want more? And that's what worries me. I may want it too much."

I pulled her into my arms and we stood there, clinging to each other in anguished silence. I could feel her hot breath on my bare shoulder. She lifted her face to me.

"Don't fight it, Joe," she said, her voice soft. "Go with it. Otherwise you'll be denying yourself—"

I kissed her on the lips.

She drew back. I didn't know where the impulse had come from, and it was a toss-up as to which of us was more surprised. We stared at each other for a few heartbeats, and then our lips were together again. We seemed to be trying to devour each other. She tugged at my towel, I pulled at her sun dress, she wore nothing beneath it, and we tumbled onto the unmade bed, skin to skin, rolling and climbing all over each other, frantic mouths and hands everywhere until we finally locked together, riding out a storm of our own making.

Ω

Afterward, we clung to each other under the sheet. I stroked her back, feeling guilty because I knew it had been better for me than her.

"Sorry that was so quick. I'm out of practice."

"Don't be sorry," she murmured, kissing my shoulder. "Maybe it's all the shocks I've taken, but orgasms seem to be few and far between for me these days. I'm just glad to have someone I can feel close to. You don't know how lonely it's been, keeping this to myself, unable to share it. It's wonderful to be able to talk about it with someone who understands."

"I wish I did understand. Why is this happening?"

"Maybe all those volts alter the nervous system, change the brain's modes of perception."

"But I've never heard of anything like this. Why don't other lightning strike victims mention seeing a dead loved one?"

"Maybe they *have* seen them and never mentioned it. You're the only one I've told. But maybe it has to be someone who died during a storm. Did Beth—?"

"No," I said quickly, not allowing the scene to take shape in my mind. "Perfect weather."

"Then maybe it has to do with the fact that they both died as children, and they're still attached to their parents. They hadn't let go of us in life yet, and maybe that carries over into death."

"Almost sounds as if they're waiting for us."

"Maybe they are."

The temperature in the room seemed to drop and Kim snuggled closer.

Ω

Later, when we went back to pick up Kim's car, we walked up to where the lightning had struck. The top of the Nelson pine was split and charred. As we stood under its branches, I relived the moment, seeing Beth again, reaching for her . . .

"I wish she'd been closer."

"Yes." Kim turned to me. "Isn't it frustrating? When I took my second hit, up in Orlando, Timmy was closer than he'd been in Texas, and I thought he might move closer with each succeeding hit. But it hasn't worked that way. He stays about fifty yards away."

"Really? Beth seemed at least twice that." I pointed to the marshy field. "She was way over there."

Kim pointed north. "Timmy was that way."

I swiveled back and forth between where I'd seen Beth, and where Kim had seen Timmy, and an idea began to take shape.

"Which way were you facing when you saw Timmy in Texas?"

She closed her eyes. "Let me think . . . the sun always rose over the end of the dock, so I guess I was facing northeast."

"Good." I took her shoulders and rotated her until she faced east. "Now, show me where Timmy was in relation to the end of the dock when he appeared in Texas."

She pointed north.

"I'll be damned," I said and trotted down the slope.

"Where're you going?"

I reached into my car and plucked the compass from my dashboard. Sometimes at night when I can't sleep I go out for long aimless drives and wind up God knows where. At those times it's handy to know which direction you're headed.

"All right," I said when I returned. "This morning Timmy was that way— the compass says that's a few degrees east of north. If you followed that line from here, it would run through New Jersey, wouldn't it?"

She nodded, her brow furrowing. "Yes."

"But in Texas—where in Texas?"

"White River Lake. West Texas."

"Okay. You saw him in a northeast direction. Follow that line from West Texas and I'll bet it takes you—"

"To Jersey!" She was squeezing my upper arm with both hands and jumping up and down like a little girl. "Oh, God! That's where we lived! Timmy spent his whole life in Princeton!"

It's also where he died, I thought.

"I think a trip to Princeton is in order, don't you?"

"Oh, yes! Oh, God, yes!" Her voice cranked up to light speed. "Do you think that's where he is? Do you think he's still at the house? Oh, dear God! Why didn't I think of that?" She settled down and looked at me. "And what about Beth? You saw her . . . where?"

"East-northeast," I said. I didn't need the compass to figure that.

"Where does that line go? Orlando? Kissimmee? Did you live around there?"

I shook my head. "No. We lived in Tampa."

"But that's the opposite direction. What's east-northeast from here?"

I stared at the horizon. "Italy."

Ω

A week later we were sitting in the uppermost part of Kim's Princeton home waiting for an approaching storm to hit.

She had to have been earning *big* bucks as an investment banker to afford this place. A two-story Victorian—she said it was Second Empire style—with an octagonal tower set in the center of its mansard roof. One look at that tower and I knew it could be put to good use.

I found a Home Depot and bought four eight-foot sections of one-inch steel pipe, threaded at both ends, and three compatible couplers. I drilled a hole near the center of the tower roof and ran a length through; I coupled the second length to its lower end, and ran that through, and so on until Kim had a steel lightning target jutting twenty-odd feet above her tower.

The tower loft was unfurnished, so I'd carried up a couple of cushions from one of her sofas. We huddled side by side on those. The lower end of the steel pipe sat in a large galvanized bucket of water a few feet in front of us—the bucket was to catch the rain that would certainly leak through my amateur caulking job at the roof line, the water to reduce the risk of fire.

I heard the first distant mutter of thunder and rubbed my hands together. Despite the intense dry heat up here, they felt cold and damp.

"Scared?" Kim said

"Terrified."

My first brush with lightning had been an accident. I hadn't known what was coming. Now I did. I was shaking inside.

Kim smiled and gave my arm a reassuring squeeze. "So was I, at first. Knowing I'm going to see Timmy helps, but still . . . it's the uncertainty that does it: *Is* it or *isn't* it going to hit?"

"How about I just say I don't believe in lightning? That'll make me feel better."

She laughed. "Hey, whatever works." She sidled closer. "But I think I know a better way to take your mind off your worries."

She began kissing me, on my eyes, my cheeks, my neck, my lips. And I began undoing the buttons on her blouse. We made love on the cushions in that hot stuffy tower, and were glazed with sweat when we finished.

A flash lit one of the eight slim windows that surrounded us, followed by a deep rumble.

"Almost here," I whispered.

Kim nodded absently. She seemed distant. I knew our lovemaking had once again ended too quickly for her, and I felt bad. Over the past week I'd tried everything I knew to bring her through, but kept running into a wall I could not breach.

"I wish—" I began but she placed a finger against my lips.

"I have to tell you something. About Timmy. About the day he died."

I knew it had been tough on her coming back here. I'd seen his room—it lay directly below this little tower. Like so many parents who've lost a child, she'd kept it just as he'd left it, with toys on the counters and drawings on the wall. I would have done that with Beth's room, but my marriage fell apart soon after her death and the house was sold. Another child occupied Beth's room now.

"You don't—"

"Shush. Let me speak. I've got to tell you this. I've got to tell *someone* before . . ."

"Before what?"

"Before I explode. I brought Timmy home from the hospital to a room that was set up like the finest ICU. All his vital signs were monitored by telemetry, he had round-the-clock skilled nursing to give him his chemotherapy, monitor his IVs, draw blood for tests, adjust his respirator."

"Why the respirator?" I couldn't help it—the doctor in me wanted to know.

"The tumor had spread to his lungs—he couldn't breathe without it. It'd also spread to many of his bones, even his skull. He was in terrible pain all the time. They radiated him, filled him with poisons that made him sicker, loaded him with dope to ease the pain, and kept telling me he had a fighting chance. He *didn't* have a chance. I knew it, and that was why I'd brought him home, so he could be in his own room, and so I could have every minute with him. But worse, Timmy knew it too. I could see it in his eyes when they weren't glazed with opiates. He was hanging by a thread but no one would let it break. He wanted to go."

I closed my eyes, thinking, Oh, no. Don't tell me this . . . I don't want to hear this . . .

"It was the hardest decision of my life. More than anything else in the universe, I wanted my little boy to live, because every second of his life seemed a precious gift to me. But why was I delaying the inevitable? For him, or for me? Certainly not for him, because he was simply existing. He couldn't read, couldn't even watch TV, because if he wasn't in agony, he was in the Demerol zone. That meant I was prolonging his agony for *me*, because I couldn't let him go. I *had* to let him go. As his mother, I had to do what was right for him, not for me."

"You don't have to go on," I said as she paused. "I can guess the rest."

Kim showed me a small, bitter smile. "No, I don't think you can." She let out a deep shuddering sigh and bit her upper lip. "So one day, as a thunderstorm came through, I dosed a glass of orange juice with some ipecac and gave it to Timmy's nurse. Ten minutes later, while she was in the bathroom heaving up her lunch, I sneaked down to the basement and threw the main breaker for the house. Then I rushed back up to the second floor to be with Timmy as he slipped away. But he wasn't slipping away. He was writhing in the bed, spasming, fighting for air. I . . . I was horrified, I felt as if my blood had turned to ice. I thought he'd go gently. It wasn't supposed to be like that. I couldn't bear it."

Tears began to stream down her face. The storm was growing around us but I was barely aware. I was focused on Kim.

"I remember screaming and running back down to the basement, almost killing myself on the way, and resetting the breaker. Then I raced back upstairs. But when I reached him, it was too late. My Timmy was gone, and I hadn't been there. He died alone. *Alone!* Because of me! I killed him!"

And now she was sobbing, deep wracking sounds from the pit of her soul. I took her in my arms and held her tight against me. She virtually radiated pain. At last I understood what was fueling the engine of this mad compulsion. What an appalling burden to carry.

"It's all right, Kim," I whispered. "What you saw were muscle spasms, all involuntary. You did the right thing, a brave thing."

"*Was* it right?" she blurted through her sobs. "I know it wasn't brave—I mean, I lost my nerve and changed my mind—but was it *right*? Did Timmy really want to go, or was it me just thinking he did? Was his suffering too much for him to bear, or too much for me? That's what I've got to know. That's why I have to see him close up and hear what he's trying to say. If I can do that, just once, I swear I'll stop all this and run for a basement every time I hear a storm coming."

As if on cue, a blast of thunder shook the little tower and I became aware again of the storm. Rain slashed the windows and the darkened sky was alive with flashes. I stared at the steel pole a few feet before me and wanted to run. I could feel my heart hammering against my ribs. This was insane, truly insane. But I forced myself to sit tight and think about something else.

"It all makes sense now," I said.

"What?"

"Why we're seeing Beth and Timmy . . . they didn't give up their lives—life was taken from them."

Kim bunched a fist against her mouth. She closed her eyes and moaned softly.

"Through love in Timmy's case," I said quickly. I cupped my hand behind her neck and kissed her forehead. "But not in Beth's."

Kim opened her eyes. "Can't you tell me about it? Please?"

She'd shared her darkest secret with me, and yet I couldn't bring myself to talk about it. I was about to refuse her when a deafening blast of thunder stopped me. I was dancing with death in this tower. What if I didn't survive? Kim should know. Suddenly I wanted her to know.

I closed my eyes and opened the gates, allowing the pent-up past to flow free. A melange of sights, smells, sounds eddied around me, carrying me back five years . . .

I steeled myself and began: "It was the first time in years I'd allowed myself more than a week away from my practice. Twelve whole days in Italy. We were all so excited . . ."

Ω

Angela was first generation Italian-American and the three of us trooped to the Old Country to visit her grandparents—Beth's great-grandparents. While Angela stayed in Positano, yakking in Italian to all her relatives, Beth and I dashed off for a quick, two-day jaunt to Venice. Yes, it's an overpriced tourist trap. Yes, it's the Italian equivalent of Disney World. But there's not another place in the world like it, and since the city is supposedly sinking at the rate of two and a half inches per decade, I wanted Beth to experience it without a snorkel.

From the day she was born, Beth and I shared something special. I don't think I've ever loved anyone or anything more than that little baby. When I was home, I'd feed her; when I wasn't on call, I'd get up with her at night. Most parents love their kids, but Beth and I *bonded*. We were soul mates. She was only eight, but I felt as if I'd known her all my life.

I wanted her to be rich in spirit and experience, so I never passed up a chance to show her the wonders of the world, the natural and the manmade. Venice was a little of both. We did all the touristy stuff—a gondola ride past Marco Polo's and Casanova's houses, shopping on the Rialto Bridge, eating gelato, crossing the Bridge of Sighs from the Doge's palace into the prison; we took boats to see the glassblowers on Murano and the lace makers on Burano, snagged a table at Harry's Bar where I treated her to a Shirley Temple while I tried a Bellini. But no matter where we went or what we did, Beth kept dragging me back to Piazza San Marco so she could feed the pigeons. She was bonkers for those pigeons.

Vendors wheel little carts through the piazza, selling packets of birdseed, two thousand lire a pop. Beth must have gone through a dozen packets during our two-day stay. Pigeons have been called rats with feathers, and that may not be far off, but these have got to be the fattest, tamest feathered rats in the world. Sprinkle a little seed into your palm, hold it out, and they'll flutter up to perch on your hand and arm to eat it. Beth loved to stand with handfuls stretched out to both sides. The birds would bunch at her feet, engulf her arms, and even perch on her head, transforming her into a giggling mass of feathers.

I wasn't crazy about her being that close to so many birds—thoughts of the avian-born diseases like psittacosis that I'd studied in med school kept darting through my head—so I tried to limit her contact. But she got such a kick out of them, how many times could I say no? I even went so far as to let her talk me into doing her two-handed feeding trick. Soon, holding my breath within a sea of fluttering wings, I was inundated with feathers. I couldn't see Beth but I could hear her distinctive belly laugh. When I finally shook off the pigeons, I found her red-faced and doubled over with laughter.

What can be better than making a child laugh? The pigeons grossed me out, but so what? I grabbed more seed and did it again.

Finally it was time to leave Venice. The only flight we could book to Naples left Marco Polo at six thirty the next morning, and the first public waterbus of the day would make a number of stops along the way and get us to the airport with only a few minutes to spare. Since I didn't want to risk missing the flight, I had the hotel concierge arrange for a private water taxi. It would pick us up at five a.m. at a little dock just a hundred feet from our hotel.

At ten of five, Beth and I were standing by our luggage at the end of Calle Larga San Marco. The tide was out and the canal smelled pretty rank. Even at this hour it was warm enough for short sleeves. I was taken with the silence of the city, the haunted emptiness of the dark streets: Venice on the cusp of a new day, when the last revelers had called it quits, and the earliest risers were just starting their morning coffee.

Beth was her usual bossy little self. As soon as she'd learned to string words together, she began giving directions like a sergeant major. She had no qualms about telling us what to wear, or what to buy in the supermarket or a department store, or setting up seating arrangements—"You sit there, Mommy, and Daddy, you sit there, and I'll sit right here in the middle." We called her "the Boss." And here in Venice, without her mother around, Boss Beth took charge of me. I loved to humor her.

"Put the suitcases right there, Daddy. Yours on the inside and mine on the outside so that when the boat gets here we can put them right on. Now you stand right over here by me."

I did exactly as she told me. She wanted me close and I was glad to comply. Her voice trailed off after that and I could see her glancing around uneasily. I wasn't fully comfortable myself, but I talked about seeing Mommy in a few hours to take her mind off our isolation.

And then finally we heard it—the sputtering gurgle of an approaching *taxi acquei*. The driver, painfully thin, a cigarette drooping from his lips, pulled into the dock—little more than a concrete step-down—and asked in bad English if we were the ones going to the airport. We were, and as I handed him our two suitcases, I noticed the heavy droop of his left eyelid. My first thought was Bell's palsy, but then I noticed the scar that parted his eyebrow and ridged the lid below it.

I also noticed that he wasn't one to make contact with his good eye, and that his taxi didn't look to be in the best shape. A warning bell sounded in my head—not a full-scale alarm, just a troubled chime—but I knew if I went looking now for another taxi, we'd almost certainly miss the plane.

If only I'd heeded my instincts.

Beth and I sat together in the narrow, low-ceilinged cabin amidships as the driver wound his way into the wider, better-lit Grand Canal where we were the only craft moving. We followed that for a while, then turned off into a narrower passage. After numerous twists and turns I was completely disoriented. Somewhere along the way the canal-front homes had been replaced by warehouses. My apprehension was rising, and when the engine began to sputter, it soared.

As the taxi bumped against the side of the canal, the driver stuck his head into the cabin and managed to convey that he was having motor trouble and needed us to come up front so he could open the engine hatch.

I emerged to find him standing in front of me with his arm raised. I saw something flash dimly in his hand as he swung it at me, and I managed to get my left arm up in time to deflect it. I felt a blade slice deep into my forearm and I cried out with the pain as I fell to the side. Beth started screaming, "Daddy! Daddy!" but that was all she managed before her voice died in a choking gurgle. I didn't know what he'd done to Beth, I just knew he'd hurt her and no way in hell was he going to hurt her again. Bloody arm and all, I launched myself at him with an animal roar. He was light and thin, and not in good shape. I took him by surprise and drove him back against the boat's console. Hard. He grunted and I swear I heard ribs crack. In blind fury I pinned him there and kept ramming my right forearm against his face and neck and kneeing him in the groin until he went limp, then I threw him to the deck and jumped on him a few times, driving my heels into his back to make sure he wouldn't be getting up.

Then I leaped to Beth and found her drenched in blood and just about gone. He'd slit her throat! Oh Lord, oh God, to keep her from screaming he'd cut my little girl open, severing one of her carotid arteries in the process. The wound gaped dark and wet, blood was everywhere. Whimpering like a lost, frightened child, I felt around in the wound and found the feebly pumping carotid stump, tried to squeeze it shut but it was too late, too late. Her mouth was slack, her eyes wide and staring. I was losing her, my Beth was dying and I couldn't do a thing to save her. I started shouting for help, I screamed until my throat was raw and my voice reduced to a ragged hiss, but the only replies were my own cries echoing off the warehouse walls.

And then the blood stopped pulsing against my fingers and I knew her little heart had stopped. CPR was no use because she had no blood left inside, it was all out here, soaking the deck and the two of us.

I held her and wept, rocking her back and forth, pleading with God to give her back to me. But instead of Beth stirring, the driver moved, groaning in pain from his broken bones. In a haze of rage as red as the sun just beginning to crawl over the horizon, I rose and began kicking and stomping him, reveling in the wonderful crunch of his bones beneath my soles. I shattered his limbs and hands and feet, crushed his rib cage, pulped the back of his skull, and I relished every blow. When I was satisfied he was dead, I returned to Beth. I cradled her in my arms and sobbed until the first warehouse workers arrived and found us.

Ω

Kim clutched both my hands; tears streamed down her cheeks. Her mouth moved as she tried to speak, but she made no sound.

"The rest is something of a blur. An official inquiry into the incident—two people were dead, so I couldn't blame the Venice authorities for that—revealed that the killer had overheard the hotel arranging our water-taxi ride. He borrowed a friend's boat and beat the scheduled taxi to the pickup spot. The court determined that he was going to kill us, steal whatever valuables we'd bought or brought, and dump our bodies in the Adriatic. They suspected that we weren't his first victims.

"I was released, but then came the nightmare of red tape trying to return Beth's body to the States. Finally we brought her home and buried her, but my life was changed forever by then. The world was never the same without Beth. Neither was my marriage. Angela never said so, but I know she secretly blamed me for Beth's death. So did I. Angela and I split a year later. She couldn't live with me. Who could blame her? I could barely live with myself. Still can't."

"But you're *not* to blame."

"I had a chance to back off before we stepped onto that water taxi, but I didn't take it. And Beth paid for it."

We sat in silence then, each mired in our pools of private guilt. Gradually I realized that the flashes outside were less frequent, the thunder not quite so loud.

"I think it's passed us by," I said.

Kim glanced around, frowning in disappointment. "Damn. We'll have to wait for another storm. That could be next week or next month around here." She pointed to the steel pole. "Oh, look. It's wet."

Fine rivulets of water were coursing down the surface of the steel.

"So much for my caulking skills. I'll see what I can do tomorrow."

Kim got on her knees and leaned forward to touch the wet surface and—

—the tower seemed to explode. I had an instant's impression of a deafening *buzz* accompanied by a rainbow shower of sparks within a wall of blazing light; boiling water exploded from the galvanized bucket as multiple arcs of blue-white energy converged from the pole onto Kim's outstretched arm. Her mouth opened wide in a silent scream while her body arched like a bow and shuddered violently, and then a searing bolt flashed from her opposite shoulder into me . . .

. . . the whiteout fades, as do the walls of the tower, leaving ghostly translucent afterimages, and I know which way to turn. I spot the tiny figure immediately, still in her yellow dress, standing so far away, suspended above the treetops. Beth! I call her name but there is no sound in this place. I try to move toward her but I'm frozen in space. I need to be closer, I need to see her throat . . . and then her hand goes to her mouth, and her eyes widen as she points to me. What? What's the matter?

I realize she's pointing behind me. I turn and see Kim's ghostly figure on the floor . . . so still . . . too still . . .

I came to and crawled to Kim. Her right arm was a smoking ruin, charred to the elbow, and she wasn't breathing. Panicked, I struggled upright and kneeled over her. I forced my rubbery arms to pound my fists on her chest to jolt her heart back to life—once, twice—then I started CPR, compressing her sternum and blowing into her mouth, five thrusts, one breath . . . five thrusts, one breath . . .

"Come on, Kim!" I shouted. I was so slick with sweat that my hands kept slipping off her chest. "Breathe! You can do it! Breathe, damn it!"

I saw her eyelids flutter. Her blue irises had lost their luster, but I sensed an exquisite joy in their depths as they fixed on me for a beseeching instant . . . the tiniest shake of her head, and then she was gone again.

I realized what she'd just tried to tell me: *Don't . . . please don't.*

But it wasn't in me to kneel here and watch the life seep out of her. I lurched again into CPR but she resisted my best efforts to bring her back. Finally, I stopped. Her skin was cooling beneath my palms. Kim was gone.

I stared at her pale, peaceful face. What was happening in that other place? Had she found her Timmy and the forgiveness she craved? Was she with him now and preferring to stay there?

I felt an explosive pressure building in my chest, mostly grief, but part envy. I let out an agonized groan and gathered her into my arms. I ached for her bright eyes, her crooked-toothed smile.

"Poor lost Kim," I whispered, stroking her limp hair. "I hope to God you found what you were looking for."

Just as with Beth, I held Kim until her body was cold.

Finally, I let her go. I dressed her as best I could, and stretched her out on the cushions. I called the emergency squad, then drove my car to the corner and waited until I saw them wheel her body out to the ambulance. Then I headed for the airport.

I hated abandoning her to the medical examiner, but I knew the police would want to question me. They'd want to know what the hell we were doing up in that tower during a storm. They might even take me into custody. I couldn't allow that.

I had someplace to go.

Ω

I arrived in Marco Polo Airport without luggage. The terminal snuggles up to the water, and the boats wait right outside the arrival terminal. I bought a ticket for the waterbus—I could barely look at the smaller, speedier water taxis—and spent the two-and-a-half mile trip across the Laguna Véneta fighting off the past.

I did pretty well leaving the dock and walking into the Piazza San Marco. I hurried through the teeming crowds, past the flooded basilica on the right—a Byzantine toad squatting in a tiny pond—and the campanile towering to my left. I almost lost it when I saw a little girl feeding the pigeons, but I managed to hold on.

I found a hotel in the San Polo district, bought a change of clothes, and holed up in my room, watching the TV, waiting for news of a storm.

Ω

And now the storm is here. From my perch atop the Campanile di San Marco I see it boiling across the Laguna Véneta, spearing the Lido with bolts of blue-white energy, and taking dead aim for my position. The piazza below is empty now, the gawkers chased by the thunder, rain, and lightning— especially the lightning. Even the brave young *Carabinieri* has discovered the proper relationship between discretion and valor and ducked back inside.

And me: I've cut the ground wire from the lightning rod above me. I'm roped to the tower to keep from falling. And I'm drenched with rain.

I'm ready.

Physically, at least. Mentally, I'm still not completely sure. I've seen Beth twice now. I *should* believe, I want to believe . . . but do I want it so desperately that I've tapped into Kim's delusion system and made it my own?

I'm hoping this will be my last time. If I can see Beth up close, see her throat, know that her wound has healed in this place where she waits, it will go a long way toward healing a wound of my own.

Suddenly I feel it—the tingle in my skin as the charge builds in the air around me—and then a deafening *ZZZT!* as the bolt strikes the ungrounded rod above the statue of St. Mark. Millions of volts slam into me, violently jerking my body . . .

. . . and then I'm in that other place, that other state . . . I look around frantically for a splotch of yellow and I almost cry out when I see Beth floating next to me. She's here, smiling, radiant, and so close I can almost touch her. I choke with relief as I see her throat—it's healed, the terrible grinning wound gone without a trace, as if it never happened.

I smile at her but she responds with a look of terror. She points down and I turn to see my body tumbling from the tower. The safety rope has broken and I'm drifting earthward like a feather.

I'm going to die.

Strangely, that doesn't bother me nearly as much as it should. Not in this place.

Then in the distance I see two other figures approaching, and as they near I recognize Kim, and she's leading a beaming towheaded boy toward Beth and me.

A burst of unimaginable joy engulfs me. This is so wonderful . . . almost too wonderful to be real. And there lies my greatest fear. Are they all—Beth, Kim, Timmy—really here? Or merely manifestations of my consuming need for this to be real?

I look down and see my slowly falling body nearing the pavement.

Very soon I will know.

1999

The Year of the Almost-Good Script.

I started off by jumping into a fourth Repairman Jack novel. *Legacies* . . . *Conspiracies* . . . let's call this one *Tendencies*. (Yes, I know—a truly awful title.)

On March 18, after months of back and forth with the hosting service and the Web designer, www.repairmanjack.com went live. One of the best things I've ever done. Somehow, people found it—Jack fans, SF fans, Adversary Cycle fans began to trickle in, hanging out at the forum's message board, getting to know one another and forming a close-knit community. I participated almost daily and still do. A year later, when I published the URL on the last page of *Conspiracies*, the membership swelled. It's still growing, averaging over two million hits per month.

Sometime around midyear Richard Chizmar asked me to do a story for the novella series Cemetery Dance had been publishing. I'd seen this article in the *New York Times* that had mentioned how chimps and humans share 98.4 percent of their DNA. It had occurred to me: What if someone increased the share to, say, 99.3 percent? What would you have?

So I began outlining this story about transgenic chimps called sims. But the more I worked on it the larger it grew, until I told him no way I could squeeze it into 40,000 words. And I couldn't commit to a major novel because of other books contracted. We talked about it and Rich suggested I do a series of novellas on the theme and he'd publish them as they were written—no deadlines. I loved the idea.

So I doodled with *Sims* while working on the RJ novel. When I finished a draft of *Tendencies*, I sent it to Steve Spruill for his input (he sees every novel first), with the added plea for a title. I couldn't come up with anything I liked. After reading it Steve suggested *All the Rage*. Perfect.

But I couldn't start *Sims* right away. In order to do it justice I had to go back and give myself a course in genetics. During my medical school days in the early seventies we knew a tiny fraction of what we do now. What we've learned in thirty years blew me away and opened up worlds of fiction possibilities. Trouble is, science is moving so fast you've got to keep running to prevent the work from being obsolete by the time it's published.

Later in the year I flew to Bermuda for some wreck diving—the island is ringed with them. I wanted to center a novel around a wreck but the story was taking its time coming.

On the film front, Beacon renewed its option on *The Tomb* for another year. I was in fairly regular e-mail contact with Craig Spector as he was working through the script. In September Barry Rosenbush sent me the latest iteration and I liked it a lot. Jack was a bit more avuncular than I'd depicted him, characters had been dropped, and a spear-carrier had been expanded to a major supporting role, but all in all it was faithful to the spirit of Jack and the novel.

Beacon's distribution deal was with Universal at that time. Universal was enthusiastic about the script, but thought it needed a polish. They wanted a certain writer to do the work, Beacon wanted someone else. Negotiations began.

This rewrite/polish process would screw up a perfectly good script and push it further and further from the source novel. But I didn't know that at the time.

Alan Clark's *Imagination Fully Dilated* anthology (containing "Lysing Toward Bethlehem") had been a success, so he decided to self-publish volume two. The same scenario: Pick one of his paintings and write a story around it. I chose "I Become My Resting Place." It's one of a series of bucolic landscapes focused on twisted pieces of wood that look like people or almost-people.

I looked at that painting and saw a wooden corpse. (Google the title if you want a peek.) I asked myself how that could come to be. The answer was "Anna," a traditional horror story that draws on one of my favorite locales.

Anna

The bushy-haired young man with long sideburns arrives on deck with two cups of coffee—one black for himself, the other laced with half-and-half and two sugars, the way his wife always takes it. Rows of blue plastic seats, half of them filled with tourists heading back to the mainland, sit bolted to the steel deck. He stops by a row under the awning. His wife's navy blue sweatshirt is draped over the back of one of the seats but she's not there. He looks around and doesn't see her. He asks a nearby couple, strangers, if they saw where his wife went but they say they didn't notice.

The man strolls through the ferry's crowded aft deck but doesn't see his wife. Still carrying the coffee, he ambles forward but she's not there either. He wanders the starboard side, checking out the tourists leaning on the rails, then does the same on the port side. No sign of her.

The man places the coffee on the seat with her sweatshirt and searches through the inner compartments and the snack bar. He begins to ask people if they've seen a blond woman in her mid-twenties wearing a flowered top and bell-bottom jeans. Sure, people say. Dozens of them. And they're right. The ferry carries numerous women fitting that description.

The man finds a member of the crew and tells him that his wife is missing. He is taken to the ferry's security officer who assures him that his wife is surely somewhere aboard—perhaps she's seasick and in one of the rest rooms.

The man waits outside the women's rooms, asking at each if someone could check inside for his wife. When that yields nothing, he again wanders the various decks, going so far as to search the vehicle level where supply trucks and passengers' cars make the trip.

When the ferry reaches Hyannis, the man stands on the dock and watches every debarking passenger, but his wife is not among them.

He calls his father-in-law who lives outside Boston. He explains that they were on their way over for a surprise visit but now his daughter is missing. The father-in-law arrives in his chauffeur-driven Bentley and joins the young man in storming the offices of the Massachusetts Steamship Authority, demanding a thorough, stem-to-stern search of the ferry and too damned bad if that will delay its departure. The father-in-law is a rich man, influential in Massachusetts politics. The ferry is detained.

The state police are called to aid in the search. The Coast Guard sends out a helicopter to trace and retrace the ferry's route. But the wife is not to be found. No one sees her again. Ever.

"Ow!"

William Morley grabbed his right heel as pain spiked through it. His knee creaked and protested as he leaned back in the chair and pulled his foot up to where he could see it.

"I'll be damned!" he said as he spotted the two-inch splinter jutting from the heel of his sock.

Blood seeped through the white cotton, forming a crimson bull's-eye around the base of the splinter. Morley grabbed the end and yanked it free. The tip was stiletto sharp and red with his blood.

"Where the hell . . . ?"

He'd been sitting here in his study, in his favorite rocker, reading the Sunday *Times,* his feet resting on the new maple footstool he'd bought just yesterday. How on earth had he picked up a splinter?

Keeping his bloody heel off the carpet, he limped into the bathroom, dabbed a little peroxide on the wound, then covered it with a Band-Aid.

When he returned to the footstool he checked the cushioned top and saw a small hole in the fabric where his heel had been resting. The splinter must have been lying in the stuffing. He didn't remember moving his foot before it pierced him, but he must have.

Morley had picked up the footstool at Danzer's overpriced furniture boutique on Lower Broadway. He'd gone in looking for something antiquey and come out with this brand-new piece. He'd spotted it from the front of the showroom; tucked in a far rear corner, it seemed to call to him. And once he'd seen the intricate grain—he couldn't remember seeing maple grained like this—and the elaborate carving along the edge of the seat and up and down the legs, he couldn't pass it up.

But careless as all hell for someone to leave a sharp piece of wood like that in the padding. If he were a different sort, he might sue. But what for? He had more than enough money, and he wouldn't want to break whoever did this exquisite carving.

He grabbed two of the stool's three legs and lifted it for a closer look. Marvelous grain, and—

"Shit!" he cried, and dropped it as pain lanced his hand.

He gaped in wonder at the splinter—little more than an inch long this time—jutting from his palm. He plucked the slim little dagger and held it up.

How the hell . . . ?

Morley knelt next to the overturned stool and inspected the leg he'd been holding. He spotted the source of the splinter—a slim, pale crevice in the darker surface of the lightly stained wood.

How on earth had that wound up in his skin? He could understand if he'd been sliding his hand along, but he'd simply been holding it. And next to the crevice—was that another splinter angled outward?

As he adjusted his reading glasses and leaned closer, the tiny piece of wood popped out of the leg and flew at his right eye.

Morley jerked back as it bounced harmlessly off the eyeglass lens. He lost his balance and fell onto his back, but he didn't stay down. He'd gained weight in his middle years and was carrying an extra thirty pounds on his medium frame, yet he managed to roll over and do a rapid if ungainly scramble away from the footstool on his hands and knees. At sixty-two he cherished his dignity, but panic had taken over.

My God! If I hadn't been wearing glasses—!

Thankfully, he was alone. He rose, brushed himself off, and regarded the footstool from a safe distance.

Really—a "safe distance" from a little piece of furniture? Ridiculous. But his stomach roiled at the thought of how close he'd come to having a pierced cornea. Something very, very wrong here.

Rubbing his hands over his arms to counter a creeping chill, Morley surveyed his domain, a turn-of-the-century townhouse on East Thirty-first Street in the Murray Hill section of Manhattan. He and Elaine had spent just shy of a million for it in the late eighties, and it was worth multiples of that now. Its four levels of hardwood floors, cherry wainscoting, intricately carved walnut moldings and cornices were all original. They'd spent a small fortune refurbishing the interior to its original Victorian splendor and furnishing it with period antiques. After the tumor in her breast finally took Elaine in 1995, he'd stayed on here, alone but not lonely. Over the years he'd gradually removed Elaine's touches, easing her influence from the decor until the place was all him. He'd become quite content as lord of the manor.

Until now. The footstool had attracted him because of its grain, and because the style of its carving fit so seamlessly with the rest of the furniture, but he wouldn't care now if it was a genuine one-of-a-kind Victorian. That thing had to go.

Tugging at his neat salt-and-pepper beard, Morley eyed the footstool from across the room. Question was . . . how was he going to get it out of here without touching it?

The owner of Mostly Maple was at the counter when Morley walked in. Though close to Morley in age, Hal Danzer was a polar opposite. Where Morley was thick, Danzer was thin, where Morley was bearded, Danzer was clean shaven, where Morley's thin hair was neatly trimmed, Danzer's was long and thick and tied into a short ponytail.

A gallimaufry of maple pieces of varying ages, ranging from ancient to brand new, surrounded them—claw-footed tables, wardrobes, breakfronts, secretaries, desks, dressers, even old kitchen phones. Morley liked maple too, but not to the exclusion of all other woods. Danzer had once told him that he had no firm guidelines regarding his stock other than it be of maple and strike his fancy.

Morley deposited the heavy-duty canvas duffel on the counter.

"I want to return this."

Danzer stared at him. "A canvas bag?"

"No." With difficulty he refrained from adding, *you idiot.* "What's inside."

Danzer opened the bag and peeked in. He frowned. "The footstool you bought Saturday? Something wrong with it?"

Hell, yes, something was wrong with it. Very wrong.

"Take it out and you'll see."

Morley certainly wasn't going to stick his hand in there. Last night he'd pulled the old bag out of the attic and very carefully slipped it over the stool. Then, using a broom handle, he'd upended the bag and pushed the stool the rest of the way in. He was *not* going to touch it again. Let Danzer find out firsthand, as it were, what was wrong with it.

Danzer reached in and pulled out the footstool by one of its three carved legs. Morley backed up a step, waiting for his yelp of pain.

Nothing.

Danzer held up the footstool and rotated it back and forth in the light.

Nothing.

"Looks okay to me."

Morley shifted his weight off his right foot—the heel was still tender. He glanced at his bandaged left hand. He hadn't imagined those splinters.

"There, on the other leg. See those gaps in the finish? That's where slivers popped out of the wood."

Danzer twisted the stool and squinted at the wood. "I'll be damned. You're right. Popped out, you say?"

Morley held up his bandaged hand. "Right into my palm. My foot too." He left off mention of the near miss on his eye.

But why isn't anything happening to you? he wondered.

"Sorry about that. I'll replace it."

"Replace it?"

"Sure. I picked up three of them. They're identical."

Before Morley could protest, Danzer had ducked through the curtained doorway behind the counter. But come to think of it, how could he refuse a replacement? He couldn't say that this footstool, sitting inert on the counter, had assaulted him. And it *was* a beautiful little thing . . .

Danzer popped back through the curtain with another, a clone of the first. He set it on the counter.

"There you go. I checked this one over carefully and it's perfect."

Morley reached out, slowly, tentatively, and touched the wood with the fingertips of his left hand, ready to snatch them back at the first sharp sensation. But nothing happened. Gently he wrapped his hand around the leg. For an awful instant he thought he felt the carving writhe beneath his palm, but the feeling was gone before he could confirm it.

He sighed. Just wood. Heavily grained maple and nothing more.

"While I was inspecting it," Danzer said, "I noticed something interesting. Look here." He turned the stool on its side and pointed to a heavily grained area. "Check this out."

Remembering the near miss on his eye, Morley leaned closer, but not too.

"What am I looking for?"

"There, in the grain—isn't the grain just fabulous? You can see a name. Looks like 'Anna,' doesn't it?"

Simply hearing the name sent a whisper of unease through Morley. And damned if Danzer wasn't right. The word "ANNA" was indeed woven into the grain. Seeing the letters hidden like that only increased his discomfiture.

Why this unease? He didn't know anyone named Anna, could not remember *ever* knowing an Anna.

"And look," Danzer was saying. "It's here on the other one. Isn't that clever."

Again Morley looked where Danzer was pointing, and again made out the name "ANNA" worked into the grain.

Morley's tongue felt as dry as the wood that filled this store. "What's so clever?"

Danzer was grinning. "It's got to be the woodworker. She's doing a Hirschfeld."

Morley's brain seemed to be stuck in low gear. "What the hell are you talking about?"

"Hirschfeld—Al Hirschfeld, the illustrator. You've seen him a million times in the *Times* and *Playbill*. He does those line caricatures. And in every one of them for the last umpteen years he's hidden his daughter Nina's name in the drawing. This Anna is doing the same thing. The shop probably doesn't allow its woodworkers to sign their pieces, so she's sneaked her name into the grain. Probably no one else but her knows it's there."

"Except for us now."

"Yeah. Isn't that great? I just love stuff like this."

Morley said nothing as he watched the ebullient Danzer stuff the replacement footstool into the canvas duffel and hand it back.

"It's all yours."

Morley felt a little queasy, almost seasick. Part of him wanted to turn and run, but he knew he had to take that footstool home. Because it was signed, so cleverly inscribed, by Anna, whoever that was, and he must have it.

"Yes," he mumbled through the sawdust taste in his mouth. "All mine."

At home, Morley couldn't quite bring himself to put the footstool to immediate use. He removed it from the canvas bag without incurring another wound—a good sign in itself—and set it in a corner of his study. He felt a growing confidence that what had happened yesterday was an aberration, but he could not yet warm to the piece. Perhaps in time . . . when he'd figured out why the name Anna stirred up such unsettling echoes.

He heard the clank of the mail slot and went down to the first floor to collect the day's letters: a good-sized stack of the usual variety of junk circulars, come-ons, confirmation slips from his broker, and pitches from various charities. Very little of a personal nature.

Still shuffling through the envelopes, he had just reentered the study when his foot caught on something. Suddenly he was falling forward. The mail went flying as he flung out his arms to prevent himself from landing on his face. He hit the floor with a brain-jarring, rib-cracking thud that knocked the wind out of him.

It took a good half minute before he could breathe again. When he finally rolled over, he looked around to see what had tripped him—and froze.

The footstool sat dead center in the entry to the study.

A tremor rattled through Morley. He'd left the stool in the corner—he was certain of it. Or at least, pretty certain. He was more certain that furniture didn't move around on its own, so perhaps he hadn't put it in the corner, merely intended to, and hadn't got around to it yet.

Right now he wasn't certain of what he could be certain of.

Morley found himself wide awake at three a.m. He'd felt ridiculous stowing the footstool in a closet, but had to admit he felt safer with it tucked away behind a closed door two floors below. That name—*Anna*—was keeping him awake. He'd sifted through his memories, from boyhood to the present, and could not come up with a single Anna. The word was a palindrome, so reversing the order was futile; the only workable anagram was also worthless—he'd never known a "Nana" either.

So why had the sight of those letters set alarm bells ringing?

Not only was it driving him crazy, it was making him thirsty.

Morley reached for the bottle of Evian he kept on the night table—empty. Damn. He got out of bed in the dark and headed for the first floor. Enough light filtered through the windows from the city outside to allow him a faint view of where he was going, but as he neared the top of the stairs, he felt a growing unease in his gut. He slowed, then stopped. He didn't understand. He hadn't heard a noise, but he could feel the wiry hairs at the back of his neck rise in warning. Something not right here. He reached out, found the wall switch, and flicked it.

The footstool sat at the top of the stairway.

Morley's knees threatened to give way and he had to lean against the wall to keep them from crumbling. If he hadn't turned on the light he surely would have tripped over it and tumbled down the steps, very likely to his death.

"That footstool! Where did you get it?"

After a couple of seconds' pause, Danzer's voice came back over the line. "What? Who is this?"

Morley rubbed his eyes. He hadn't slept all night. After kicking the footstool down the hallway and locking it in a spare bedroom, he'd sat up the rest of the night with the room key clutched in his fist. As soon as ten a.m. rolled around—the time when Danzer opened his damn store—he'd started dialing.

"It's Bill Morley. Where did you buy that footstool?"

"At a regional woodworker's expo on Cape Cod."

"From whom? I need a name!"

"Why?"

"I just do! Are you going to tell me or not?"

"Hold your horses, will you? Let me look it up." Papers shuffled, then: "Here it is . . . Charles Ansbach. 'Custom and Original Woodwork.'"

"Charles? I thought it was supposed to be 'Anna.'"

Danzer laughed. "Oh, you mean because of the name in the grain. Who knows? Maybe this Anna works for him. Maybe she bought his business. Maybe—"

"Never mind! Where can I find this Charles Ansbach?"

"His address is Twelve Spinnaker Lane, Nantucket."

"Nantucket?" Morley felt his palm begin to sweat where it clutched the receiver in a sudden death grip. "Did you say Nantucket?"

"That's what's written here on his invoice."

Morley hung up the phone without saying good-bye and sat there trembling.

Nantucket . . . of all places, why did it have to be Nantucket? He'd buried his first wife, Julie, there. And he'd sworn he'd never set foot on that damn island again.

But now he must break that vow. He had to go back. How else could he find out who Anna was? And he must learn that. He doubted he would sleep a wink until he did.

At least he hadn't had to take the ferry. No matter how badly he wanted to track down this Anna person, nothing in the world could make him ride that ferry again.

After jetting in from LaGuardia, Morley stepped into one of the beat-up station wagons that passed for taxis on Nantucket and gave the overweight woman behind the wheel the address.

"Goin' to Charlie Ansbach's place, ay? You know him?"

"We've never met. Actually, I'm more interested in someone named Anna who works for him."

"Anna?" the woman said as they pulled away from the tiny airport. "Don't know of any Anna workin' for Charlie. Tell the truth, don't know of any Anna connected to Charlie at all."

That didn't bode well. Nantucket was less than fifteen miles long and barely four across at its widest point. The islanders were an insular group who weathered long, isolated off-seasons together; as a result they tended to know each other like kin, and were always into each other's business.

As the taxi took him toward town along Old South Road, Morley marveled at the changes since his last look in the seventies. Decades and an extended bull market had transformed the island. New construction was everywhere. Even now, in post-season October, with the oaks and maples turning gold and orange, new houses were going up. Nantucket ordinances allow little variation in architecture—clapboard or cedar shakes or else—but the newer buildings were identifiable by their unweathered siding.

Nantucket had always been an old-money island, a summer hideaway for the very wealthy from New York, Connecticut, and Massachusetts—Old Money attached to names that never made the papers. The Kennedys, the Carly Simons and James Taylors, the Spike Lees and other spotlight-hungry sorts preferred Martha's Vineyard. Morley remembered walking through town here in the summer when the island's population explodes, when the streets would be thick with tourists fresh off the ferry for the day. They'd stroll Main Street or the docks in their pristine, designer leisure wear, ogling all the yachts. Salted among them would be these middle-aged men in faded jerseys and torn shorts stained with fish blood, who drove around in rusty Wagoneers and rumbling Country Squires. Deck hands? No, these were the owners of the yachts, who lived in the big houses up on Cliff Road and on the bluffs overlooking Brant Point. The more Old Money they had, the closer to homeless they looked.

"Seems to be houses everywhere," Morley said. "Whatever happened to the conservancy?"

"Alive and well," the driver replied. "It's got forty-eight percent of the land now, and more coming in. If nothing else, it'll guarantee that at least half of the island will remain in its natural state, God bless 'em."

Morley didn't offer an amen. The conservancy had been part of all his troubles here.

The cab skirted the north end of town and hooked up with Madaket Road. More new houses. If only he'd held on to the land longer after Julie's death, think what it might be worth now.

He shook his head. No looking back. He'd sold off the land piece by piece over the years, and made a handsome profit. Prudent investing had quadrupled the original yield. He had no complaints on that score.

He noticed groups of grouselike birds here and there along the shoulder of the road, and asked the driver about them.

"Guinea hens. Cousins to the turkey, only dumber. We imported a bunch of them a few years ago and they're multiplying like crazy."

"For hunting?"

"No. For ticks. We're hoping they'll eat up the deer ticks. Lymes disease, you know."

Morley was tempted to tell her that it was *Lyme* disease—no terminal s-but decided against it.

Spinnaker Lane was a pair of sandy ruts through the dense thicket of bayberry and beach plum south of Eel Point Road. Number twelve turned out to be a well-weathered Cape Cod with a large work shed out back.

"Wait for me," Morley told the driver.

He heard the whine of an electric saw from the shed so he headed that way. He found an angular man with wild salty hair leaning over a table saw, skinning the bark off a log. A kiln sat in the far corner. The man looked up at Morley's approach, squinting his blue eyes through the smoke from the cigarette dangling at the corner of his mouth.

"Charles Ansbach?"

"That's me." His face was as weathered as the siding on his shed. "What's up?"

Morley decided to cut to the chase. These islanders would talk your head off about nothing if you gave them half the chance.

"I'm looking for Anna."

"Anna who?"

"She works for you."

"Sorry, mister. No Anna working for me, now or ever."

"Oh, no?" Morley said, feeling a flush of anger. He was in no mood for games. "Then why is she working her name into the grain of your furniture?"

Ansbach's blue eyes widened, then he grinned. "So, you spotted that too, ay?"

"Where is she?"

"Told you: Ain't no Anna."

"Then *you're* doing it?"

"Ain't me, either. It's in the grain. Damnedest thing I ever seen." He glanced down and blew sawdust off the log he'd been working on. He pointed to a spot. "Here's more of it, right here."

Morley stepped closer and leaned over the table. The grain was less prominent in the unstained wood, but his gut began to crawl as he picked out the letters of "ANNA" fitted among the wavy lines.

"It's uncanny," he whispered.

"More than uncanny, mister. It's all through every piece of wood I got from that tree. Downright spooky, if you ask me."

"What tree?"

"From the old Lange place. When I heard they was taking down one of the big maples there, I went to see it. When I spotted the grain I realized it was a curly maple. You don't see many curly maples, and I never seen one like this— magnificent grain. I bought the whole tree. Kept some for myself and sold the rest to a coupla custom wood workers on the mainland. Got a good price for it too. But I never . . ."

Ansbach's voice faded into the growing roar that filled Morley's ears. The strength seemed to have deserted his legs and he slumped against the table.

Ansbach's voice cut through the roar. "Hey, mister, you all right?"

All right? No, he was not all right—he was *far* from all right. All right for him was somewhere out near Alpha Centauri. But he nodded and forced himself to straighten and stagger away.

"What's wrong, mister?" Ansbach called after him but Morley didn't reply, didn't wave good-bye. He sagged into the rear seat of the taxi and sat there trying to catch his breath.

"You look like you just seen a ghost!" the driver said.

"Do you know the old Lange place?" Morley gasped.

"Course. Ain't been a Lange there for a long time, though."

"Take me there."

My tree! My tree! Morley thought. Have they cut it down?

Perhaps not. Perhaps it had been another tree. He couldn't remember any other maples on the house property, and yet it must have been another tree, not *his* tree. Because if they'd cut down his tree they would have removed the stump. And in doing so they inevitably would have found Julie's bones.

The taxi pulled off Cliff Road and stopped in front of the Lange place. The house itself looked pretty much the same, but Morley barely recognized its surroundings. Once the only dwelling on a fifty-two-acre parcel between Cliff and Madaket Roads, it now stood surrounded by houses. Morley's doing. He'd sold them the land.

Panic gripped him as he searched the roof line and saw no maple branches peeking over from the backyard. He told the driver to wait again and hurried around the north corner of the house, passing a silver Mercedes SUV on the way. He caught his breath when he reached the rear. His maple was gone, and in its place sat . . . a picnic table.

As he staggered toward it, he noticed the table's base—a tree stump. His tree was gone but they hadn't pulled the stump!

Morley dropped into a chair by the table and almost wept with relief.

"Can I help you?"

Morley looked up and saw a mid-thirties yuppie type walking his way across the lawn. His expression was wary, verging on hostile. With good reason: Who was this stranger in his yard?

Morley rose from the chair and composed himself. "Sorry for intruding," he said. "I used to live here. I planted this tree back in the seventies."

The man's expression immediately softened. "No kidding? Are you Lange?"

"No. It was the Lange place before I moved in, and remained the Lange place while I was living here. It will always be known as the Lange place."

"So I've gathered."

"What happened to my tree?"

"It got damaged in that nor'easter last fall. Big branch tore off and stripped a lot of bark. I had a tree surgeon patch it up but by last spring it was obvious the tree was doomed. So I had it taken down. But I left the stump. Put it to pretty good use, don't you think?"

"Excellent use," Morley said with heartfelt sincerity. Bless you, sir.

"The center is drilled to hold an umbrella in season."

"How clever. It's a wonderful addition to the yard. Don't ever change it."

Morley suffered through a little more small talk before he could extract himself. He rode back to the airport in silent exhaustion. When he finally reached his first-class seat for the return to LaGuardia, he ordered a double Macallan on the rocks and settled back to try to sort out what the hell was going on. But when he glanced out his window and saw the Nantucket ferry chugging out of the harbor far below, the events of the most nerve-wracking and potentially catastrophic twenty-four hours of his life engulfed him in a screaming rush . . .

The trouble with Julie Lange was that she was a rich girl who didn't know how to play the part. She didn't appreciate the finer things money could buy. She was just as happy with something from the JCPenney's catalog as a one-of-a-kind designer piece. She had no desire for the style of life and level of comfort to which her new husband desperately wished to become accustomed.

But young Bill Morley hadn't realized this when he started courting her in the big-haired, long-sideburned, bell-bottomed late sixties and early seventies. All he knew was that she was pretty, bright, fun, and rich. And when they eventually married, he was ecstatic to learn that her father was giving them the Nantucket family summer house and adjacent acreage as a wedding present.

That was the good news. The bad news was that Julie wanted to live there year round. Bill had said he wanted to write, hadn't he? Nantucket would be the perfect place, especially in the winter when there were no distractions.

No distractions . . . a magnificent understatement. The damn island was virtually deserted in the winter. Bill contracted island fever early on and was a raw nerve by the time spring rolled around. He begged Julie to sell the place and move to the mainland.

But oh no, she couldn't sell the family home. She'd spent almost every summer of her life at the Lange place. Besides, who would want to leave Nantucket? It was the best place on earth.

She just couldn't see: The island was paradise to her, but to him it was hell on earth.

Bill fumed. He could *not* survive another winter on this island. He cudgeled his brain for a way out, and came up with a brilliant solution: How about we keep the house but sell off the fifty acres of undeveloped land and use the money from that to buy a place near Boston? We can live there in the winter and still summer here. Cool, huh?

But Julie simply laughed and said she couldn't bear the thought of anyone but a Lange living on the land where she'd roamed and camped out during her childhood. In fact, she'd been looking into donating it to the conservancy so that it would always remain in its wild, undeveloped state.

Which left Billy three choices, none of which was particularly appealing. He could stay with Julie on Nantucket and devolve into drooling incoherence.

Or he could file for divorce and never see this island again, but that would mean cutting himself off from the Lange estate, all of which would go to Julie when her old man died.

Or Julie could die.

He reluctantly opted for the last. He wasn't a killer, and not a particularly violent man, but an entire winter on this glorified sandbar had shaken something loose inside. And besides, he deserved to come out of this marriage with something more than a bad memory.

But he'd have to make his move soon, before Julie handed fifty acres of prime land over to the stupid damn conservancy.

So he convinced Julie that the backyard needed some landscaping. And on a bright Friday afternoon in June, after solidifying the plan and setting up all the props he'd need, Bill Morley sat on his back porch and watched the landscapers put the finishing touches on the free-form plantings in the backyard. He waved to them as they left, then waited for Julie to return from town where she'd been running errands and shopping and doing whatever she did.

Carrying a three-iron casually across a shoulder, he met her in the foyer when she came home, and she looked so bright, so cheery, so happy to be alive that he gave her one last chance to change her mind. But Julie barely listened. She brushed off the whole subject, saying she didn't want to talk about selling houses or land or moving because she had something to tell him.

Whatever it was, she never got the chance. He hit her with the golf club. Hard. Three times. She dropped to the floor like a sack of sand, not moving, not breathing.

As soon as it was dark, Bill began digging up one of the landscapers' plantings. He removed the burlap-wrapped root ball of a young maple and dug a much larger hole under it. Julie and the three iron went into the bottom of that, the maple went on top of her, and everything was packed down with a nice thick layer of dirt. He wheelbarrowed the leftover soil into the woods she'd planned to give away, and spread it in the brush. He cleaned up before dawn, took a nap, then headed for town.

He parked their car in the Steamship Authority lot and bought two tickets to Hyannis on the next ferry, making sure to purchase them with a credit card. Then he ducked into the men's room. In a stall, he turned one of Julie's dark blue sweatshirts inside out and squeezed into it—luckily she liked them big and baggy. He put on the fake mustache he'd bought in Falmouth two weeks before, added big, dark sunglasses, then pulled the sweatshirt hood over his head.

The mustachioed man paid cash for his ticket and waited in line with the rest of the ferry passengers. As he stood there, he used the cover of his sunglasses to check out the women with long blond hair, cataloging their attire. He spotted at least four wearing flowered tops and bell-bottom jeans. Good. Now he knew what he'd say Julie was wearing.

Once aboard, the mustachioed man entered one of the ship's rest rooms where he broke the sunglasses and threw them in the trash. After flushing the mustache he emerged as Bill Morley with the sweatshirt—now right-side out—balled in his hand. While passengers milled about the aft deck, he discreetly draped the sweatshirt over the back of a chair and headed for the snack bar.

After that he played an increasingly confused, frightened, and eventually panicked young husband looking for his lost wife. He'd gone to get her a cup of coffee, and when he came back she was . . . gone.

Morley smiled at how perfectly the plan had worked. The police and his father-in-law had been suspicious—wasn't the husband always suspect?—but hadn't been able to punch a hole in his story. And since Julie wasn't carrying a speck of life insurance, no clear motive.

The disguise had proved a big help. If he'd stood on line as Bill Morley, someone very well might have remembered that he'd been alone. But as it turned out, no one could say they'd noticed Bill Morley at all, with or without his wife, until he'd begun wandering the decks, looking for her.

But it had been his fellow passengers who'd helped him the most. A number of them swore they'd seen a woman aboard matching Julie's description. Of course they had—Morley had made sure of that. One couple even identified Julie's picture. As a result, the long, unsuccessful search focused on the thirty-mile ferry route. No one gave a thought to digging up the yard back on Nantucket.

Final consensus: 1) Julia Lange Morley either fell or jumped unnoticed from the ferry; or 2) she was a victim of foul play—killed or knocked unconscious and transported off the ferry in the trunk of one of the cars riding on the lower deck.

Neither seemed likely, but once one accepted the fact that Julie had embarked but not debarked, those were the possibilities that remained.

Morley had kept the house for a while but didn't live there. Instead he mortgaged it and used the money to lease an apartment in Greenwich Village. It was the disco seventies, with long nights of dancing, drugs, and debauchery. In the summers he rented out the Lange place for a tidy sum, and forced himself to pay a visit every so often. He was especially interested in the growth of a certain young maple—*his* maple.

And now it seemed his maple had come back to haunt him.

Haunt . . . poor choice of words.

And perhaps he should start calling it Julie's maple.

All right: What did he know—really *know*?

Whether through extreme coincidence, fate, or a manipulation of destiny, he had purchased a piece of maple furniture made from the very tree he'd placed over Julie's corpse nearly thirty years ago. That seemed to be the only hard fact he could rely on.

After that, the assumptions grew murky and fantastic. Much as he hated saying it, he had no choice: The wood from that tree appeared to be possessed.

Two days ago he would have laughed aloud at the very suggestion of a haunted footstool, but after numerous injuries and one potentially fatal close call, Morley was unable to muster even a sneer today.

He didn't believe in ghosts or haunted houses, let alone haunted footstools, but how else to explain the events of the past two days?

But just for the sake of argument, even if it *were* possible for Julie's soul or essence or whatever to become a part of that young maple as it grew—after all, its roots had fed on the nutrients released by her decomposing body—why wasn't JULIE worked into the grain? Why ANNA?

Morley's second scotch hit him and he felt his eyelids growing heavy. He let them close and drifted into a semiconscious state where floating woodgrains morphed from JULIE to ANNA and back again . . . JULIE . . . ANNA . . . JULIE . . . ANNA . . . JULIE—

"Dear God!" he cried, awakening with a start.

The flight attendant rushed to his side. "Is something wrong, sir?"

"No," he gasped. "I'm all right. Really."

But Morley wasn't all right. His insides were strangling themselves in a Gordian knot. He'd just had an inkling about Anna, and if he was correct, *nothing* was all right. Nothing at all.

As soon as Morley was through the airport gate, he found a seat, pulled out his cell phone, and dialed Nantucket information. He asked the operator to read off all the names on the short list of doctors practicing on the island. She did, but none of them rang a bell.

"He might not be in practice anymore." Might not even be alive, though Morley prayed he was. "He was a GP—my wife saw him back in the seventies."

"That was probably Doc Lawrence. He's retired now but his home phone's listed."

Lawrence! Yes, that was it! He dialed the number and a moment later found himself talking to Charles Lawrence, M.D., elderly, somewhat hard of hearing, but still in possession of most of his marbles.

"Of course I remember your wife. Saw Julie Lange at least twice a summer for one thing or another all the years she was growing up. Did they ever find her?"

"Not a trace."

"What a shame. Such a nice girl."

"She certainly was. But let me ask you something, Doctor. I was just out visiting the old place and it occurred to me that Julie had an appointment with you the day before she disappeared. Did you . . . discover anything that might have upset her?"

"Not at all. In fact, quite the opposite. She was absolutely overjoyed about being pregnant."

Morley was glad he was already sitting as all of LaGuardia seemed to tilt under him. Even so, he feared he might tumble from the chair.

"Hello?" Dr. Lawrence said. "Are you still there?"

"Yes," he croaked. His tongue felt like Velcro.

"You sound as if this is news to you. I assumed she told you."

"Yes, of course she did," Morley said, his mind racing. "That's why we were heading for the mainland—to surprise her father. I never had the heart to tell him after she . . ."

"Yeah, I know. That made it a double tragedy."

Morley extricated himself from the conversation as quickly as possible, then sat and stared at nothing, the cell phone resting in his sweating palm, cold damp terror clutching at his heart.

On the last day of her life, Julie had driven into town to run some errands and to see Doc Lawrence for "a check-up." A check-up . . . young Bill Morley had been too involved in planning his wife's demise to question her about that, but now he knew what had been going on. Julie must have missed her period. No such thing as a home pregnancy test back then, so she'd gone to the doctor to have it done. That was what she'd wanted to tell him before he cracked her skull with the three iron.

Julie had often talked about starting a family . . . not if—*when*. When she talked of a son, she never mentioned a name; but whenever she spoke of having a daughter, she knew what she wanted to call her. A name she loved.

Anna.

Julie had always intended to call her little girl Anna.

Morley felt weak. He closed his eyes. Something had invaded the wood of that tree, and the wood of that tree had invaded his house, his life. Was it Anna, the tiny little life that had been snuffed out along with her mother's, or was it Julie, seeking vengeance in the name of the child who would never be born?

How did it go? Heaven has no rage like love to hatred turned, Nor hell a fury like a woman scorned.

But what of a woman never allowed to be born?

Morley shuddered. It didn't matter who, really. Either way, measures had to be taken, and he knew exactly what he needed to do.

Night had fallen by the time Morley got home. He entered his house cautiously, turning on lights in each room, hallway, and staircase before he proceeded. When he reached the living room he went directly to the fireplace, opened the flue, and lit the kindling beneath the stack of aged logs on the grate.

He waited until he had a roaring fire, then went to the hall closet and removed a heavy winter blanket. With this tucked under his arm, Morley headed up the stairs—turning lights on as he went—to the floor where he'd locked the footstool in the spare bedroom.

He hesitated outside the door, heart pounding, hands trembling. He tried the knob—still locked, thank God. He turned the key and opened the door just enough to snake his hand in and turn on the light. Then, taking a deep breath, he pushed the door open.

The footstool lay on its side, exactly as he had left it.

He felt a little silly now. What had he been afraid of? Had he been half expecting it to jump at him?

But Morley was taking no chances. He threw the blanket over the stool, bundled it up, and carried it downstairs where he dumped it in front of the fireplace. Using the log tongs, he pulled the stool free and consigned it to the flames.

He watched the curly maple burn.

He wasn't sure what he expected next. A scream? The legs of the stool writhing in pain? None of that happened. It simply lay there atop the other logs and . . . burned. At one point he leaned closer, trying for one last peek at the name hidden in the grain, but the heat drove him back before he could find it.

Anna . . . his child's name . . . he thought he should feel something, but he was empty of all emotions except relief. He never knew her . . . how could he feel anything for her? And as for Julie . . .

"It's too bad you had to die," he whispered as the varnish on the wood bubbled and blackened. "But you left me no choice. And as for coming back and interfering with my life, that's not going to happen. I'd all but forgotten about you—and now I'll go about forgetting you again."

Morley watched the fabric and padding of the stool dissolve in a burst of flame, watched the wood of the seat and legs char and smoke and burn and crumble. He remained before the fire until every last splinter of the stool had been reduced to ash.

Finally he rose and yawned. A long, hard day, but a fruitful one. He looked around. His home was his again, purged of a malign influence. But how to keep it from re-entering?

Easy: Morley resolved never to buy another stick of furniture that wasn't at least a hundred years old.

With that settled, he headed upstairs for a well-deserved night's rest. In his bedroom he pulled out the third drawer in his antique pine dresser. As he bent to retrieve a pair of pajamas, the top drawer slid open and slammed against his forehead.

Clutching his head, Morley staggered back. His foot caught on the leg of a chair—a chair that shouldn't have been there, *hadn't* been there a moment ago—and he tumbled to the floor. He landed on his back, groaning with the pain of the impact. As he opened his eyes, he looked up and saw the antique mahogany wardrobe tilting away from the wall, leaning over him, *falling!*

With a terrified cry he rolled out of the way. The heavy wardrobe landed with a floor-jarring crash just inches from his face. Morley started to struggle to his feet but froze when he saw the letters worked into the grain of the wardrobe's flank: ANNA.

With a hoarse cry he lunged away and rose to his hands and knees—just in time to see a two-foot splinter of wood stab through the oriental rug—exactly where he'd been only a heartbeat before. He clambered to his feet and ducked away as his dresser tumbled toward him. On its unfinished rear panel he saw the name ANNA wrapped around one of its knots.

Caught in the ice-fisted grip of blind, screaming panic, Morley lurched toward the door, dodging wooden spears that slashed through the rug.

Julie . . . Anna . . . or whoever or whatever it was had somehow seeped out of the footstool and infected the entire room. He had to get out!

Ahead of him he saw the heavy oak door begin to swing shut. No! He couldn't be trapped in here! He leaped forward and ducked through the door an instant before it slammed closed.

Gasping, Morley sagged against the hallway wall. Close. Too close. He—

Pain lanced into his ankle. He looked down and saw a foot-long splinter of floorboard piecing his flesh. And all up and down the hall the floorboards writhed and buckled, thrusting up jagged, quivering knife-sharp spikes.

Morley ran, dodging and leaping down the hall as wooden spears stabbed his lower legs, ripping his clothes. Where to go? Downstairs—out! He couldn't stay in the house—it was trying to kill him!

He reached the stairs and kept going. He felt the wooden treads tilting under his feet, trying to send him tumbling. He grabbed the banister and it exploded into splinters at his touch, peppering him with a thousand wooden nails. He slammed against the stairwell wall but managed to keep his footing until the next to last step when he tripped and landed on the tiled floor of the front foyer.

What now? his fear-crazed mind screamed. Would the tiles crack into ceramic daggers and cut him to shreds?

But the foyer floor lay cool and inert beneath him.

Of course, he thought, rising to his knees. It's not wood. Whatever was in the footstool has managed to infiltrate the wood of the house, but has no power over anything else. As long as I stay on a tile or linoleum floor—

Morley instinctively ducked at the sound of a loud *crack!* behind him, and felt something whiz past his head. When he looked up he saw one of the balusters from the staircase jutting from the wall, vibrating like an arrow in a bull's-eye. At that instant the upper border of the wainscoting splintered from the wall and stabbed him in the belly—not a deep wound, but it drew blood.

And then the entire foyer seemed to explode—the wainscoting panels shredding and flying at him, balusters zipping through the air, molding peeling from the ceiling and lancing at him.

Morley dashed for the front door. Moving in a crouch, he reached the handle and pulled. He sobbed with joy when it swung open. He stumbled into the cool night air and slammed the door shut behind him.

Battered, bruised, bleeding, he gripped the wrought iron railing—metal: cold, hard, wonderful, reliable metal—and slumped onto the granite slabs of his front steps where he sobbed and retched and thanked the stars that years ago he'd taken a contractor's advice and replaced the original oak door with a steel model. For security reasons, the contractor had said. That decision had just saved his life.

He'd lost his home. No place in that building was safe for him—even being this close to it could be dangerous. He fought to his feet and staggered across the glorious concrete of the sidewalk to lean against the magnificent steel of one of the parked cars. Safe.

And then something bounced off his head and dropped to the sidewalk. Morley squinted in the darkness. An acorn. Dear God!

He lurched away from the overhanging oak and didn't stop moving until he was a good dozen feet from the tree.

An accident? A coincidence? After all, it was October, the time of year when oaks began dropping acorns.

But how could he be sure that even the trees hadn't turned against him?

He needed a safe place where he could rest and tend his wounds and clear his head and not spend every moment fearing for his life. A place with no wood, a place where he could *think!* Tomorrow, in the light of day, he could solve this problem, but until then . . .

He knew the place. That newly restored hotel on West Thirty-fifth Street—the Deco. He'd been to an art show there last month and remembered how he'd loathed its decor—all gleaming steel and glass and chrome, so completely lacking in the warmth and richness of the wood that filled his home.

What a laugh! Now it seemed like Mecca, like Paradise.

The Deco wasn't far. Giving the scattered trees a wide berth, Morley began walking.

"Sir, you're bleeding," said the clerk at the reception desk. "Shall I call a doctor?"

I know damn well I'm bleeding, Morley wanted to shout, but held his tongue. He was in a foul mood, but at least he wasn't bleeding as much as before.

"I've already seen a doctor," he lied.

"May I ask what happened?"

This twerp of a desk clerk had a shaved head, a natty little mustache, and a pierced eyebrow that rose as he finished the question. His name tag read Wölf. Really.

"Automobile accident." Morley fumbled through his wallet. "My luggage is wrecked, but I still have this." He slapped his Amex Platinum down on the black marble counter.

The clerk wiggled his eyebrow stud and picked up the card.

"I must stress one thing," Morley said. "I want a room with no wood in it. None. Got that?"

The stud dipped as the clerk frowned. "No wood . . . let me think . . . the only room that would fit that is the Presidential Suite. It was just refurbished in metal and glass. But the rate is—"

"Never mind the rate. I want it."

As the clerk nodded and got to work, Morley did a slow turn and looked around. What a wonderful place. Steel, brass, chrome, marble, glass, ceramic. Lovely because this was the way the future was supposed to look when the here-and-now was the future . . . a future without wood.

Lovely.

He did not let the bellhop go—though Morley had no luggage, the man had escorted him to the eighth floor—until he had made a careful inspection. The clerk had been right: not a stick of wood in the entire suite.

As soon as he was alone, Morley stripped and stepped into the shower. The water stung his wounds, but the warm flow eased his battered muscles and sluiced away the dried blood. He wrapped himself in the oversized terry cloth robe and headed straight for the bedroom.

As he reached for the covers he paused, struck by the huge chrome head-board. At its center, rising above the spread wings that stretched to the edges of the king-size mattress, was the giant head of a bald eagle with a wickedly pointed beak. So lifelike, Morley could almost imagine a predatory gleam in its metallic eye.

But no time for aesthetics tonight. He was exhausted. He craved the oblivion of sleep to escape the horrors of the day. Tomorrow, refreshed, clear-headed, he would tackle the problem head on, find a way to exorcise Julie or Anna from his home. But now, tonight . . .

Morley pulled back the covers and collapsed onto the silk sheets. Hello, Morpheus, good-bye, Anna . . .

Wölf spots the night manager crossing the lobby and motions him over.

"Mr. Halpern, I just had a guest here who insisted on a room with no wood—absolutely no wood in it. I gave him the Presidential Suite. I believe that's all metal and glass and such, right?"

"It was until yesterday," Halpern says. He's fortyish and probably thinks the curly toupee makes him look thirtyish. It doesn't. "The designer moved in a new headboard. Said he found it in a Massachusetts wood shop. Brand new and carved out of heavily grained maple. But he went and had it coated with so many layers of chrome paint it looks like solid steel. Said he couldn't resist the

eagle. Can't say as I blame him—looks like it came straight off the Chrysler Building."

"Should I inform the guest?"

"What? And disturb his sleep?" Halpern waves a dismissive hand and strolls away. "Let the man be. What he doesn't know won't hurt him."

2000–2002

Now I go three years without a short story.

I have a good explanation for that. No, I didn't return to the interactive field. Novels . . . novels and novellas were to blame.

2000

I guess you could call this my Cemetery Dance year.

I started off writing the first two *Sims* novellas back to back, finished them, then sent them to Rich Chizmar. I wanted to keep rolling on the story but I was under contract to deliver the fifth Repairman Jack novel in the fall, so that took precedence. I decided to call it *Hosts*.

The *Conspiracies* trade edition was published in February and Dark Delicacies, the famous Burbank bookstore, flew me out for a signing. Afterward I sat down with Craig Spector and Richard C. Matheson who convinced me to throw some of my backlist in with a new publisher named Stealth Press. It didn't take much convincing: Pat Lobrutto was the editor and he wanted to put my old sf back into print. He'd been one of the editors with Doubleday back in the 1970s who'd first put it into print. (Amazing how the wheel turns.) What else did I have to hear?

On the movie front, a guy named Scott Nimerfro was chosen to rewrite *Repairman Jack*. Since things seemed to be flowing smoothly, I okayed another option renewal. By June the Nimerfro rewrite was "not quite there yet." In October, while out in L.A. for an *All the Rage* signing at Dark Delicacies, I had breakfast with producers Barry Rosenbush and Bill Borden who told me that Nimerfro was out, all scripts had been scrapped, and they were looking for a new writer. They eventually hired a guy named Trevor Sands. I didn't know it then, but this was the beginning of a recurring scenario.

In March I traveled to St. Augustine to see the opening of "Syzygy." A modest production, to say the least, but an enthusiastic cast. And the audience screamed and laughed in all the right places.

While talking to Rich Chizmar in June he asked me if I had anything lying around that he could publish. I said the only unpublished piece was a Christmas story I used to read to my daughters when they were young. I thought it was still on a disk somewhere. He wanted to see it so I sent him *The Christmas Thingy.* He called back the next day and said he wanted to publish it. In fact, he'd already lined up Alan Clark to do the art. How could I say no?

Sims-1 (*La Causa*) was published in July and quickly sold out. I finished a draft of *Hosts* in September and started in on *Sims-3.*

Here I ran into a bit of a problem. I hadn't fully outlined the series (I'm one of those anal types who likes to travel with a map, but here I thought I'd indulge in a tightrope-without-a-safety-net approach), and now when I went back to the story I discovered things I wished I'd put in the first two novellas. But it was too late: *La Causa* was in print and the second, *The Portero Method,* was on its way.

So I adjusted. I finished the third, *Meerm,* by mid-October and *Zero* by early December. *The Portero Method* had yet to appear.

By now a number of the regulars on the repairmanjack.com forum had become so close and were in contact so often in virtual space that they decided to get together in person. They chose the last weekend in October in Baltimore for what they called the Grand Unification (after the story cross-reference graphic on the Web site). I shocked them by driving down and joining them for dinner on Saturday night. (How could I not? One fellow had come all the way from England.) Great fun, great people. They love each other like family and I feel like a proud father for having brought them together. The GU, as it's called, has become an annual event, and each year it gets a little bigger.

All the Rage was published in October, *The Christmas Thingy* in November, and the Stealth Press reprint of *Healer* in December.

Two new novels, a novella, and a Christmas story published, plus my first novel resurrected. But no short story.

2001

A nothing-special year.

Beacon wanted to extend the film option on *The Tomb* for eighteen months this time. I gathered that Trevor Sands was not wowing anyone with his rewrite. It occurred to me to say no. I'd signed the original option when there had been only one Repairman Jack novel. Now there were four and a fifth due soon. My agent was getting calls from one studio or production company after another asking about film rights to Jack. I could auction them for a tidy piece of change. And if not for Barry Rosenbush, a true believer in putting Jack on the screen since the 1980s, I would have. Instead we renegotiated a few points and I signed.

I finished the last *Sims* novella and handed in volumes three, four, and five to Cemetery Dance in a single package. Then I started Repairman Jack number 6. The working title was *Spirits* which I later changed to *The Haunted Air*.

Sims-2 was being held up by delayed art but Rich assured me that all five parts would be published within the next twelve months.

I'd written the *Sims* novellas with an eye toward collecting all five in one volume after CD published them. So I melded them, changing the order of some events for a smoother flow, and took the novelized version to Forge. They bought it but said it couldn't be scheduled until 2003. This was fine with me because that would give Rich extra time to get all five novellas into print first.

I'd optioned the *Midnight Mass* novella to a local fellow named Tony Mandile who managed to come up with half a million in financing. He began shooting his film.

And that got me thinking about *Midnight Mass* again. I'd long intended to blend it with "Good Friday" and "The Lord's Work" and expand them to a novel. Now seemed like the time to do it. Since a good portion of the novel had already been published elsewhere, I doubted a regular trade publisher would be interested. So on the way back from Baltimore one Sunday morning in October I had breakfast with Rich and offered it to him. He wanted it.

Later on my agent reminded me that Forge had first look at my next novel—it was in all my contracts. Fine. I sent the stories and a treatment of how the rest of the novel would go to my editor, David Hartwell. I figured he'd pass. But no. He wanted it. So now I had to tell Rich the deal was off. He did do a beautiful, Harry Morris–illustrated limited edition, however.

The paperback of *All the Rage* was a September release, followed by the *Hosts* hardcover in October. Both tanked for an obvious reason.

I was in Nantucket, speeding through the last quarter of *The Haunted Air*, when Bin Laden's puppets destroyed the World Trade towers. Like everyone else, I was a long, long time recovering from the shock (but not the rage—that's a keeper). When I finally returned to the novel I found myself, for the first time in my life, unable to write. Thriller fiction seemed so . . . pointless. Who was I kidding? I was a piker. Nothing I put on paper could hold a candle to present-day reality. But I pushed into it. I wasn't writing about the real world. In the novel I was in control. I could make sure the bad guys got what they deserved. I found some comfort in that.

2002

The Haunted Air came in much longer than I'd anticipated (150,000 words) and I didn't finish it until the end of January—two months late. I immediately started on the *Midnight Mass* novel.

Meanwhile my agent had found a publisher for *The Fifth Harmonic*: a new-age imprint in Virginia called Hampton Roads. The money wasn't much, but at least the novel would be available.

On the movie front, Trevor Sands was out and another screenwriter was in. I'd heard that somewhere along the line, studio head Army Bernstein had written his own *Repairman Jack* script and sent it out to a number of directors. Chuck Russell (*The Scorpion King*) and Jim Gillespie (*I Know What You Did Last Summer*) reportedly told him they were Repairman Jack fans and that the Jack in his script was not the guy they knew. Whatever. I was fed up. I let it be known that there'd be no new option for Beacon.

In May I was impaneled as a judge for the World Fantasy Award. More than two hundred books and magazines would arrive at my door over the next few months.

In July I finished *Midnight Mass* and jumped into *Gateways* the following week. I didn't want to deliver late again.

In the summer Beacon Films got a *Repairman Jack* script they loved from a writer named Chris Morgan. A day before the option ran out they triggered their right to buy. They now owned film rights to my guy. It was a bittersweet situation: I received a nice fat check but I'd lost control of my novel and my character. Repairman Jack belonged to someone else.

Sims-3 (*Meerm*) was published in August, and *The Haunted Air* in October.

In November I was wined and dined by the Beacon folks, invited to the premiere of their latest film, *The Emperor's Club*, and told that Touchstone's projected budget for *Repairman Jack* was in the $70 to 80 million dollar range. Nothing but open road ahead, baby.

Yeah, right.

2003

Finally, a year with a short story—two, in fact.

I finished *Gateways* in mid-January—late again. Luckily David Hartwell wanted no significant changes.

I immediately began outlining Repairman Jack number eight—I had no title yet.

In March I was approached by Tom and Elizabeth Monteleone about doing special, limited, uniform editions of my six Adversary Cycle novels. I thought it was a great idea. We started with *The Keep*. They sent me the scans and I began to proof the pages. I was pleased to see how well the novel held up after more than two decades—much better than *The Tomb*. But I couldn't help tweaking the prose.

Out in Hollywood they were looking for a guy to play Repairman Jack—a name who could "open" the film. They weren't finding any. Hugh Jackman was everyone's pick, but between *Van Helsing* and then his upcoming Broadway show, he was unavailable. Some folks talked about the Rock, others Vin Diesel. I damn near had a heart attack. Here's this character who so average looking he can slip through a crowd completely unnoticed, and they wanted the Rock or Diesel? Come on!

The months passed and still no actor for Jack.

Sims the novel was published in April and went back to press for two more printings. The last two novellas still hadn't appeared from Cemetery Dance.

Touchstone and Beacon appeared to be at an impasse. Touchstone wouldn't go ahead with the big budget without an opener star and they couldn't get one to fit the part. So Beacon decided to downsize the huge finish of the script and bring it closer to the book; this way they'd be able to lower the budget to where Touchstone would let them choose the right actor for Jack.

Meanwhile I was chugging away on the as-yet-untitled Repairman Jack number eight and loving it. But synching up the timelines of two parallel plots was turning out to be a more complex process than I'd anticipated. Finally I printed out the plotlines and cut them into discrete scenes. Then I laid them out on the floor side by side and mixed and matched scenes until they crisscrossed in a smooth flow.

Hey . . . crisscross.

I had my title.

I finished in October and immediately started in on a relatively gentle medical mystery—almost a cozy—starring a young female internist in a small town. *Crisscross* had been so unrelentingly grim and dark that I needed a change of pace, something light and fluffy to clear the gloom.

November saw the almost simultaneous publication of *The Fifth Harmonic* and *Gateways*.

Three new novels published in a single calendar year. A new record for me.

"SOLE CUSTODY"

Kealan Patrick Burke contacted me in the spring about *Quietly Now*, a tribute anthology to Charles L. Grant. I was long out of the short story groove and told him so. But because this was for Charlie, a master of quiet horror and a good guy I've known forever, I said I'd give it a shot.

It took me six weeks of off-and-on writing to get it to where I felt it worthy of Charlie. I tried my best to keep it quiet and think I succeeded. Okay, the truck accident, the falling safe, and the drive-by shooting with machine pistols weren't so quiet, but the horror was quiet, and that's what counts.

This one's for you, Charlie, wherever you are.

Sole Custody

"Yergundye am'row."

The sound, a small, high voice, jars me from sleep. I roll over and lift my head. A pale wash of light from the streetlamp outside reveals a short, slim form standing close to my bed.

My son.

"Jason?" I shake the cobwebs from my brain and glance at the glowing numbers on the clock. "What're you doing up at this hour? Is something wrong?"

"You're going to die tomorrow."

Now I'm awake. Believe me—fully awake.

"What?" I lever up to sitting and swing my legs from under the sheet. I grab his thin, knobby, seven-year-old shoulders. "What did you say?"

"You're going to die tomorrow."

Those words, spoken by my boy, my darling little boy, twist my gut. I fumble for the bedside lamp, find the switch, turn it on.

Jason stands stiff and straight; with his buzz-cut dark hair he looks like a soldier at attention; his brown eyes are wide and staring through me. I shake him. Gently.

"Jason! Jason, wake up! You're having a dream!"

Jason doesn't blink, doesn't say a word. He simply turns and begins walking away.

"Jason?"

I say it softly this time because I realize he's sleepwalking and I heard somewhere once that you shouldn't wake a sleepwalker.

I follow. I'm scared for him, don't want him falling down the cellar stairs. But he heads straight to his room. I'm close behind, turning on the light so neither of us will trip. I watch him slip under the covers. I stand over him as he closes his eyes . . . a few heartbeats later I can tell by his soft, even breathing that he's back into normal sleep.

I stare down at my son.

You're going to die tomorrow.

Christ, what a terrible thing for anyone to hear, but when it comes from your own little boy . . .

Then again, maybe not from Jason. Maybe from his grandmother.

Yeah. That would explain it.

Ralda hates me. Always has, always will. She never said so when Maria was alive. She didn't have to. If actions speak louder than words, then Ralda's body is the PA system at Dodger Stadium.

It all comes down to this: Ralda—her real name is Esmeralda but no one calls her that—has never forgiven me for stealing her daughter. If falling in love and getting married is stealing, then here—put on the cuffs and lock me up. I'm guilty.

Of course, eloping only made matters worse, but we didn't see that we had much choice. No way we could have had a traditional wedding with both families in the same room. Maria was *rom*, a gypsy, and that translated to the uptight Brits who comprised most of my kin as thieves, whores, and ne'er-do-wells. To Maria's side I was *gadje*, a non-gypsy, and a rom marrying a gadje was unthinkable.

So we hopped a flight to Vegas and got married. When we returned and Maria told her mother, well, it was something to see. Ralda put on a day-long display of screaming and cursing, tearing her own clothes and throwing Maria's out the front door. After that came the silent treatment, which was okay with me but damn near broke Maria's heart. Over the years she had to endure a passel of silent treatments. Ralda has an advance degree in creative silence and a triathelete's stamina.

She couldn't spew all her anger at her only child—despite Ralda's many faults, she truly loved Maria—and she couldn't rail at her own husband who'd been dead (gratefully, I'll bet) half a dozen years, so I became the target, the *numero uno* focus of her rage. Fine. Like I cared. It made for some uncomfortable meals at holidays, but I handled it.

I may not be the brightest bulb in the chandelier, but I was a good provider. I got through high school and made it halfway through year one at a community college before deciding I had a brighter future in the workforce than in the classroom. I was right. By the time Maria and I tied the knot I was bringing home decent money from my own little heavy equipment transport and specialty moving business. We began building a life together, and when Maria learned she was pregnant, I didn't think life could get no better.

Ralda softened somewhat after Jason was born. Even though he was half *gadje,* she adored her grandson and lavished him with attention. It was almost scary the way she fixated on him when we came to visit. Like Maria and I weren't there.

Life was good. My business was growing, Maria and I were talking about another baby, and then some rich eighteen-year-old fuck tooling around in his daddy's Mercedes sport coupe plowed into the driver's side of our minivan at ninety miles an hour. Maria and Jason were inside. J—that was what we'd started calling him—was strapped into his baby seat in the rear passenger side and, thank God, not even scratched. Maria didn't last twenty-four hours.

At the funeral Ralda jabbed a bony finger at my heart and screamed, "*You! You* should have been driving!"

I couldn't argue. I wished that too. Still wish it.

My brain and my life put themselves on hold for a while. I did a lot of couch time, remote in hand, switching channels like a robot, not watching nothing. I felt like I was coming apart. I kept thinking, What's the use?

But I held it together for J's sake, and we're doing all right now. Not great. I mean, how good can a kid's life be without his mother? How good can his dad's life be without the love of his life? But we're hanging in there.

The only problem has been Ralda. She'd like a recurring speed bump. Lately she's been filling Jason's head with her gypsy garbage—about how, even though he's not a pure-blood rom, he's still special, still has certain "gifts." I've been doing my best to act like a counterweight, to drag him back to the real world, and I thought I'd been doing a decent job.

Obviously I've been fooling myself.

Jason awakens the next morning with his usual cheeriness. I quiz him gently as I pour his orange juice and nuke his frozen waffles—he likes them drowning in syrup and melted butter—but he don't remember nothing about what he said or did last night.

So, after dropping him off at school, I pay a visit to Ralda's little bungalow in Lomita.

As she opens the front door I get in her face, jabbing a finger right at her nose. "You've gone too far this time, lady!"

I've been thinking about last night all the way down here and by now I'm pissed. I mean *really* pissed.

She gives me her usual why-do-I-have-to-share-the-planet-with-this-gadje look. She's wearing a pink housedress and fuzzy white slippers, her graying black hair is pulled back tight from her face. God, she's ugly. She looks like that puppet Madame that used to be on *Hollywood Squares*. How Maria ever sprang from her has always been beyond me. Way, way, way beyond.

"What are you talking about?" She has this thin accent that ever so slightly rolls the r.

"What'd you do, hypnotize him?"

She squints at me. "You're drinking again, aren't you."

I had a little problem after Maria's death, but I'm well over that now. And I'm sure as hell not going to let her change this from being about her to being about me.

"Not a drop. But what about you? What've you been pouring into my boy? I know you've been filling his head with all your Gypsy bullshit, which is bad enough, but after what you made him do last night, your ass is cooked."

"What?" She spreads her hands, palms up, like the whole world is turning against her and she don't know why. "What did my little Jason do that was so terrible?"

"You know. You know damn well. And he's not your little Jason. He's *mine*. And that custody deal you worked out with the judge? That's gonna be history when I tell him the games you've been playing with a little boy's head!"

"Vincent, what are you talking about? What did he do?"

Her using my first name hangs me up for a second or two. She never uses my name. I've always been "him" or "that man." Like she couldn't get my name to pass her lips. But it passes today.

"He said just what you wanted him to say." I turn and start stomping back to my pickup. "I never thought much of you, Ralda, but I never dreamed you'd use your own grandson to try to work a number on my head!"

"What did he say? Tell me what he said!"

Oh, she's good, she's really, really good. I didn't know her better, I'd think she really and truly didn't know.

But I ain't gonna play her game. I give her an I'm-outta-here wave and hop in behind the wheel. I don't have to crank up the truck because I never turned her off. As I put her in gear I hear Ralda's voice calling to me.

"Whatever he said, Vincent, listen to him! He has the gift! Do you hear me? The gift!"

And I'm thinking, He ain't got no gift, lady. He's got a curse: you.

I'm not a crazy hothead. Really, I'm not. It's just that this has been simmering for years and now I'm at the boiling point.

When Maria died, J was four and in preschool. Just the morning session. She hadn't wanted to let him go, even for those few hours, but figured it would help with his socialization. Yeah, she used that word. She was always reading books on raising kids.

After Maria's death, when I was lower-lip deep in my funk, J was the only thing that kept me from going under. I kept him in the morning session just so he could keep something of his old daily rhythm. But after I pulled my act together and got back to work, I had to add on the afternoon.

That worked out most of the time. But not all.

I had no trouble getting him there in the morning, but afternoons tended to be a problem. We live in a nice little two-bedroom ranch—the kind the real estate folk like to call "cozy"—in an okay neighborhood in Gardena. But sometimes me and my crew have jobs in places like Sylmar or Costa Mesa, which may not be all that far in miles, but in time . . . let me tell you, take anything bad you've heard about L.A. traffic and multiply it by ten for the reality. I just couldn't guarantee that I'd make it back in time every day. So I arranged for aftercare, which is new speak for after-school daycare.

That was when Ralda played her hand.

Old bitch took me to court. Can you believe it? To family court! Petitioned the judge for some strange kind of joint custody where she could take care of Jason after school until I got home from the job. Let me tell you, she made a real heartstring yanker of a case for herself: Lived alone, J was her only grandchild, all that was left of her beloved daughter. Wasn't it better that he spend his after-school hours with a loving grandparent than in the company of strangers?

Sounded good to the judge—who I think was a grandmother herself—and Ralda was awarded after-school custody. I had to hire a lawyer to try and get it undone but he was useless. Money down the sewer.

I wound up feeling more like a divorcé than a widower. I mean, my mother-in-law had joint custody of my kid.

Ralda loves J, I know that, and to be honest, for a while there it looked to be working out. J seemed happy with the arrangement and I have to admit I felt better knowing he was staying with someone who'd die rather than let anything happen to him.

But then J started coming home with Gypsy words and expressions and talking about having "gifts"—you know, second sight, clairvoyance, talking to animals, crazy stuff like that. I went right to Ralda and told her—no, wait, I *asked* her, real polite-like, to stop putting ideas like that into his head. People would think he was crazy.

Know what she said? She told me that into every third generation of her family is born a child with a "gift," that J is that one, that there are many gifts and she is only trying to find out which one he has.

I asked her to stop. (See? I was still asking.) She said she couldn't, that it would be a terrible sin to let his gift go undetected, undeveloped, that he's been neglected too long already.

Neglected? I blew my stack at that and told her if she didn't cease and desist—yeah, I said that; heard it on *Law & Order* or someplace—if she didn't stop filling my little boy's head with her garbage, I'd have her joint custody thing tossed out on its ear.

She gave me this hard look and said that I'd never have sole custody again. Then she slammed the door in my face.

Things were kind of at a stalemate for a while. J stopped using Gypsy talk around me, but that didn't mean he wasn't getting an earful from his grandmother and being told not to use or mention it at home.

But last night changes everything. I don't care if the judge is a grandmother ten times over, no one can get away with teaching a child to say something like that to his own father.

So all this crapola is on my mind as I drive to today's job in downtown. Yeah, there really is a downtown L.A. That's where the city's skyscrapers cluster in the basin. That's where you find the convention center and city hall, that big tapering building everyone knows from *Dragnet*. The whole rotten situation's on my mind when I park in a municipal lot, and I'm still steaming about it as I step off the curb to cross Figueroa.

I hear a voice behind me yell, "Oh, shit!" and I hear a horn blaring, and I look up to see this Ford F-150 pickup running the red light and making a beeline for me. I see the guy behind the wheel and he's got one hand holding a cell phone against his ear and the other wrapped around a Starbucks cup, leaving his left pinky for steering; he's looking down and I know, I just know he's spilled some coffee in his lap. He ain't got a clue as to what's happening and I realize I'm a goner and somewhere in my head J's voice is saying, *You're going to die tomorrow.*

All this takes place during a single heartbeat and just as I start into a much-too-late dive back toward the curb this eighteen-wheeler tools into the intersection from the left, cruising with the green, and knocks the shit out of the pickup, knocks it into next week, leaving me in the middle of the lane shaking and sweating and sick and hoping I haven't peed my pants.

I stagger to the other side and lower myself to the curb. I sit bent forward, holding my floating head in my shaking hands. Nobody notices me, which is fine. I'm not keen on having people watching as I hurl breakfast. Everybody's gravitating toward the wreckage in the intersection. Everybody except this bent old black guy with a cane and a Fred Sanford beard.

"You gotta be the luckiest-assed man on God's earth," he says as he stops a couple of feet from me.

I look up at him but say nothing. I'm not lucky. I'm *un*lucky. I've got a witch for a mother-in-law. Oh, not a witch who casts spells and cooks up magic spells. No, she's a witch who plays with your head. Because that's what Gypsies do, and they're good at it.

I see how this works now. She hypnotizes or does whatever she does to Jason to make him say whatever she wants him to say. *You're going to die tomorrow* is a brilliant choice, especially when it comes from your son. It puts you on edge, throws you off your rhythm, distracts you. Distracts you to the point where you're on autopilot. You see the little green walking man sign light up and you step off a curb without checking to see if anything's coming your way.

"Here," says the old guy. He's holding out a pint bottle swathed in a paper bag. "Take a pull. You could use it."

I wave him off and struggle to my feet. "Thanks, but I'm wobbly enough already."

"Lucky guy," he says as I walk away. "One lucky fucking guy."

I'm better by the time I get to the job, but I'm still not right. Taking charge though, dividing up the crew into details and telling them to get their asses in gear takes my mind off what almost happened.

The job is in one of downtown's older buildings. Real old. One of those narrow three-story dinosaurs that hung on through the ferro-concrete building boom. Me and my guys have been hired to move a big old Kelvinator-sized safe out of the third-floor office. Ordinarily not a problem, but in this case the building's been renovated umpteen times since the safe was moved in, and one of those renovations was a major overhaul of the staircase. Mainly narrowing it to increase the square footage of rentable space around it. The result: the safe can't go down the way it came up. The solution: knock out a window and enough wall around it to get the safe through, then winch it down to the sidewalk.

Yeah, I know, sounds like a mess, but trust me, the window and its wall are a much easier fix than a ripped-up stairwell.

By noon we've broken through the wall, the winch is in place, and the safe chained up and ready to go for a ride. I head downstairs to guide it from there and to make sure the landing pad stays clear of the curious. I've got about a mile of yellow caution tape wound around the area but over the years I've learned never to underestimate the stupidity of the average L.A. pedestrian. Even though my safety record's just about perfect, my liability premium is still through the roof. One bad accident, just one, will put it on the space shuttle.

Nobody gets to play the old *Looney Toons* flattened-under-a-safe scene on my watch.

As I hit the sidewalk I see the old black dude from over on Figueroa standing at the front of the gaggle pressing against the tape.

I nod. "What's up?"

He shrugs and smiles, showing two, maybe three teeth. "Nothing better to do."

"Retired, huh?"

"You could say that."

I get to work directing the guys on the roof with the winch and the guys inside with the safe. Pretty soon we've got the safe out and dangling in space. I signal the winch guys to start easing her down. As the winch starts cranking I look across the touchdown area and see some kid, a little Korean girl, no more than three, standing a couple of feet inside the tape. It's not like she's in danger or nothing, but I want her back where she belongs. I start toward her but I don't go two steps before something squishes under my right boot.

I look down. "Shit!"

Which is exactly what it is. A nice fat pile of dog shit.

Behind me I hear the old man laugh and say, "Maybe you ain't so lucky after all!"

As I stop to kick my boot against the concrete I hear a screech of stressed-out metal and hoarse shouts from above. Before I can look up, the safe slams onto and into the sidewalk directly in front of me.

For the next few seconds, all around me, there's no sound. Then someone says *"Madre!"* and another voice laughs and soon it's a babble that I barely hear. Because I'm looking at the safe and knowing that's exactly where I would've been when it hit . . . if I hadn't stepped in that dog shit.

I sense someone beside me. I turn and it's that old black guy. He's come through the tape and his wide brown eyes with yellowish whites are staring at me from inches away. He grabs my forearm and squeezes.

"Wh-what are you doing?" I feel like I've got a mouth full of epoxy.

"Jus wanna touch you, man. Thas all. I ain't never had one lick of good luck in my whole damn life, and you . . . you gots enough for two, three even. Maybe some of it will rub off."

I yank my arm free and pull away. Not toward the building and my guys. Away. Just away.

Half an hour later I'm in a bar, having lunch—a golden liquid with a foamy cap. Every since I pulled myself out of my post-Maria binge, I haven't had a drink before five or six at night. Not one. But today is different. I'm quivering down to my intestinal lining.

Because now I know what's happening. I had it all wrong. I thought Jason had been coached to tell me I was going to die today, but it wasn't that at all.

It's Ralda. She's put some kind of Gypsy curse on me. The joint custody agreement ain't enough for her. She wants J all to herself.

And J . . . the old lady's always said he has a "gift" . . . maybe some part of his subconscious sensed what his grandmother was up to and tried to warn me.

Or maybe . . .

Christ, what am I thinking? I don't believe in any of this shit. Never have. And yet . . .

Something's wrong today. I can feel it. Not just that I was almost killed twice. Something more.

Maybe *almost* is the key word. I should've been flattened by that pickup, but the eighteen-wheeler saved me. I should've been crushed by that safe, but I stepped on a juicy dog turd at just the right moment to delay me just enough to stay alive.

Almost as if I'm caught in the middle of a tug of war. Ralda is out to get me, no question, but something—some*one*—else has been pulling me back from each brink she pushes me to.

Who? Only two possibilities that I can see. One is Jason—not consciously, because he would have told me about it last night or this morning. But maybe unconsciously he's using his "gift" to fight for his dear old dad.

The thought brings tears to my eyes. My little boy, taking my side against his grandmother's black magic.

The other possibility is Maria. I've never believed in an Other Side. I've always figured when you're dead, you're dead. But what if I'm wrong? I mean, I've been wrong about lots of things in my life, so why not add the afterlife to the list.

What if Maria's here, invisible but hanging close to me, shielding me from her mother's curse?

But what if it's simply luck that's keeping me alive? What if that old street dude is right? That I'm the luckiest man alive.

Fine. Great. But nobody's luck lasts forever. When does mine run out? Maybe I've used up my share for the day or the week or the month and from now on I'm on my own.

Which means I have to *make* my luck.

I raise my beer glass but stop it halfway to my mouth. It's only my second, but maybe that's part of Ralda's curse: drown my fears, get sloshed, and splatter my truck and myself against a bridge abutment.

No way. She doesn't get me that easy.

I leave a sawbuck and the rest of my beer on the bar and get the hell out. I stand blinking in the sunlight, wondering where I can go to be safe. Not downtown L.A. Any second now someone could lose control of their car, jump the sidewalk, and flatten me against a wall like a swatted fly. I wish I was home but I'm sure as hell not risking the freeway to get there. Like jumping into a lion's den.

I need a place that's wide open. And public. Away from trucks and safes. Someplace I can get to without crossing too many streets. Only one place comes to mind.

I start walking, eyes on the move to check for threats above, below, and around. I hang back from the curbs at crosswalks, I don't step onto the street until everything's come to a dead stop, and then I stick close to my fellow pedestrians, figuring their presence will dilute the curse or whatever it is that's dogging me.

It takes me longer than I ever could have imagined to reach Pershing Square, but I make it in one piece. I've been here before, just out of curiosity. It's a pretty cool place with all this modern architecture-sculpture and landscaping and fountains, but I can't appreciate any of that now. All I want is a safe spot, and I think this is it. If I hang out at the center here, no car can get to me, even if the driver's been paid to run me down. It's open enough so that nobody can sneak up on me. And it's far enough from any buildings so that even if there's an earthquake nothing can fall on me.

I buy a paper, find a good spot near Pershing's statue, and hang here, reading, watching. Every so often someone from my crew calls my cell and I tell them what to do, but I never say where I am. Don't want nobody knowing that.

My stomach starts to growl as the sun settles behind one of the taller buildings but I'm afraid to eat. What if it's poisoned? Not like the hot dog guy is out to get me, but if I've got a curse on me and if there's one poisoned frank in the city, it'll find its way to me. Same goes for a drink. Never know when you might pick up a tampered cola.

I'm cursing myself for being so crazy paranoid, but all I need to do is survive the day, make it till midnight, and I'll have beaten her.

So I keep waiting and watching. I should call to let Jason know I'll be late, but I'd have to talk to *her*, and the last person on earth I want to talk to is *her*.

I hold my safe perch well into the dark. Finally I look at my watch: 10:58. Just a tad more than an hour to go.

And suddenly I want to be there in Ralda's bungalow, eye to eye as the clock strikes twelve. I know it's crazy but I can't resist the urge. I want to laugh in her face when that moment arrives.

Real careful-like, I make my way back to the garage, get in my pickup, and start the trip to Lomita. My guts are tied in knots as I get on the 110 and head south. I keep my sweaty hands tight on the wheel and stick to a middle lane where I won't be in the way of the speeders and won't have to deal with on-ramps and off-ramps.

The Lomita exit is coming up and I'm checking my rearview to see if it's safe to ease right when I spot two low-slung cars, one bright orange, the other canary yellow, racing my way through the traffic like candy-colored bullets, weaving in and out at suicidal speed.

Every muscle in my body clenches as I somehow know without a doubt that one of them is going to kill me. Not on purpose, but it's going to happen. He's being controlled by an unseen hand, just like me.

I realize now that the whole stupid idea of seeing Ralda at the last minute didn't come from me, but from her, pushing me out of my safe spot and onto the road where she can finish me off.

Panicked, I freeze. Go left? Go right? Stay where I am? All I can be sure of is that whatever move I make will be wrong. But I've got—

What's that popping noise? Oh, no, oh God, they're shooting at each other. It's some sort of gang thing and I'm going to be caught in the middle of it.

A sudden calm slips over me. The panic, the fear, the indecision melt away. I give myself over to the inevitability of what's about to happen. It's over . . . all over. This is where it ends for me and there's not a damn thing I can do about it.

In this strange, peaceful mood, I hang in the center lane. The traffic seems to slow. The air thickens as the world around me grinds down into second gear, then into first. I hear rapid-fire pops, see flashes blooming from the windows of the onrushing cars as the orange one veers to my right, the yellow to my left. They continue their barrage as they flank me. The sound is deafening. My windows shatter on both sides, peppering me with an ice storm of semi-sharp safety glass. I can feel the *whoosh* of the slugs as they hurtle through the car, even feel one tug at the hair at the back of my head. I see—or at least think I do—the bullets whizzing past my face from opposite directions. And I brace for the one that will end me.

And then the two cars are past. They're still shooting at each other but they're moving on. And I'm still alive. The guy ahead of me ain't so lucky. He winds up in the gunfire sandwich, just like me, only I see the silhouette of his head jerk left as it catches one and suddenly his car veers onto the shoulder and jumps the railing.

I roll my own car onto the shoulder a little past where he went over. I stop, open the door, and vomit. Or at least try to. I ain't had a thing to eat since breakfast and so only a little bile comes up.

I look around and see other cars pulled over, people out and jumping the railing to go check on the guy who went over, others talking on their cell phones—to the cops, I hope.

I close the door and slump against the steering wheel, gasping for air. I should be dead. No way I should have survived that barrage. I should be down in that ravine with the other poor bastard.

But I'm not. And the only reason I can come up with is protection: Here's further proof, damn near undeniable proof, that someone's protecting me.

With that thought fixed firmly in my head and heart, I slip the car back into gear and head for Ralda's house.

I have her beat. I want to see her face when she realizes it.

"Vincent!" Ralda says as she opens her front door. She's traded this morning's housedress for a ratty purple robe, but she's still wearing those fuzzy white slippers. "Where have you been?"

I brush past her and turn to face her.

"Worried about me?" I say with a wolfish grin—at least it *feels* wolfish.

In fact I'm feeling pretty wolfish all over—tough and mean and pretty goddamn near invincible.

"Yes. And so was Jason. He kept listening to the news for word that you'd been killed like his mother. He was terrified."

Some of the wolf dies. I hadn't thought of that. One parent gets killed on the road and J can't help worrying about the same thing happening to the other half of the team.

I look around but don't see him.

"Where is he?"

"In my bed." Ralda fixes me with this you-should-be-ashamed stare. "He fell asleep watching the late news, hoping he wouldn't hear about you, praying you'd call soon."

I feel like a shit, but only for an instant.

"I'd've been home on time if it wasn't for you."

Her eyes widen. "Me?"

"Yeah. You. You!" I hear my voice rising and I let it go. "Don't think I don't know about the curse you put on me. You were out to kill me today, but it didn't work. First off, Jason warned me. And second, someone's been protecting me. Someone more powerful that you, Ralda." I laugh and I don't particularly like the sound. "Christ, I couldn't have died today if I *tried*!"

She's looking at me like I'm a crackhead or something.

"Vincent, are you mad? Where did you ever get the idea that I could lay a curse on anyone? Others have that power, but I do not. And even if I could, do you think I would deprive Jason of his father, his only surviving parent? I may not like you, and I may think you're hurting Jason by ignoring his gift, but I would never wish another tragedy on that poor boy."

Something in what she's saying and how she says it strikes home, hits true:

Ralda don't give a damn about me beyond what I mean to J. And she'd never do anything that might hurt him.

My head's spinning. What's been happening to me all day? I could have been killed three times but I walked away. What—?

"You're going to die tomorrow."

I jump at the sound of Jason's voice. I turn and see him standing in Ralda's bedroom doorway, looking through me with that same thousand-mile stare as last night.

And suddenly I'm furious again.

"Jesus Christ, Ralda, will you give it up!"

Her eyes are fixed on J as she waves me to silence.

"He has the gift," she whispers. "I've been telling you that but you won't listen."

"Aw, don't start in about gifts again. I told you—"

"He has the Sight."

I'm getting more and more steamed.

"Ralda—"

"Listen to me. When he gets like this he can see the future. Only a day or two ahead now, and only as it applies to him—but with nurturing, that will improve."

"Bullshit. Last night you had him say I was going to die today, and I didn't, so now you've got him saying I'm going to die tomorrow. And what'll happen *tomorrow* night at"—I check my watch—"eleven fifty-eight? Same thing?"

She whirls toward me. "What time was it when he first told you?"

"Who cares?"

"You do! It's important!"

I think back to last night when he woke me up. I know I looked at the clock, but what did it say? And then I remember . . .

"One ten . . . ten after one."

And then she's staring at me with wonder and terror in her eyes and I know I've got to be looking back at her with the same.

I can barely hear her voice.

"It was after midnight when he told you. He wasn't talking about today, he was talking about tomorrow." She turns toward my lost-looking son. "He's *still* talking about tomorrow."

"SEX SLAVES OF THE DRAGON TONG"

Yellow Peril . . . how can a phrase that reeks so of racism and paranoia yield a body of fiction so . . . cool?

The term originated in the late nineteenth century. Chinese immigrants were flooding our western shore and spreading throughout the country at a time when their homeland was growing more and more militaristic. Could this mass immigration be a silent first wave of an eventual invasion?

In polite conversation they were called Chinamen or Orientals (not "Asian," as political correctness now dictates). Down on the street they were chinks and coolies.

Chinese villains became regulars in the penny dreadfuls. In 1913 Sax Rohmer created the paradigm for all Oriental evil from then on: Fu Manchu. I became enthralled with the good doctor at age fifteen when I met him in the pages of the Pyramid reprint of *The Insidious Doctor Fu Manchu*. I became a fan of the pulps and particularly enjoyed the exotic yellow-peril stories they regularly featured. (Even the Shadow had an archnemesis named Shiwan Khan.)

So when Joe Lansdale asked me to contribute to an anthology called *Retro Pulp Tales*, I said it had to be Yellow Peril. I did a lot of research to find the right tone. I decided it would involve a face-off between two fictional titans of the times.* I came up with the most lurid title I could think of, and after that the story pretty damn near wrote itself.

---

*If you are unable to identify them, you are forbidden from reading any more of my fiction.

Sex Slaves of the Dragon Tong

"You'll find my Margot, won't you?" Mr. Kachmar said. "Please?"

Detective Third Grade Brad Brannigan felt the weight of the portly man's imploring gaze as Chief Hanrahan ushered him out of his office.

"Of course he will," the chief told him. "He's one of our best men."

Brannigan smiled and nodded with a confidence as false as the chief's words. He was baffled as to why he, the greenest detective in the San Francisco PD, had been called in on this of all cases.

When the door finally closed, sealing out Mr. Kachmar, the chief turned and exhaled through puffed cheeks.

"Lord preserve us from friends of the mayor with wayward daughters, aye, Brannigan?"

As Hanrahan dropped into the creaking chair behind his desk, Brannigan searched for a response.

"I appreciate the compliment, Chief, but we both know I'm not one of your best men."

The chief smiled. "That we do, lad. That we do."

"Then why—?"

"Because I'll be knowing about Margot Kachmar and she's a bit of a hellion. Twenty years old and not a thought in her head about anyone but herself. Probably found a fellow she sparked to and went off with him on a lark. Wouldn't be the first time."

"But her father looked so worried."

"I'd be worried too if I had a daughter like that. Kachmar has only himself to blame. Rich folks like him give their kids too long a leash. Make it tough for the rest of us. You should hear my own daughter." He mimicked a young woman's voice. " 'This isn't the dark ages, Daddy. It's nineteen thirty-eight.' "

He huffed and returned to his normal tone. "I wouldn't care if it was nineteen *fifty*-eight, you've got to be after watching your daughters every single minute. Watching 'em like a hawk."

While trying his best to look interested in the chief's domestic philosophy, Brannigan cut in as soon as he had a chance.

"Where was she last seen?"

"Washington and Grant."

"Chinatown?"

"At least that's what her girlfriend says." Hanrahan winked. "Covering for her, I'll bet. You give that one a bit of hard questioning and she'll be coming around."

"But Chinatown is . . ."

"Yes, Sorenson's beat. But I can't very well be asking him to look into it, can I."

Of course he couldn't. Sorenson was laid up in the hospital with some strange malady.

"And," Chief Hanrahan added, "I can't very well be pulling my best men off other cases and sending them to No-tickee-no-shirtee-ville to question a bunch of coolies about some young doxy who'll show up on her own in a day or two. So you're getting the nod, Detective Brannigan."

Brad felt heat in his cheeks and knew they were reddening. For a fair-skinned redhead like him, a blush was always waiting in the wings, ready to prance onstage at an instant's notice.

The chief's meaning was clear: I don't want to waste someone useful, so you take it.

Brad repressed a dismayed sigh. He knew this was because of the Jenkins case. Missing a vital clue had left him looking like an amateur. As a result the rest of the detectives at the station had had weeks of fun at his expense. But though the razzing was over, Chief Hanrahan still hadn't assigned him to anything meaty. Brannigan wound up with the leftovers. If he didn't get some arrests to his credit he'd never make second grade.

Stop feeling sorry for yourself, he thought. Your day will come. It just won't be today.

Brannigan took the chief's suggestion and called on Margot's friend Katy Webber for a few answers. Katy lived in her parents' home, a stone mansion in Pacific Heights.

Five minutes with her were all it took to convince him that she wasn't covering for Margot. She was too upset.

"One moment she was with me," she said through her tears, "and the next minute she wasn't! I turned to look in a jewelry store window—that was why we went there, to look for some jade—and when I turned back to point out a necklace, she was gone!"

"And you didn't see anyone suspicious hanging about? No one following you?"

"Not that I noticed. And Margot never mentioned seeing anyone. The streets were crowded with people and cars and . . . I don't understand how she could have disappeared like that."

Neither did Brannigan. "You must have seen *something*."

"Well . . ."

"What?"

"It might be nothing, but I saw this black car pulling away and I thought . . ." She shook her head. "I thought I saw the back of a blond head through the rear window."

"Margot's head?"

Katy shrugged and looked miserable. "I don't know. It was just a glimpse and then the car turned the corner."

"Do you remember the license plate? The make? The model?"

Katy responded to each question with a shake of her head. "I don't know cars. I did notice that it had four doors, but beyond that . . ."

Swell, Brannigan thought. A black sedan. San Francisco had thousands and thousands of them.

But Katy's story convinced him that someone had kidnapped Margot Kachmar. In broad daylight to boot. He'd start where she was last seen, at Washington and Grant, and move out from there.

But he'd move on his own. This was his chance to get himself out of Dutch with the chief, so he'd keep it to himself for now. If Hanrahan got wind that this was a real kidnapping, he'd pull Brannigan and put someone else on it sure.

Someone in that area of Chinatown had to remember something. All he needed to do was ask the right person. And that meant his next step was good old-fashioned door-to-door detective work.

"Wah!" Yu Chaoyang cried. "Slow the car!"

Jiang Zhifu looked around, startled. He and Yu occupied the back of one of the black Packard sedans owned by Yan Yuap Tong. An underling Yu had brought from Singapore sat behind the wheel. All three wore identical black cotton outfits with high collars and frog-buttoned fronts, although Yu's large girth required twice as much fabric as Jiang's; each jacket was embroidered with a golden dragon over the left breast; each man wore his hair woven into a braid that dangled from beneath a traditional black skullcap.

"What is wrong?" Jiang said as the car slowed almost to a stop.

"Nothing is wrong, my *tong* brother. In fact, something is very right." A chubby finger pointed toward the sidewalk. "Look and marvel."

Jiang peered through the side window glass and saw a typical Chinatown scene: pushcarts laden with fruits and vegetables, fish live and dead, fluttering caged birds and roasted ducks; weaving among them was the usual throng of shoppers, a mix of locals and tourists.

Yu had come to America just last month on a mission for his father, head of the Yan Yuap Tong's house in Singapore; Jiang had volunteered to guide him through the odd ways of this strange country.

Yu was proving to be a trial. Arrogant and headstrong, he did not give proper face to his tong brothers here in San Francisco. Some of that might be anticipated from the son of a tong chief from home, but Yu went beyond proper bounds. No one expected him to kowtow, but he should show more respect.

"I don't understand," Jiang said.

Yu turned to face him. He ran a long sinuous tongue over his lips, brushing his thin drooping mustache in the process. His smile narrowed further his puffy lids until they were mere slits through which his onyx eyes gleamed.

"Red hair! Red hair!"

Jiang looked again and saw a little girl, no more than ten years old, standing by a cart, looking at a cage full of sparrows. She wore a red dress with white trim; but her unruly hair was even redder: a bushy flame, flaring around her face like the corona of an eclipse.

"Look at her." Yu's voice became a serpent, slithering through the car. "What a price I can fetch for her!"

"But she's a child."

"Yes! Precisely! I have a buyer in Singapore who specializes in children, and a red-haired child . . . aieee! He will pay anything for her!"

Jiang's stomach tightened. A child . . .

"Are you forgetting the conditions set by the Mandarin?"

"May maggots eat the eyes of your Mandarin!"

Jiang couldn't help a quick look around. He thanked his ancestors that the windows were closed. Someone might have heard.

"Do not speak of him so! And do not even think of breaking your agreement with him!"

Yu leaned closer. "Where do your loyalties lie, Jiang? With your tong, or with this mysterious Mandarin you all kowtow to?"

"I am loyal to Yan Yuap, but I am also fond of my skin. And if you wish to keep yours, you will heed my warning. Those who oppose his will wind up dead or are never seen again."

"Eh-yeh!" Yu waved a dismissive hand. "By tomorrow night I will be at sea with this barbarous country far behind me."

"Yes. You will be gone, but I will still have to live here."

Yu grinned, showing mottled teeth, stained from his opium pipe. "That is not my worry."

"Do not be so sure. The Mandarin's reach is long. He has never been known to break his word, and he has no mercy toward those who break theirs to him. I beg you not to do this."

The grin turned into a sneer. "America has softened you, Jiang. You shake like a frightened old woman."

Jiang looked away. This man was a fool. Yu had come to America for women—white women he could sell to the Singapore brothels. The lower level houses there and the streets around them were full of dolla-dolla girls shipped in from the farmlands. But the upper echelon salons that provided gambling as well as sex needed something special to bring in the high rollers. White women were one such draw. And *blond* white women were the ultimate lure.

Since nothing in San Francisco's Chinese underworld happened without the Mandarin's consent—or without his receiving a share of the proceeds—Yu had needed prior approval of his plan. How he had raged at the ignominy of such an arrangement, but he had been persuaded that he would have no success without it.

The Mandarin had set two conditions. First: take only one woman from San Francisco, all the rest from surrounding cities and towns. The second: no children. He did not care to weather a Lindbergh-style investigation.

Jiang said, "We took a girl here only yesterday, and now a child from these same streets. You will be breaking both conditions with this act."

Yu smiled. "No, Jiang. *We* will be breaking them. We will watch and wait, and when the time is right, you will pluck this delicious little berry from her branch."

Jiang agonized as Yu had the driver circle the block again and again. Yes, he was a member of the Yan Yuap Tong, but he was also a member of a more powerful and far-flung society. And the Mandarin was one of its leaders. Jiang was the Mandarin's eyes within the Yan Yuap Tong, and as such he would have to report this. Not that he would mind the slightest seeing the worst happen to Yu, but he prayed to his ancestors that the Mandarin wouldn't make him pay too for his part in the transgression.

"Wah!" Yu said. "She has turned the corner. There is no one about! Now! Now!"

Fumes filled the car as Jiang poured chloroform onto a rag. He jumped out, the soft slap of his slippers on the pavement the only sign of his presence; he clamped the rag over the child's face and was dragging her back toward the car's open door when a ball of light brown fur darted across the sidewalk toward them. Jiang heard a growl of fury, saw bared fangs, and then the thing was upon him, tearing at the flesh of his arm.

He cried out for help and received it in the report of a pistol. The dog yelped and tumbled backward to lie twitching on the sidewalk. The child's wild struggles—she was a tough little one—slowed and ceased as the chloroform did its work. Jiang shoved her into the backseat between Yu and himself. The car lurched into motion. Jiang glanced back and saw a pool of blood forming around the head of the sandy-haired dog.

He looked at the now unconscious child and saw Yu caressing one of her pale, bare thighs.

"Ah, my little quail," he cooed, "I would so like to use the trip home to teach you the thousand ways to please a man, but alas you must remain a virgin if I am to take full profit from you."

Jiang closed his eyes and trembled inside. He had to tell the Mandarin of this. He prayed he'd survive the meeting.

"I've run into a blank wall," Brannigan said.

"And so you've come to me for help."

Looking at Detective Sergeant Hank Sorenson now, Brannigan wished he'd gone elsewhere.

He'd had a nodding acquaintance with Sorenson at the station, but the figure pressed between the sheets in the hospital bed before him was a caricature of the man Brannigan had known.

He tried not to stare at the sunken cheeks, the glassy, feverish eyes, the sallow, sweaty skin as pale as his hospital gown. The slow smile that stretched Sorenson's lips and bared his teeth was ghastly.

"You mean to tell me you walked up to Chinatown residents and asked them what they saw?"

The whole afternoon had been a frustrating progression of singsong syllables, expressionless yellow faces with gleaming slanted eyes that told him nothing.

"I didn't see that I had any other option."

"You can't treat chinks like regular people, Brad. You can't ask them a direct question. They're devious, crafty, always circling."

Brannigan bristled at Sorenson's attitude, like a teacher chiding a student for not knowing his lesson.

"Well, be that as it may, no one saw anything."

Sorenson barked a phlegmy laugh. "Oh, they saw all right. They're just not going to tell an outsider. Not if they know what's good for them."

"What's that mean?"

"The Mandarin. You do not cross the Mandarin."

Sorenson went on to explain about Chinatown's lord of crime. Then he added, "If this Kachmar girl is a blond, you might be dealing with a white slave ring. The Yan Yuap Tong—also called the Dragon Tong because their symbol is a dragon—has been involved in that before. The tongsters probably have your missing girl's photo on its way back to Singapore already, to get the bidding started."

Brannigan had heard of Oriental rings that abducted white women for sex slaves, but he'd never expected that Margot Kachmar—

"Check Oakland and Marin and maybe San Jose," Sorenson was saying. "See if they've had a blonde or two gone missing recently."

"Why there?"

"Because police departments don't communicate nearly enough. Someday they will, but with things as they are, spreading out the abductions lessens the chances of anyone spotting a pattern."

Oakland . . . San Jose . . . that seemed like a lot of legwork with slim chance of turning up anything useful.

"Why don't I go straight to the source? This Mandarin character . . . where do I find him?"

Sorenson began to shake with ague. His head fell back on the pillow. When the tremors eased . . .

"No one knows. He hides his identity even from his fellow Chinese. Just as well—you don't want to find him. I came close and look what it got me."

"I don't understand."

"I was homing in on the Mandarin's identity, getting closer than anyone before me, and then, a week ago, something got into my house and bit me."

"Something?"

"A giant millipede, bright red, at least eight inches long, crawled into my bed and bit me on the shoulder. I managed to smash it with a shoe as it raced away, but only got the back half. The front half broke off and escaped. Bug scientists over at the university say it only exists in Borneo."

"But what's that got to do—?"

"It was *put* in my house, you idiot!" Sorenson snapped, a faint tinge of color seeping into his cheeks. "By one of the Mandarin's men. And look what it's done to me!"

He pulled the hospital gown off his left shoulder to reveal a damp dressing. He ripped that off.

"It's due for a change anyway. Have a look."

Brannigan saw an ulcerated crater perhaps two inches across penetrating deep into the flesh of Sorenson's shoulder. Its base was red and bloody. A quick look was more than enough for Brannigan, but as he was turning away he thought he saw something move within the bloody fluid. He looked again—

And jumped back.

Many little things were moving in the base of the ulcer.

"What—?"

Sorenson's expression was bleak. Brannigan could see he was trying to keep up a brave face.

"Yeah. The bug didn't poison me. I wish it had. Instead it laid a bunch of eggs in me, a thousand, maybe a million of them. And they keep hatching. I think they're getting into my system, eating me alive from the inside."

"Can't the doctors stop it?"

He shook his head. "They've never seen anything like—"

He clasped a hand over his mouth as he broke off into a fit of coughing. The harsh barks seemed to be coming from somewhere around his ankles. With a final wet hack he stopped.

A look of horror twisted his features as he stared at his palm. It was filled with bloody phlegm, and Brannigan could swear he saw something wriggling within the glob, something with many, many legs.

"Oh, God!" Sorenson wailed, his composure finally broken. "Call the doctor! Get the nurse in here! Hurry!"

Brannigan turned and ran for the hallway. Behind him he heard the wrenching sound of a grown man sobbing.

Jiang could not keep his body from shaking as he knelt with his forehead pressed against the cold stone floor. The Mandarin stood over him, eerily silent. Jiang had told him what had transpired on the street. It had been hours ago, but he had come as soon as he could get away.

At last the master spoke, his voice soft, the tone sibilant.

"So . . . Yu Chaoyang has disobeyed me and endangered all we have worked for here. I half expected this from such a man. The Japanese are overrunning our China, slaughtering its people, and Yu thinks only of adding to his already swollen coffers."

"Venerable, I tried to dissuade him but—"

"I am sure you did your best, Jiang Zhifu, but apparently it wasn't enough."

No-no-no! cried a terrified voice within Jiang. Let him not be angry!

But Jiang's outer voice was wise enough to remain silent.

"However," the master said, "I will allow you to redeem yourself."

"Oh, Illustrious! This miserable offspring of a worm is endlessly grateful."

"Rise."

Jiang eased to his feet and stood facing the master, but looked at him only from the corner of his eye. The man known throughout Chinatown as the Mandarin—even Jiang did not know his true name—was tall, lean, high-shouldered, standing bamboo straight with his hands folded inside the sleeves of his flowing turquoise robe; his hair was thin and covered with a brimless cap beaded with coral. He had a high, domed forehead and thin lips, but his eyes—light green, their color intensified by the shade of his robe—were unlike any Jiang had ever seen.

"Where is the child now?"

"Yu has her in the tonghouse, but soon he will head for his ship and set sail. Shall I stop him? Shall I see to it that he suffers the same fate as that too-curious detective?"

The master shook his head. "No. Did the child see you?"

"No, Magnificent. I took her from behind and she was soon unconscious."

"Then she cannot point a finger of blame at a Chinaman. Good. You will return to the tonghouse and light a red lamp in the room where the child is kept. I will send a few of my dacoits to see that she is returned to the streets. You must be present so that no suspicion falls on you. Then let Yu go to his ship and set sail with the rest of his cargo. He will never see home. He—Jiang, you are bleeding."

"It is nothing, Eminent. The child's dog bit me as I pulled her into the car. It is nothing."

"The red-haired little girl had a dog, you say? What kind of dog?"

"A scruffy mongrel. May this unworthy snail ask why such an Esteemed One as you would ask?"

When the master did not answer, Jiang dared a glance at his face and saw the unimaginable: a look of uncertainty in those green eyes.

"Exalted . . . did this miserable slug say something wrong?"

"No, Jiang. I had a thought, that is all . . . about a certain little red-haired girl who must not be touched . . . ever." He turned and stepped to the single high small window in the north wall of the tiny room. "It could not possibly be she, but if it is . . . and if she is harmed . . . all the ancestors of all the members of the Yan Yuap Tong will not save it from doom . . . a doom that could spread to us as well."

Brannigan leaned against the center railing of the hospital's front steps and sucked deep draughts of the foggy night air.

Sorenson . . . a tough, no-nonsense cop . . . reduced to a weeping child. It gave him a bad case of the willies. Who was this Mandarin? And more important, was he involved in Margot Kachmar's disappearance?

Feeling steadier, Brannigan stepped down to the sidewalk and headed for his radio car. He needed to call in. A catchy song by Frances Day, "I've Got You Under My Skin," echoed unwelcomed his head. From somewhere in the fog a newsboy called out the headlines of the evening edition. As he passed a silver Rolls Royce its rear door opened and an accented voice spoke from the dark interior.

"Please step inside. Someone wishes to speak to you."

Someone? That could very well be the Mandarin. Well, Brannigan damn well wanted to speak to him too, but on his terms, not in the back of a mysterious limousine.

He backed away. "Have him meet me down at the station," he said. "We'll have a nice long chat there."

Brannigan jumped at the sound of another voice close behind him, almost in his ear.

"He would speak to you now. Into the car, please."

Brannigan reached for his pistol but his shoulder holster was empty. He whirled and found himself face-to-face with a gaunt Chinaman dressed in a black business suit, a white shirt, and a black tie. A black fedora finished off the look. His expression was bland, his tone matter-of-fact, but his features had a sinister, almost cruel cast.

He held up Brannigan's .38 between them but did not point it at him. He gestured to the car with his free hand.

"Please."

Brannigan's first instinct was to run, but he figured all he'd gain by that was a slug in the back. Probably better than a millipede in his bed, but he decided on the car option. Maybe he'd find an opening along the way to make a break.

With his bladder clenching, he ducked inside. The door slammed behind him, drenching him in darkness. He could sense but not see whoever was seated across from him. As the car began moving—the thin chink was also the driver, it seemed—Brannigan leaned forward, straining to see his host.

"Are you . . . ?" His mouth was dry so he wet his lips. "Are you the Mandarin?"

A soft laugh. "Oh, no. I would not serve that one."

"Then why do you want to speak to me?"

"It is not I, Detective Brannigan. It is another. Hush now and save your words for him."

The glare from a passing streetlight illuminated the interior for a second, leaving Brannigan in a state of shock. The other occupant was a turbaned gi-ant who looked as if he'd just stepped out of Arabian Nights.

The car turned west on California, taking them away from Chinatown. A few minutes later they stopped at a side entrance to the Fairmont Hotel, perched atop Nob Hill like a granite crown. The driver and the giant escorted Brannigan to an elevator in an empty service hallway. Inside the car, the driver inserted a key into the control panel and up they went.

After a swift, stomach-sinking ride, the elevator doors opened into a huge suite, richly furnished and decorated with palm trees and ornate marble col-umns reaching to its high, glass-paned ceiling.

An older man rose from a sofa. He was completely bald with pale gray eyes. He wore black tuxedo pants and a white dress shirt ornamented with a huge diamond stickpin. Brannigan spotted a black dress jacket and tie draped over a nearby chair. A long thick cigar smoldered in his left hand; he extended the right as he strode forward.

"Detective Brannigan, I presume. Thank you for coming."

Brannigan, flabbergasted, shook the man's hand. This wasn't at all what he'd expected.

"I didn't have much choice."

He eyed his two escorts as they took up positions behind his host. The driver had removed his hat, revealing a bald dome; glossy black hair fringed the sides and back of his scalp.

"Oh, I hope they didn't threaten you."

Brannigan was about to crack wise when he realized that they hadn't threatened him at all. If anything they'd been overly polite.

He studied the bald man. Something familiar about him . . .

"I've seen you before."

The man shrugged. "Despite my best efforts, my face now and again winds up in the papers."

"Who are you?"

"Let's just say I'm someone who prefers to move in and out of large cities without advertising his presence. Otherwise my time would be consumed by a parade of local politicians with their hands out, and I'd never get any work done."

"What do you want with me?"

"You were in Chinatown today asking about a missing girl, Margot Kachmar."

The statement startled Brannigan at first, but then he glanced at the Ori-ental driver and realized he shouldn't be surprised.

"That's police business."

"And now it's *my* business." A sudden, steely tone put a knife edge on the words. "My daughter was abducted from that same area this afternoon."

"She was? Did you tell the police?"

"That's what I'm doing now."

"I mean an official report and—never mind. Are you sure she was abducted?"

The bald man hooked a finger through the air and Brannigan followed him to the far side of a huge couch. Along the way he glanced out the tall windows and saw Russian Hill and San Francisco Bay stretching out below. This had to be the penthouse suite.

The man pointed to a sandy-furred mutt lying on a big red pillow. A thick bandage encircled its head.

"That's her dog. She goes nowhere without him. He was shot—luckily the bullet glanced off his skull instead of piercing it—and that can only mean that he was defending her. He almost died, but he's a tough one, just like his little owner."

Two in two days from the same neighborhood . . . this was not the pattern Sorenson had described.

"How old is your daughter, and is she blond?"

"She's a ten-year-old redhead—her hair's the same shade as yours."

Cripes. A kid. "Well, I'm sorry about what happened to her, but I don't think she's connected to the Kachmar girl. I—"

"What if I told you they were both dragged into a black Packard sedan? Most likely the same one?"

Katy Webber had described a black sedan. Maybe there was a connection after all.

The bald man said, "I have men out canvassing the neighborhoods right now, looking for that car."

"That's police business. You can't—"

"I can and I am. Don't worry—they'll be very discreet. But I'll make you a deal, detective: You share with me, I'll share with you. If I locate Miss Kachmar, I'll notify you. If you find my daughter alive and well I will see to it that you never have to worry about money for the rest of your life."

Brannigan felt a flush of anger. "I don't need to be bribed to do my job."

"It's not a bribe—it will be gratitude. Anything of mine you want you can have. I've made fortunes and lost them, gone from living in mansions to being penniless on the street and back to mansions. I'm good at making money. I can always replace my fortune. But I can't replace that little girl." The man seemed to lose his voice and Brannigan saw his throat work. When he recovered he added, "She means everything to me."

The nods from the turbaned giant and the driver said they felt the same.

Brannigan was touched. He couldn't help it. And from the looks on all three faces he knew that if they were the first to discover the child's abductor, the mugg would never see trial.

He couldn't condone or allow the vigilantism he sensed brewing here. And for that reason he couldn't tell them what Sorenson had said about the Dragon Tong. He'd keep that to himself.

"I promise you that if I find her, you'll be the first to know."

The bald man put his hand out to the Chinese driver who placed Brannigan's pistol in it, then he fixed the detective with his pale gaze. "That is all I ask. Can my associates offer you a lift?"

"No thanks." He'd seen enough of the old man's chums for one evening. "I'll grab a cab."

He took the elevator down to the lobby level, but before going outside, he stopped at the front desk.

"Who's staying in the penthouse suite?" he asked the clerk. He flipped open his wallet, showing his shield. "And don't give me any malarkey about hotel policy."

The man hesitated, then shrugged. After consulting the guest register he shook his head.

"Sorry. It's unoccupied."

"Baloney! I was just up there."

Another shake of the head. "No occupant is listed. All I can tell you is this: The penthouse suite is on reserve—permanent reserve—but it doesn't say for whom."

Frustrated, Brannigan stormed from the hotel. He had more important things to do than argue with some hotel flunky.

Ten minutes later Brannigan was standing in the shadows across the street from the headquarters of the Dragon Tong. Its slanted cupola glistened with moisture from the fog. A few of the upper windows were lit, a pair of green-and-yellow paper lanterns hung outside the front entrance, but otherwise the angular building squatted dark and silent on its lot.

What now? Sorenson had told him how to find it, but now that he was here he couldn't simply walk in. Much as he hated to admit it, he was going to have to call Hanrahan for backup.

As he turned to go back to his radio car he noticed movement along the right flank of the tonghouse. Three monkeylike shadows were scaling the wall. He hurried across the street and crept closer to investigate. He found a rope hanging along the wall, disappearing into a third-story window lit by a red paper lantern.

Apparently someone else was interested in the tonghouse. He knew the three he'd seen shimmying up this rope were too small and agile to have been the bald guy and company.

He looked at the rope, tempted. This was one hell of a pickle. Go up or get help?

The decision was taken out of his hands when the rope snaked up the wall and out of reach. He cursed as he watched it disappear into the window.

But then he noticed a narrow door just to his right. He tried the handle—unlocked—and pushed it open. The slow creaks from the old hinges sounded like a cat being tortured. He cringed as he slipped into some sort of kitchen. He pulled his pistol and waited to see if anyone came to investigate.

When no one came, he slipped through the darkness, listening. The tonghouse seemed quiet. Most of the tongsters were probably home at this hour. But what of the hatchetmen the tongs reputedly used as guards and enforcers? Did they go home too? Brannigan hoped so, but doubted it.

He stepped through a curtain into a small chamber lit by a single oil lamp, its walls bare except for a black lacquered door ornamented with gold dragons uncoiling from the corners. The door pulled outward and Brannigan found himself in an exotic, windowless room, empty except for a golden Buddha seated in a corner; a lamp and joss sticks smoked before it, their vapors wafting toward the high ceiling.

Something about the walls . . . he stepped closer and gasped as he ran his fingers over what he'd assumed to be wallpaper. But these peacock plumes weren't painted, they were the genuine article. And all four walls were lined with them.

Dazzled by its beauty, Brannigan stepped back to the center of the room and turned in a slow circle. No window, no door other than the one he'd come through. The room appeared to be a dead end.

But then he noticed the way the smoke from the joss sticks wavered on its path toward the ceiling. Air was flowing in from somewhere. He moved along the wall, inspecting the plumes until he found one with a wavering fringe. And another just below it. Air was filtering through a narrow crevice. He pushed at the wall on either side until he felt something give. He pushed harder and a section swung inward.

Ahead of Brannigan lay a long, dark, downsloping corridor, ending in a rectangle of wan, flickering light. The only sound was his own breathing.

He hesitated, then took a breath and started forward. He'd come this far . . . in for a dime, in for a dollar.

Pistol at the ready, he crept down the passage as silently as his heavy regulation shoes would allow, pausing every few steps to listen. Nothing. All quiet.

When he reached the end he stopped. All he could see ahead was bare floor and wall, lit by a lamp in some unseen corner. Still hearing nothing, he risked a peek inside—

—and ducked back as he caught a flash of movement to his left. A black-handled hatchet whispered past the end of his nose and buried itself in the wall just inches to the right of his head.

And then a black-pajama-clad tongster with a high-cheeked, pockmarked face lunged at him with a raised dagger. His brutal features were contorted with rage as he shouted rapid-fire gibberish.

The report from Brannigan's pistol was deafening as it smashed a bullet through the chink's chest and sent him tumbling backward. Another black-clad tongster, a raw-boned, beady-eyed bugger, replaced him immediately, howling the same cry as he swung a hatchet at Brannigan's throat. He too fell with a bullet in his chest.

But then the doorway was filled with two more and then three, and more surging behind them. With only four rounds left in his revolver, Brannigan knew he had no chance of stopping this Mongol horde. He began backpedaling as the hatchetmen leaped over their fallen comrades and charged.

Brannigan fired as he retreated, making good use of his remaining rounds, slowing the black-clad gang's advance, but a small, primitive part of him began screeching in panic as it became aware that he was not going to leave the tonghouse alive. Not unless he reached the door to the joss room in time to shut it and hold it closed against the swarm of hatchetmen.

After firing his last shot he turned and ran full tilt for the door. His foot caught on the sill as he rushed through and he tumbled to the floor. The horror of knowing that he was about to be hacked to death shot strength into his legs but he slipped as he started to rise and knew he was done for.

As he rolled, tensing for the first ax strike, preparing a last stand with his bare hands, he was startled by the sound of gunfire, followed immediately by shouts and screams of pain. He looked up and saw the old man's turbaned Indian wielding a huge scimitar that lopped off heads and arms with slashing swipes, while the driver hacked away with a cutlass. The old man himself stood in the thick of it, firing a round-handled, long-barreled Mauser at any of the hatchetmen who slipped past his front line.

Brannigan pawed fresh shells from his jacket pocket and began to reload. But the melee was over before he finished. He sat up and looked around. More than joss-stick smoke hung in the air; blood had spattered the feathered walls and pooled on the floor. The old man and the Indian were unscathed; the driver was bleeding from a gash on his right arm but didn't seem to notice.

"What . . . how . . . ?"

The old man looked at him. "I sensed you weren't telling us everything you knew, so we followed you. Good thing too, I'd say."

Brannigan nodded as he struggled to his feet. He felt shaky, unsteady. "Thank you. I owe you my—"

"Is she here?" the old man said. "Have you seen her?"

"I have her right here, Oliver," said a sibilant, accented voice.

Brannigan turned and raised his pistol as a motley group filed into the small room: a green-eyed, turquoise-robed Chinaman entered, followed by a trio of gangly, brutal-looking, dark-skinned lugs dressed in loincloths and nothing else; one carried a red-haired girl in his arms; two black-pajamaed tongsters brought up the rear, one thin, one fat, the latter with his hands tied behind his back and looking as if he'd wound up on the wrong end of a billy club.

The lead Chinaman spoke again. "I feared you might have been drawn into this."

"So it's you, Doctor," the old man said. At least Brannigan knew part of his name now: Oliver. "Striking at me through my child? I knew you were ruthless but—"

"Do not insult me, Oliver. I would gladly cut out your heart, but I would not break it."

The doctor—doctor of what? Brannigan wondered—removed a bony, long-fingered hand from within a sleeve and gestured to the loinclothed crew. The one carrying the little girl stepped forward and handed her over to Oliver. She looked drugged but as the old man took her in his arms, her eyes fluttered open. Brannigan saw her smile.

The word was a whisper. "Daddy."

Tears rimmed Oliver's eyes as he looked down at her, then back to the doctor. "I don't understand."

"This was not my doing." Without looking he flicked a finger toward the fat, bound tongster. "This doomed one broke an agreement."

"I thought I left you back in Hong Kong. When was it . . . ?"

"Three years ago. I understand you recently closed your factory there."

He nodded. "The political climate in the Far East has accomplished what you could not. I'm gathering my chicks closer to the nest, you might say. A storm is brewing and I want to be properly positioned when it strikes."

The doctor's smile was acid. "To profiteer, as usual."

Oliver shrugged. "Nothing wrong with doing well while doing good."

Who were these two? Brannigan wondered. They stood, each with his own personal army, like ancient mythical enemies facing each other across a bottomless divide.

"And what of you, Doctor?" Oliver continued. "With your homeland being invaded, why are you here?"

"You heard what the Japanese dogs did in Nanking?"

"Yes. Ghastly. I'm sorry."

"Then you can understand why I am here. To raise money from the underworld for weapons to repel the insects."

Oliver's faint smile looked bitter. "And all along you thought the enemy was people like me."

"You still are. My goal remains unchanged: To drive all foreigners from Chinese soil. I will admit, however, that I singled out the white western world as the threat, never realizing that a yellow-skinned neighbor would prove a far more vicious foe."

Something the doctor had said rang through Brannigan's brain: *To raise money from the underworld* . . . that could only mean—

He pointed his pistol at the green-robed chink. "You're the Mandarin! You're—"

The green eyes glanced his way and the pure malevolence in them clogged the words in Brannigan's throat. Before he could clear it, Oliver pointed to the bound chink and spoke.

"I'll take him from here. My associates and I have a score to settle."

"No, he is mine. He broke his word to me. I have experts in the Thousand Cuts. He will die long after he wishes to, I promise."

Brannigan couldn't believe his ears. These two acted like laws unto themselves. It was like listening to two sovereign nation-states argue over extradition of a prisoner.

"Hey, wait just a minute, you two." He stepped closer to the Mandarin. "Neither of you is going to do anything." The green eyes turned on him again. "I'm arresting you and your tongster buddy here for—"

Something smashed against the back of Brannigan's skull, dropping him to his knees. He tried to regain his feet but the edges of his vision went blurry and he toppled forward into darkness.

Jiang Zhifu poised his fist over the fallen detective's neck and looked to the master for permission to finish the worm. The master nodded. But as Jiang raised his hand for the death blow a shot rang out and a bullet plowed into the feathered wall beside him.

"That will be enough," said the man called Oliver.

The master motioned Jiang back toward Yu and he obeyed, albeit reluctantly. He was confused. Who was this white devil to give orders in the master's presence, and have the master acquiesce? Although this Oliver and the master seemed to be old enemies, the master treated him as an equal.

Something became clear to Jiang. It must have been because of this man that the master had sent Jiang to the Fairmont Hotel where he'd been instructed to ask a certain question of the kitchen staff. When Jiang returned with word that yes, meals were indeed being delivered to the penthouse suite, the master had changed his plans.

Jiang looked at the little red-haired girl in Oliver's arms. Yu had brought all this to pass by abducting her. The master had hinted that consequences most dire and relentless would befall anyone even remotely connected with harming that child.

Jiang had doubted that, but looking around the joss room now, he believed. So many of his tong brothers dead, shot or hacked to pieces. He and Yu were the only two members of Yan Yuap left alive in the house. Jiang would have to leave and return at dawn with the rest of the members, feigning shock at the carnage here.

"As I was saying, Oliver, before we were interrupted, this worthless one is mine to deal with, but if you wish I can have some expert seamstresses stitch his skin back together and make you a gift of it."

"Thanks for the offer," he said but did not look grateful. "I think I'll pass on that."

"Then I shall nail it to the wall of this tonghouse as a warning."

Jiang jumped as a slurred voice said, "The only thing you'll be doing is looking the wrong way through the bars of a jail cell."

Aiii! The detective was conscious again. He must have a skull as thick as the walls of the Imperial Palace!

The master spoke without a trace of fear. "You have at most six shots, Detective. My dacoits will be upon you before you can shoot all of them."

The detective leveled his pistol at the master's heart.

"Yeah, but the first one will go into you."

Yu started to move forward, crying, "Yes! Arrest me! Please!"

But Jiang yanked him back and struck him across the throat—not a killing blow, just enough to silence him.

The master only smiled. "You may arrest me if you wish, Detective, but that will doom the ten women this bloated slug collected for export."

The detective's eyes widened. "Ten? Good Christ, where are they?"

"In a ship in the harbor, moored at Pier Twelve. A ship wired to explode at midnight."

"You're lying!"

"He doesn't lie, Brannigan," said Oliver. "Over our years of conflict I've learned that the doctor is capable of just about anything, but he never lies."

"If you look at your watch," the master said, "you will see that you have time to bring me to your precinct house or rush to the harbor and save the women. But not both."

Jiang could see the detective's resolve wavering.

The master continued in a silky, almost seductive voice. "May I suggest the former course? Think what bringing in the mysterious and notorious Mandarin will do for your career. It will guarantee you the promotion you most surely desire."

The detective looked to Oliver. "Will you hold him here until—?"

The older man cut him off with a quick shake of his head. "This is your show, kid." He looked down at the child stirring in his arms. "I have what I came for. You choose."

He backed toward the door.

"Damn you all!"

Then he turned and ran.

Jiang knew that if the young detective broke all speed records, he might reach the docks in time. Fortunately for him, he would meet little resistance aboard ship; most of the crew had deserted once word leaked out that Yu had displeased the Mandarin.

When the detective was gone, Oliver smiled. "Dear Doctor, you never fail to find interesting ways to test people. I'm glad he chose what he did, otherwise I'd have had to send my associates to the waterfront. As it is, I've got someone here who needs some attending to, and I have a call to make."

He turned to go, then turned back.

"Oh, and those weapons your people need . . . if you have trouble buying through the usual channels, call me. I'm sure we can work something out."

And then the master shocked Jiang by doing the unthinkable. He inclined his head toward this man named Oliver.

There's still a chance, Brannigan thought as he jumped behind the wheel of his radio car. He'd call the station and send a squad of cars to the docks while he returned to the tonghouse and collared the Mandarin.

But when he snatched the microphone from its holder he noticed the frayed end of its coiled wire dangling in the air.

"Damn!"

He tossed the useless piece of garbage against the passenger door. No options left. He started the car, threw it into gear, and floored the gas pedal. He didn't think he could make it, but he was going to try.

Traffic was light and with his siren howling he reached the docks in five minutes. He found Pier Twelve and raced up the gangplank of a rustbucket freighter, his pistol held before him.

He reached the deck and, with only that wash of light from the city behind him for illumination, looked around. The tub looked deserted. Two of the three cargo hatches lay open. He ran to the third and rapped on it with the gun butt.

"Hello! Anyone in there?"

The muffled chorus of female voices from below was a sweet symphony. He found the fasteners, released them, and pulled off the cover.

"Detective Brad Brannigan," he said into the square of darkness below him, and the words had never sounded so good on his tongue. "Let's get you gals out of there."

As the captives shouted, cried, and sobbed with relief, Brannigan grabbed the rope ladder coiled by the hatch and tossed it over the edge.

"Squeeze the minutes, girls! We haven't got much time."

As the first climbed into view, a rather plain blonde, he grabbed her arm and hauled her onto the deck.

"Run! Get down the gangplank and keep going!"

He did this with each of the girls—amazingly, all blondes.

"I thought there were ten of you," he said as he helped the ninth over the rim.

"Margot hurt her ankle when they grabbed her. She can't climb up."

Hell and damn. Margot Kachmar, the one who started all this for him. He wished he could see his watch. How much time did he have left, if any?

Didn't matter. He hadn't finished the job.

He directed number nine to the gangway, then leaned over the rim and called into the darkness below.

"Margot? Are you near the ladder?"

"Yes, but—"

"No buts. Put your good foot on a rung and hold on tight."

"O-okay." He felt the ropes tighten. "I'm on. Now what?"

"I bring you up."

Brannigan sat on the deck, braced his feet against the hatch rim, and began hauling on the rope ladder. The coarse coils burned his palms and his back protested, but he kept at it, pulling rung after ropy rung up and over the edge until he saw a pair of hands grip the rim.

"Keep coming!" he shouted, maintaining tension on the rope.

When her face was visible and she had both elbows over the rim, he grabbed her and hauled her onto the deck.

"Oh, thank you!" she sobbed as she looked at the city. "I'd given up hope of ever seeing home again!"

"Don't thank me yet." He lifted her into his arms and carried her toward the gangway. "C'mon, kiddo. Your daddy's waiting for you."

His haste gave him a bad moment on the gangway as he slipped halfway down and nearly fell off. He was just stepping onto the dock with his burden safe and unharmed when a bright flash lit up the night.

"Hold it!" a man's voice said. "One more!"

The purple afterimage of the flash blotted out whoever was talking.

"What?"

A second flash and then another voice saying, "Joe Stenson from the *Chronicle*. Your name's Brannigan, right?"

"Yes, but—"

"That's with a double 'n'?"

"Get out of here!" Brannigan shouted as he began carrying Margot away from the ship. "The ship's going to blow at midnight!"

"Blow?"

"As in explode!"

"But it's already after midnight," Stenson said.

Brannigan slowed for a few steps. Had he been duped? Then he remembered what Oliver had said about the Mandarin always keeping his word and resumed his frantic pace.

"Just get away from the ship!"

"If you say so."

Stenson was pacing him to his left. A photographer ambled on his right.

"How come you two are down here?" Brannigan asked.

"Got a tip. Guy didn't give his name, just told me to get down to Pier Twelve if I wanted to catch a hero cop in action, and am I ever glad I listened. The girls told me what happened to them, and that picture of you carrying this little lady down the gangplank—hoo boy, if that's not front-page stuff, I'll quit and open a flower shop."

Ahead Brannigan could see the rest of the girls waiting near the street, cheering when they saw he had Margot. He set her down on the curb and they all gathered around, hugging her, hugging him, while the photographer flashed away.

"What was that about the ship exploding at midnight?" Stenson said. "Were you—?"

And then the pavement shook and the night lit up like day as huge explosions ripped through the old freighter, rupturing her hull and shooting hundred-foot columns of flame up from the hatches.

Stenson turned to his photographer. "Are you getting this, Louie?"

"I'm getting it, Joe. Am I ever getting it!"

The adrenaline began seeping away then, leaving Brannigan fagged. He'd missed collaring the Mandarin, but looking at these ten girls, all alive and well because of him, he couldn't help but feel on top of the world.

But who in the world had called the *Chronicle*?

He sensed motion behind him and turned to see a silver Rolls Royce gliding by. A little red-haired girl smiled and waved from the rear window before the car was swallowed by the fog.

2004

I finished a first draft of my cozy medical mystery (a short novel which I wouldn't be able to sell), then began outlining Repairman Jack number nine. This time I had a title from the get-go: *Infernal*.

While signing at a Manhattan Barnes & Noble I was approached by a comic book artist named Matthew Dow Smith. He wanted to develop some of my work into graphic novels. I told him he could pitch around and see if anyone was interested. I never shrink from finding a new audience to listen to my stories. By the end of the year we agreed with IDW to do *The Keep* as a five-issue series which would later be combined into a graphic novel: I would script and Matt would illustrate. I was looking forward to this. This graphic novel would show what the movie coulda-shoulda been.

Both *Sims* and *Gateways* were nominated for the 2004 Prometheus Award. *Sims* won and I traveled to the World SF Convention in Boston to accept the award from the Libertarian Futurist Society. As glad as I was to see my novel recognized for its sense of life and defense of human dignity—and asking what exactly does "human" mean?—I experienced no thrill of victory. Maybe because at this stage in my career awards don't mean much. It's an honor to be in the running, to have people who care about reading and writing find worth in my work, but the awards themselves . . . I'll certainly accept them if offered, but I no longer see much point in them.

Midnight Mass was published in April but I put off my signing at Dark Delicacies until May, during the Electronic Entertainment Expo (E3) in L.A. Beacon wanted to arrange a meeting between me and Hideo Kojima, the genius who created the *Metal Gear Solid* series of video games. Kojima-san is a major Repairman Jack fan and wants to do a Jack video game. Beacon owns the gaming rights, so Kojima-san has to go through them.

We had lunch at Ivy at the Shore in Santa Monica, one of those places where the elite meet to eat and greet. Saw lots of familiar faces from films and TV that I couldn't put a name to. (I'm awful at names.)

As of this writing, Kojima and Konami are still waiting for the final film script. (Which may or may not appear in my lifetime.)

We've stayed in contact. He sends me his latest games as they come out. I'd send him books but he doesn't speak English.

As for the script, the producers were underwhelmed with the latest iteration. I sensed a drastic loss of momentum. Then a young, big-name star expressed interest in playing Repairman Jack. His tender age would necessitate some significant rewriting, but his involvement lit a match under the project.

I'd ridden this Hollywood roller coaster before. The best approach was put it on the back burner and not think about it until something happened. At the start of this process (ten years now in development hell) I might have been concerned about a mid-to-late twenties actor playing mid-thirties Jack. But this was Beacon Films. By the time they got around to exposing some film, he'd be just the right age.

Somewhere around midyear I did an extensive edit on *The Tomb* for the Borderlands Press limited edition—excised a lot of extraneous prose. They published the leaner, cleaner, meaner version under my original title, *Rakoshi*.

In November I returned to L.A. for another Dark Delicacies signing (*Crisscross*, this trip). While there I met with folks from Lions Gate TV who wanted to adapt *Sims* into a miniseries. Over the next few weeks the screenwriter, producer, and I discussed changes in the story line to make *Sims* fit a four-hour, two-night format. I was okay with all of them. In fact, one of them struck me as brilliant.

So it was decided: Lions Gate would option *Sims* and pitch it to the networks come January. (SciFi Channel appeared to be the best fit.) LG-TV seemed sanguine about placing it but I wasn't on the train yet. I've learned over the years to wait until the check clears, and even then don't consider it a lock.

About that time Steve Spruill pointed out a major glitch in *Infernal,* so I went deep into revision mode.

Then I proofed *Reborn* for the Borderlands Press edition. I hadn't read it since 1989 and had forgotten its wild finale. Wow. Some over-the-top scenes. I wonder if I'd do the same now.

For the few of you who haven't heard my decades-long whine, listen: In 1983 Paramount released *The Keep*, a film by Michael Mann (yes, that Michael Mann) that happened to share a title and not much else with my novel. A dreadful movie. I learned from a number of sources that Paramount Home Entertainment planned to issue a DVD version late in November with no commentary track. To remedy that I took matters into my own hands by recording an unauthorized commentary track. Along for the ride were Douglas E. Winter (critic, biographer, novelist, columnist for *Video Watchdog*) and David J. Schow (novelist and screenwriter—e.g., *The Crow*), both acerbic wits with strong opinions about the film. We invited Mann's input but he passed. (Heh.)

We didn't exactly trash the film, but we were hard on it—justifiably so. We called the commentary *The Keep Chronicle (Dude, Where's My Book?)* and planned to release it in a double CD package to be played along with the film. We even had a deal with Pascal Records in L.A. Then we learned that the release was put off indefinitely.

Well, they can run but they can't hide. When Paramount does release it, we'll be ready.

"PART OF THE GAME"

During one of my signings at Dark Delicacies, Del Howison (co-owner with his wife, Sue) told me that he and Jeff Gelb were putting together an anthology of stories by people who'd signed at the store. They were calling it—surprise!—*Dark Delicacies*. He had no theme other than a riff on the title.

Delicacies . . . edibles . . .

I'd had such fun with my yellow-peril story that I decided to revisit the scene and write a new story, as pulpy as the last, that would intersect "Sex Slaves of the Dragon Tong."

Some of the epithets might offend those of you with tender ears, but that's the way they wrote 'em back in the 1930s.

Part of the Game

"You have been brought to attention of a most illustrious one," Jiang Zhifu said.

The Chinaman wore long black cotton pajamas with a high collar and onyx-buttoned front. He'd woven his hair into a braid that snaked out from beneath a traditional black skullcap. His eyes were as shiny and black as his onyx buttons and, typical of his kind, gave nothing away.

Detective Sergeant Hank Sorenson smiled. "I guess the Mandarin heard about my little show at Wang's pai gow parlor last night."

Jiang's mug remained typically inscrutable. "I not mention such a one."

"Didn't have to. Tell him I want to meet him."

Jiang blinked. Got him! Direct speech always set these chinks back on their heels.

Hank let his cup of tea cool on the small table between them. He'd pretend to take a sip or two but not a drop would pass his lips. He doubted anyone down here would make a move against a bull, but you could never be sure where the Mandarin was concerned.

He tried to get a bead on this coolie. A call in the night from someone saying he was Jiang Zhifu, a "representative"—these chinks made him laugh—of an important man in Chinatown. He didn't have to say who. Hank knew. The chink said they must meet to discuss important matters of mutual interest. At the Jade Moon. Ten a.m.

Hank knew the place—next to a Plum Street joss house—and he'd arrived early. First thing he'd done was check out the rear alley. All clear. Inside he'd chosen a corner table near the rear door and seated himself with his back to the wall.

The Jade Moon wasn't exactly high end as Chinkytown restaurants went:

dirty floors, smudged tumblers, chipped lacquer on the doors and trim, ratty-looking paper lanterns dangling from the exposed beams.

Not the kind of place he'd expect to meet a minion of the mysterious and powerful and ever-elusive Mandarin.

The Mandarin didn't run Chinatown's rackets. He had a better deal: He skimmed them. Never got his hands dirty except with the money that crossed them. Dope, prostitution, gambling . . . the Mandarin took a cut of everything.

How he'd pulled that off was a bigger mystery than his identity. Hank had dealt with the tongs down here—tough mugs one and all. Not the sort you'd figure to hand over part of their earnings without a fight. But they did.

Well, maybe there'd been a dustup and they lost. But if that was what had happened, it must have been fought out of sight, because he hadn't heard a word about it.

Hank had been running the no-tickee-no-shirtee beat for SFPD since 1935 and had yet to find anyone who'd ever seen the Mandarin. And they weren't just saying they'd never seen them—they meant it. If three years down here had taught him anything, it was that you never ask a chink a direct question. You couldn't treat them like regular people. You had to approach everything on an angle. They were devious, crafty, always dodging and weaving, always ducking the question and avoiding an answer.

He'd developed a nose for their lies, but had never caught a whiff of deceit when he'd asked about the Mandarin. Even when he'd played rough with a character or two, they didn't know who he was, where he was, or what he looked like.

It had taken Hank a while to reach the astonishing conclusion that they didn't *want* to know. And that had taken him aback. Chinks were gossip-mongers—yak-yak-yak in their singsong voices, trading rumors and tidbits like a bunch of old biddies. For them to avoid talking about someone meant they were afraid.

Even the little people were afraid. That said something for the Mandarin's reach.

Hank had to admit he was impressed, but hardly afraid. He wasn't a chink.

Jiang had arrived exactly at ten, kowtowing before seating himself.

"Even if I knew of such a one," the Chinaman said, "I am sure he not meet with you. He send emissary, just as my master send me."

Hank smiled. These chinks . . .

"Okay, if that's the way we're going to play it, you tell your master that I want a piece of his pie."

Jiang frowned. "Pie?"

"His cream. His skim. His payoff from all the opium and dolla-dolla girls and gambling down here."

"Ah so." Jiang nodded. "My master realize that such arrangement is part of everyday business, but one such as he not sully hands with such. He suggest you contact various sources of activities that interest you and make own arrangements with those establishments."

Hank leaned forward and put on his best snarl.

"Listen, you yellow-faced lug. I don't have time to go around bracing every penny-ante operation down here. I know your boss gets a cut from all of them, so I want a cut from *him*! Clear?"

"I afraid that quite impossible."

"*Nothing* is impossible!" He leaned back. "But I'm a reasonable man. I don't want it all. I don't even want half of it all. I'll settle for an even split of just his gambling take."

Jiang smiled. "This a jest, yes?"

"I'm serious. Dead serious. He can keep everything from the dope and the heifer dens. I want half of the Mandarin's gambling take."

Hank knew that was where the money was in Chinatown. Opium was big down here, but gambling . . . these coolies gambled on anything and everything. They had their games, sure—parlors for fan-tan, mah-jongg, pai gow, sic bo, pak kop piu, and others—but they didn't stop there. Numbers had a huge take. He'd seen slips collected day and night on street corners all over the quarter. Write down three numbers, hand them in with your money, and pray the last three Dow Jones digits matched yours at the end of trading.

They'd bet on just about any damn thing, even the weather.

They didn't bother to hide their games either. They'd post the hours of operation on their doors, and some even had touts standing out front urging people inside. Gambling was in their blood, and gambling was where the money was, so gambling was where Hank wanted to be.

No, make that *would* be.

Jiang shook his head and began to rise. "So sorry, Detective Sorenson, but—"

Hank sprang from his chair and grabbed the front of Jiang's black top.

"Listen, chink-boy! This is not negotiable! One way or another I'm going to be part of the game down here. Get that? A big part. Or else there'll *be* no game. I'll bring in squad after squad and we'll collar every numbers coolie and shut down every lousy parlor in the quarter—mah-jongg, sic bo, you name it, it's history. And then what will your boss's take be? What's a hundred percent of nothing, huh?"

He jerked Jiang closer and backhanded him across the face, then shoved him against the wall.

"Tell him he either gets smart or he gets nothing!"

Hank might have said more, but the look of murderous rage in Jiang's eyes stalled the words in his throat.

"Dog!" the chink whispered through clenched teeth. "You have made this one lose face before these people!"

Hank looked around the suddenly silent restaurant. Diners and waiters alike stood frozen, gawking at him. But Hank Sorenson wasn't about to be cowed by a bunch of coolies.

He jabbed a finger at Jiang. "Who do you think you are, calling me a—?"

Jiang made a slashing motion with his hand. "I am servant of one who would not wipe his slippers on your back. You make this one lose face, and that mean you make *him* lose face. Woe to you, Detective Sorenson."

Without warning he let out a yelp and slammed the knife-edge of his hand onto the table, then turned and walked away.

He was halfway to the door when the table fell apart.

Hank stood in shock, staring down at the pile of splintered wood. What the—?

Never mind that now. He gathered his wits and looked around. He wanted out of here, but didn't want to walk past all those staring eyes. They might see how he was shaking inside.

That table . . . if Jiang could do that to wood, what could he do to a neck?

Fending off that unsettling thought, he left by the back door. He took a deep breath of putrid, back-alley air as he stepped outside. The late morning sun hadn't risen high enough yet to break up the shadows here.

Well, he'd delivered his message. And the fact that Jiang had struck the table instead of him only reinforced what he already knew: no worry about bull busting down here. No chink would dare lay a hand on a buzzer-carrying member of the SFPD. They knew what would happen in their neighborhoods if anyone ever did something like that.

He sighed as he walked toward the street. At least during his time in the restaurant he'd been thinking of something other than Tempest. But now she came back to him. Her face, her form, her voice . . . oh, that voice.

Tempest, Tempest, Tempest . . .

"I should have killed the dog for his insult to you, Venerable," Jiang said as he knelt before the Mandarin and pressed his forehead against the stone floor.

Instead of his usual Cantonese, Jiang spoke in Mandarin—fittingly, the language the Mandarin preferred.

"No," the master said in his soft, sibilant voice. "You did well not to harm him. We must find a more indirect path to deal with such a one. Sit, Jiang."

"Thank you, Illustrious."

Jiang raised his head from the floor but remained kneeling, daring only a furtive peek at his master. Many times he had seen the one known throughout Chinatown as the Mandarin—not even Jiang knew his true name—but that did not lessen the wonder of his appearance.

A high-shouldered man standing tall and straight with his hands folded inside the sleeves of his embroidered emerald robe; a black skullcap covered the thin hair that fringed his high, domed forehead. Jiang marveled as ever at his light green eyes that almost seemed to glow.

He did not know if his master was a true mandarin—he had heard someone address him once as "Doctor"—or merely called such because of the dialect he preferred. He did know the master spoke many languages. He'd heard him speak English, French, German, and even a low form of Hindi to the dacoits in his employ.

For all the wealth flowing through his coffers, the master lived frugally. The money went back to the homeland for to serve a purpose higher than mere creature comfort.

"So this miserable offspring of a maggot demands half the gambling tribute. Wishes to be—how did he put it?—'part of the game'?"

"Yes, Magnificent."

The master closed his eyes. "Part of the game . . . part of the game . . . by all means we must grant his wish."

Jiang spent the ensuing moments of silence in a whirlpool of confusion. The master . . . giving in to the cockroach's demands? Unthinkable! And yet he'd said—

An upward glance showed the master's eyes open again and a hint of a smile curving his thin lips.

"Yes, that is it. We shall make him part of the game."

Jiang had seen that smile before. He knew what usually followed. It made him three times glad that he was not Detective Sorenson.

Hank held up his double-breasted tuxedo and inspected it, paying special attention to the wide satin lapels. No spots. Good. He could get a few more wears before sending it for cleaning.

As always, he was struck by the incongruity of a tux in his shabby two-room apartment. Well, it should look out of place. It had cost him a month's rent.

All for Tempest.

That babe was costing him a fortune. Trouble was, he didn't have a fortune. But the Chinatown games would fix that.

He shook his head. That kind of scheme would have been unthinkable back in the days when he was a fresh bull. And if not for Tempest it would still be.

But a woman can change everything. A woman can turn you inside out and upside down.

Tempest was one of those women.

He remembered the first time he'd seen her at the Serendipity Club. Like getting gut-punched. She wasn't just a choice piece of calico; she had the kind of looks that could put your conscience on hold. Then she'd stepped up to the mike and . . . a voice like an angel. When Hank heard her sing "I've Got You Under My Skin," that was it. He was gone. He'd heard the song a hundred times on the radio, but Tempest . . . Tempest made him feel like she was singing to him.

Hank had stayed on through the last show. When she finished he followed her—a flash of his buzzer got him past the geezer guarding the backstage door—and asked her out. A cop wasn't the usual stage-door Johnny and so she'd said okay.

Hank had gone all out to impress her, and they'd been on the town half a dozen times so far. She'd tapped him out without letting him get to first base. He knew he wasn't the only guy she dated—he'd spied her out with a couple rich cake eaters—but Hank wasn't the sharing kind. Trouble was, to get an exclusive on her was going to take moolah. Lots of it.

And he was going to get lots of it. A steady stream . . .

He yawned. What with playing the bon vivant by night and the soft heel by day, he wasn't getting much sleep.

He dropped onto the bed, rolled onto his back, and closed his eyes. Tempest didn't go on for another couple of hours, so a catnap would be just the ticket. He was slipping into that mellow, drowsy state just before dropping off to sleep when he felt a sharp pain in his left shoulder, like he'd been stabbed with an ice pick.

As he bolted out of bed Hank felt something wriggling against his undershirt. He reached back and felt little legs—*lots* of little legs. Fighting a sick revulsion he grabbed it and pulled. It writhed and twisted in his hand but held fast to his skin. Hank clenched his teeth and yanked.

As the thing came free, pain like he'd never known or imagined exploded in his shoulder, driving him to his knees. He dropped the wriggling creature and slapped a hand over the live coal embedded in his shoulder. Through tear-blurred vision he saw a scarlet millipede at least eight inches long scurrying away across the floor.

"What the—?"

He reached for something, anything to use against it. He grabbed a shoe and smashed it down on the thing. The heel caught the back half of its body and Hank felt it squish with a crunch. The front half spasmed, reared up, then tore free and darted under the door and out into the hallway before he could get a second shot.

Hell with it! His shoulder was killing him.

He brought his hand away and found blood on his palm. Not much but enough to shake him. He struggled to his feet and stepped into his tiny bathroom. The bright bulb over the speckled mirror picked up the beads of sweat on his brow.

He was shaking. What was that thing? He'd never seen anything like it. And how had it got in his room, in his *bed,* for Christ sake?

He half turned and angled his shoulder toward the mirror. The size of the bite surprised him—only a couple of punctures within a small smear of blood. From the ferocity of the pain he'd expected something like a .38 entry wound.

The burning started to subside. Thank God. He balled up some toilet tissue and dabbed at the wound. Looky there. Stopped bleeding already.

He went back to the front room and looked at the squashed remains of the thing. Damn. It looked like something you'd find in a jungle. Like the Amazon.

How'd it wind up in San Francisco?

Probably crawled off a boat.

Hank shuddered as he noticed a couple of the rearmost legs still twitching. He kicked it into a corner.

"The usual table, Detective?" Maurice said with a practiced smile.

Hank nodded and followed the Serendipity's maître d' to a second-level table for two just off the dance floor.

"Thank you, Maurice."

He passed him a fin he could barely afford as they shook hands. He ordered a scotch and water and started a tab. This was the last night he'd be able to do this until the Mandarin came across with some lucre.

He shook his head. All it takes is money. You don't have to be smart or even good-looking, all you need is lots of do-re-mi and everybody wants to know you. Suddenly you're Mr. Popularity.

As Hank sipped his drink and waited for Tempest to take the stage, he felt his shoulder start to burn. Damn. Not again. The pain had lasted only half an hour after the bite and then felt as good as new. But now it was back and growing stronger.

Heat spread from the bite, flowing through him, burning his skin, breaking him out in a sweat. Suddenly he had no strength. His hands, his arms, his legs . . . all rubbery. The glass slipped from his fingers, spilling scotch down the pleated front of his shirt.

The room rocked and swayed as he tried to rise, but his legs wouldn't hold him. He felt himself falling, saw the curlicue pattern of the rug rushing at him.

Then nothing.

Hank opened his eyes and found himself looking up at a woman in white. She looked about fifty. He looked down. More white. Sheets. He was in a bed.

"Where—?"

She flashed a reassuring smile. "You're in St. Luke's and you're going to be just fine. I'll let your doctor know you're awake."

Hank watched her bustle out the door. He felt dazed. The last thing he remembered—

That bite from the millipede—poison. Had to be.

The pain had tapered to a dull ache, but he still felt weak as a kitty.

A balding man with a gray mustache strode through the door and stepped up to the bed. He wore a white coat with a pair of pens in the breast pocket and carried a clipboard under his arm.

"Detective Sorenson," he said, extending his hand, "I'm Doctor Cranston, and you've got quite a boil on your back."

"Boil?"

"Yes. A pocket of infection in your skin. You shouldn't let those things go. The infection can seep into your system and make you very ill. How long have you had it?"

Hank pulled the hospital gown off his shoulder and gaped at the golf ball–size red swelling.

"That wasn't there when I put on my shirt tonight."

Dr. Cranston harrumphed. "Of course it was. These things don't reach that size in a matter of hours."

A flash of anger cut through Hank's fuzzy brain. "This one did. I was bitten there by a giant bug around seven o'clock."

Cranston smoothed his mustache. "Really? What kind of bug?"

"Don't know. Never seen anything like it."

"Well, be that as it may, we'll open it up, clean out the infection, and you'll be on your way in no time."

Hank hoped so.

Bared to the waist, Hank lay on his belly while the nurse swabbed his shoulder with some sort of antiseptic.

"You may feel a brief sting as I break the skin, but once we relieve the pressure from all that pus inside, it'll be like money from home."

Hank looked up and saw the scalpel in Cranston's hand. He turned away. "Do it."

Cranston was half right: Hank felt the sting, but no relief.

He heard Cranston mutter, "Well, this is one for Ripley's."

Hank didn't like the sound of that.

"What's wrong?"

"Most odd. There's no pus in this, only serous fluid."

"What's serous fluid?"

"A clear amber fluid—just like you'd see seeping from a burn blister. Most odd, most odd." Cranston cleared his throat. "I believe we'll keep you overnight."

"But I can't—"

"You must. You're too weak to be sent home. And I want to look into this insect. What did it look like?"

"Send someone to my place and you'll find its back half."

"I believe I'll do just that."

Two days cooped up in a hospital room hadn't made Hank any better. He had to get out to seal the deal with the Mandarin. But how? He was able to stand and walk—shuffle was more like it—but he still felt so weak. And the pounds were dropping off him like leaves from a tree.

The boil or whatever it was had gone from a lump to a big open sore that wept fluid all day.

He was sitting on the edge of the bed, looking out at the fogged-in city when Cranston trundled in.

"Well, we've identified that millipede."

Here was the first good news since he'd been bitten.

"What is it?"

"The entomologists over at Berkeley gave it a name as long as your arm. Other than that they weren't much help. Said it was very, very rare, and that only a few have ever been seen. Couldn't imagine how it managed to travel from the rain forests of Borneo to your bed."

"Borneo," Hank said. Everybody had heard of the Wild Man from Borneo but . . . "Just where the hell is Borneo?"

"It's an island in the South China Sea."

"Did you say South *China* Sea?"

Cranston nodded. "Yes. Why? Is that important?"

Hank didn't answer. He couldn't. It was all clear now.

Good Christ . . . China . . .

The Mandarin had sent his reply to Hank's demand.

"There's, um, something else you should know."

Cranston's tone snapped Hank's head up. The doctor looked uneasy. His gaze wandered to the window.

"You mean it gets worse?" Cranston's nod sent a sick, cold spike through Hank's gut. "Okay. Give it to me."

Cranston took a breath. "The millipede may or may not have injected you with venom, but that's not the problem." His voice trailed off.

Hank didn't know if he wanted to hear this.

"What *is* the problem then?"

"You remember when we did a scraping of the wound?"

"How could I forget?"

"Well, we did a microscopic examination and found what, um, appear to be eggs."

Hank's gut twisted into a knot.

"Eggs!"

"Yes."

"Did you get them all?"

"We don't know. They're quite tiny. But we'll go back in and do another scraping, deeper this time. But you should know . . ."

"Know what?"

Cranston's gaze remained fixed on the window.

"They're hatching."

Next day, one of the green soft heels, a grade-one detective named Brannigan, stopped by to ask about Chinatown. He'd been assigned to look for a missing white girl last seen down there. He was asking about the Mandarin. Hank warned him away, even went so far as to show him the big, weeping ulcer on his shoulder.

Suddenly he was seized by a coughing fit, one that went on and on until he hacked up a big glob of bright red phlegm. The blood shocked him, but the sight of the little things wriggling in the gooey mass completely unnerved him.

"Oh, God!" he cried to Brannigan. "Call the doctor! Get the nurse in here! Hurry!"

The eggs had hatched and they were in his lungs! How had they gotten into his lungs?

Sick horror pushed a sob to his throat. He tried to hold it back until Brannigan was out the door. He didn't think he made it.

Hank stared at the stranger in the bathroom mirror.

"It's not unprecedented," Cranston had said. "Larva of the ascaris round worm, for instance, get into the circulation and migrate through the lung. But we've no experience with this species."

He saw sunken cheeks; glassy, feverish eyes; sallow, sweaty skin as pale as the sink, and knew he was looking at a dead man.

Why hadn't he just played it straight—or at least only a little bent—and taken a payoff here and there from the bigger gambling parlors? Why had he tried to go for the big score?

He was coughing up baby millipedes every day. That thing must have laid thousands, maybe tens of thousands of eggs in his shoulder. Her babies were sitting in his lungs, sucking off his blood as it passed through, eating him alive from the inside.

And nobody could do a damn thing about it.

He started to cry. He'd been doing that a lot lately. He couldn't help it. He felt so damn helpless.

The phone started to ring. Probably Hanrahan. The chief had been down to see him once and had never returned. Hank didn't blame him. Probably couldn't stand looking at the near-empty shell he'd become.

Hank shuffled to the bedside and picked up the receiver.

"Yeah."

"Ah, Detective Sorenson," said a voice he immediately recognized. "So glad you are still with us."

A curse leaped to his lips but he bit it back. He didn't need any more bugs in his bed.

"No thanks to you."

"Ah, so. A most regrettable turn of events, but also most inevitable, given such circumstances."

"Did you call to gloat?"

"Ah, no. I call to offer you your wish."

Hank froze as a tremor of hope ran through his ravaged body. He was almost afraid to ask.

"You can cure me?"

"Come again to Jade Moon at three o'clock this day and your wish shall be granted."

The line went dead.

The cab stopped in front of the Jade Moon. Hank needed just about every ounce of strength to haul himself out of the rear seat.

The nurses had wailed, Dr. Cranston had blustered, but they couldn't keep him if he wanted to go. When they saw how serious he was, the nurses dug up a cane to help him walk.

He leaned on that cane now and looked around. The sidewalk in front of the restaurant was packed with chinks, and every one of them staring at him. Not just staring—pointing and whispering too.

Couldn't blame them. He must be quite a sight in his wrinkled, oversize tux. Used to fit like tailor-made, but now it hung on him like a coat on a scarecrow. But he'd had no choice. This had been the only clothing in his hospital room closet.

He stepped up on the curb and stood swaying. For a few seconds he feared he might fall. The cane saved him.

He heard the singsong babble increase and noticed that the crowd was growing, with more chinks pouring in from all directions, so many that they blocked the street. All staring, pointing, whispering.

Obviously Jiang had put out the word to come see the bad joss that befell anyone who went against the Mandarin.

Well, Hank thought as he began his shuffle toward the restaurant door, enjoy the show, you yellow bastards.

The crowd parted for him and watched as he struggled to open the door. No one stepped up to help. Someone inside pushed it open and pointed to the rear of the restaurant.

Hank saw Jiang sitting at the same table where they'd first met. Only this time Jiang's back was to the wall. He didn't kowtow, didn't even rise when Hank reached the table.

"Sit, Detective Sorenson," he said, indicating the other chair.

He looked exactly the same as last time: same black pajamas, same skullcap, same braid, same expressionless face.

Hank, on the other hand . . .

"I'll stand."

"Ah so, you not looking well. I must tell you that if you fall this one not help you up."

Hank knew if he went down he'd never be able to get up on his own. What then? Would all the chinks outside be paraded past him for another look?

He dropped into the chair. That was when he noticed something like an ebony cigar box sitting before Jiang.

"What's that? Another bug?"

Jiang pushed it toward Hank.

"Ah no, very much opposite. This fight your infestation."

Hank closed his eyes and bit back a sob. A cure . . . was he really offering a cure? But he knew there had to be a catch.

"What do I have to do for it?"

"Must take three time a day."

Hank couldn't believe it.

"That's it? No strings?"

Jiang shook his head. "No, as you say, strings." He opened the box to reveal dozens of cigarette-size red paper cylinders. "Merely break one open three time a day and breathe fine powder within."

As much as Hank wanted to believe, his mind still balked at the possibility that this could be on the level.

"That's it? Three times a day and I'll be cured?"

"I not promise cure. I say it fight infestation."

"What's the difference? And what is this stuff?"

"Eggs of tiny parasite."

"A parasite!" Hank pushed the box away. "Not on your life!"

"This is true. Not on my life—on *your* life."

"I don't get it."

"There is order to universe, Detective Sorenson: Everything must feed. Something must die so that other may live. And it is so with these powdery parasite eggs. Humans do not interest them. They grow only in larvae that infest your lung. They devour host from inside and leave own eggs in carcass."

"Take a parasite to kill a parasite? That's crazy."

"Not crazy. It is poetry."

"How do I know it won't just make me sicker?"

Jiang smiled, the first time he'd changed his expression. "Sicker? How much more sick can Detective Sorenson be?"

"I don't get it. You half kill me, then you offer to cure me. What's the deal? Your Mandarin wants a pet cop, is that it?"

"I know of no Mandarin. And once again, I not promise cure, only *chance* of cure."

Hank's hopes tripped but didn't fall.

"You mean it might not work?"

"It matter of balance, Detective. Have larvae gone too far for parasite to kill all in time? Or does Detective Sorenson still have strength enough left to survive? That is where fun come in."

"Fun? You call this *fun*?"

"Fun not for you or for this one. Fun for everyone else because my master decide grant wish you made."

"Wish? What wish?"

"To be part of game—your very words. Remember?"

Hank remembered, but . . .

"I'm not following you."

"All of Chinatown taking bet on you."

"On me?"

"Yes. Even money on whether live or die. And among those who believe you soon join ancestors, a lottery on when." Another smile. "You have your wish, Detective Sorenson. You now very much part of game. Ah so, you *are* game."

Hank wanted to scream, wanted to bolt from his chair and wipe the smirk off Jiang's rotten yellow face. But that was only a dream. The best he could do was sob and let the tears stream down his cheeks as he reached into the box for one of the paper cylinders.

2005

Call this The Year of Hollywoodus Interruptus.

It started off well enough. The chairwoman of the 2005 World Horror Convention called to inform me that I'd been elected this year's Grand Master. That meant joining the likes of Bloch, Bradbury, Matheson, King, and Straub. Cool. Very cool.

IDW (the company doing *The Keep* graphic novel) was planning a new anthology comic modeled on the old *Creepy* and *Eerie* magazines of yore ("yore" being the Hindi word for mid-1960s). They were calling it *Doomed* and asked me to adapt one of my short stories for it. I chose my nasty, bitter Hollywood horror, "Cuts." They liked that so much they asked me to adapt three more. Over the next few months I scripted "Slasher," "Pelts," and "Faces." After they appeared in *Doomed*, all four stories were to be combined into a graphic mini-collection.

On the Hollywood front, Beacon hired Joel Fields to rework the *Repairman Jack* script to accommodate the young star. I met with Joel in NYC and we talked character. He seemed to have a firm grasp on Jack and I had a good feeling about the work he'd do. After many meetings with the studio and the star, and a number of rewrites, he was able to deliver a new script by the end of the year.

Elsewhere in Hollywood, Lions Gate TV pitched the *Sims* miniseries to the SciFi Channel. After a four-week wait, they passed. Even so, I was told the project was still very much alive (everyone was still "very excited"—*excited* is a word you hear *ad nauseam* in Hollywood) but I wasn't buying. The *Sims* miniseries died with a whimper.

I got busy on Repairman Jack number ten. The delivery date had been moved from December up to September. I had to start cranking. Once again, I was lost as to a title.

My agent contacted me about Amazon Shorts, a new feature at Amazon.com that would allow readers to download a short story for a nominal fee. Could I write something for them?

Let's see . . . what's on my plate? The tenth Jack novel, an RJ short story for International Thriller Writers' *Thriller*, scripting five issues of *The Keep* miniseries, adapting four short stories for *Doomed*, revising the text and writing a foreword to the Infrapress edition of *Wheels Within Wheels*, revising *Reprisal* for Borderlands Press, revising *The Tery* and "The Last Rakosh" for Overlook Connection Press.

No, I couldn't do a short story.

But I did have a long-lost Repairman Jack piece called "The Long Way Home." It appeared in Joe and Karen Lansdale's four-hundred-copy *Dark at Heart* anthology in 1992 and hadn't been seen since. Show them that.

On the morning of May 11, Amazon, adamant about no previously published material, rejected it. By afternoon they'd reversed themselves. I was told that Jeff Bezos himself had said to screw the technicality in this case.

So I revised the story to bring it into the twenty-first century and sent it in. Amazon Shorts launched in August. "The Long Way Home" became the second most downloaded story during the program's first six months.

The deadline for Repairman Jack number ten was fast approaching. I was going to make the delivery date, but still had no title. I offered a few story points on the repairmanjack.com forum and asked for suggestions. Lisa Krause came up with *Harbingers*, which I thought was perfect. She was honored in the acknowledgments. (See, it pays to hang out at the forum.)

In September Hollywood came a-calling on two fronts.

First, an offer from Showtime's *Masters of Horror* to adapt "Pelts" for its second season. A fellow named Matt Venne did a great script. Now all we needed was one of their stable of famous directors (the "Masters of Horror" of the title) to choose it for filming. This was not a guarantee: *MoH* commissioned more scripts than it could use.

Next, an offer from Twentieth Century Fox TV to develop *The Touch* into a TV series. Kevin Falls (writer-producer of shows like *Sports Night*, *Arliss*, *West Wing*) would be the show runner.

Kevin and I had a lot of contact—calls, e-mails, dinner—over the next few months. We discussed the changes necessary to turn the book into a series and they were all fine with me. ABC approved the outline for the pilot. The network was very "excited." (The "e" word again.) He sent me the pilot script in December and I loved it. So did the development people at ABC. Now it went to the head honchos for the greenlight decision. We were competing against ninety pilot scripts, of which only twelve would be shot. We wouldn't hear until sometime in January.

So the 2005 scorecard ran something like this: All writing obligations successfully completed; one TV miniseries shot down; a TV movie, a TV series, and a theatrical film still in the air.

And all I could do was wait.

"INTERLUDE AT DUANE'S"

In January David Morrell and I were instructors at the Borderlands Bootcamp for Writers. David had helped start the International Thriller Writers organization and induced me to join. Then ITW induced me to donate a Repairman Jack story to their anthology (*Thriller*) to raise funds for the organization.

Thus was "Interlude at Duane's" born. All contributors were limited to a 5,000 word count. I could have used more. Toward the end I was on fire, burning up the keyboard. I wish I could write with that speed and intensity all the time.

As you will see, this one was *fun*.

Interlude at Duane's

"Lemme tell you, Jack," Loretta said, blotting perspiration from her Fudgsicle-colored skin, "these changes gots me in a baaaad mood."

They'd just finished playing some real-life *Frogger* jaywalking 57th and were now chugging west.

"Real bad. My feets killin me too. Nobody better hassle me afore I'm home and on the outside of a big ol glass of Jimmy."

Jack nodded, paying just enough attention to be polite. He was more interested in the passersby and was thinking how a day without your carry was like a day without clothes.

He felt naked. Had to leave his trusty Glock and backup home today because of his annual trip to the Empire State Building. He'd designated April 19th King Kong Day. Every year he made a pilgrimage to the observation deck to leave a little wreath in memory of the Big Guy. The major drawback to the outing was the metal detector everyone had to pass through before heading upstairs. That meant no heat.

He didn't think he was being paranoid. Okay, maybe a little, but he'd pissed off his share of people in this city and didn't care to run into them naked.

After the wreath-laying ceremony, he ran into Loretta and walked her back toward Hell's Kitchen. Oh, wait. It was Clinton now.

They went back a dozen or so years to when both waited tables at a now-extinct trattoria on West Fourth. She'd been fresh up from Mississippi then, and he only a few years out of Jersey. Agewise, Loretta had a good decade on Jack, maybe more—might even be knocking on the door to fifty. Had a good hundred pounds on him too. Her Rubenesque days were just a fond, slim memory, but she was solid—no jiggle. She'd dyed her Chia-Pet hair orange and sheathed herself in some shapeless, green-and-yellow thing that made her look like a brown manatee in a muumuu.

She stopped and stared at a black cocktail dress in a boutique window.

"Ain't that pretty. Course I'll have to wait till I'm cremated afore I fits into it."

They continued to Seventh Avenue. As they stopped on the corner and waited for the walking green, two Asian women came up to her.

The taller one said, "You know where Saks Fifth Avenue?"

Loretta scowled. "On Fifth Avenue, fool." Then she took a breath and jerked a thumb over her shoulder. "That way."

Jack looked at her. "You weren't kidding about the bad mood."

"You ever know me to kid, Jack?" She glanced around. "Sweet Jesus, I need me some comfort food. Like some chocolate-peanut-butter-swirl ice cream." She pointed to the Duane Reade on the opposite corner. "There."

"That's a drugstore."

"Honey, you know better'n that. Duane's got everything. Shoot, if mine had a butcher section I wouldn't have to shop nowheres else. Come on."

Before he could opt out, she grabbed his arm and started hauling him across the street.

"I specially like their makeup. Some places just carry Cover Girl, y'know, which is fine if you a Wonder Bread blonde. Don't know if you noticed, but white ain't zackly a big color in these parts. Everybody darker. Cept you, a course. I know you don't like attention, Jack, but if you had a smidge of coffee in your cream you'd be *really* invisible."

Jack expended a lot of effort on being invisible. He'd inherited a good start with his average height, average build, average brown hair, and nondescript face. Today he'd accessorized with a Mets cap, flannel shirt, worn Levi's, and battered work boots. Just another guy, maybe a construction worker, ambling along the streets of Zoo York.

Jack slowed as they approached the door.

"Think I'll take a raincheck, Lo."

She tightened her grip on his arm. "Hell you will. I need some company. I'll even buy you a Dew. Caffeine still your drug of choice?"

"Guess . . . till it's time for a beer." He eased his arm free. "Okay, I'll spring for five minutes, but after that, I'm gone. Things to do."

"Five minutes ain't nuthin, but okay."

"You go ahead. I'll be right with you."

He slowed in her wake so he could check out the entrance. He spotted a camera just inside the door, trained on the comers and goers.

He tugged down the visor of his cap and lowered his head. He was catching up to Loretta when he heard a loud, heavily accented voice.

"*Mira! Mira! Mira!* Look at the fine ass on you!"

Jack hoped that wasn't meant for him. He raised his head far enough to see a grinning, mustachioed Latino leaning against the wall next to the doorway. A maroon gym bag sat at his feet. He had glossy, slicked-back hair and prison tats on the backs of his hands.

Loretta stopped and stared at him. "You better not be talkin a me!"

His grin widened. "But señorita, in my country it is a privilege for a woman to be praised by someone like me."

"And just where is this country of yours?"

"Ecuador."

"Well, you in New York now, honey, and I'm a bitch from the Bronx. Talk to me like that again and I'm gonna Bruce Lee yo ass."

"But I know you would like to sit on my face."

"Why? Yo nose bigger'n yo dick?"

This cracked up a couple of teenage girls leaving the store. Mr. Ecuador's face darkened. He didn't seem to appreciate the joke.

Head down, Jack crowded close behind Loretta as she entered the store.

She said, "Told you I was in a bad mood."

"That you did, that you did. Five minutes, Loretta, okay?"

"I hear you."

He glanced over his shoulder and saw Mr. Ecuador pick up his gym bag and follow them inside.

Jack paused as Loretta veered off toward one of the cosmetic aisles. He watched to see if Ecuador was going to hassle her, but he kept on going, heading toward the rear.

Duane Reade drugstores are a staple of New York life. The city has hundreds of them. Only the hoity-toitiest Upper East Siders hadn't visited one. Their most consistent feature was their lack of consistency. No two were the same size or laid out alike. Okay, they all kept the cosmetics near the front, but after that it became anyone's guess where something might be hiding. Jack could see the method to that madness: The more time people had to spend looking for what they had come for, the greater their chances of picking up things they hadn't.

This one seemed fairly empty and Jack assigned himself the task of finding the ice cream to speed their departure. He set off through the aisles and quickly became disoriented. The overall space was L-shaped, but instead of running in parallel paths to the rear, the aisles zigged and zagged. Whoever laid out this place was either a devotee of chaos theory or a crop circle designer.

He was wandering among the six-foot-high shelves and passing the hemor-rhoid treatments when he heard a harsh voice behind him.

"Keep movin, yo. Alla way to the back."

Jack looked and saw a big, steroidal black guy in a red tank top. The over-head fluorescents gleamed off his shaven scalp. He had a fat scar running through his left eyebrow, glassy eyes, and held a snub-nose .38 caliber revolver—the classic Saturday night special.

Jack kept his cool and held his ground. "What's up?"

The guy raised the gun, holding it sideways like in movies, the way no one who knew squat about pistols would be caught dead holding one.

"Ay yo, get yo ass in gear fore I bust one in yo face."

Jack waited a couple more seconds to see if the guy would move closer and put the pistol within reach. But he didn't.

Not good. On the way to the rear, the big question was whether this was personal or not. When he saw the gaggle of frightened-looking people—the white-coated ones obviously pharmacists—kneeling before the rear counter with their hands behind their necks, he figured it wasn't.

A relief . . . sort of.

He spotted Mr. Ecuador standing over them with a gleaming nickel-plated .357 revolver.

Robbery.

The black guy pushed him from behind.

"Assume the position, asshole."

Jack spotted two cameras trained on the pharmacy area. He knelt at the end of the line, intertwined his fingers behind his neck, and kept his eyes on the floor.

Okay, just keep your head down to stay off the cameras and off these bo-zos' radar, and you'll walk away with the rest of them.

He glanced up when he heard a commotion to his left. A scrawny little Sammy Davis–size Rasta man with his hair packed into a red, yellow, and green striped knit cap appeared. He was packing a sawed-off pump-action twelve and driving another half dozen people before him. A frightened-looking Loretta was among them.

And then a fourth—Christ, how many were there? This one was white and had dirty, sloppy, light-brown dreads, piercings up the wazoo, and was hump-ing the whole hip-hop catalog: peak-askew trucker cap, wide, baggy, ass-crack-riding jeans, huge New York Giants jersey.

He pointed another special as he propelled a dark-skinned, middle-aged Indian or Pakistani by the neck.

Both the Rasta and the new guy had glazed eyes. Stoned. Maybe it would make them mellow.

What a crew. Probably met in Rikers. Or maybe the Tombs.

"Got Mister Maaaanagerrrr," the white guy singsonged.

Ecuador looked at him. "You lock the front door?"

Whitey jangled a crowded key chain and tossed it on the counter.

"Yep. All locked in safe and sound."

"*Bueno.* Get back up there and watch in case we miss somebody. Don't wan nobody gettin out."

"Yeah, in a minute. Somethin I gotta do first."

He shoved the manager forward, then slipped behind the counter and disappeared into the pharmacy area.

"Wilkins! I tol you get up front!"

Wilkins reappeared carrying three large plastic stock bottles. He plopped them down on the counter. Jack spotted PERCOCET and OXYCONTIN on the labels.

"These babies are mine. Don't nobody touch em."

Ecuador spoke through his teeth. "*Up front!*"

"Dude, I'm gone," Wilkins said and headed away.

Scarbrow grabbed the manager by the jacket and shook him.

"The combination, mofo—give it up."

Jack noticed the guy's name tag: J. PATEL. His dark skin went a couple of shades lighter. The poor guy looked ready to faint.

"I do not know it!"

Rasta man raised his shotgun and pressed the muzzle against Patel's quaking throat.

"You tell de mon what he want to know. You tell him *now!*"

Jack saw a wet stain spreading from Patel's crotch.

"The manager's ou-out. I d-don't know the combination."

Ecuador stepped forward. "Then you not much use to us, eh?"

Patel sagged to his knees and held up his hands. "Please! I have a wife, children!"

"You wan see them again, you tell me. I know you got armored car pickup every Tuesday. I been watchin. Today is Tuesday, so give."

"But I do not—!"

Ecuador slammed his pistol barrel against the side of Patel's head, knocking him down.

"You wan die to save you boss's money? You wan see what happen when you get shot inna head? Here. I show you." He turned and looked at his prisoners. "Where that big bitch with the big mouth?" He smiled as he spotted Loretta. "There you are."

Shit.

Ecuador grabbed her by the front of her dress and pulled, making her knee-walk out from the rest. When she'd moved a half dozen feet he released her.

"Turn roun, bitch."

Without getting off her knees, she swiveled to face her fellow captives. Her lower lip quivered with terror. She made eye contact with Jack, silently pleading for him to do something, anything, *please*!

Couldn't let this happen.

His mind raced through scenarios, moves he might make to save her, but none of them worked.

As Ecuador raised the .357 and pointed it at the back of Loretta's head, Jack remembered the security cameras.

He raised his voice. "You really want to do that on TV?"

Ecuador swung the pistol toward Jack.

"What the fuck?"

Without looking around, Jack pointed toward the pharmacy security cameras.

"You're on *Candid Camera*."

"The fuck you care?"

Jack put on a sheepish grin. "Nothing. Just thought I'd share. Done some boosting in my day and caught a jolt in Riker's for not noticing one of them things. Now I notice—believe me, I *notice*."

Ecuador looked up at the cameras and said, "Fuck."

He turned to Rasta man and pointed. Rasta smiled, revealing a row of gold-framed teeth, and raised his shotgun.

Jack started moving with the first booming report, when all eyes were on the exploding camera. With the second boom he reached cover and streaked down an aisle.

Behind him he heard Ecuador shout, "Ay! The fuck he go? Wilkins! Somebody comin you way!"

The white guy's voice called back, "I'm ready, dog!"

Jack had hoped to surprise Wilkins and grab his pistol, but that wasn't going to happen now. Christ! On any other day he'd have a couple dozen 9mm hollowpoints loaded and ready.

He'd have to improvise.

As he zigged and zagged along the aisles, he sent out a silent thank-you to the maniac who'd laid out these shelves. If they'd run straight, front to back, he wouldn't last a minute. He felt like a mouse hunting for cheese, but this weird, mazelike configuration gave him a chance.

He hurried along, looking for something, anything to use against them. Didn't even have his knife, damn it.

Batteries . . . notebooks . . . markers . . . pens . . . gum . . . greeting cards . . .

No help.

He saw a comb with a pointed handle and grabbed it. Without stopping, he ripped it from its package and stuck it in his back pocket.

He heard Ecuador yelling about how he was going this way and Jamal should go that way, and Demont should stay with the people.

Band-Aids . . . ice cream . . . curling iron—could he use that? Nah.

Hair color . . . humidifiers . . . Cheetos . . . beef jerky—

Come *on*!

He turned a corner and came to a summer cookout section. Chairs—no help. Umbrella—no help. Heavy-duty spatula—grabbed it and hefted it. Nice weight, stainless steel blade, serrated on one edge. Might be able to do a little damage with this. Spotted a grouping of butane matches. Grabbed one. Never hurt to have fire.

Fire . . . he looked up and saw the sprinkler system. Every store in New York had to have one. A fire would set off the sprinklers, sending an alert to the FDNY.

Do it.

He grabbed a can of lighter fluid and began spraying the shelves. When he'd emptied half of it and the fluid was puddling on the floor, he reached for the butane match—

A shot. A *whizzz!* past his head. A quick glance down the aisle to where Scarbrow—who had to be the Jamal Ecuador had called to—stood ten yards away, leveling his .38 for another go.

"Ay yo I found him! Over here!"

Jack ducked and ran around a corner as the second bullet sailed past, way wide. Typical of this sort of oxygen waster, he couldn't shoot. Junk guns like his were good for close-up damage and little else.

With footsteps behind him, Jack paused at the shelf's endcap and took a quick peek at the neighboring aisle. No one in sight. He dashed across to the next aisle and found himself facing a wall. Ten feet down to his right—a door.

EMPLOYEES ONLY

He pulled it open and stuck his head inside. Empty except for a table and some sandwich wrappers. And no goddamn exit.

Feet pounded his way from behind to the left. He slammed the door hard and ran right. He stopped at the first endcap and dared a peek.

Jamal rounded the bend and slid to a halt before the door, a big grin on his face.

"Gotcha now, asshole."

In a crouch, gun ready, he yanked open the door. After a few heartbeats he stepped into the room.

Here was Jack's chance. He squeezed his wrist through the leather thong in the barbecue spatula's handle, raised it into a two-handed kendo grip, serrated edge forward.

Then he moved, gliding in behind Jamal and swinging at his head. Maybe the guy heard something, maybe he saw a shadow, maybe he had a sixth sense. Whatever the reason, he ducked to the side and the chop landed wide. Jamal howled as the edge bit into his meaty shoulder. Jack raised the spatula for a backhand strike, but the big guy proved more agile than he looked. He rolled and raised his pistol.

Jack swung the spatula at it, made contact, but the blade bounced off without knocking the gun free.

Time to go.

He was in motion before Jamal could aim. The first shot splintered the doorframe a couple of inches to the left of his head as he dove for the opening. He hit the floor and rolled as the second went high.

Four shots. That left two—unless Jamal had brought extras. Jack couldn't imagine a guy like Jamal thinking that far ahead.

On his way toward the rear, switching aisles at every opportunity, he heard Ecuador shouting from the far side of the store.

"Jamal! You get him? You get him?"

"No. Fucker almost got me! I catch him I'm gonna skin him alive."

"Ain't got time for that! Truck be here soon! Gotta get inna the safe! Wilkins! Get back here and start lookin'!"

"Who's gonna watch the front, dog?"

"Fuck the front! We're locked in, ain't we?"

"Yeah, but—"

"Find him!"

"A'ight. Guess I'll have to show you boys how it's done."

Jack now had a pretty good idea where Ecuador and Jamal were—too near the barbecue section to risk going back. So he moved ahead. Toward Wilkins. He sensed that if this chain had a weak link, Wilkins was it.

Along the way he scanned the shelves. He still had the spatula, the comb, and the butane match but needed something flammable.

Antibiotic ointments . . . laxatives . . . marshmallows . . .

Shit.

He zigged and zagged until he found the hair-care aisle. Possibilities here. Needed a spray can.

What the—?

Every goddamn bottle was pump action. He wanted fluorocarbons. Where were fluorocarbons when you needed them?

He ran down to the deodorant section. Everything here was either a roll-on or a smear-on. Whatever happened to Right Guard?

He spotted a green can on a bottom shelf, half hidden behind a Mitchum's floor display. Brut. He grabbed it and scanned the label.

DANGER: Contents under pressure . . . flammable . . .

Yes!

Then he heard Wilkins singsonging along the neighboring aisle, high as the space station.

"Hello, Mister Silly Man. Where aaaare youuu? Jimmy's got a present for you." He giggled. "No, wait. Jimmy's got six—count em—six presents for you. Come and get em."

High as the space station.

Jack decided to take him up on his offer.

He removed the Brut cap as he edged to the end of the aisle and flattened against the shelf section separating him from Wilkins. He raised the can and held the tip of the match next it. The instant Wilkins's face came into view, Jack reached forward, pressing the nozzle and triggering the match. A ten-inch jet of flame engulfed Wilkins's eyes and nose.

He howled and dropped the gun, lurched away, kicking and screaming. His dreads had caught fire.

Jack followed him. He used the spatula to knock off the can's nozzle. Deodorant sprayed a couple of feet into the air. He shoved the can down the back of Wilkins's oversized jeans and struck the match. His seat exploded in flame. Jack grabbed the pistol and trotted into an aisle. Screams followed him toward the back.

One down, three to go.

He checked the pistol as he moved. An old .38 revolver with most of its bluing rubbed off. He opened the cylinder. Six hardball rounds. A piece of crap, but at least it was his piece of crap.

The odds had just become a little better.

A couple of pairs of feet started pounding toward the front. As he'd hoped, the screams were drawing a crowd.

He heard cries of "Oh, shit" and "Oh, fuck!" and "What he *do* to you, bro?"

Wilkins wailed in a glass-breaking pitch. "Pepe! Help me, man! I'm dyin!"

Pepe . . . now Ecuador had a name.

"*Sí,*" Pepe said. "You are."

Wilkins screamed, "No!"

A booming gunshot—had to come from the .357.

"Fuck!" Jamal cried. "I don't believe you *did* that!"

A voice called from the back. "What goin on dere, mon? What happening?"

"S'okay, Demont!" Pepe called back. "Jus stay where you are!" Then, in a lower voice to Jamal: "Wilkins jus slow us down. Now find that fuck fore he find a phone!"

Jack looked back and saw a plume of white smoke rising toward the ceiling. He waited for the alarm, the sprinklers.

Nothing.

What did he have to do—set a bonfire?

He slowed as he came upon the employee lounge again. Nah. That wasn't going to work twice. He kept going. He was passing the ice cream freezer when something boomed to his right and a glass door shattered to his left. Ice cream sandwiches and cones flew, gallons rolled.

Jack spotted Demont three aisles away, saw him pumping another shell into the chamber of his shotgun. He ducked back as the top of the nearest shelf exploded in a cloud of shredded tampons.

"Back here, mon! Back here!"

Jack hung at the opposite endcap until he heard Demont's feet crunch on broken glass in the aisle he'd just left. He eased down the neighboring lane, listening, stopping at the feminine hygiene area as he waited for Demont to come even.

As he raised his pistol and held it two inches from the flimsy metal of the shelving unit's rear wall, he noticed a "personal" douche bag box sitting at eye level. *Personal?* Was there a community model?

When he heard Demont arrive opposite him, he fired two shots. He wanted to fire four but the crappy pistol jammed. On the far side Demont grunted. His shotgun went off, punching a hole in the dropped ceiling.

Jack tossed the pistol. Demont would be down but not out. Needed something else. Douche bags had hoses, didn't they? He opened the box. Yep—red and ribbed. He pulled it out.

Footsteps pounded his way from the far side of the store as he peeked around and spotted Demont clutching his right shoulder. He'd dropped the shotgun but was making for it again.

Jack ran up and kicked it away, then looped the douche hose twice around his scrawny neck and dragged him back to the ruined ice cream door. He strung the hose over the top of the metal frame and pulled Demont off his feet. As the little man kicked and gagged, Jack slammed the door, trapping the hose. He tied two quick knots to make sure it didn't slip, then dove through the empty frame for the shotgun. He pumped out the spent shell, chambered a new one, and pulled the trigger just as Jamal and Pepe rounded the corner.

Pepe caught a few pellets, but Jamal, leading the charge, took the brunt of the blast. His shirtfront dissolved as the double-ought did a pulled-pork thing on his overdeveloped pecs. Pepe was gone by the time Jack chambered another shell. Looked back: Demont's face had gone pruney, his kicks feeble. Ahead: Jamal lay spread-eagled, starting at the ceiling with unblinking eyes.

Now what? Go after Pepe or start that fire?

Fire. Start a big one. Get those red trucks rolling.

But which way to the barbecue section? He remembered it being somewhere near the middle.

Three aisles later he found it—and Pepe too, who was looking back over his shoulder as he passed it. Jack raised the shotgun and fired, but Pepe went down just before the double-ought arrived. Not on purpose. He'd slipped in the spilled lighter fluid. The shot went over his head and hit the barbecue supplies. Bags of briquettes and tins of lighter fluid exploded. Punctured cans of Raid whirli-gigged in all directions, fogging the air with bug killer.

Pepe slipped and slid as he tried to regain his feet—would have been funny if he hadn't been holding a .357. Jack pumped again, aimed, and pulled the trigger.

Clink.

The hammer fell on an empty chamber.

Pepe was on his knees. He smiled as he raised his pistol. Jack ducked back and dove for the floor as one bullet after another slammed through the shelving of the cough and cold products, smashing bottles, drenching him with Robitussin and Nyquil and who knew what else.

Counted six shots. Didn't know if Pepe had a speed loader and didn't want to find out. Yanked the butane match from his back pocket and lit her up. Jammed a Sucrets pack into the trigger guard, locking the flame on, then tossed it over the shelf. He heard no *whoomp!* like gasoline going up, but he did hear Pepe cry out in alarm. The cry turned to screams of pain and terror as the spewing Raid cans caught.

Jack crept back and peeked around the corner.

Pepe was aflame. He had his arms over his eyes, covering them against the flying, flaming pinwheels of Raid as he rolled in the burning puddle, making matters worse. Black smoke roiled toward the ceiling.

And then it happened. Clanging bells and a deluge of cold water.

Yes.

Jack saw the .357 on the floor. He sprinted by, kicking it ahead of him as he raced through the downpour to the pharmacy section. After dancing through an obstacle course of Popsicles and gallons of ice cream, he found Loretta and the others cowering behind the counter. He picked up the key ring and tossed it to Patel.

"Out! Get everybody out!"

As the stampede began, he heard Loretta yelling.

"Hey, y'all! This man just saved our lives. You wanna pay him back, you say you never seen him. He don't exist. You say these gangstas got inna fight and killed each other. Y'hear me? Y'hear?"

She blew Jack a kiss and joined the exodus. Jack was about to follow when a bullet smashed a bottle of mouthwash near his head. He ducked back as a second shot narrowly missed. He dove behind the pharmacy counter and peeked over the top.

A scorched, steaming, sodden Pepe shuffled Jack's way through the rain with a small semiauto clutched in his outstretched hand. Jack hadn't counted on him having a backup. Hell, he hadn't counted on him doing anything but burn. The sprinkler system had saved him.

Pepe said nothing as he approached. Didn't have to. He had murder in his eyes. And he had Jack cornered.

He fired again. He bullet hit the counter six inches to Jack's right, showering him with splinters as he ducked.

Nowhere to hide. Had to find a way to run out Pepe's magazine. How? A lot of those baby semis held ten shots.

Another peek. Pepe's slow progress had brought him within six feet. Jack was about to duck again when he saw a flash of bright green and yellow.

Loretta.

Moving faster than Jack ever would have thought possible, she charged with a gallon container of ice cream held high over her head in a two-handed grip. Pepe might have heard her without the hiss and splatter of the sprinklers. But he remained oblivious until she streaked up behind him and smashed the container against the back of his head.

Jack saw his eyes bulge with shock and pain as he pitched toward the floor. Probably felt like he'd been hit with a cinder block. As he landed face-first, Loretta stayed on him—really on him. She jumped, landing knees first on the middle of his back . . . like Gamera on Barugon. The air rushed out of him with an agonized groan as his ribs shattered like glass.

But Loretta wasn't finished. Shouting, she started slamming the rock-hard container against his head and neck, matching the rhythm of her words to the blows.

"NOW you ain't NEVER pointin NO gun to MY head EVER aGAIN!"

Jack moved up beside her and touched her arm.

"Hey, Lo? Lo! *Loretta barada nikto.*"

She looked up at him. "Huh?"

"I think he's got the message."

She looked back down at Pepe. His face was flattened against the floor, his head canted at an unnatural angle. He wasn't breathing.

She nodded. "I do believe you right."

Jack pulled her to her feet and pushed her toward the front.

"Go!"

But Loretta wasn't finished. She turned and kicked Pepe in the ribs.

"Told you I was a bitch!"

"Loretta—come on!"

As they hustled toward the front she said, "We even, Jack?"

"Even Steven."

"Did I happen to mention my bad mood?"

"Yes, you did, Loretta. But sometimes a bad mood can be a good thing."

This will be my last short fiction collection. I may put together some sort of omnibus volume in the future, or perhaps a special collection of stories from the Secret History of the World, but all those will be culled from *Soft and Others, The Barrens and Others,* and this volume. I'm pretty much done with short fiction. I can't give you a reason for that. Simply put, the form no longer appeals to me.

Since I'll have no fourth collection, I thought I'd catch you up on the threads I left hanging in the biographical sections.

"The Long Way Home" was the most downloaded story on Amazon Shorts for 2006. That sounds impressive, and conferred some bragging rights, but at twenty cents per download, it did not make me rich.

Dario Argento chose "Pelts" for his second *Masters of Horror* feature. I consider it one of the goriest tales I've ever written, but he upped the gore factor to extreme levels and added a lot of explicit sex. I suppose you could call the result soft-core gorn. But thanks to Matt Venne's script, the film remains true to the heart of the story. If you have a strong stomach, it's available for rent, but be prepared for some look-away moments.

The Touch TV series never passed beyond the script stage. No pilot. No future. No taking the script anywhere else without ABC's permission and we weren't going to get that. Seems they once passed on a pilot for a show called *CSI* and let the writers take it to a rival network. They're not going to make that mistake again.

As for the Repairman Jack film, the agony continues. The Joel Fields script didn't fly and the too-young star passed on it. (Thank you!) So Beacon turned to Chris Morgan and told him to go back to Craig Spector's original script and juice it up. The result blew me away. As of this writing, Ryan Reynolds has been attached to star as Jack. But Beacon can't seem to nail down a direc-tor. The problem is that a number of previous and inferior versions of the script circulated through Hollywood during the film's many, many years in development hell. As a result, directors and their agents think they've already read it—and they remember not liking it (with good reason). But they haven't read Chris's new and vastly improved version that sticks to the novel. The big challenge is getting people to give it another look.

As far as books go, I've branched out into young-adult fiction, going back in time to 1983 when Jack was fourteen and just beginning to discover his talents. The first, *Jack: Secret Histories,* was a lot of fun and I plan to write a few more.

I continue to write the adult Repairman Jack novels as well. I've decided to end the series with number fifteen. I made a promise early on not to run Jack into the ground, and I'm keeping it.

After that I'll try different things. I've kept other ideas in holding patterns for years. I'll let them land when I've completed Jack's saga.

The beat goes on. . . .

—F. Paul Wilson
the Jersey Shore
July 2008

<www.repairmanjack.com>